Once Walked With Gods

ELVES
BOOK 1

Once Walked With Gods

ELVES
BOOK 1

James Barclay

GOLLANCZ
LONDON

Copyright © James Barclay 2010
All rights reserved

The right of James Barclay to be identified as the author
of this work has been asserted by him in accordance with
the Copyright, Designs and Patents Act 1988.

First published in Great Britain in 2010 by
Gollancz
An imprint of the Orion Publishing Group
Orion House, 5 Upper St Martin's Lane, London WC2H 9EA
An Hachette UK Company

A CIP catalogue record for this book is available
from the British Library

ISBN 978 0 575 08501 5 (Cased)
ISBN 978 0 575 08502 2 (Trade Paperback)

1 3 5 7 9 10 8 6 4 2

Typeset at The Spartan Press Ltd,
Lymington, Hants

Printed and bound at CPI Mackays,
Chatham, Kent

The Orion Publishing Group's policy is to use papers that
are natural, renewable and recyclable products and made
from wood grown in sustainable forests. The logging and
manufacturing processes are expected to conform to the
environmental regulations of the country of origin.

www.jamesbarclay.com
www.orionbooks.co.uk

For Mollie

Chapter 1

Only in harmony can we build. Only in trust can we fulfil our destiny.

They had been tracked for the last five miles of their approach. Sildaan had sensed them but even she had not seen them. Those she brought with her were completely oblivious. They had no conception of the risk they ran. Of course they didn't. Typical of men. Strangers. Puffed up with notions of their own strength and power. Ignorant. And alive only because she was with them.

Yet she had placed her life squarely in their hands. She sighed to herself. Here, just beyond the sanctuary of the rainforest and gazing on the majesty of the temple of Yniss at Aryndeneth, it seemed a wholly ridiculous decision.

The great green and gold dome of the temple rose over two hundred feet into the air. The dome sat on a circular stone structure. Both dome and walls held multiple windows in coloured glass to beam in light across the rainbow spectrum. Every stone in the walls was carved with one of Yniss's gifts, whether it be light, water, animal, vegetable or mineral. Great iron-bound wooden doors over-looked a carved path that ran through a grand stone apron and out into the forest.

It was on this carved path that they stood, the thirty men grouped behind Sildaan, staring out, mouths open at the sight of the temple. For a while, they barely registered those that stood on the apron in front of it.

Nine TaiGethen. Three cells of the elite warrior class of Yniss, father of the elven race. The cell that had tracked them joining the two others. Their faces were painted in green and brown camouflage and they wore clothes that mimicked the colours of the rainforest floor. In the shadows of the canopy, they were simply invisible.

Sildaan had never been on this side of them before. Their stillness was unnerving. Their unwavering gaze bored holes in her courage. Swords were sheathed in back-mounted scabbards. Jaqrui throwing crescent pouches were clasped shut. Perhaps that was why the humans appeared unworried. She pitied them their ignorance. A TaiGethen needed no edged weapon in order to kill.

'Stop, Priest Sildaan,' said Myriin. 'They will not desecrate this temple.'

Sildaan felt the first ugly cut of guilt through her soul. She steeled herself. What they had come to do *had* to be done. She clung to that certainty as if it might escape her grasp and blow away above the canopy, taking her courage with it.

'Myriin.' Sildaan bowed her head and touched fingers to her forehead. 'These are unusual times. Yniss forgive me for the company I am forced to keep.'

Myriin raised her eyebrows fractionally. 'Unusual indeed. We noted you travelled here free of duress. As if you chose to bring them here.'

'I did,' said Sildaan. A ripple of anger spread across the TaiGethen. 'Because we have no other choice.'

'There will never come a time when elves will stand side by side with men. And these have seen Aryndeneth. You have brought them to their deaths. Why?'

'They are not dying at your hand,' said Sildaan quietly. 'They are staying. This temple needs greater protection than even you can provide.'

A growl emanated from the throat of each TaiGethen. Behind Sildaan, the men tensed. Hands went to sword hilts and there was a whispering of words that she could not understand.

'Don't be stupid,' hissed Sildaan in the tongue of men. 'You cannot defeat them with blades.'

'I will not leave my people defenceless,' said Garan, the leader of the men.

Sildaan glanced at him, standing just behind her and in front of all of his charges. He was ugly, his chin obscured by coarse hair. He was covered in the sores and blisters of exposure to all the rainforest could throw at him, as were they all. Sildaan could have helped them but she chose not to. It was a fitting reminder of where they were and where the power truly lay.

'You have no idea, Garan.'

'I know they cannot beat magic.'

'You'd better be right,' said Sildaan. 'Or we're all going to die.'

'Just do what you feel you must,' said Garan. 'This talking seems an unnecessary risk.'

Sildaan ignored him and turned back to Myriin. The TaiGethen warrior had moved a pace away from the others.

'I will speak with you.'

Sildaan felt a shiver run down her back. She prayed Garan's words would not turn out to be prophetic. She walked out onto the apron, feeling the eyes of the TaiGethen on her. Anger, deference and suspicion. They were sworn to protect the priests of Yniss but were ready to kill her the instant she proved herself a traitor. She could feel it through her feet and smell it in the air. Close to, she could see the fury in Myriin, evidenced by the slightest tremble in her hands.

'I bring them here with the purest of intentions,' said Sildaan.

'You are a priest of Yniss!' Contempt flashed across Myriin's face. She shook her head. 'You contradict yourself.'

'And you have spent too long hidden in the rainforest. A thousand years of stability are about to be swept away and the Ynissul are not numerous enough to combat what will inevitably come at us.'

Myriin straightened. 'You're speaking of the denouncement of Takaar?'

'You doubt it will happen?'

'I doubt Aryndeneth will be a target for Tuali mobs if it does.' Myriin stabbed a finger at the men. 'What are they doing here?'

'Myriin. You know I respect you as I do every TaiGethen. Without you, the Garonin would have killed so many more in the last days on Hausolis. But that was ten years ago and the mood has turned against Takaar. For all those you saved, he cost all of those lives when he fled. His was the backward step. Elves of every thread are shouting betrayal. It was never possible to hide the truth. These men are here to protect the Ynissul and our faith.'

Myriin's eyes were cold. 'Takaar's legacy is a thousand years of unity and harmony. Only the faithless will turn against him. We do not need the protection of men.'

'Yniss is at the centre of our faith. Not Takaar.' Sildaan found her anger eclipsing her fear. 'The faithless are those who revere one elf above their god.'

'Takaar saved the elven race. Not just the Ynissul thread. Every elf owes him a debt they can never repay.'

'You don't sit in the Gardaryn to feel the public fury. Neither do you hear the words spoken in every temple in Ysundeneth. You are out of touch.'

'Clearly,' said Myriin. 'I missed the moment when it became acceptable for a priest of Yniss to bring heretics to the home of our faith.'

Sildaan saw the smallest tension flow through Myriin's facial muscles. Time was short.

'Because I care for you and your people, Myriin, I will give you this one chance. Stand down and leave the temple grounds. You cannot stop what is coming. Only those I have with me can do that. Gather your people and go. Disappear. It is the only way to save yourselves.'

Sildaan could see the word coming and it brought tears to her eyes and a veil of guilt across her heart.

'Traitor.'

TaiGethen blades whispered from scabbards. The warriors moved. Myriin held up a hand. They paused.

'Sildaan, you will consider yourself in my custody, there to await trial for your crimes.'

Sildaan squeezed her eyes shut. She had known it would come to this but she had had to try anyway.

'I'm sorry, Myriin. Yniss will bless you on your journey.' She bowed her head. 'Garan.'

'Go prone,' said Garan.

Sildaan dropped. She felt the TaiGethen surge towards the company of human warriors and mages. The temperature plummeted all around her. A howling wind roared over her, chilling her body. She felt ice crowding her hair and blocking her nostrils. Her mouth was raw with frost when she inhaled.

She could hear nothing but the gale of ice. She kept her face close to the freezing stone of the apron. If there were screams, they were lost to her so she added her own. Her voice sounded like her throat was being dragged over rocks. And once her breath was exhausted, pulling in another was agony.

Sildaan thought the gale was brief. Garan had said that most magic was. Yet it seemed a lifetime before the din subsided. Sildaan lay unmoving, waiting for the swift death of a TaiGethen blade. Yet all she heard were the footsteps of the men advancing towards her and her temple.

Sildaan pushed herself away from the ground, her arms unsteady beneath her. She was stunned by the cold and turned a numb face towards the temple. She barely recognised it. Ice sheathed it, obscuring the stone and hanging in spears from ledges and sills. Frost rimed the stone apron and threw a shroud across the canopy at the edge of the temple clearing. All was white.

Sildaan felt a strong hand under her arm and allowed Garan to help her to her feet.

'Careful,' he said. 'It's slippery.'

Sildaan nodded, watching the frost begin to puddle and run away to feed all of Beeth's roots and branches. It melted from the bodies of the TaiGethen. Sildaan put a hand to her mouth. Their faces were blackened, ruined by frostbite and burned beyond all recognition. They lay in pieces. Like statues pushed violently onto their backs. Limbs had sheared from bodies, whose attitudes at the moment of their deaths relaxed as the ice deserted them.

A bird called across the apron. Sildaan started.

'It's so quiet,' she breathed. She rubbed her hands together and blew on them to try and get some feeling back. 'What did you do?'

'I told you our magic was powerful,' said Garan.

'Not the half of it,' said Sildaan. She managed a timid smile and looked at her hands. The trembling had nothing to do with the cold. Her voice fell to a whisper. 'Still. It looks like this might be easier than I thought.'

Auum hissed in a breath through his teeth. The damage was an affront to Beeth, the god of root and branch. Crude, careless, ugly. Split branches, broken vine and trampled brush. Caused by those not born to the forest. Those whom the TaiGethen were blessed by Yniss to hunt down.

Auum knelt and traced his fingers over ground that still retained the faintest vestiges of heavy-shod footprints. Here in the middle of the rainforest. Almost as far from the coast as it was possible to get. Auum left his hand in the dirt while the rain cascaded over his body from a huge leaf just above his head. He let Gyal's tears refresh him and the sounds of the downpour rush through him.

He stood and faced his mentor, the Priest Serrin, whom it had been his honour to protect these ten years since his escape to Calaius. The priest was tall. His head was shaven. His body, naked but for a loincloth and leather shoes, was painted entirely white. Studs and rings adorned his ears and nose.

Serrin was one of the Silent. Dedicated to mute observance of Yniss in his temples, a keeper of archives and relics.

'Strangers,' Auum said, rising to his feet. 'Closing on Aryndeneth.'

Serrin's large oval eyes narrowed. Auum could see him weighing up a decision to speak. Out here it was permitted, though the Silent struggled with the occasional necessity nonetheless.

'Which?' asked Serrin, his voice hoarse and quiet.

'This is not the Terassin. It's too clumsy for them. Men. Fifteen at least.' Auum spat. 'A thousand years of blessed isolation. Why couldn't they leave us alone?'

Serrin's eyes betrayed his concern. The first sails had been spotted fifteen years ago. Men. Promising friendship and stinking of treachery and deceit. They had been warned away from the forest. It seemed that warning had gone unheeded.

'We'll catch them long before they reach Aryndeneth,' said Auum. 'This trail is fresh and they'll be slow. They're carrying too much weight.'

Auum moved off along the trail. The day was half done. Rain had been falling incessantly, feeding the ground and filling the leaves of the canopy that reached up high to grab Gyal's tears as they fell. Down on the ground it was dark. Banyan, balsa, fig, liana and vine choked the forest floor. Dense low bush spread thick tendrils that snagged the careless foot. Too much had been hacked aside. A pathway had been cut wide enough for three walking abreast.

Auum growled. It was time.

Serrin reached into a pouch on his belt and pulled out a small lidded clay pot, closed with a leather band. He opened it and dipped two fingers of his right hand into it. Keeping his face to the ground he smeared the white paint across his cheeks, nose and forehead, working it to re-cover every pore.

Auum watched him for a moment, seeing the deliberate movements and the intensity in every stroke before re-applying his own camouflage. The brown and green paints felt cool against his skin. And empowering. Auum sent a prayer to Yniss to guide his hands and keep his senses sharp. When he had finished, he saw Serrin watching him. The priest, face startling white and eyes gleaming with passion, nodded.

'Now we hunt.'

'Move on, it's nothing,' said Haleth, scratching ineffectually at his sword arm through his leather. 'Just one of those stupid little pig things.'

'Tapir,' said Arshul, the whisper-thin assassin.

Haleth shrugged. 'If you say so.'

'No,' said another. Herol, it was. Called himself One-Eye. Confusing considering he was blind in neither. 'I saw something. Just a flicker. Pale like a spirit.'

'I saw it too,' said Rissom, the big bull-headed Racheman.

He was suffering with a fever after a bite from something horrible. He wasn't alone of course. But at least he wasn't whining about it though the discharge from his nose and one ear looked bad. Haleth grimaced.

'All right, you saw it. Congratulations. But let's move on. Unless you want to be chasing your phantom until you drop dead from snake or frog or burrowing insect. The temple is still a day away. But if it makes you feel better, Herol, drop back twenty. Take three others with you. Rissom, take two and flank right. Kuthan, do likewise on the left. Keep in sight, keep calling out what you find. And nothing heroic, all right? This is a dangerous place. Let's go.'

Haleth set off, hacking aside the dense trailing vines that grabbed and snagged at clothing and face. Thick branches hung low from trees to grasp them and the damn roots formed hoops to trip them. On Balaia, roots went underground. Haleth cursed the Calaian rainforest, its thick sludge underfoot and its blasted insect life. Why did he ever agree to come back?

His face was a mass of bites despite the poultices and drinks the elves who'd met their ship had given them. And there were eggs in his arms and legs. Apparently, there was something at the temple that would sort that out. A leaf not present in this part of the forest. There was something particularly hideous about having insects hatching under your skin, feasting off your flesh. Haleth shuddered and scratched. He'd rather get snake bite.

'Fucking place gets worse by the hour,' said Arshul. 'Don't the rain ever stop?'

'Stop your moaning and get up here and help me,' said Haleth. 'I can barely make out which way the sun is going. Your eyes are better than mine.'

'Well you're going to have bugs coming out of yours soon, aren't you? No wonder they're failing you.' Arshul came up to Haleth's left and chopped away with smooth movements of his blade. He looked at the light and shade ahead. 'We're still going in the right direction. Mainly.'

'Good,' said Haleth. He tripped on a hidden root and stumbled, bracing himself against a balsa trunk. 'Bugger it.'

'What happened to our guide? Sildaan promised us one.'

'Sharp ears are good at promises, not so good at delivering,' said Haleth.

Something rushed across their path, perhaps ten yards ahead. Light and shade. Quick and gone as soon as he had seen it. Arshul pointed.

'That's it,' he said, voice trembling. 'A ghost in the trees.'

'Sighting dead ahead,' called Haleth, his heart thudding hard in his chest. 'Ten yards moving left to right. Heads up, One-Eye, coming your way.'

'I hear you, boss.'

The company was still moving but very slowly. Every eye strained to see whatever it was. Haleth had a nagging feeling he recognised it, but in the downpour and almost lost in the shadows and ridiculously dense vegetation, there was no telling for sure.

He could sense the nerves of those around them. This was not in any of their experience. They'd all been on Calaius for over a hundred days, trying to acclimatise. But there was no getting used to the rainforest. Rumours had run riot about what travelled inside the canopy. Haleth knew.

'Nothing yet,' said One-Eye. 'Wait. Movement. Up ahead, fifteen yards. Haven't we—'

The shriek from Haleth's left was drawn from the deepest well of fear. Birds took flight and a rush of movement was heard in the canopy all around them. There was a crashing on the forest floor. Haleth, Arshul and the eight others in the central group turned, holding their swords ready. Haleth already knew it wasn't an enemy coming. But an enemy might be right behind the runner.

A young man appeared, his face white in the gloom, his weapon gone and his mind with it. He burst through the vines and fell to the ground just in front of Haleth.

'Kuthan!' he wailed. 'Kuthan's head . . . So quick. Nothing to see. Nothing to hear.'

'Talk to me, Ilesh. I need more sense than that.' Haleth dropped to his knees and grabbed Ilesh's shoulders. The young man looked up. 'That's better. Speak.'

'There is nothing more. Kuthan's dead. Beheaded and I didn't even see anything. But there was something there. And then gone.'

A keening wail carried over the drumming of the rain. For a moment, Haleth thought it had to be a wounded animal. Then he heard the slicing of vegetation, terribly close. He jerked back reflexively. Ilesh's head jolted violently to the left. Blood sprayed out over Haleth's face. He dropped the man and scrabbled back to his feet, grabbing his sword from the mud.

Something jutted from Ilesh's neck. A crescent blade with indented finger grips at one end. It had carved deep, slicing the jugular and lodging in the windpipe. The poor fool juddered and slumped sideways. Haleth didn't take his eyes from the weapon. Sildaan had spoken of these things. Jaqrui, she'd called them. A signature weapon.

'Shit,' he breathed. 'TaiGethen.'

A scream rang out from behind them. Shouting followed it and cries for help floated across the forest floor. Haleth turned full circle, seeing another glimpse of the ghost in the trees.

'Everyone to me. Now! I want a circle. Clear some ground, dammit. And stand together. Stand. Arshul, behind me. One-Eye, get back here. Archers and mages in the centre. To my left. Move!' Haleth could see fear in every face. Action helped, but only a little.

His men chopped at the vegetation at their feet, desperately trying to make enough space to stand and defend. The rain still rattled down and the gloom had deepened if anything, meaning there was yet more to come. One-Eye was leading his two back to the fold. They were trying to cover every angle, hacking at the foliage in front of them to make a path.

'We're watching for you,' said Haleth. 'Come on. Quickly.'

A shadow flashed behind One-Eye. Haleth's throat went dry. The man to One-Eye's left pitched forwards. Haleth saw the pale gleam of a blade. Gone in an instant.

'Run, One-Eye!' he yelled. 'Run!'

Around him his men were jittery, staring out into the forest, trying to pierce the impenetrable. The ground around them was still treacherous but it would have to do. Tree trunks, vines and thick branches were going to get in the way of free swordplay. And the circle was too small. Haleth could understand their reluctance. Still . . .

'Move out. Give the mages and bowmen some space. Don't wait for a command to shoot or cast. Come on. Space. Space to fight.'

Haleth took two deliberate steps forward and gestured with his arms for those to his left and right to come with him.

'How many of them are there?' asked one.

'Do I look like a seer?'

One-Eye and his sole charge ran into the rough circle. Survivors of the left flank and rear joined too. Seventeen stood and waited. Three of them with bows. Two mages. There was the sound of feet seeking firm purchase. Muttered curses and demands for more room. The whisper of spell shapes forming.

Yet around them, barring the dripping, drumming and splashing of rain, the forest had fallen silent.

Chapter 2

Complacency is your greatest enemy.

Auum and Serrin watched the men. The three already dead would be reclaimed by the forest. Auum prayed that Shorth visited torment on them for eternity. A prayer sure to be answered. Shorth would be greedy for the souls of men. Merciful Shorth whose wrath when betrayed was more terrible than that of Yniss himself.

'They have courage,' said Serrin.

Auum sniffed. 'They have organisation. Courage, no. We will wait long enough for the fear to eat away what little belief they have. Tual's denizens will create doubt and false thought. Gyal's tears will obscure real threat. And then you and I will complete Yniss's work.'

'Their leader. He has courage.'

'It will not save him.'

'One must survive.'

'Is that an order?' asked Auum.

Serrin shrugged. 'Advice.'

Auum inclined his head. 'I understand.'

He turned back to study his prey and chose his next target.

'Where are they?' asked Arshul, his voice a hiss into the cacophony of animal and insect calls that had sprung up with a sudden slackening of the rain.

This was not what he had signed up for. Decent money but unacceptable conditions. He was a man who lived with total certainty. With the knowledge that he had all the answers, was in complete control. He was here to fulfil specific tasks. Remove specific targets. This jaunt into the rainforest was billed as little more than an educational stroll. A way to understand better the complexities of this ridiculous society. Being under attack from lethal elves was not in the brief.

'Out there,' said One-Eye.

'Very helpful. Any of you, can you see anything?'

'Focus,' said Haleth from the other side of the circle. 'Remember the way it's gone so far. The pale one is a distraction. The others will come from another direction. Keep talking, and whatever you do, do not break ranks. If we stand together, we'll get through this.'

'A ghost in the forest,' said Arshul. 'Not everything you hear turns out to be rumour.'

'It's no ghost,' said Haleth. 'Trust me.'

The group fell silent. Out there, they were watching. Arshul felt a moment of pure guilt. Was this how his marks felt? Knowing he was coming for them and unable to do anything but note the sun travel across the sky. Wait for the blade to issue through the ribs or the poison to take a hold. And die wondering who it was that had ordered their death at the hands of a paid stranger.

The hoots and calls of monkeys and birds filled the air above. The buzz and chitter of insects brought a phantom itch to the ear. The undergrowth was alive. Animals took the opportunity to see what the rain had unearthed. They didn't have long. Thunder rumbled above the canopy. Another downpour was coming.

But out there, in the infinite shadows the rainforest provided, the enemy awaited the perfect moment. No doubt they would pick it. And the delay was having precisely the desired effect. The men were twitchy, wondering how long they would have to stand here. How long they had to live. Some would be thinking about escape.

'A song, anyone?' said Arshul.

'You've got to be kidding,' said a voice, nervous and small.

'Not at all. Might break the mood. Get the blood flowing. Give us energy. Get our feet going and our courage together.'

'Good idea, Arshul,' said Haleth. 'It's about time this hell hole heard the beauty of Balaian song. A chorus of "Break the Chains"?'

'We won't be able to hear them coming.'

'You won't hear them anyway, not even if every beast in the forest fell silent and the sun dried the rain,' growled One-Eye. 'Sing, you bastards. And keep your eyes open.'

Tentatively at first, but growing in volume, the battle chant rose. And with every word, Arshul felt warmer and stronger. He surprised even himself.

'Blade aloft and arrow nocked
Break the Chains!
Break the Chains!
Armour bright and soul alight
Break the Chains!
Break the Chains!
Enemies hear and cower in fear
Break the Chains!
Break the Chains!
Shake them, break them, bring them down
Break the Chains!
Break the Chains!'

Warm fluid sprayed over Arshul's face. He looked left. The one with the white face was in front of Jinosh, his fingers buried in Jinosh's neck. Arshul brought up his blade. The white face dragged his fingers clear, the filed nails tearing out flesh. Jinosh screamed and fell forward. Arshul moved his blade to strike. The white face dropped to his knees. Feet ploughed into Arshul's chest, driving him back onto the sodden ground.

Arshul saw a blade flash. Another man cried out, clamping his hands to his midriff. Arshul was disoriented. He saw the TaiGethen's feet lift from his chest. Noise exploded all around him. He heard the thud of bows but not the sound of a hit. Arshul tried to scramble to his feet. The elf was inside the ring. A blade came at him but he moved so fast the edge carved empty air.

An archer dropped his bow, tried to get a knife. A palm slapped up into his nose, snapping his head back, smashing bone high up into his head. Haleth was shouting. Arshul made it to his haunches. The elf struck again, short sword taking a second archer through the eye.

'Cast!' yelled Haleth. 'One of you bastards. Cast!'

'At what?' shrieked a mage, his voice tattered by fear.

Every swordsman had turned now. And the elf had gone, springing up and out of the circle, using a vine to speed his progress. Arshul watched him, gaping because he could do nothing else. In the cloying confines of the rainforest, the elf moved without impediment. A creature at one with his environment. He brought his legs into a tuck, unwound it as he landed, spun and delivered a ferocious kick into the back of One-Eye's neck. The big man crumpled, head flopping on his shattered vertebrae.

'Turn, turn!' yelled Haleth. They weren't listening to him any more. The group scattered. 'No! Stick together.'

The pale face appeared again, as if stepping out of nowhere. He lashed his fingers across the face of a running mage, tearing out his eyes and sending him crashing into a tree. The TaiGethen pounced on another, landing two kicks more quickly than Arshul could follow and delivering a killing blow to the heart with his blade.

Arshul began to back away. The elves were intent on those in front trying in vain to escape.

'Stand with me,' hissed Haleth.

But the fire drops of terror were turning Arshul's heart to ash and he shook his head.

'No. You'll be next. Alone I can hide, escape.'

'You will never escape them alone.'

'I can try. I'm sorry, Haleth.'

Arshul clung to the threadbare remnants of his will and moved quietly away.

'Stand, you bastard!' roared Haleth. 'Craven scum. Worthless piece of shit. Stand! Anybody. Stand with me!'

Haleth didn't come after him. Arshul knew he wouldn't. Too much pride. Too much belief in the crew he had assembled. Look at that faith now. Being picked off, one after another. So Arshul, a very quiet man, a man used to leaving no trace, crept further away.

The screams of terrified men, so like their womenfolk when all was said and done, echoed through a mist that rose from the forest floor. Arshul could track the enemy from the sounds of rushing in the undergrowth, growing a little more distant now. That and the feeble cries for help that would never come.

Only Haleth still bellowed true defiance and his voice was taking on a curious quality now, seemingly coming from all points of the compass but gently, like the incoming tide in Korina Bay. A brave man. It was almost a shame to sacrifice him, but in the end there was only one option.

You had to hand it to the elves. Just two of them if his eyes did not deceive him, and almost, almost, they would claim the full complement of twenty men. Impressive. But Arshul was a lone man. And his tally was far higher. His skill was consummate. And his tasks henceforth would be more suited to his talents.

Arshul felt the reassuring bulk of a banyan tree trunk behind him and looked up into its welcoming branches. Death, so he was told, lurked amidst the twining boughs and the great rain-scooping leaves. Yet nothing so deadly and quick as that which stalked the forest floor.

Arshul paused to listen. The forest had quietened once more. The work had been done. Haleth, like the rest, would be bleeding his last drop of life into the ever-hungry earth. There was poetry in that. It was something the elves believed and it was easy to see why.

He looked down at his hands. They were quivering. Lucky he wasn't being asked to shoot a bow this afternoon. He smiled. The forest had closed around him. Even he could not see where he had just been. Good. So still. Peaceful despite the drenching noise of animal life.

Arshul turned to look for his first handholds. The elf stood very close, barely a pace away. Studying him. Arshul's bladder let go and he had to cling onto his bowels. The elf's eyes were cold with inevitability.

Arshul knew that tears spilled down his cheeks. He knew his mouth was open to beg for mercy but all that emerged was a scream. The scream of a woman.

Auum and Serrin looked down on the last of the men. Just as clumsy as the rest, though perhaps a little quieter. The blood had stopped flowing from his heart. The bubbles from his mouth, where his face lay half in the mud, had begun to burst.

'We made a mistake letting the other one go. He is a leader of men. He can cause us problems. This one would have better suited us. A loner,' said Auum.

'No. The other will be heard, believed. Fear will grow.'

Auum nodded. 'There's sense in that. Come on. The temple is a day from here.'

Serrin was still looking down on the body of the mercenary.

'There may be others,' said Auum. 'We need to warn the Tai-Gethen, prepare the temple. What is it?'

'Someone helps them.'

Auum nodded. 'Or they'd never find the temple. I know. We will find whoever is behind this. Yniss will guide our hands. They cannot touch us here, my priest. This is our land.'

Chapter 3

Solitude is the harshest of punishments, for an elf is never alone, not even in death.

'I saved as many of my people as I could.'

You left countless thousands to die.

'I had no choice.'

You had the choice to stand and fight. But you turned and ran.

'I was defending those I could save.'

You were deserting those who needed you. You are a coward.

'I am *not*—'

Coward, craven, recreant. Gutless and exiled. You deserve to die. Why do you still draw breath?

'Because Yniss, my lord god of harmony, wishes to punish me further by keeping me alive.'

Pah! How convenient. Blame your god for your pathetic, self-pitying life. They turned from you the day you betrayed your people. They await the moment you drag up the courage to do what you should have done the day of your humiliation. The day the blood of so many innocents stained your hands.

'I could not have done more.'

You could have died in the service of the people who loved you. You should have. Give them that satisfaction now. Admit your guilt. Face your god. Know your true nature.

Takaar turned from the stone on which his tormentor had chosen to sit, unable to stare the truth in the face any longer. Takaar watched the rushing waters of the River Shorth hundreds of feet below. Beguiling, even from such a height. The waters swirled and thrashed across and around the exposed rocks.

Behind him, the immensity of the rainforest taunted him. Every creature that lived, breathed and died in the service of their god,

Tual, set up a cacophony that rang through his head, muddying his reason.

He raised his eyes to the sky, imploring Gyal to give him answers. And so she did, the god of rain unleashing a storm that drowned the calls of the forest and drummed on his head, cleansing and purifying. Calling forth his memories.

Red light grew behind the mist. The song died away. The mist dispersed as if brushed aside by the hand of Yniss himself, displaying the enemy ranged against them. Along the parapet, warriors tensed. Takaar stared, aware of the current sweeping across the defending forces. He breathed deep, trying to calm his heart, which tolled hard in his chest.

Takaar blinked. This wasn't right. A generation of fighting couldn't result in this. The forest floor was covered in Garonin foot soldiers. Dense like ants. Moving forward slowly. Thousand upon thousand. Behind them, driving straight over trees, never deviating, the machines. Hundreds of them.

Takaar crouched, hugging his knees to his chest. He rocked gently back and forth, his bare toes gripping the edge of the cliff. As he rocked he let his gaze travel up the opposite cliff and into the rainforest beyond. His vision fogged and his tears rolled down his cheeks. Today, like every day, he knew the truth.

'I am a coward. Innocent blood stains my soul,' he whispered.

Good, good.

Takaar stood. The thrashing waters boomed loud, mingling with the drum of the rain on the exposed rock and rippling through the canopy. His mind was blank. Not even the memories plagued him. The void inside was worse than the visions.

You can stop it. Step forward. So simple. So final.

Takaar edged his feet forward, feeling the crumbling mud beneath his arches. He straightened and breathed in the pure air of the rainforest. The glorious home, blessed by Yniss and tainted by the blood of so many who never had the chance to feel its earth beneath their feet. Trapped in the old world and surely dead.

And all his fault.

'I do not deserve to breathe this air or witness the beauty of this dawn.'

No.

Takaar stared down to the rocks on which his body would break and to the foaming spitting rapids that would flush away his blood and flesh. And his shame, his humiliation and his cowardice. He would be consumed by the rainforest and returned to Yniss. Purified. Forgiven.

'But I do not deserve forgiveness.'

We all deserve forgiveness.

'My death is not justice for those I caused.'

Do not confuse justice with forgiveness. There can never be justice. Only vengeance. Do to yourself what the victims of your cowardice would wish done to you. And within, forgiveness will be yours. Yniss loves you still.

'I do not deserve the love of Yniss. Any god.'

Mercy and forgiveness go hand in hand. But only when accompanied by sacrifice. Do what you must.

Takaar bowed his head. Above him, the rain intensified. Gyal's tears fell, lamenting the final act of a fallen hero. Thunder clattered across the heavens. Lightning sheeted inside the thunderheads.

Takaar wiped a hand across his skull. He found it hot and wet with sweat despite the cool of the dawn. But he felt cold. Deep down in his soul. He watched them advance. The defence mustered perhaps three thousand. Without, ten times that number and the promise of more in the gloom behind the machines.

'Takaar?'

Takaar flinched. He snapped his head round and almost lost his balance.

'Pelyn.' He swallowed. 'What is it?'

Pelyn frowned and upturned her palms. 'Orders.'

Takaar nodded. 'Yes. Orders.'

He looked out over the massive force ranged against them and now less than two hundred yards from them, close to the killing zone. The barrels of the machines were rotating around and angling up. He could hear the cranks of heavy bows. The sounds echoed in his head, fogging his mind.

Takaar could feel the burning heat that clutched his heart as if it were happening again this instant. The narrowing of his vision, the trembling of his hands and the weakening of his legs. Breath came hard. Gasping. His body shuddered and his eyes twitched.

You judged them.

Takaar's hands shook and when he took them from his face, the wetness was from more than rain.

You judged them. And most you found unworthy. Another excuse for your craven acts. Pushing aside the old and the sick to save your filthy life.

'I did the only thing left to do. And some were saved.'

Takaar's voice set birds to flight in the lessening rain. He spun round to face his tormentor but the rock was empty. Empty as it always had been.

You are alone. And you lie only to yourself.

How often had these words played in his head. He knew what came next. He had heard it countless times before. His mouth moved in unison.

'With courage so lacking you cannot even take your own life.'

'Are we standing or going out to meet them?'

It was Pelyn again but from somewhere more distant.

'All these lives,' said Takaar, shaking his head and rubbing the backs of his hands across his eyes. 'Is the evacuation complete?'

'Complete?' It was Katyett this time. Or he thought it was. His ears weren't right. They were ringing and muted. 'Pelyn told you. Ten more days to get them all through. We have to hold. Takaar. Decide.'

'Decide what?' he said. 'Which way to die? Out there or in here. No way out. Yniss has deserted us.'

Takaar smiled at Pelyn. She was staring at him. Confused.

'You said . . .'

'It's too late.' Takaar was shaking his head again. 'It's too late. I'm sorry. So sorry.'

Takaar took a backward step.

The rain had stopped. Gyal's tears had ceased to flow. She turned her face from him once more and he deserved nothing less. Takaar glanced at the cliff top and the worn patch where he had stood, knowing he would be back. Knowing he had no choice.

'Tomorrow,' he said. 'Tomorrow will be different.'

He took his lies and ducked back under the dripping rainforest canopy.

At Sildaan's assurance that they were safe, Leeth led the temple priests out onto the apron. From the depths of the temple they had heard so little but the sense of wrong had pervaded every stone. When the cold had swept in, the priests had begun to pray. Leeth had felt sorry for them then and so he did now that they were outside their sanctuary and facing the first day of a new world. Or, more accurately, a return to the old one.

Taking his first step out into the light and seeing the bodies of the TaiGethen on the ground and the frost still clinging to the shadowed crevices of the temple, Leeth realised he was not ready. The ugly shapes of men haunted the periphery of the apron. One stood with Sildaan. The leader, Garan.

Behind Leeth, the five priests muttered and cursed. More prayers were uttered. Accompanying their anger was confusion. There stood Sildaan. One of their number. Standing with enemies amongst the mutilated bodies of Yniss's finest warriors. The air smelled wrong. Tainted. That would be the magic Sildaan had spoken of, and on which she pinned such hope.

'Wait here,' said Leeth. He walked towards Sildaan. 'What have you done?'

'This is a fight for survival, Leeth,' said Sildaan. 'Don't pretend you didn't realise that.'

'And we win this fight by killing our own, do we?'

'There will inevitably be sacrifice.'

'Is that what you call it?'

'The TaiGethen will never join us. Ynissul or not, they are an impediment. We've discussed this. It is the only way.'

'We discussed taking them prisoner,' said Leeth.

Sildaan laughed. 'Oh yes, you mentioned that. I operate in the real world. Yet out of respect for you and them, I did offer them a way out. Guess the reaction that provoked?'

'I can't see a way that we're doing the right thing.' Leeth shook his head. 'Me and you, we agree about what is happening here. We know we have to reinstate the old order, the right order. But there have to be enough of us left to rule. You know the problems the Ynissul face – that all elves face, come to that. We cannot afford to kill our brothers so casually. Not even the TaiGethen.'

Sildaan stepped up to Leeth. She was taller than him. She was faster and better skilled too. But he would not flinch. Sildaan gazed deep into his eyes, trying to unsettle him.

'We've been through this, Leeth. Those of our thread that stand against us are of no use to us. And we have to own the temple. We have to make a statement that will reverberate through the forest and into the cities. This is the right first step.'

'Taking the temple, yes. Now Jarinn has left for Ysundeneth. But this? This is senseless slaughter. These were your friends. You've turned your back on too much. And now I look, I find it distasteful that we sully our temple with these *men*.'

'You've lost your nerve, Leeth. These men will keep you alive. You need to work out where you stand.'

Sildaan pushed Leeth in the chest with both hands. He staggered back, swiping at the steadying hands of Garan.

'Don't touch me,' he said.

'Sildaan is right: you have to make a statement.'

'What would you know of it, stranger?'

Leeth spun round to stare at red eyes in a face bitten raw. Garan's heavy brows distorted his forehead. Like them all he was powerful, wore the sort of heavy leathers and furs that were totally inappropriate for the rainforest, and carried weapons of little use beyond a clearing.

'I see what needs doing. You want war; you need to provoke it, not ask it politely,' said Garan.

'We don't want war. We—'

'Leeth,' Sildaan said, keeping her voice calm and quiet.

Leeth tensed a little more and turned back to her.

'You want this,' he said. 'Don't you?'

'I want an end to the folly that is Takaar's law, yes. We both do. And this is a message that will be heard across Calaius.'

'You will bring them all down on us,' hissed Leeth. 'And their magic will not be enough. Subtlety, you said.'

'This is hardly the place to be discussing this. Our allies do not need to hear us squabble.'

But Leeth shook his head. Sildaan felt a wash of fury through her body.

'They shouldn't be here. None of them. This is our business.'

'You know why,' snapped Sildaan. 'We need help. We are not numerous.'

'And about to get less so.'

Sildaan struck fast, her right fist breaking Leeth's nose. Blood sprayed over her hand and began to run from his nostrils. Leeth jerked back and put both hands to his face. His eyes were wide and he coughed hard at the sudden pain.

'What was that for?'

'You're not my damned conscience, Leeth. Yniss knows I don't need anyone telling me what to do or how to act. I need to know you're with us. I need to know you trust me. Well?'

Leeth stared at her over his hands while blood ran down to his chin and dripped onto his jerkin. He tightened his fingers against his nose and moved the bone carefully back into place, provoking grunts from the men nearest him. Leeth didn't so much as wince. When he was done, he removed his hands and let the blood run freely.

'You and I have known each other for over eight hundred years,' he said, his voice a little clogged. 'And you know I won't lie to you.'

He spat blood onto the ground and wiped his mouth.

Sildaan sighed. 'Now might be a good time to start.'

'Why? Sildaan, I know you better than this. What's happened to you? We don't need allies. We cannot trust them. This is not our way. They are not welcome and they will never be accepted. Who sanctioned their coming here to lend us their belligerent assistance anyway?'

'What happened was that I realised time was short. Shorter than anyone standing over there in their pathetic huddle thinks. You know what's going to happen in Ysundeneth, at the Gardaryn. Today. You need to learn to move with the times.'

'But you're talking about unravelling the harmony. Taking us back to the War of Bloods. Why would you want that?'

'Leeth, I hear you. But we need to move on. Please?'

But she could see that he'd planted his feet. She groaned inwardly. He shook his head.

'Fucking sharp-ears,' muttered Garan.

Leeth snapped. He was shorter and slighter than Garan but that did not make him any the less threatening. That much he knew. He spoke in the tongue of the northern continent.

'What's it to you, blink-life?' Leeth stood a pace away from Garan. Space to strike and kill with his bare hands. 'This is not your fight. This is not your land. You'll get your dues whether you raise a blade or stand in the rain where we choose. We own you. Your lives are in our hands right now. We could disappear into our forest and you would never get out.

'So I will stand and talk with my sister at the temple of my god for as long as I need. And should you choose to insult me again, I will kill you. Do you understand?'

'I understand,' said Garan, speaking fluently in elvish. 'I under-stand that standing here is wasting time you don't have. I know that Sildaan is right and that those who refuse to see what is coming risk bringing disaster on the Ynissul.'

'I have no need to debate this with you,' said Leeth. 'You are nothing. Hired muscle.'

'You are driving me spare, Leeth,' said Sildaan. 'Why must you do this?'

'Because we must do this right or we are betraying every elf and leaving scum like this to march unhindered into Yniss's blessed country.'

Sildaan beckoned him away from Garan.

'What is it that you want, Leeth?'

'I want you to promise me you will not strike down another Ynissul. TaiGethen or otherwise. I want you to accept you are not the arbiter of the fate of any of our people. You nor those above you. Sildaan?'

'I cannot do that,' said Sildaan, speaking quietly, voice barely audible over new rain falling in a torrent. 'And I am desolate that I cannot make you understand why.'

'Then I cannot walk with you,' said Leeth, and there were tears in his eyes. 'We cannot return to a rule by fear. It is you who must move with the times. We must command respect to be obeyed.'

Sildaan walked up to him and placed a hand on his shoulder. He felt a surge of sadness. Almost grief.

'I know. But we cannot achieve that goal without conflict. No elf will bend the knee simply because we ask them. Why won't you see that?'

'If they will not then we are not fit to rule again.'

'Oh, Leeth. We cannot miss this chance because if we do we will be in thrall to Tualis or Beethans. They will not be so timid as you.'

'Takaar has taught us that conflict is not the way forward. What-ever his failings, he was the one who ended the War of Bloods. This path will lead to disaster.'

'Then you must follow a different one.'

Sildaan pulled him into an embrace. After the briefest pause, he clung to her and began to weep. Not for a moment did he expect the knife which slid up under his ribs and pierced his heart. He gasped and clung on tighter.

'Safe journey to the ancients. One day you will bless my way and we will walk again together.'

Leeth felt no pain. His legs gave way and Sildaan knelt with him. He stared at her while she wiped blood from his mouth and nose.

'Your way will see us all to death,' managed Leeth.

'Quiet now. Leave your hate here. Travel free.'

Leeth's eyes closed. He could not stop his body sliding to the ground. The stone was chill on his cheek. He prayed to Shorth to embrace his soul. Dimly, he felt Sildaan withdraw her knife. He could not muster any anger, just an overwhelming sadness.

Leeth breathed in but blood was filling his lungs, drowning him. He tried to open his eyes but he had not the strength. He heard voices echoing around him.

'Shorth, take your soul to the blessed embrace of Yniss. Let Tual's denizens use your body. Let the forest reclaim you. Let your sacrifice not be in vain,' said Sildaan.

'It was the only option you had,' said Garan.

'I loved him. But what we face is greater than any love for one *ula*. You, I detest. Work out how much I value your life.'

Leeth shed a single tear.

Chapter 4

Belief in your body is the root of survival.

'Look at you, beautiful beast.'
And look at you crawling on your belly like the reptile you love so well. Appropriate.

Takaar twitched in anger, his legs rattling undergrowth. The snake turned in his direction, lifted and flattened its head. Its body curled in under it. It stared at him, deep brown iris surrounding a black pupil. Takaar stilled completely, ignoring the entreaties of his tormentor to reach out a hand and embrace his death at the bite of this stunning creature.

Instead, he continued his study. Around him and across him, insects crawled and leeches clung. The taipan's tongue sampled the air. It was better than eight feet long and a reddish dark brown in colour on its back and sides. Underneath, the scales were a yellower colour. It had a round, snouted head and its neck was quite dark, an almost glossy black.

It could kill him if it so chose. Or it thought it could.

'So shy,' he whispered. 'So powerful.'

The most venomous in the forest, he thought, but that was still to be determined for sure.

'Will you help me, I wonder? I will not hurt you, I promise.'

The taipan relaxed its posture; its head moved back to the forest floor. It nosed into the leaf litter. Takaar came very slowly to a crouched position. The snake ignored him for the moment, intent on some prey or other.

'But that will have to wait, deadly friend.' Takaar chuckled. 'First a test for you.'

Takaar rustled a handful of leaves. The taipan was poised in an instant, no more than four feet from him. The pair stared at each other, the taipan's body moving slowly beneath it. Takaar moved his body gently from side to side, noting the mirror movement of the snake's raised neck.

'Good,' said Takaar. 'Now then . . .'

Takaar twitched his body. The taipan struck, head moving up and forward with astonishing speed. Takaar's right hand shot out. His fist closed around the snake's neck, right behind its head. Its jaws opened and shut, scant inches from Takaar's face. Its body coiled and jerked, furious at its capture. Takaar held on. The snake coiled hard around his arm, squeezing.

Takaar pressed his fingers against the hinges of the snake's jaws, forcing them open. The taipan's fangs were not long, less than an inch. Not hinged like some vipers he had examined. The inside of the mouth was pink and soft. So much death contained within. Takaar smiled.

'You're a fierce one, aren't you? I've been wanting one of you for a long, long time, you know that? Hmm.'

Takaar turned and walked back to his shelter, which lay a short distance inside the edge of the rainforest where the trees met the cliffs overlooking the glory of the delta at Verendii Tual. The air was fresher here, beyond the suffocating humidity deep under the canopy. His shelter had become a sprawling affair. Part skin bivouac, part thatch and mud building. He headed for the building, next to which stood his third and best attempt at a kiln. A few trial pots rested on a rack next to it.

The taipan had relaxed, its struggles ceasing. Takaar could feel its weight on his arm. A fascinating creature. He glanced down at it. Those eyes stared where he determined, his grip on its head as firm as in that first moment. Takaar ducked his head and entered the building. It was dark inside but his eyes adjusted very quickly.

Shame you didn't choose to let it bite you. Why do you continue this pathetic charade?

'If it was any of your business, which it isn't, I would explain in greater detail. But suffice to say that the mind must be active or the inevitable descent to madness begins.'

Begins? For you that journey is a fading memory.

'Madness is subjective. All of us exhibit the signs to a greater or lesser extent. I have some. So do you. It is the way of things. At least I am building something useful. What is it that you will leave behind you?'

Your corpse being devoured by the beasts you worship.

'I will leave truth.'

And you have been so diligent in constructing your own truth, haven't you?

'Can we talk about this later? I'm a little busy.'

I just fail to see why you pursue this folly. How can you leave a legacy in a place where no one will ever find it? That is why you're here, right? To make sure no one ever finds you, alive or dead.

'You miss the point of my penance.'

I miss the point of your continued existence entirely.

Takaar focused back on his task. There was a table along one wall of the building, the result of a number of experiments in binding legs to tabletops. The surface was a little rough and uneven, cut from a fallen hardwood tree, similarly the legs. They were notched and grooved to slot together and then bound with liana and some young strangler vine. The table rocked a little but it served.

The tabletop was tidy. Obsessively so, said his tormentor, but it did not do to be confused about what lay in each of the small, wood-stoppered clay pots. They stood in rows down the left- and right-hand sides, leaving space in the centre for new work. He had etched a symbol into each stopper representing a particular herb or animal extract. He recorded the code, carving into pieces of hardwood he'd polished for the purpose.

A single clay pot half the size of Takaar's hand sat in the middle of the table. Across it was stretched and tied a circle of cloth from Takaar's dwindling supply of fine fabric. He picked up the pot, forced open the jaws of the taipan and hooked its fangs over the lip of the vessel. The cloth triggered the bite reflex and the taipan released its venom against the side of the jar. Impossible to see exactly how much, but he carried on milking until the snake tried to withdraw.

'There, my friend. No pain. You are one of Tual's denizens and I have no wish for you to come to harm.'

I doubt it feels the same way about you.

Takaar ignored the comment. He ducked outside the hut, walked away forty or so yards and released the reptile back into the forest, watching it slide quickly and effortlessly away, disappearing beneath the deep undergrowth and leaf fall.

'Now then. To work.'

Takaar had eaten well that morning. Fish from the tributary of the River Shorth that ran not three hundred yards from him, spouting into a fabulous waterfall down the cliffs a little way to the south. He would need all the strength of that last meal in the hours to come, if his suppositions were correct.

Going back into his hut, Takaar glanced around at the walls and table as he always did.

'Should I die today, what will be the judgement of the elves when my work is found?'

That you are a filthy coward who has researched a thousand ways to die and yet has not the courage to use any of them on purpose. The fact that your death was an accident would be the final insult.

'Why do I listen to you?'

Because deep down in the dying embers of your sanity and morality, you know that I am right.

Three hundred pots sat on rough shelves around the walls. Each one marked and named on the carved wood hanging at the right-hand end of each shelf. Too few had detailed descriptions of properties, effects and the more complex notes on mixing and various cooking methods, but even if he did die today, if was a start. A bright TaiGethen or Silent priest could take it on.

Takaar pulled his fine knife from his boot. He'd spent day upon day honing the blade to little more than a spike with a needle tip. He took the cloth lid from the venom pot and looked inside. The taipan had yielded a decent amount of the toxin. More than enough to kill him a hundred times over.

Takaar dipped his knife point into the pot and withdrew it, assessing the small teardrop glistening on it. It was mid-sized in his terms. A gamble given what he'd seen out in the wild. He did his last equipment check. Saw the food, the water, the cloths and the hollowed-out log bucket. They sat next to a hammock raised three feet from the ground between the two tree trunks around which he'd built the hut.

Takaar pricked his skin with the blade point, just on the underside of his wrist. He breathed very deeply. This was the time when he felt exhilaration and empowerment. The time to join with nature in a way no TaiGethen, no elf, had ever done. To survive was to understand more. And to find another weapon to use against the Garonin.

Are you really so deluded? Actually, I suppose you are. The Garonin are gone. You ran away from them and slammed the door in their faces, remember? Or does that not fit with your convenient truth?

'Now there you really are wrong. You never escape the Garonin. Trust me. They'll be back.'

Trust is not something anyone will have in you ever again.

'That is part of my penance. Now shush. I have symptoms and reactions to feel.'

The world will be a richer place if you have overdosed this time.

Takaar ignored his tormentor. He stood tall and breathed deeply, trying to speed the venom around his body. He ran on the spot, pumping his arms, feeling his heart rate increase. Nothing. Nothing while the sun crept around the forest a notch and the rain began to fall from the clouds that moved to cover it.

'Too slow,' he said. 'Too slow.'

The poisonous secretions of the yellow-backed tree frog were far quicker to act on the elven body. Indeed, he'd have been unable to stand already and he'd be fighting to breathe. The taipan's venom was slow and that was a disappointment. So far, all he could note was a slight blurring of his vision and an unsteadiness in his step. Still, everything had its uses.

Takaar moved towards his hammock. His head felt thick and there was an ache beginning to grow at the back of his skull. He swallowed. Or he tried to. There was difficulty there. Takaar raised his eyebrows.

'Better.'

Takaar put a hand on the left tree trunk, ready to lever himself into the hammock. He felt hot. Sweat was beading on his brow and under his arms. A pain in his stomach added to that in his head. His eyes misted over and he swayed. The symptoms may be slow to appear but they were comprehensive when they arrived.

Takaar found he had his whole arm wrapped around the tree trunk to keep himself upright. He didn't remember making the move. He lifted a leg to get himself in—

Sildaan was screaming at someone. Words that Silent Priest Sikaant could not make out had disturbed his meditation. The priest broke the seal on the chamber of relics in which he had spent the last three days and pushed open the door. From his left, grief and anger was coming from the worker village set behind the temple. To his right, across the dome and out onto the apron, the air smelled wrong. Sildaan's voice echoed against the walls of Aryndeneth, ugly and discordant.

Sikaant shivered. There was a deeper chill in the temple than the blessed cool imparted by the ancient stones. He crossed soundlessly beneath the dome, his eyes fixed on the bright square of the open doors. Two priests stared out from the shadow. They stood shoulder to shoulder and just to the left of the opening.

Sildaan's words began to reach him with a clarity he regretted when he heard them. No longer shouted but strident and terrible. Heretic.

'How can you look so forlorn? Why can't you grasp this? I have *never* agreed with Takaar's law. And I am very, very far from being alone. You cannot enforce harmony. It grows or it doesn't. You have been presiding over a veneer, nothing more. And it is about to be shattered into a million fragments and scattered into oblivion.

'What is desirable about relinquishing our position as the ruling thread? Do you really think that merely by telling a Tuali or a Gyalan that we love them as equals makes it so? They don't believe it. They retain their hatred of us. Every thread does. And the truth of that is about to be seen. First in Ysundeneth and soon, everywhere. Even here.'

Any confusion in Sikaant's mind was cleared up the moment he could see the scene on the temple apron. Men defiled it. A few of the thirty stared out into the forest, guarding in vain against an attack that, if it came, they would not see until it was upon them. Most watched Sildaan pacing around three kneeling priests. All had their heads up and proud though their hands were bound. All of them had swords held to their throats by human warriors.

'You will see, should I let you live, that the price of this false peace has been too high. I agree with those in every thread who consider that Takaar's actions on Hausolis were the ultimate message of failure of Takaar's law. And of Takaar himself.'

One of the priests spoke. Ipuuran. Ever a fearless advocate.

'You think the denouncement will tear the threads apart. You are wrong. A thousand years of peace is too long a time to throw away. Peace that cost nothing.'

'*Nothing?*' Sildaan was screaming again. 'It cost the Ynissul every-thing. Our position, our birthright. Our respect. The love of our own god. You're blind if you cannot see what is coming. You like Myriin and all the TaiGethen and Silent who hide under the canopy have no notion of what simmers beneath the lid of the harmony.'

'Lorius will—' began Ipuuran.

'*Lorius*. Ha! Lorius is going to do exactly what he has been urged to do. You think he will be able to quell what is coming while standing and denouncing Takaar? Oh dear. He is as stupid as you. He firmly believes in the harmony and that it will endure whatever obstacles he removes from the path of chaos. He thinks his words will give him position among the lesser threads, but they hate him almost as much as they do every living and breathing Ynissul. Barring Jarinn, perhaps.

'What happens at the Gardaryn is happening at our design, O great temple priest. *That* is why the humans are here. Because only they can prevent the slaughter of those born to rule. And so we will. When the blood-letting is done, the power of the elves will once again rest with the Ynissul. Just as it should be.'

In the shadows, Sikaant moved again. Up to the shoulders of the priests looking on. He hated what he had to do. Speaking beneath the dome was an affront to his order. But not so great as the words he had just heard. Sikaant was quick. Almost as quick as a TaiGethen. His long-fingered hands, each finger ending in a sharpened nail, slid around the exposed necks of the two priests and rested there. He put his head in between theirs. They dared not move.

'Those watching from safety are surely won to the cause of heresy,' he whispered.

'We had not realised you were here,' said one whose name escaped Sikaant.

'Evidently,' said Sikaant.

His hands closed. His nails bit, dragged and tore. He ripped his hands clear. Blood flooded from ruined throats. Voices gurgled. Legs collapsed beneath dying bodies. Sikaant held them both upright. Their struggles were weak and their resistance minimal. He dragged them both into the light.

Sildaan saw him, her words choking in her mouth. Men began moving towards him.

'You need more heretics,' said Sikaant. 'These two have failed you.'

He turned and fled where no man would dare follow.

Back on the ledge. Watching the river. Wishing for a push. Perhaps he could train a monkey to do it. He laughed. Train a monkey. Hardly. All they were good for was stealing his food. Or becoming food themselves.

'That's the cycle of life. Tut tut, round and round. Can't be stopped.'

Yes, it can. For you, anyway.

Takaar waved a hand dismissively. 'Stupid. One death does not a cycle break. One death adds to the cycle. One death is one more body to be reclaimed. One more to be shared. One more to enrich the forest.'

You make it sound such a positive step. Why don't you take it?

'Pfff. So much work to do. Reparations to be made. Every day a little more. Every day to even the score. Were I to lie down, I would be failing all who walk in my footsteps.'

You wrote the book on failure so I won't challenge you on that one.

'Do I believe in redemption? I can't tell. Perhaps not. Not deserved. Not sought. The sentence for my crime is life. And I am immortal.'

Only if you choose it.

'Can't repeat myself. Not a choice. Run, run, not again. Death is running. Life is suffering. Life is penance. I can climb a tree and fall. I can leap from this edge and none will mourn me. I don't want grief; I want hatred and I want anger. These are deserved. Hmm. Deserved and sought.'

You do none of it. You seek nothing but solitude and introversion. Want anger? Ysundeneth has more of it than you can possibly desire.

'No. Not. People. Gods. Yes.'

I hate you.

'Then I win today.'

You never win. You merely delay the inevitable while you toy with your death and your immortality.

'Ah, now I understand you. You hate me because the taipan could not kill me.'

Ah, but it was close

'Ah, but not close enough.'

Takaar felt himself shudder. His tormentor had no idea just how close, not really. It had not been the swelling at the point of the injection of the venom. That had been excruciating and he would suffer for days from the cuts he had to make to relieve pressure on his flesh. Nasty nasty. Nor was it the strange effects on his blood, thinning it so that when he awoke from the collapse across his hammock, the tiny pinprick in his wrist was still dripping and his nose streamed red.

No, it had been the paralysis. First of his limbs, rendering him unable to move from his position lying across his hammock, head hanging over one side, legs the other. And later of his throat and lungs, forcing him to fight for every breath. A day had it been? So hard to know. He had seen light and dark. He had heard the sounds of day and night but he had no real idea how often he had been conscious and how often not.

When the paralysis had eased, he'd vomited bile and fouled himself. Hours later, he had dragged together the strength to move. The weakness remained with him and, alongside it, a furious mind, charting potential uses. Slow to start, this venom, but devastating. He dared not try more than the tiny tear he had used.

Takaar smiled.

Smug. Like you used to be.

'Belief in your body is the root of survival.'

Spare me.

'Never.'

Chapter 5

Flinch and perish.

In a thousand years the seat of government had not witnessed such ferment and unrest within its walls. The floor in front of the stage was heaving. The galleries back and sides crammed like never before. Every window and door was filled. Outside on the piazza, thousands more were gathered, hoping to get inside.

Properly built at the heart of Ysundeneth, the ocean home and first city of Calaius, the building was called Gardaryn in the ancient tongue but less grandly termed the 'beetle' by the local population. It dominated the cobbled southern piazza and its spires could be seen from all points of the city. Its shape resembled the carapace of the liana beetle. A metaphor for immense strength. The carapace would not crush under a careless boot.

Stone walls, carved from the quarries at Tolt Anoor, were all but hidden beneath the splendid wooden roof, whose edges swept almost to the ground either side. It curved up above the grand entrance and staircase, rising almost a hundred and fifty feet at the top of its spine. The spires rose at four corners and in its centre. When the Gardaryn was in session, red flags flew from the spires and ceremonial guards in classical deep-green livery took up station in small turrets.

Katyett had climbed high into the lattice of rafters with her TaiGethen cell. Up the stairs to the central gantry and then further up into the shadows. There, away from the unsettling closeness of the huge crowd that had filled every seat, bench, aisle and ledge, they could see everything.

At the head of the large public areas, a stage rose. At its back, an arc of five stepped rows of seats. The seats were plain, though cushioned, one for each of the high priests, the Amllan of every village, town and city, and further representatives of each thread of the elven race.

In front of the seating were three lecterns, each adorned with a carved image of Yniss at work creating the earth and the elves. They were arranged in a semicircle around a dark stain on the otherwise scrubbed white stone floor. Blood had been spilled just once in the Gardaryn. The day of its inauguration would forever be a bleak one. The large irregular shape was preserved as a reminder of days apparently not all hoped were buried for good.

The air was charged. A thunderstorm had moved across Ysundeneth an hour before, lightning and torrential rain accompanying it. A message from the gods, some would be saying. Katyett gave that no credence. The elves had to look to themselves if they were to escape this. That was what the gods had placed them on this land to do. Live in harmony. Live in peace. Love the land and all that lived and grew there.

Too many had forgotten that. And too many of them were here. The crowd bayed for the speeches to begin, practically salivating at the prospect of the denouncement. It brought Katyett a profound sadness. She knew the root of their fury but not one of them had been there on that fateful day ten years before when Takaar had taken his backward step. Not one. She wondered who was really behind it and why they had waited so long to set their plan rolling. Perhaps today they would find out.

Katyett looked down at the most senior representatives of the Ynissul. Jarinn, high priest of Yniss, who clearly wished he was back at the temple at Aryndeneth. Llyron, high priest of Shorth, whose gaze never faltered. Kalydd, the Amllan of Deneth Barine, who fidgeted with his hands. And Pelyn, Arch of the Al-Arynaar, the army of Yniss who, like always, looked angry and defiant. Of course, not an Ynissul herself but a disciple of Takaar. The direction of the Al-Arynaar, an army drawn from every thread, would be critical in the times to come.

Katyett let her gaze travel to the tapestries that adorned the wall behind the ranks of seats on the stage. They were beautiful. They told the story of the final battles, of ultimate heroism and of the tasks of Takaar. They were inaccurate. Incomplete. She wondered how long they would remain there.

'We could do with him right now,' shouted Grafyrre over the howling of the crowd.

Katyett turned to her Tai. He was sitting astride a beam, leaning on another that angled up towards the carapace. She raised her eyebrows.

'We could do with him as he was then,' she said.

Grafyrre nodded. 'Yes. Sorry. That was insensitive.'

Katyett smiled. 'Only a little. Yniss knows you are right.'

'You should be down there,' said Merrat, a mischievous twinkle in her eye.

'Your hold appears precarious,' said Katyett. She bit her lip and looked down at the gathering again. 'Not for all the blessings of Yniss would you find me down there today.'

'A reckoning?' asked Merrat.

'That implies some measure of rationality,' said Katyett. 'I doubt we'll see that in today's proceedings.'

The aggression rose from the floor in waves. It added to the stultifying humidity. Outside the air was utterly still, and though every door and shutter was open, no draught could be felt. Heat bloomed and rose, sweat mingling with timber and animal odours to cloy in the nostrils. Stares followed the heat upwards. Angry eyes. Disdainful.

'All right, here we go,' said Merrat.

The Speaker of the Gardaryn was on his feet to an extraordinary explosion of noise from the public. His name was Helias and he wore the green and white robes of his office with a confident ease. He was an ambitious young Tuali. Revered and reviled in equal measure. It was a position in which he revelled. Conversation in the galleries and on the floor died away as Helias approached the centre lectern. A couple of shouts bounced about the walls. Normally good-natured. Not today.

'Now we come to it!' called Helias. 'You've all felt it. You all have your opinion. You all wonder why we have been so long reaching this juncture. Now hear it from the mouths of those who would have your heart and your soul to believe their words.'

'Good of him to try and ease the tension,' muttered Katyett.

'Think he's taking sides?' asked Merrat.

'Perish the thought.' Katyett smiled. 'He's as neutral as any slighted Tuali.'

'I call to the debate, Jarinn, high priest of Yniss, keeper of the temple of Aryndeneth and defender of the memory of Takaar!'

A storm of boos and jeers greeted Jarinn's announcement. A classically tall Ynissul, he wore his black hair long and tied back with gold threads. His face was proud, an accident of birth, he always said, and his eyes, large angled ovals, were a beautiful blue. His robes were plain, as Yniss demanded. Brown, unadorned and without a hood. He went barefoot, a symbol of his trust in Yniss to keep him safe from harm. Katyett hoped his prayers had been particularly fervent this morning.

Reaching the lectern, Jarinn looked square at the public. There may have been a slight shake of his head. He focused then on the lectern opposite him, ignoring the opportunity to appeal to the Speaker for protection from the abuse that rained on him. He did, however, pause to nod his thanks at those in the arc of seats who had stood to applaud him. It merely served to intensify the noise from the floor.

'So where's the public support?' asked Grafyrre, when Helias belatedly raised his hands for quiet.

'Jarinn advised Takaar's followers to stay away,' said Katyett and again she smiled. 'Anyway, most of us are up here.'

There were five Tai cells watching from the rafters. Quite an assembly of Yniss's elite warriors. Five further cells were dispersed around the city, watching likely trouble spots should the denouncement be carried. Katyett needed to know the mood of the city quickly in the event Jarinn required a secure exit back to Aryndeneth.

Below them, a rhythmic thumping and stamping had begun. A powerful sound reminiscent of ancient battles, the prelude to chant and dirge. Katyett let the reverberations roll over her, taking her back to a time before the harmony, before Takaar's law.

'I call to the debate—' began Helias.

The voices of the public grew from a bass rumble to a thundering, battering shout.

'Lor-i-us, Lor-i-us, LOR-I-US!'

Over and over. Helias held up his hands for quiet but he saw he was going to get nowhere. Katyett could just hear him over the tumult, his voice rising into the rafters.

'I call to the debate, Lorius, high priest of Tual, keeper of the temple at Tul-Kastarin and denouncer of Takaar!'

The rhythmic chanting and stamping gave way to a frenzy of adulation. Some ran towards the front of the stage. Al-Arynaar guards blocked any further advance. Fists punched the air, heat and tension rose. Grafyrre blew out his cheeks. Katyett knew how he felt.

Lorius rose, meandered more like, to his feet. Lorius was old. Very old for a Tuali. He predated the resetting of the calendar to record the harmony. The years of peace. A shame that his memories of the times before the harmony were so confused.

Lorius moved with agonising slowness to his lectern. He spread his papers and studied them for a time before lifting his head to gaze out over the floor of the chamber. His face was deeply lined, his eyes still blazed with hazel passion and his chin, which trembled slightly, still held a few wisps of the huge beard he had once boasted.

He tipped back his hood to reveal a bald dark-spotted head and ears whose points had sagged outwards. Lorius held up his hands and the tumult stilled on an instant. He nodded his thanks.

'Dark days are upon us,' he said, his voice phlegm-filled and hoarse. 'Dark forces move beneath the veneer of benevolence.'

'Pompous idiot,' muttered Katyett.

'It is a creeping disease that threatens us and all we have built. Most are unaware it is happening, yet the evidence is all around us, plain to see for those who choose to look. A tragedy will overcome us unless we act now.'

Theatrical boos rang out from all corners of the public areas. Lorius held up his hands again. Jarinn shook his head.

'Yes, and the tragedy is this. Takaar and all his grand ideas, his harmony, all his deeds. A sham. All of it. A sham!'

'How can a thousand years of peace be a sham?' shouted Jarinn before the yells of the crowd drowned out anything more.

The sound of a gong echoed out over the Gardaryn. The Speaker had called for order. The gongs were hung in frames to the left and right of the stage. *Ula* with beaters as long as their arms stood ready for the Speaker's order. The echoing tone rolled out over the Gardaryn, quietening the crowd. Mob.

'I will have decorum in this chamber. The public will refrain from drowning out the debate,' said Helias before looking square at Jarinn. 'And High Priest Jarinn will await his turn to make his opening remarks.'

The crowd exploded into noise, cheers, jeers and a concerted wagging of fingers at Jarinn. The high priest spread his hands and shrugged, playing the villain for the moment but only drawing more abuse. Lorius quietened the crowd again.

'Thank you, Helias. I am not telling any of you anything you don't already know. We all believed Takaar's words. We all believed the myth of the harmony of the elves. And why is it a myth? I'll tell you why and it is two-fold. First.'

And the finger he held up was mimicked by thousands on the floor.

'Takaar may have begun with pure ideals but what happened when his own life and those of his Ynissul brothers were threatened? He ran like the dog coward that he is. He ran to the gateway, his acolytes trailing in his wake. And through it he dived, consigning a hundred thousand elves to death. So much for the harmony on that day. So much for the harmony on that day!'

You had to hand it to Lorius: he didn't shrink from milking a volatile crowd. Katyett scanned the faces that she could see. Puffed up with anger and righteous indignation. Looking for an outlet for the fury they felt and finding it at the lectern opposite their hero. The vocal barrage that flew at Jarinn was truly shocking. And Helias stood by and watched it. For his part, Jarinn kept his face carefully neutral.

'Second!' thundered Lorius and a forest of V-signs shot into the air to accompanying cheers. 'Just what is it we have seen in the decade since Takaar appeared through the gate from Hausolis and fled into the forest as it collapsed behind him? Have we seen the returning Ynissul working like slaves to maintain the harmony their coward imposed upon us?'

Lorius paused. The public hushed. 'Let me take you back in history just for a moment. There have been elves living here in the rainforest for over a thousand years. All of us faithfully following Takaar's harmony, Takaar's law. And there are none among us – few enough that remember the first days here – who would deny that it worked. And, Tual knows, we needed to live in peace with the challenges that we faced here.

'All threads pulled together to make sure we not only survived but thrived. The Ynissul too.'

Boos and jeers stalled his speech, and for the first time Lorius displayed anger. He moved from behind his lectern and faced the crowd full on. For a moment, Katyett wondered if he'd dropped them as easily as he'd caught them. There he stood, an *ula* alone in front of a hooting mob that paid him no attention. For a second time, though, she had to admit a grudging respect.

Not for a heartbeat did his expression change. Nor did he gesture for calm or let his eye move away from the scene in front of him. And slowly, slowly they quietened, realising perhaps that their show had ceased and their principal actor had walked from the stage.

'Thank you,' said Lorius quietly. And he returned to his lectern, daring them to begin again. 'Why do you jeer at the truth? Perhaps your memories are short. The Ynissul were instrumental in the success of the harmony and High Priest Jarinn a central figure in that success. Jeer now if you don't believe me.'

Silence. Almost. Merrat chuckled.

'Good, isn't he?'

'Very,' said Katyett. 'And just look at the space he's created for whatever lie is coming next.'

'So why is it that we stand here now knowing that our people are unhappy? That they feel undermined? That tension grows by the day and knowing that there have been incidents of violence between threads. A dark place we thought never to revisit. The answer is as simple as it is tragic.

'In the wake of Takaar's abject failure, the Ynissul, bolstered by the return of so many with him – mysterious when brother and sister threads suffered so badly – have set about reinstalling themselves as the dominant thread.'

Now the boos began again and Lorius nodded.

'Yes. Yes. Across our land, they take charge. The Amllans of Ysundeneth, Tolt Anoor and Deneth Barine?'

'YNISSUL!'

'The high priest of Shorth?'

'YNISSUL!'

'The Lord of the Fleet?'

'YNISSUL!'

Lorius spread his hands and let the applause grow. He wagged a finger when it was at its height and began again.

'I could go on.' He snatched up a sheaf of papers. 'From judges to landowners, civil servants to the keepers of the exchequer, Ynissul are everywhere. And while the Lord of the Al-Arynaar might be a Tuali, her love for Takaar renders her Ynissul in all but name. The insidious, growing influence is everywhere. Even up there in the rafters!'

Every face swung up to sneer at the TaiGethen high above the floor. Missiles were thrown, mainly fruit. The TaiGethen in the rafters swayed and dodged economically, catching much that reached them, Merrat cocked her arm, a hard, unripe mango in her fist.

'No,' said Katyett. 'Or at least, not yet.'

'Look at them.' Lorius continued the taunt. 'Like monkeys swinging from the branches of a banyan, too fearful to put their feet on the ground lest we see the deception in their eyes. Too haughty to nestle among their brothers in case we should give them something unmentionable. And do they, our oh-so-glorious immortals, do they hide up there to protect us all from harm? To police thread unity? I think not. Every TaiGethen is an Ynissul. EVERY SINGLE ONE! And there they sit, waiting for the call to defend their own and only their own.

'Takaar is the reason the Ynissul alone refuse to interbreed. They use Takaar's law against us. Why is every position of power being eaten up by the Ynissul? Same reason. Takaar's law. The law that demands that the holder of any position of authority must be given to the brother or sister best able to enhance the harmony. Takaar's harmony!

'The harmony that meant a hundred thousand non-Ynissul died. The harmony that would enslave us all again beneath the heel of the Ynissul. We must free ourselves before it is too late. We must live the harmony as it was first conceived. Before it was perverted as a weapon to oppress our lesser, mortal souls.'

The crowd's anger and volume intensified and increased with every phrase, every punch of the air.

'Before the true harmony is destroyed we must claim back the life we enjoyed before Takaar failed us all. I say to hell with Takaar's law! I say rip it from the statute. I denounce Takaar for the coward he is. I denounce all that he stands for and I say wipe the slate clean of his influence. I denounce Takaar. Vote with me!'

Chapter 6

Yniss is perfect. Those who follow him, not so.

Haleth took a long swallow of the leaf and root infusion Sildaan had ordered made for him by one of the cowed and fearful temple workers. Actually, it wasn't too bad. It started off bitter but had a sweet aftertaste. Mind you, it could have tasted like fox shit and he'd have drunk the lot for the promise of an end to the burrowing insects and their eggs in his flesh.

He had run onto the temple grounds mid-afternoon, exultant to be alive but with an anger at his treatment that burned bright.

'You left us for target practice,' he said, handing back the clay mug. 'No guide and just the sun to lead us. I still can't believe I'm still alive. Even less that I made it here. It was a slaughter out there. Why did you split us up?'

Sildaan passed the mug to a worker. At least she had the good grace to look apologetic. Mostly, the sharp-ears didn't give anything away so it had to mean something.

'I spilt us up to draw the sentry TaiGethen cell away from you. It seems to have worked.' She shook her head. 'You ran into a Silent Priest, didn't you? It's the only explanation.'

Haleth nodded. 'Right. One with the white face and his body-guard. And I'm looking at corpses everywhere. Anyone else make it here?'

Next to Sildaan, Garan sighed. 'Not so far.'

'And they won't,' said Sildaan. 'Sorry. This is most unfortunate.'

'Bloody hell,' said Haleth. 'I'll say it's unfortunate. We've lost almost half our force. Two mages as well. It was a big mistake coming here first. We should have gone straight for Ysundeneth with the main force. That's where the power lies.'

'That's why I'm calling the shots,' said Sildaan. 'You don't under-stand the elven mind. All we are is the rainforest. It is where we truly live. The cities cover less than one half of one per cent of Calaius. They might be our marketplaces and our seat of government but our soul is here. And it is secure.

'If we're to truly remove the harmony, return to the right order of things, we have to undermine that security. Taking the temple will do that. Because those that hear about it will take the message to their homes and beyond, that the TaiGethen could not defend Aryndeneth. It is a blow to the heart. But it will take time for the message to spread.'

'You want to make them mistrust the TaiGethen?'

'They have a mystique and it needs to be torn aside. And they all still follow Takaar's way. They have to be beaten, and that happens as much in the mind as it does with the blade and your magic. Trust me. This was the right thing to do. I am sorry you lost some of your people. We need every one but we have to expect some to die.' Sildaan gave a half shrug. 'It's dangerous here.'

'Oh, you noticed.'

'At least you're still alive, Haleth,' said Garan, but he was frowning. 'Sildaan, perhaps you'd like to tell us why that is? I didn't realise the TaiGethen were so careless.'

'They aren't,' said Sildaan.

Haleth felt a chill despite the stultifying heat outside the temple.

'Meaning?'

'Meaning they let you go,' said Sildaan.

Haleth's gaze flicked to the forest that pressed in on all sides. It could be hiding an army. His mouth was dry and the terrified screams of his men echoed about his head again.

'So they'll be coming here,' he said.

'Yes,' said Sildaan. 'But not immediately.'

'I beg your pardon?' Garan had clicked his fingers at someone Haleth couldn't see before turning his attention to Sildaan. 'Why not?'

'Well, first, they have no need to follow you so closely. Their trail skills are quite extraordinary. And second, they want to give you time to recount your tale of terror to all who will hear before they come to finish the job they started.'

Haleth couldn't cover every angle at once, so whichever way he turned, he felt eyes from the depths of the forest boring into his back. He realised he was shaking. He eyed the sanctuary offered by the temple. The place made him uneasy but at least he could put his back to a wall in there. Or hide somewhere very dark and quiet.

'Then we must prepare,' said Garan. 'Ah, Keller, there you are.'

Garan's lead mage was a man of average height, average features and wholly above average talent.

'What do you need?'

'I need you to infest the edges of this apron with wards. Alarms, disablers and destroyers. Plenty for my guards to stand behind anyway. We—'

'What are you doing?' asked Sildaan.

Less of a question, thought Haleth. More of a demand. Garan gave her a look that suggested she was simple. Her eyes just bored into him. Emotionless like the ghost in the forest.

'I'm making us safe,' said Garan. 'Anyone who puts a foot on your stone will regret their final step. And anyone who survives that will face the swords of my warriors. Good, eh?'

'Ridiculous,' said Sildaan.

Haleth tensed. Garan's face was stone.

'This is fighting,' he said. 'This is my domain.'

Sildaan shook her head. 'I will deal with these two. Clear the apron. Keep all your men out of sight. Now is probably a good time to give that order.'

Garan stared at her, Haleth watching him examining her for doubt and treachery. 'You'd better know what you're doing.'

'This is my land,' said Sildaan.

'And what about the other Silent? The one who made such an easy mess of your loyal priests?'

'By the time he chooses to return, we'll be long gone.' Sildaan looked at them each in turn. 'So are we clear what needs doing?'

She strode away towards the temple. Garan huffed out a breath.

'Patronising bitch.'

'Yeah but you know what, boss?' said Haleth.

'What?'

'Her dealing with those bastards while I'm somewhere else entirely seems to me the perfect plan.'

'Except you can't trust the sharp-ears. However far you think you are away, don't turn your back, all right? I need you.'

'I hear you, boss.'

*

The afternoon was on the wane when Auum and Serrin reached Aryndeneth. They had tracked the man's footsteps easily. Evidence of desecration increased the nearer they approached the temple. They had to assume there had been an attack.

Auum brought Serrin to the fringe of the forest and together they looked over the empty apron towards the doors, which stood open. Inside, the temple was dark. It was so quiet.

'It seems there will be no Feast of Renewal this year,' said Auum. 'Where are my brothers and sisters? And where are yours?'

Auum knew. Serrin knew. The temple was never left unguarded. It was never empty of worshippers and priests. There was only one reason the TaiGethen would be absent. Auum swallowed. He was staring at the unbelievable, the inconceivable. He felt nauseous. Only his fury at the defiling of his temple calmed his body, quelled the shaking in his limbs.

'We must go in,' said Serrin.

Auum nodded. He led Serrin around the edge of the apron and silently up to the doors. There were dark stains on the stone. Flies buzzed and swarmed. The whole place stank of death. He feared what they would find within. Waving Serrin into his wake, he entered.

The cool inside the temple, its peace and reverence, was instantly calming, yet Auum could not be at one with his favourite place on Calaius. No TaiGethen stood around the walls of the dome. No priests were at prayer in front of the statue of Yniss that dominated the huge space.

Between the precisely set windows, the walls and domed ceiling were covered in intricate murals. They depicted the coming of Yniss to Calaius before the first elves set foot there and the trials of the elven peoples to earn the right to live with the land. They charted the work of Takaar when he split his time between the two elven homes. And above the doors was a pictorial representation of the text Takaar had written regarding the energies he claimed to have felt on Calaius, energies that came to represent the heart of the harmony.

But no mural or historical record could vie for attention with the statue of Yniss, which rose seventy feet into the dome. Yniss, the father of the elves. Yniss, who gave them the gift of living as one with the land and its denizens, with the air and with the natural earth energies that were grasped in the hand of Ix, the most capricious of gods. Auum, as ever, let his eyes feast on the statue, which was carved from a single block of flint-veined polished pale stone.

Yniss was sculpted kneeling on one leg, head looking down along the line of his right arm. The arm was extended below his bended knee, thumb and forefinger making a right angle with the rest of the fingers curled half-fist. The god was depicted as an old elf, age lines around the eyes and across the forehead. His long full hair was carved blowing back over his right shoulder.

Yniss's body was athletic perfection. A single-shouldered robe covered little more than groin and stomach, leaving open the bunching shoulders, beautifully defined arms and powerful legs. Yniss's eyes seemed to sparkle with life, nothing more than a trick of the water at his feet and the light in the temple.

Yniss channelled his life energy along forefinger and thumb into the harmonic pool by which he knelt, from where it spread throughout the land, bringing glory where it touched. Pipes concealed beneath the statue's thumb and forefinger fed water from an underground spring into the pool beneath the statue's outstretched hand.

Some believed the statue and its precisely measured water flow was the final piece in the completion of the harmony, a circle of life in effect. Auum believed in the energy that maintained the earth but the statue had been created by elves, not their gods. It was not credible to believe anything deific had been bestowed upon it.

Auum and Serrin knelt before pool and statue and prayed to Yniss to preserve them for the tasks to come. Auum felt his prayer uncertain for the first time in his life and realised it was because, uniquely, he felt *uncomfortable* in here. When he caught Serrin's gaze he knew the Silent felt the same way too.

'Walk behind me,' said Auum.

Serrin nodded. Auum kept the pool close on his right and walked around by the statue of Yniss. It was not unheard of for the temple to be empty but it was for the doors to the contemplation chambers and reading cells to be free of guards. Within, all the greatest treasures of the elven religion were kept. A lone figure was approaching along the passageway towards them. Auum felt a euphoric relief.

'Sildaan,' he said. 'We feared the temple taken. There's blood all over the stones.'

Sildaan started, stared open-mouthed and just about managed to continue walking forward. She made a quick glance back over her shoulder.

'I wasn't expecting to see you,' she said. 'You aren't due here.'

Sildaan was wearing the robes of a scripture priest, every part of the cream material sewn with favourite quotes and maxims. She appeared distracted and a little confused. Auum's presence seemed to unsettle her.

'You're in shock. I'm sorry we weren't here to help repel the strangers.' Auum paused. 'Sildaan. Where is everyone? The Tai-Gethen. The priests?'

Sildaan frowned. 'Why are you here?'

'Men are here. Their mark is all over the forest. Or it was.'

Sildaan's head came up sharply. 'What do you mean?'

'I am TaiGethen,' said Auum. 'I am a cleanser of the rainforest.'

Sildaan gaped. 'It was *you*?'

Auum shared a look with Serrin. The Silent Priest spread his hands. He didn't understand her either. Auum tried again.

'There were twenty men approaching the temple. We spared one to take the story back to whoever brought him here. We tracked him here. We feared others had sacked the temple. We're blessed to be wrong.'

Sildaan had paled but she managed a smile.

'The temple is secure,' she said, looking over her shoulder again.

'What's wrong, Sildaan? There's no danger back there. But we need to place guards. Where are the TaiGethen?'

Sildaan gestured behind her. 'I've forgotten something. If you'll excuse me?'

'Of course. Yniss bless you, Sildaan, we are very happy to see you alive.'

Sildaan's smile was thin. She turned. A moment too late as it proved.

'Sildaan. It's time to go. I'm sick of whining mages. Where are—'

The voice belonged to a man. One of two striding out of one of the cells a few doors down the corridor and marching towards the temple dome as if he owned it. Auum's twin blades hissed out, everything Sildaan had said, her every reaction, horribly clear now. He cursed himself blind. Serrin's body was rigid, the rage dragging a hiss from his lips. His hands shaped into claws.

The men pulled up short just behind Sildaan, staring at Serrin and Auum. One smiled.

'Good of you to let me live,' he said in good modern elvish. Haleth.

That's what the others had called him. 'Not where you thought I'd lead you, eh?'

'Your reprieve was only ever temporary,' said Auum.

He moved towards the man, already knowing where he would strike. Sildaan blocked his path and placed a hand on his chest. She was a priest. He could do nothing but acquiesce. For now.

'You will not spill blood in this temple,' she said, all traces of vagueness gone from her voice and a hard strength in its place that Auum didn't recognise.

'Elven blood, no,' said Auum. 'I will wait for you outside, *cascarg*. They are dead already.'

'Back off, Auum. You don't know what you're dealing with,' said Sildaan.

'I am dealing with a man who saw all his friends die. He knows he cannot beat me. You know you cannot stop me getting him. Or his friend.'

'Please, Auum,' said Sildaan. 'There are powers at work here you cannot beat. The TaiGethen are finished. Go run the rainforest. Your work in Aryndeneth is done.'

Auum recoiled as if slapped, his blades flat against his legs. Confusion roared through him. He couldn't gainsay her. He was merely a bodyguard, not of the temple elite. Authority under Yniss had to be maintained. He was dismissed. There was nothing he could do. He backed off a pace, switching his gaze to Haleth, who flashed his eyebrows and waved a goodbye hand.

Auum could not disobey her. And Serrin should not. Within the temple walls at least. But these were times when nothing was certain. The Silent stalked into the gap and gripped Sildaan's neck with one long-fingered hand, his sharpened nail points digging in where he gripped.

'Auum is my guard. He does my work. I order him to ignore the words of a traitor,' hissed Serrin, having to drag every word out under the dome.

Sildaan's eyes widened. Her hand went to her belt only to find Serrin's other clamping down on her wrist. Auum growled and once again looked at Haleth. The smugness was gone from the man's face and he muttered a curse Auum did not understand. Auum's blades came to ready.

Haleth was smart. He stepped behind Sildaan and held a dagger past the side of her head, its point coming to rest a hair's breadth from Serrin's left eye. Serrin froze. The other man turned and called out. Auum could not understand the human language but very quickly there was the sound of hurrying feet. Four men came down the corridor. None were warriors. There was a brief exchange and the quartet began to make small hand movements, odd gestures and mutterings. The air cooled. Auum felt a throbbing in his body and an uncomfortable pulling sensation.

The other man cleared his throat and addressed himself to Auum and Serrin.

'Now what's going to happen is that the sharp-fingered one is going to let Sildaan go. He will do so very carefully or Haleth may stumble and he will die in a sheet of pain. And you, my TaiGethen friend, will sheathe your blades and walk backwards until you can feel the statue behind you. I will then move in the opposite direction with Sildaan and we can all make our escapes. Be assured that if you feel you still want us dead, my colleagues here will freeze you such that a flick of my finger will shatter you to a million fragments. Do I make myself clear?'

Auum shrugged. 'I can kill all of you before you make the first cell door.'

'Auum, you can't,' said Sildaan. 'I know you hate me but believe this. I have seen what these mages can do. There is no TaiGethen fast enough to outrun one of their castings.'

'What is a "mage"?' said Auum, staring at them. Helpless, un-armed humans. 'They do not frighten me.'

Haleth laughed. 'Of course. Not seen magic before, have you? Perhaps a little demonstration?'

'No!' snapped Sildaan. 'You will do no such thing. Auum, please, I implore you. Do what Garan says. Survive today and do what you will tomorrow.'

'I will come after you,' said Auum.

'So be it. What I am doing makes the Ynissul stronger. It will return us to where we belong.'

Auum closed his eyes briefly, an intense sadness in his heart. 'Anything that destroys the harmony and goes against Takaar can only finish us. We will stop you.'

'It is already too late for that,' said Sildaan.

Serrin had released Sildaan's throat and wrist and stepped back away from the heretic priestess. The *cascarg*. Traitor. Auum had a clear run on her and Garan but Serrin gestured him to hold his thought. The Silent knew him too well. Auum reached up and sheathed his twin short blades in the scabbards on his back. He took a pace back, then another, as slowly as he could muster.

Garan smiled.

'Why thank you,' he said.

He shouted something in the human language and dragged Sildaan over backwards, the pair of them crashing to the floor.

'No! NO!' yelled Sildaan.

Down the passageway, the mages all opened their eyes and brought their hands together. Auum knew in that instant that Sildaan had been telling the truth. He grabbed Serrin by the arm, dragged him around and pushed him into a run. He held a hand against his priest's back and sprinted towards the statue of Yniss.

The air pressed in on Auum's ears. It chilled and froze. He could feel the ice on his neck and the back of his head. There was a roaring sound all around him. He heaved his hand forward, practically throwing Serrin over the left arm of Yniss. The pair of them plunged into the harmonic pool. Auum held on, and with his free hand grabbed a feed pipe beneath the hand of the statue.

An extraordinary cold passed overhead. The pool froze. Inch upon inch of ice formed in a moment, crackling and spitting, forcing down towards them. Serrin was beginning to struggle in his grasp. Auum cupped his priest's chin, forcing the *ula* to look at him. He saw the panic in Serrin's eyes and shook his head. Auum put a hand to his heart, the gesture of trust for a TaiGethen. Serrin calmed.

Auum let him go and looked up. The ice was thick but not impenetrable. The water around them was cold. Colder than anything he had ever experienced. He had about six feet of water between the base of the pool and the thick ice above his head. He could see no movement around the pool yet but it wouldn't be long.

Auum chose the centre of the pool. He drew both blades and turned them hilt up in his hands. He smacked them both against the underside of the ice again and again, watching for the telltale lattice of cracks. Same as for cracking a dried mudslide. He hoped the other part worked as well.

Serrin saw what he was doing. Auum switched his grip, pointed the blade tips up. Serrin grabbed at his waist and hauled him to the bottom of the pool, allowing him to crouch and stare up at the tiny weakness he had made. Auum nodded at Serrin.

The priest let him go.

Auum powered up. His feet were planted, his thighs, honed from a life running in the forests of Hausolis and Calaius, did not fail him. He focused on the lattice of cracks, and hammered his blade tips into them, praying to Yniss that he had done enough. Praying his blades did not shatter.

He had the blades right in front of his face, his elbows tight into his chest to soak up the impact. At the last, he tucked his head in and trusted Yniss to guide his hands. Auum felt the blades strike the underside of the ice. He heard cracking and popping. He felt the frozen layer give.

Auum exploded through the shattering remains of the ice, roaring in a fresh breath, exulting in the warmth that had already invaded the temple to cover the cold the mages had used to try and kill him. He brought his arms to his sides, fury making him shudder. The men were just gathering at the side of the pool. Mages, whatever the hell they were, admiring their work. Haleth too, tracking his movements, his mouth hanging open.

Someone was shouting a warning. Auum landed on the lip of the pool, already moving forward. Around him, the mages were backing off, muttering and gesturing again. Auum thrashed his blades around left to right, the leading edge of the right blade cutting through the face of one mage, that of the left blade thumping into the arm of another.

Auum balanced instantly on his right leg and kicked out high with his left, the flat of his foot slamming into a third mage's nose. He drew the leg back in, still balanced on his left, and roundhoused the last of them, the top of his foot slapping into the mage's ear, sending him clattering to the floor.

'Shorth take you to eternal torment,' he said.

His path was clear to Haleth. The man had a blade drawn. He crabbed sideways, looking for an angle. Auum ran forward, dropped and slid across the slick stone floor. Haleth tried to chop down with his sword. Auum's feet crashed into the man's knees. His own blades crossed above him, catching Haleth's blow.

Haleth fell sideways. Auum pivoted on his right knee and rose smoothly to his feet. Haleth scrabbled back, trying desperately to get his sword in front of him and his feet beneath him. Auum stood over him.

'Pathetic,' he said. 'Reprieve over.'

Auum batted Haleth's blade aside with one blade and punctured his heart with the other. He withdrew the blade and turned back to the mages. All four were still alive. Auum strode forwards and drove his right blade into the chest of a screaming mage already pouring blood from a deep gash in his face that had ripped his lower lip down to his chin, taken an eye and cut his nose to hang across one cheek. Stopping his heart was a blessing he did not deserve. His blood defiled the stone of Yniss's temple.

To his left, the one with the smashed nose was back on his feet and running towards the doors. Not a backward glance at his injured comrades. Hardly a surprise. Auum dropped the blade from his left hand, pulled a jaqrui throwing crescent from his belt pouch, cocked his arm and threw in one smooth motion.

The cruel blade whispered away and buried itself in the back of the mage's neck. Auum turned. Serrin was hauling himself out of the pool, nodding that he was fine. Auum picked up his blade. The mage he had roundhoused was barely conscious. Auum ensured the next time he opened his eyes it would be in the presence of Shorth. The last survivor stared at his ruined arm, too shocked by pain to be afraid.

Auum stalked over to him. He saw his blade had half-severed the arm and cut deep into the mage's stomach. Blood was pooling quickly beneath him.

'Your blood will feed my forest. Your soul will shriek in endless torment. Nothing can save you.'

He turned to run back around the statue after Sildaan and Garan. Serrin stopped him with a curt hand gesture. He indicated the main doors and the two trotted outside.

'Live today, Auum.'

'We have to take the head from the beast,' said Auum.

Serrin carried on running, straight into the rainforest to the right of the stone apron.

'Assemble the faithful. Then return.'

'How do we know who they are? Sildaan has betrayed us. *Sildaan.* Who else?'

Serrin sighed and stopped where they could see the temple but were hidden by the embracing foliage. Auum felt detached. It wasn't shock at what he'd seen inside the temple, more a cold dread at what they faced. Serrin's eyes were brimming with tears.

'We will start with your brothers and sisters.' Serrin put a hand on Auum's shoulder and kissed his forehead. 'You saved my life.'

Auum inclined his head. 'And I will be here to do so again for as long as you need me at your side.'

'You are destined for better things than guarding Silent Priests.'

Serrin was frowning and Auum could see his eyes had misted over.

'We'll get Aryndeneth back,' said Auum. 'We'll right this wrong. Yniss will not turn from us.'

'Can't you feel it, Auum? Everything we believe in. All that we are as elves is at risk. The blood of men is staining the floor of our temple and an Ynissul priest invited them inside. The harmony is failing.'

'That is an inescapable conclusion.' Auum's smile was hollow. 'Talkative for a Silent Priest, aren't you?'

'These are unusual times. And they call for unusual solutions.'

'Meaning?'

Auum could see Serrin nagging at his lower lip as he wondered whether to say what he wanted to suggest.

'The threads will tear themselves apart. The elves will be in conflict again. Just like the War of Bloods.'

'Worse,' said Auum. 'This time, we don't have Takaar to unite us.'

Serrin stared at him. 'Don't be so sure.'

Auum almost lost his balance.

'He will not come. He turned his back ten years ago. We don't know if he is even still alive.'

But despite his protestations Auum's heart began to race and something that felt like hope coursed through his body.

'Do you really believe him dead? Takaar?' Serrin paused. 'You have to find him, convince him. I have to take word of what's happened here back to Ysundeneth, to Jarinn and Katyett. News of your mission too.'

'I am your shadow. I will not leave you.'

Serrin placed a hand on his shoulder. 'Our paths will cross again soon enough. Do this for me. Bring him towards Ysundeneth. I'll find you.'

Auum nodded. 'Where is he?'

'Verendii Tual,' said Serrin. 'He is an *ula* with more power than he knows but be careful. Ten years of solitude will not have been kind.'

'This is the plan of a monkey-brain,' said Auum.

'In a land being consumed by those with their eyes turned from God, he with a monkey-brain will reign.'

'That is not in the scriptures.'

'Not yet,' said Serrin. 'Not yet.'

Chapter 7

When you enter battle you are always fighting three enemies at once.
Your fear, your foe and his courage.

The heat in the Gardaryn was stultifying. The bedlam that had
greeted the end of Lorius's address had gone on and on, with Helias
apparently unwilling to bring the chamber to order as protocol
demanded. But Jarinn did not look for help or support. He merely
waited for the noise to recede.

'Lorius displays much passion,' he said eventually.

Katyett waited for the baying of the crowd to begin again but
instead they stilled and turned to face him, listening.

'And he speaks with some measure of truth,' continued the high
priest of Yniss.

'Look at that,' breathed Merrat.

'There's still hope while they remember they love him,' said
Katyett, and a little warmth stole into her heart.

'I will not speak for long. I am an old elf, though I might not look
it, and standing is tiring.'

The glint in Jarinn's eyes was picked up by those close to the stage.
Laughter broke out and one wag even reminded the high priest of his
immortality.

'Ah but, my friend, though you are right, no Ynissul is impervious
to illness, steel or other infirmity. And I can assure you that immortality can seem a curse when one suffers from arthritis.'

A theatrical 'Ahhh!' rose from the crowd. Jarinn raised his hands.

'But I am not here to garner sympathy; I am here to return our
people to a state of reason and logic and to avoid a descent into
blood.'

The boos and catcalls began again.

'Well what did you expect – that I would agree with him? Now let
me address one of the things he said which worries me deeply. I hear

that Ynissul are being inserted into all positions of authority that come available. This is unacceptable. I will consult with Lorius and we will right that balance. I apologise that I was not fully aware before today. Aryndeneth is a distant temple.'

Silence, then thunderous applause.

'They believe him,' said Grafyrre.

'That shouldn't surprise you,' said Katyett. 'Let's face it: if anyone is trusted to always tell the truth, it is Jarinn.'

'For the most part, I am not going to respond to High Priest Lorius, an *ula* that I respect and am proud to call a friend,' said Jarinn. 'I will tell you what I believe and you will have to judge whether my beliefs are worthy of today's harmony. Will you listen to me?'

A few hoots of contempt but in the main a respectful silence fell.

'Thank you. Here is what Takaar means to us. He means twelve hundred years of peace. He means the War of Bloods is a distant memory. He means a society that embraces all its threads and strives to treat them with equality. Why would you tear that up?

'Lorius speaks of Takaar's failure as a catalyst for an Ynissul attempt to return to dominance. He is mistaken. I stand here before you, high priest of Yniss, and I tell you that the Ynissul do not wish for dominance. I do not wish for dominance. All I want to do is serve my god, serve my people and serve our glorious land.

'If Takaar's law has taught us anything, it is that we are one. We cannot exist as warring threads. Look how our population has grown during the harmony. Look how all our gods are stronger. Look at how much more we *know*. Temples bulge with scriptures. Our rainforest provides everything we need to keep our bodies healthy. Working together has brought us comfort of mind and body.

'Why would you tear that up?'

Jarinn paused. He scanned the crowd, who stared at him, utterly silent now. Jarinn's voice had a compelling quality to it. He didn't speak at great volume. He didn't have to. Katyett knew what each and every *ula* and *iad* in the chamber felt. It was like Jarinn was talking to them, and them alone.

'Takaar ever was an enigma. Most of you here probably never met him, much less saw him in action. A braver elf there has never been, and will never be. Two hundred and more years before any of us travelled here, before Takaar opened the gateway, it was he who saw the path to our salvation. He was the first to openly declare his love for every elf who walked the land under the gaze of our gods. And it was he who cut to the heart of the conflict and made us understand our stupidity.

'The War of Bloods. Very grand in name but we were merely fighting about who lived the longest. We might just as well have been fighting over the size of our hands or the colour of our hair. These things are not within our control. I did not choose to be born an Ynissul, nor did Lorius choose to be born a Tuali. Accidents of birth.

'Are you cursed if you are Gyalan and relatively short-lived? No. You enjoy a purity of soul that no Ynissul can ever know. There is joy in that. And ask any man from the north if they would consider a lifespan of four hundred years and more short? The blink-lives are jealous of all of our longevities. Theirs is such a brief ember, is it not? If you were human, you could understand that causing conflict, yes?'

Laughter spread around the chamber.

'Takaar taught us to embrace our differences. To use our strengths to help each other, not to divide us. And he succeeded, didn't he? Yes, he did. So that is what Takaar and Takaar's law has brought us. Twelve hundred years of peace, harmony and understanding. Remember that. It is an indisputable truth.'

Jarinn paused again and surveyed the crowd.

'So to the events of a decade ago and the reason we are all in here, rather than without, enjoying the beauty of our land. Takaar failed. His courage faltered on that fateful day. A great many elves lost their lives. All these facts are irrefutable.

'Consider this also. That in the forty days before Takaar fell from grace, his actions with the Garonin pressing on towards the walls of Tul-Kenerit saved hundreds of thousands of lives. Indeed on the day before, nine thousand came through the gate from Hausolis to find sanctuary here on Calaius. These facts are irrefutable. We have every scrap of paperwork to prove it.

'And finally, think on this. When Takaar's courage faltered, he ran. And that is a shame he must forever bear. And he ran through the portal and into the streets of Ysundeneth. There is an argument that it was his only hope of escaping the Garonin. And that is probably true. But it also demonstrates a mind still keen despite the torture he must have been experiencing. Popular hatred dictates that he ran through and marooned a hundred thousand. Imagine if he had not? We all know that the Garonin wanted the gateway more than any elven heart. Takaar stopped them when the gate collapsed in his wake. And in doing so, he saved each and every one of you.'

There was a murmuring in the chamber. Lorius scoffed loudly.

'It does not matter if this salvation was an unintended consequence of his flight. He achieved it anyway. I am not here to defend Takaar personally; I am here to tell you what will happen if his law is denounced along with him, if it is torn up and is no longer presided over by our gods.

'Takaar's law binds us. Tuali, Beethan, Ixii, Gyalan, Orran, Ynissul, whoever our god and whatever our longevity in our land. It is a guiding hand when there is doubt. It is the spine of our race. The fire in the darkest of places and the sun after the rains have come. It is rooted as deeply within us now as is the air we breathe here. It links us, gives us strength and unity. It stays the hand of the wronged. It is the embrace for those who need succour.

'Takaar's law is the heart of the elves. Rip it out and you will reap sorrow and bloodshed. No one denies we have problems but we must work through them together. As Takaar taught us. Denounce him and his law and be lessened. Be turned from the path to greatness. Be no better than men.

'Do not turn from Takaar. Not now. Not ever. Every challenge is surmountable. Every grievance can be resolved. But not if you tear the spine from our body. Walk with me and, as Takaar once did, walk with gods.

'Thank you for hearing me.'

The applause was deafening but not so febrile as that which had followed Lorius's speech. Eloquent, empathetic, sincere. But Katyett's smile was sad.

'Has he done enough?' asked Grafyrre.

'Oh, Graf, what do you think?'

'I think we'd better be ready to do exactly what Lorius accused us of waiting to do,' said Grafyrre.

'Yniss preserve us for what is to come,' whispered Merrat.

Katyett gathered herself to see the inevitable unfold. A few spoke in support of Lorius and were cheered to the rafters. A few, a very few including Pelyn, spoke for Jarinn and were taunted and shouted down. Agitators were moving among the crowd and the calm Jarinn had engendered dissolved into a broiling expectancy.

Pelyn had stood before a withering barrage of abuse. They called her traitor and coward. They called her slave to the Ynissul. Only once did she raise her eyes to the rafters and Katyett saw in her eyes all the pain of memory that she carried with her. Al-Arynaar warriors were gathering in the wings, ready to augment those already stretched across the front of the stage. Much of the crowd was on its feet now and there was a distinct bunching forward.

Katyett called the TaiGethen to her. Fifteen of them, five cells, swarming over the timbers and barely even disturbing the dust.

'You all know which way this is going to go. You know our priorities. No blades. We cannot afford blood on our hands. Positions. May Yniss bless your every move.'

Katyett led Grafyrre and Merrat towards the front of the stage, where they stopped directly above the trio of lecterns. Others moved further back to wait above the stage in front of the ranks of seats. There was nervousness among the dignitaries below and some could be seen clearly eyeing up escape routes should things turn nasty.

Katyett kept her eyes on the crowd. She could see four Tualis near the front of the chamber. They were spread across the front of the stage and about three rows back in the press. She could see them shouting, leaning in to whisper and leading chants against Takaar.

'See them?' asked Katyett.

'Yes,' said Grafyrre.

'If it comes to it, take them down quickly.'

Pelyn had stopped speaking and the howls of abuse and bile followed her back to her seat. Katyett watched her and saw the hand signals she gave to her warriors. The TaiGethen Arch bit her lip. It could all get out of hand very quickly. She couldn't catch Pelyn's eye and the Al-Arynaar leader had turned an expression full of anger on the crowd.

Helias raised his hands for quiet and the room stilled like the sky before thunder. Jarinn and Lorius moved back to their positions.

'Now we come to it,' said Helias, and Katyett had to smile at his penchant for the dramatic. 'You have heard the speeches from both sides of the debate. Words of passion, energy and belief. But it is you who will decide on this most critical of matters. Which way will you go? Think on it and hear the closing lines from Jarinn and, first, from Lorius. And may I remind you all of protocol at this time. Respect your priests, respect your gods and respect the history of this place. Lorius, please.'

Lorius nodded. 'Brothers and sisters. A vote to denounce is not a vote to destroy the harmony. It is a vote to embrace a new way forward, an equal way forward, for all elves of all threads. A vote for peace and the glory of all our gods.'

'Jarinn, please,' said Helias.

Jarinn nodded. 'Brothers and sisters. Denouncing Takaar's law rips the spine from the body of elven harmony. The one cannot exist without the other. Vote to keep the law. Vote to keep the harmony and avoid a headlong fall into bloodshed and hatred.'

Helias nodded at each priest in turn.

'Thank you. And now the chamber shall be seated.'

Katyett's heart was thundering in her chest. Across the chamber, elves found chair, bench and floor space. Many could only crouch. Others sat on friends. The murmur of conversation was loud and constant, the buzz of anticipation like a plague of approaching insects.

'Now we vote,' said Helias. 'I will have silence. And I will have decorum throughout or the vote shall be called void.'

The buzz and hum died away. The sounds of the crowd outside mingled with the cacophony of the surrounding rainforest and the drumming of rain on the roof.

'Those who would see Takaar's law remain, who would see Takaar's name still held in reverence by Yniss, stand now.'

Behind Helias perhaps two thirds of the dignitaries stood, but in defiance of protocol the public did not follow them. Only a handful rose to their feet to be greeted by jeers and laughter. On the stage Jarinn's head dropped. Helias waited. A ripple ran around the chamber, elves straining to leap up on his word, barely in check.

'Those who would see Takaar denounced and Takaar's law torn from the statute, stand now.'

The storm of noise was staggering. Elves surged to their feet, their voices booming up into the rafters, washing across the stage and rebounding. Immediately, Katyett could see fighting on the floor, those few supporters of Jarinn paying for their courage. She could not worry about them now. Hundreds began to bunch and move towards the stage. From nowhere, she saw torches brandished and lit. She saw the flash of metal, weapons being uncovered in direct contravention of the laws of the Gardaryn.

'I call the vote to denounce carried!' yelled Helias into the deafening tumult though none needed his words to know the result.

Helias retreated, beckoning to both Jarinn and Lorius. Neither priest moved, though Jarinn glanced back at the tapestries hung on the walls, the symbols of Takaar's heroism and the law that had governed the elves for so long.

All around her, Katyett felt the eyes of the TaiGethen on her. She shrugged and nodded.

'Tais, we move.'

Elite elven warriors hung down from the rafters and dropped seventy feet to the stage, their landings soft and sure. They rose as one, two cells moving in front of the lecterns, the other three moving quickly back to begin clearing the seats. Katyett stood in the centre of the stage. Down on the floor, the line of Al-Arynaar braced.

'No weapons,' she shouted. 'Disarm and disable.'

The roaring of the crowd was extraordinary. Her voice could not possibly carry to all who needed to hear it. She spun around. Helias was still backing away.

'Helias. Order the gongs. We have to clear the floor.' But Helias wasn't listening; he was leaving. 'Damn you.'

Katyett touched Grafyrre's shoulder. The TaiGethen turned half round.

'They'll try and take the flanks,' he said. 'We can't let the treasures be destroyed.'

'Split the Tais. Have the Al-Arynaar hold the centre.'

Katyett scanned the floor. The density in front of the stage was growing again, having dispersed a little when the TaiGethen dropped down. Agitators were galvanising a chant, a demand that the Takaar tapestries be destroyed, and all the words in the ancient language too. Malevolent. Foreboding.

She swung back to the lecterns and saw behind them the seats emptying quickly. Dignitaries were heading into the antechambers, kitchens and offices behind the stage towards the three sets of doors usually used by caterers and staff. She walked onto the bloodstain at centre stage.

'My Lord Jarinn, you need to leave. One cell will guard you. Head straight back to Aryndeneth. The city is going to be ugly for a while. High Priest Lorius, you too. I'll detail a cell to take you to a place of safety.'

'I have no need of your help, TaiGethen.'

'Suit yourself,' said Katyett. 'But we are clearing this building. I suggest you go in safety while you still can.'

'Lorius, don't be stupid,' said Jarinn. 'I'll see to it, Katyett. You're needed elsewhere.'

'Thank you, Jarinn. Olmaat! Your Tai to guard the priests.'

Olmaat nodded his acceptance of the honour. He was a superb warrior. The fastest of the TaiGethen. Katyett turned back to the front of the stage. The noise was growing steadily. A distinct divide had grown between those facing the stage, chanting and taunting, and those behind, waiting and watching. Katyett headed left to join her Tai.

'Altogether too organised,' said Merrat.

'Watch the torch carriers. We—'

An order was barked from down on the floor. A volley of missiles arced overhead. Clay broke against the stone walls behind the tapestries and liquid spilled on stone, seat and wool. Katyett sniffed the air.

'Oil.' She knew what was coming next. 'Tai, with me.'

Katyett leapt out over the Al-Arynaar in front of the stage and crashed into the crowd feet first. Elves scattered from around her. Merrat and Grafyrre landed close by, both moving towards targets to the left. Screams erupted. Katyett rose fluidly. A Tuali *ula* stood no more than three yards from her, torch in hand, cocked to throw.

'Don't do it,' she warned.

'Keep her from me,' shouted the agitator. 'She's only one.'

In the roar of the crowd down here on the public floor, Katyett let her senses take over. One with nature, Yniss at her side, she focused, her mind clear of encumbrance and distraction. Most continued backing away from her. One came in from her left, swinging an unlit torch towards her head. Katyett moved a pace forward and blocked up and out with her left forearm. The torch broke over her wrist.

In front of her, the agitator caught her gaze. When he threw the torch she had already plotted its trajectory, was already in the air as it left his hand. She snatched it from its path, landed and kept moving. The agitator had no chance to escape. Katyett dropped the torch, crushed the flame underfoot, took another pace and snapped out her right fist, catching him square on the chin. His head rolled back and he crumpled.

Katyett stood over his prone form. She was standing in open space. No one was within five yards of her. But this was not victory. To the right, torches spun end over end to strike the stage, its seating and walls. And in the centre of the press the crowd had bunched and, as she watched, they rushed the stage.

*

Pelyn ran in from the back offices, eight Al-Arynaar behind her, the sounds of violence sending a shiver through her back. Her mind was still aflame at the memory of her treatment at the hands of the public and the smirking contempt of Helias. Making sure he was safe had taken a significant effort of will.

She saw the crowd run right through her thin line of Al-Arynaar guard and onto the stage. She saw torches strike tapestry and wood, and sheets of flame leap up where the oil she could smell had splashed. There were TaiGethen powering in from left and right but of Katyett she could see no sign.

'Get those fires out,' she shouted, waving a hand to her right. 'Keep people away from the tapestries. I want this stage clear.'

Two Al-Arynaar moved right, taking cushions from the chairs to act as beaters. Two more came with them, moving to head off those intent on seeing the fires consume a national treasure. Pelyn headed directly for the centre of the stage, where the first of the public were closing on the lecterns. She saw knives in hands, faces contorted with righteous rage. But no direction. Nowhere to truly vent the anger that had eclipsed the joy of their victory.

Pelyn and the four with her were a woefully inadequate number. She ran forward, throwing her arms out.

'Back. Get back. Get off the stage.'

But her voice was lost. Pelyn led her Al-Arynaar across the lectern space. Below, at the front of the stage, her warriors were still trying to keep as many from the stage as they could. Right in front of her, an *ula* hefted a hand axe, clearly intent on taking it to the lectern carvings. He was Tuali like her, and his face was full of contempt. From behind him, sudden movement. Katyett and her Tai leapt over the crowd, executing tuck and roll before stretching out to land softly and turn, backing her up. To the right, Al-Arynaar pressed elves back, allowing the two with beaters to attack the flames.

Pelyn's warriors moved to her sides. The *ula* with the axe stepped up, backed by others.

'Out of my way.' His voice was a snarl, his face ugly in his fury. 'Takaar is denounced. We will remove his image.'

'Stand down. Sheathe the axe.'

The Tuali laughed. 'You no longer have the authority to stop me.'

Pelyn pushed her face right into his.

'Don't make me embarrass you,' she said. 'You are Tuali. Act like it.'

'Run back to your Ynissul friends,' he said. 'You are no more Tuali to me than a dog. *Efra*.'

The *ula* spat on her, the saliva spattering over her nose and right eye. Pelyn felt her control give. She smashed a fist in his gut. He doubled over. Pelyn stepped aside and cracked her elbow into the side of his head. He went down, rolling onto his back. Pelyn took a knife from her belt sheath, dropped to her knee and raised her hand to strike into his heart.

A hand grabbed her wrist. A strong hand.

'No.' Katyett. 'Don't give them what they want.'

Pelyn was aware of silence sweeping out over the chamber. Her mind was clouded and she couldn't shift the fury.

'He—'

'Pelyn. Listen to me.'

Pelyn jerked her arm, but Katyett's grip merely hardened and all she succeeded in doing was dropping the knife.

'They want a fight,' said Pelyn.

'They want a martyr,' said Katyett. 'Please, Pelyn. Not by your hand.'

Pelyn nodded. 'All right. I'm all right.'

Katyett let go her wrist. Pelyn turned back to the *ula*. He displayed no fear. Instead a half smile played on his lips.

'See?' he said. 'You are still their slave.'

Pelyn balled her fist and cracked it into the *ula*'s nose. Knocking him out cold against the stone stage.

'Get him out of here,' she said.

She stood up and straightened her clothes. Dozens more Al-Arynaar were entering the chamber from front and rear. Pelyn faced the subdued crowd.

'The next one of you that calls me *efra* will be the martyr you so crave. Clear the chamber.'

Katyett put a hand on her shoulder.

'You and I need to talk. Now.'

Chapter 8

Politicians seek victory to taste further glory. Soldiers seek victory to taste further life.

'You cannot let them goad you like that,' said Katyett, the moment the door to the records office was closed behind her and Pelyn.

Outside, the Gardaryn was being forcibly cleared by Al-Arynaar and TaiGethen. The aggression had dissipated, water through a cracked jug, and Katyett had left behind her a sullen cowed mob. No doubt they would find more targets for their frustration outside.

'You heard what he called me. You saw what he did.'

'Yes, and you nearly gave him what he was looking for.'

'He deserved nothing less.'

Pelyn had her back to Katyett. She was wringing her hands and her whole body was shaking. Her rage clung on, giving way slowly to shock. Katyett took a pace and went to reach out. She stopped herself midway.

'Pelyn, look at me.' There was a slight turn of the head, nothing more. 'Pelyn, please.'

Pelyn turned. There were tears on her young face, smearing the dust and dirt that had filled the air of the chamber when the riot began. There was power within her, great charisma too. Yet in this moment she was the frail *iad* in whom Takaar had seen such potential when he was building the Al-Arynaar to back the Tai-Gethen's elite skills. Pelyn stared at Katyett with all the old pain in her face.

Katyett's heart fell.

'He cannot have known what he was saying,' she said.

'He knew *exactly* what he was saying.'

'No, I mean, he knew the word he used, sure, but not what . . . happened to you on Hausolis. No one, almost no one, knows about that.'

Pelyn covered her face with her hands and drew them down to the point of her jaw.

'Plenty know and enough of them escaped through the gate. You think I'm being naive but you're as bad. Takaar's denouncement didn't just happen today. It's been happening for a decade. And if you think there aren't those in Ysundeneth capable of using every bit of information about those . . . those closest to him, against them, then you need to understand a little more about the nature of the embittered elven mind.'

'But what Takaar did, he did for you. You know that, don't you?'

Pelyn's fury returned and she advanced on Katyett.

'What I know is that he rejected me three times. In the prime of my fertility he looked in another direction. Rendered me worthless. Unworthy of carrying his child. And even back then, before the Garonin came, people called me *efra*.

'And I know that despite what he did to me, despite the humiliation, I still loved him. I still love him today.'

Katyett sighed. 'He never stopped loving you, either.'

'Really?' Pelyn's tone was bitter-edged. 'He believed in my ability on the battlefield but that is hardly the same thing.'

'It was exactly the same thing to Takaar. He saw greatness in you and he brought it to the fore. Showed everyone what you could do.'

'Out of guilt, I expect.'

'Don't be so stupid, Pelyn. You think he rejected you because he didn't care? Wouldn't have been proud to father a child with you; a Tuali–Ynissul union? He did it because he could see a better destiny.'

'What could be better than being the mother of Takaar's child!' Pelyn cried. 'Do you think I'm stupid, Katyett? Do you really? I know why he rejected me. It had nothing to do with my skills as a general. Having a baby wouldn't change that, would it? It's because he had eyes elsewhere. Didn't he? Didn't he!'

Pelyn's hand came round, open-palmed. Katyett caught her wrist and held it like she held Pelyn's gaze.

'Yes, he did. And you know what happened? Nothing. I bore him nothing. My love for him was as desperate as yours. Yniss knows it still is and ever will be. But I could not give him what he wanted. All that time I was away from the TaiGethen, when people suspected I was pregnant, I was hiding my shame, trying every method, herbal and mystic, to make myself more fertile. And I failed. I failed, Pelyn, and he and I both know he should have chosen you.'

Pelyn had relaxed completely and Katyett let go her wrist. Pelyn rubbed it and then took Katyett's hand.

'I'm sorry,' she said quietly. 'I had no idea.'

'I wish I was termed *efra*,' said Katyett, believing it too. 'At least that way I could hold my head up and say I *might* have been the mother.'

'You don't wish that. Trust me.'

Both *iads* smiled. They embraced.

'Takaar has no heir,' said Katyett, breaking away but not letting go.

Pelyn bit her lip. 'And you. Will you enter fertility again?'

'Perhaps,' said Katyett. 'But I have to live through all this first. And find Takaar and persuade him he needs a child. Yniss preserve us, he's probably dead.'

'Despite all that he has caused, to have no child would be terrible,' said Pelyn.

'There are precious few out there who would agree with you. How old are you?'

'Three hundred and seven,' said Pelyn.

'Still fertile?'

Pelyn shrugged. 'Yes, but my prime has passed by twenty years. And I only get one season, long though it feels sometimes.'

Katyett nodded. 'We really could do without this war, if it comes to it.'

'I hear you. We'd be right back to the days of pressure to conceive.'

'Funny isn't it that Takaar effectively gave the *iads* choice of partner and then demonstrated how easy it is to get it wrong.'

'Oh, Katyett, he didn't get it wrong. Wanting you to mother his child was the least surprising decision he ever made.'

Katyett burst into tears and hugged Pelyn close.

'Yours is the most generous of souls,' she whispered.

'And yours the strongest,' said Pelyn. 'We cannot fall back into war.'

'Then let's stop pining after lost love for a moment and go and sort the rabble out.'

Pelyn laughed and pulled away.

'Thank you, Katyett,' she said. 'I nearly lost myself.'

'Want to know another truth? Anyone else calls you *efra* and you'll need to beat me to the killing blow.'

'I'll take the challenge.'

The door to the office opened.

'Katyett. Trouble at the temple piazza,' said Grafyrre.

Katyett sighed. 'Looks like it might be a long old day. Come on.'

It was a heartbreaking run through the city. So much bile, stored up for so long. Katyett had been spat at by people she knew. People she might have called friend. Today, as if some delicate strand had been torn to shreds, she was Ynissul, they were anything else but. Damned because they were loyal to an *ula* who had failed after saving so many of their brothers and sisters.

They ran past the Lanyon Jail, its gates standing open. Nothing like a random assortment of bitter criminals to stoke the fires. They moved quickly along the Path of Yniss towards the temple piazza, which rested on higher ground bordering the rainforest to the north-east. Everywhere, elves had formed into gangs.

Katyett shook her head. Most of them were single-thread gangs only. While the Ynissul were the principal targets of the, presumably Tuali-backed, aggression at the moment, history told them the flimsy unification of other threads would not last. No group that they passed offered anything more than verbal abuse to the TaiGethen cells and the thirty Al-Arynaar. Hardly surprising.

There was a fire burning up at the piazza. Tall flames licked up and smoke billowed, black and oily. Katyett increased her pace, breaking into a sprint as she ran into the piazza and saw the crowd building there. She glanced at the sky, hoping for the rain to return, praying to Yniss to nudge the elbow of Gyal and set her tears to fall.

The temple piazza was a place of beauty and tranquillity. Or rather it used to be. A circular open space a quarter of a mile across, centred around lawns and gardens, bordered by the city temples. Structures built with the passion of faith, reflecting the best qualities of elven dedication and flamboyance. From the stunning carved helical spires of the temple of Beeth, god of Root and Branch; to the spectacular entrance and mural-covered vestibule of the temple of Cefu, god of the Canopy; and the dominating temple of Shorth carved as a prone body, the piazza was testament to elven creativity.

All of it at risk now but none more so than the relatively modest temple of Yniss. The temple was a circular structure with a low green-painted dome and a thirty-foot spire at each corner. It had timber steps leading up to brightly painted wooden doors. Upwards of two hundred elves surrounded the entrance. Many carried torches and their intentions for the temple were clear enough.

A thin line of Al-Arynaar stood on the edge of the apron leading to the steps and more blocked access down the sides and to the rear. A few others stood on the steps, bows ready, but Katyett could see there was no desire to shoot.

'Let's get through this crowd, Pelyn. We need to hold them off until the rain comes.'

'I'll skirt left,' said Pelyn, already motioning her warriors to move with her.

Katyett headed straight through the centre of the crowd.

'Tais, make a path. No weapons. We move.'

Those at the rear of the crowd had sensed them coming and most were quick to move aside. Further in, attention was entirely on the temple. Katyett used her arms to ease people aside.

'Move. Now. Disperse.'

The Tais came after her, fanning out into a chevron behind her. She heard muttered curses and insults. One *ula* turned and stood his ground. Katyett walked on.

'Move or fall. Your choice,' said Katyett. 'I will walk to my temple unhindered.'

'Time changes, TaiGethen. I name my right to stand here. You cannot touch me. Not any more.'

Katyett shook her head, dropped to her haunches and swept the *ula*'s feet from under him. He fell onto his side and rolled onto his back. Katyett stood astride him.

'Wrong,' she said.

The TaiGethen filled in around her, pushing back any who might come to his defence. The *ula* bunched his fists. Katyett sniffed.

'I don't want to hurt you. But if that's what it takes to stop you, that is what I will do.' She leant down towards him. 'You are foolish if you think you can threaten the TaiGethen. Yniss guides us. Yniss keeps us for greater tasks. You are simply in the way. An impediment to be moved.'

'There are too few of you. Not enough to stop what is coming.'

'Go home, *ula*. Look to your real enemies. Those within your ranks who desire war and care nothing for your soul.'

Katyett stepped over the *ula* and reached down a hand. He looked on it with contempt and pushed himself quickly to his feet. Around them, the crowd had closed in, menacing, chanting the names of Tual and Lorius.

'The time when you can tell me what to think and what to do is gone. Remember that.'

Katyett turned away from him and breasted through the crowd once more, ignoring the resistance, the shoulders turned into her chest and the feet seeking to trip her. In their midst, only one *ula* had displayed any courage, misplaced though it was. Unfortunately, one was enough.

When she broke through the front rank of the crowd, Katyett saw Pelyn deploying her Al-Arynaar across the temple apron. She stood on the steps just behind them. Katyett trotted up to join her, turning to look down on the gathering from which a little impetus had been taken.

'Where's the priest?' asked Katyett.

'Still on her way here from the beetle. Or hiding out somewhere until we can organise some calm, if she has any sense.'

'How do we disperse them?'

'I don't know,' said Pelyn. 'I will not fire on them and I will not strike them with even the flat of a blade. I know some of these people. Ordinary folk. Woodworkers, bakers and potters. We can't attack them.'

'Then we must speak to them.'

'Think they'll listen?'

'Not to me,' said Katyett. 'I appear to be of the wrong thread today.'

Pelyn spared her a wry smile. 'All right. I'll do what I can.'

'Talk like Takaar. Engage them.'

'I'll bear it in mind.'

Katyett glanced up to the heavens. Cloud was moving in fast, bearing new rain. Those intent on firing the temple would have seen it too.

'Tais,' she said, confident the chanting crowd would not hear her. 'Like in the chamber, watch the torches. Intercept when you must.'

Pelyn raised her hands.

'Please. Please. Respect the piazza. Let me speak.'

Her voice was lost in the chanting and the howling of the crowd. Katyett clicked her tongue and the TaiGethen turned to her.

'Call. Like Takaar when he raced to save his Tai, my friend, lost now on Hausolis.'

Katyett paused then raised her face and hands to the sky, leading her warriors.

'Jal-e-a! Jal-e-a!'

Over and over, they called her name. Their voices joined, rose and resonated. Reverberating against the faces of the temples around the piazza and echoing into the canopy, where Cefu carried it to the heavens. A haunting sound, capturing the ear of every elf gathered before them. When the last echo of the TaiGethen voices had died away, there was relative silence. Pelyn nodded her thanks.

'Lorius and Jarinn left the Gardaryn together. Friends just as when they entered but on two sides of a debate. No one denies the passion Takaar inspires—' she glanced quickly at Katyett '—but passion must not be allowed to degenerate into violence and hate. Whatever Takaar's crimes in your eyes, does this make Yniss and his temple a valid target? We are all the subjects of Yniss.

'I am Tuali; my Al-Arynaar before you are drawn from every thread. Remember what Lorius said. The harmony must remain. Reduce this to a fight between threads and we risk wiping ourselves out. Just like before, when Takaar rose to save us.

'Whatever our personal grievances. Whatever we believe the Ynissul to have done while hidden behind the coat-tails of Takaar, we cannot, must not descend into mindless conflict. We must not desecrate the places of our gods. If we rip down temple walls we are all truly lost.

'I ask you, as your sister, as the leader of your Al-Arynaar, as a Tuali happy to work with every thread to bring our race prosperity and happiness, to disperse. Go to your homes. You really want to destroy a *temple*? I don't think so.'

She paused. There were catcalls, there was insult and there was abuse of the Ynissul. But it was not concerted. However, the crowd did not move. Not a single one turned away. And the agitators saw they had not lost their hold just yet.

'Disperse,' said Pelyn. 'We will not allow any damage to be caused to this or any other temple. Extinguish your torches and stopper your oil. The Al-Arynaar and the TaiGethen are sworn to protect Yniss from those who threaten it. Attack this temple and you attack Yniss. You also attack us. We have no wish to harm any of you but we will do what we must.'

Unease swept the crowd and Katyett wondered whether Pelyn had misjudged her last words. But they seemed to have the desired effect. Those with no real desire to face Yniss's elite began to break away.

But then the first drops of rain began to fall.

And someone threw a torch.

Chapter 9

Trust is a powerful ally and a deadly enemy.

Jarinn and Lorius were bustled through the back of the Gardaryn. With them ran Olmaat and his TaiGethen cell. Comforting. The sounds of the city were haunting, like the rainforest before a hurricane struck. Full of echoes and aggression.

Outside the Gardaryn in the small delivery yard, Al-Arynaar were gathering. Olmaat paused to speak to one of them, an *iad* that Jarinn didn't recognise. She was Gyalan by her slight build, frightened and angry.

'There's trouble already at the temple piazza,' she said.

'Are we clear to the river moorings?' asked Olmaat.

'Only the south-eastern bank. Take the route above the spice market, head through Beeth's Retreat. It's quiet there. Most of the trouble is brewing harbourside or on the Ultan bridge, what's not herding towards the temples anyway.'

'Good,' said Olmaat. 'Katyett should still be inside. Speak to her. Tell her about the temple piazza. We can't afford desecration. Not of any temple. This isn't a time to anger the gods.'

'They are already angry,' said the Al-Arynaar.

'No,' said Jarinn and Lorius as one. Jarinn moved to the *iad* and put a hand on her shoulder. 'Our gods issue us with challenges, such that we may prove ourselves worthy of living in this paradise. What happened inside the Gardaryn is not an act against the gods. Yniss blesses the independence of every elf to make his or her decisions. That is part of our strength. What neither Yniss, nor Tual, nor Beeth, nor Gyal will accept is wanton destruction of hallowed building and earth. That is what Olmaat rightly fears. And it is what you must stop.'

Jarinn could see the doubt on her face and he smiled as warmly as he could.

'This is a worrying time. A time of change. I fear the consequences but I must face them, as must Lorius. We remain friends, merely on opposite sides of a fierce debate. Remember that. The removal of Takaar's law does not necessarily render the harmony broken. Only elves can do that.'

'Jarinn is right,' said Lorius. 'I merely seek a new way to maintain and strengthen what we already have. We will never be enemies. The day that happens, when priest fights priest, all hope will be lost. Have faith. Pray to your god. And do the work of Yniss who blesses us all.'

'Thank you,' she said, managing a weak smile.

'Go,' said Olmaat. He turned to Jarinn and Lorius. 'My priests? This way.'

He and his Tai moved out of the yard, their footfalls making nothing more than a whisper on the cobbles. In comparison, Lorius and his boots seemed to ring out to all who wanted to find them. The pace was necessarily slow. Lorius had problems with both of his knees and Jarinn's arthritis was always worse at times of particular stress.

Overhead, clouds were gathering. Another deluge was very close. The air was close and hot. The tallest trees of the canopy reached up, greedy for it to start. The hoots and calls and chitters of myriad species exhorted Gyal's tears to fall. Thunder rattled high above, booming through the heavens.

Olmaat turned left into the wide Avenue of Gyaam. Ahead, the expanse of the spice market beckoned. It only operated every tenth day, and never when the Gardaryn was in session. A few elves could be seen looking at displays in the shops that bordered the stone-flagged and pitch-marked marketplace, and that was strange enough.

'I would have thought spices the least of their concerns right now,' muttered Lorius.

As rain began to fall, footsteps could be heard behind them. Running fast. Olmaat stopped and turned, ready in an instant. Jarinn turned too and smiled.

'Hithuur,' he said. 'I'm glad you're safe.'

The tall gaunt scripture scholar lived at Aryndeneth, rarely travelling to the city. He had come to the temple a broken *ula*. His family lost to the Garonin. Only in Yniss had he found solace and he was a fervent student. Jarinn suspected his aspirations went further than a reader of the *Aryn Hiil*, the core text of the Ynissul faith.

Hithuur had never said but surely he wanted to be accepted as one of the Silent. There was a passion in his eyes and a determination in the set of his body and the questions he asked. And he did not seek the love of another *iad*. He clung to the belief that his family was still alive, one day to be found and freed.

'I had to know you would be safe,' said Hithuur, trotting up while gathering his shirt collar against the rain.

'I am with Olmaat. How much safer can I get?'

Hithuur did not smile. 'You're running into trouble if you go through the spice market. I have a safe place just to the north.'

The rain fell in stair rods, bouncing from the cobbles and setting up a roar on domed and steep-pitched roofs all around them. Olmaat set himself between Jarinn and Hithuur.

'What's the problem beyond the market?' asked Olmaat.

'We've had information that—' Hithuur looked briefly at Lorius '—elves of other threads want to kidnap you. Use you as currency in a power struggle. They all know the limited ways you can leave the city from the Gardaryn. You should lie low, High Priest Jarinn. We can move again when passions falter.'

'It makes sense, Olmaat,' said Jarinn, feeling the edge of anxiety and the full force of sadness filling him. 'See, Lorius? Your plans are poorly thought out.'

'Where is this place?' asked Olmaat.

'The Hausolis Playhouse.'

'A major public building,' said Olmaat. 'Surely you could have found something a little more obvious? The lawn of the temple piazza perhaps.'

Hithuur's face darkened a shade. 'It has significant benefits. Not least that it is closed during the grieving period for Jilad Kantur. And from the rear, no one overlooks those arriving or leaving. It is secure.'

'I'll be the judge of that,' said Olmaat. 'Tai. A hundred paces ahead. Left and right. Quick and silent.'

Olmaat's Tai turned north. At the corners of a side street, they swarmed up the sides of houses as fast as most elves could run. Scaling tiled roofs designed to channel the heaviest of rainfall into gully, gutter and storm drain as if they were climbing an easy flight of stairs. Jarinn watched them go, a smile on his lips despite the situation, the rain and the pain in his joints.

'They are something to behold,' he said to Hithuur, looking across at the adept. Hithuur turned to him, his expression one Jarinn could easily mistake for worry. 'Something wrong?'

Hithuur tried a smile. 'No, no. Just regret that I am not good enough to be one of them.'

'But you will make a fine addition to another order,' said Jarinn. 'You are meant for great things.'

Olmaat gestured his charges before him and followed along behind. The front of the playhouse bordered an area of gardens. They were a popular gathering place where people ate, drank and watched entertainment provided by a legion of jugglers, singers and minstrels before the main event.

With the theatre dark while they grieved for their principal actor, the lawns were empty of the revellers who would shelter under leathers when the heaviest rains fell. Jarinn approached at a half-trot; it was as much as his arthritis would allow. He saw Olmaat's Tai emerge from the shadows on either flank and disappear to the left and right of the playhouse. Olmaat held up a hand. Jarinn, Lorius and Hithuur stopped.

'What's wrong?' asked Jarinn.

'Nothing,' said Olmaat. 'I need to be sure we aren't observed.'

He moved on at some signal Jarinn did not see, heading to the left of the main doors, whose great double latches were carved in the shape of masked dancers. The shadows were deep here. Behind the playhouse were its workshops and stores. Timber stacks rose against high wooden walls beyond which was cleared waste ground, ear-marked for warehousing and a new marketplace for fine wooden and stone goods.

Hithuur was right: the rear access was secure. But you had to get there unseen too. Olmaat stopped in the yard, in the lee of the playhouse and spoke to his Tai. One of them scaled the gates and headed into the waste ground. The other pulled open the rear door and vanished inside. Olmaat gestured the others to him. The rain battered against the playhouse and drummed high from the stone flags that paved the yard.

Jarinn wiped his face. A pointless reflex. More rain ran down his face. He shifted his bare feet to keep them warm in the puddles in which he stood.

'Hithuur,' said Olmaat. 'What will my Tai find inside? What will I see?'

Hithuur nodded. 'The staging area is behind this door. It is clear and empty. Directly ahead is the auditorium. The curtains are drawn, and beyond them steps up to the stage. We'll be safe here. There is food and others are coming to ensure we get to Aryndeneth safely.'

'High Priest Jarinn does not need greater numbers,' said Olmaat. 'He has the TaiGethen.'

The door to the playhouse edged open. Olmaat's Tai emerged.

'It is empty,' she said. 'The auditorium is silent.'

Olmaat nodded and led them inside. Jarinn had never been back-stage at the Hausolis Playhouse though he had been on the stage a number of times, normally called from the audience to take prayers or speak from the *Aryn Hiil*. Here, the space echoed. Parts of sets were leant against walls and there were a few chairs and a couple of tables looking lost in the middle of the floor.

Directly ahead, the curtains were closed and still. Beyond them, the oval stage was surrounded by benches on the ground floor and two tiers of balcony seating above. It was a wonderful place. Warm and light and full of emotion. Much of the emotion hung in the air even now. But that wasn't what Olmaat was sensing. The TaiGethen was sniffing at the air. He gestured his Tai towards the curtains.

'Olmaat?'

Olmaat raised a hand. 'A moment, my priest. Something smells wrong.'

'What do you mean?'

'There is something in here not of the rainforest.'

'Hithuur?' Jarinn turned to his adept.

Hithuur spread his hands. 'I've no idea what he's talking about.'

'Olmaat?'

'Something is not right.'

Jarinn felt suddenly tired. 'Do what you must. I'm going to sit down. Lorius?'

'I thought you'd never ask.'

The two priests walked towards chairs and a table a few yards to the right of the curtains.

'Hithuur?' Jarinn beckoned his adept.

'It's more comfortable in the auditorium.'

He moved towards the curtains. Olmaat tensed. Jarinn felt suddenly vulnerable and frightened but still couldn't place why.

'Olmaat?' he said a third time.

Olmaat's Tai stepped back through the curtains.

'The floor of the playhouse is empty,' she said, moving back to Olmaat.

Hithuur broke into a run. There was noise behind the curtains. Slapping impacts like people landing after a jump. Olmaat's head snapped round. The curtains were dragged aside. Six figures stood in the space. Not elves. Strangers. Blink-lives. Jarinn stopped, halfway to his seat. The blink-lives had no weapons but spread their hands, palms up. He could hear murmuring.

'Takaar betrayed us!' yelled Hithuur, standing by the strangers. 'He killed my family. The harmony is dead.'

Olmaat's Tai launched herself at the blink-lives. A jaqrui throwing crescent whispered out and chopped deep into the neck of one, who toppled back grabbing at his ruined throat as his life bled away. She took a sword from her back and thrashed it through the waist of another. An arrow from the depths of the auditorium took her through the throat.

Olmaat did not attack. Instead he turned and began sprinting towards Jarinn.

'Run!' he shouted. 'Get out, get out!'

Jarinn gaped. More figures were rushing up behind the line of strangers. There was a tightness in the air. Hithuur's words hung in his mind, a blade to the heart.

'The new order will sweep Takaar's law away,' shouted Hithuur. 'You are the old way, Jarinn. And Lorius will be the first martyr of the Tuali.'

Jarinn backed away. Olmaat was nearly on him, still shouting at him to go. There was a whine in his ears and his body felt as if it had been plunged into hot water. There was a rush of energy, like his soul flaring. He felt confused. He stared at the strangers. The four remaining moved their hands together.

Heat. And soul-scourging light.

Chapter 10

Respect those you kill in battle for we are all brothers in the eyes of Shorth.

Takaar couldn't control the nausea. He twisted out of his hammock, flopped onto the ground four feet below and vomited. Green and brown flecked with red. His head pounded and his stomach twisted. He vomited again, helpless as the constriction in his gut intensified. He hauled himself up onto his hands and knees, his whole body convulsing.

He was aware of a roaring sound. He assumed it was the blood rushing around his head but it was more distant than that. As his body calmed a little, and the breaths he gasped ceased to bring more convulsions, he found he could focus outside himself.

The roaring and growling was a panther. More than one. The guttural sounds echoed his own pain and were a mirror for the confusion he was beginning to experience. He rolled away from the stinking pool and lay on his back, grabbing air in grateful gulps. The rainforest was quiet. Unnaturally so.

Takaar sat up. He plucked a leech from his right arm and walked a little shakily to the edge of his bivouac, where he rested against the bole of a fig tree. He took a few deep breaths and tried to replay the instants before he was sick. He didn't like what his body told him.

You're scared. Should be a familiar feeling but you seem to believe otherwise.

'These are unusual times.' Takaar refused to turn to his tormentor, who sat behind him underneath the shelter. 'They are unpicking everything I have ever lived for.'

All the more reason to jump when I tell you to.

Takaar shook his head and walked away from the shelter. He had experienced a trio of events. Events? It seemed the only way to describe them. Far more complex than any emotion and far more overwhelming than mere feelings. They dipped into the core of him, of his race, and toyed with it.

It had begun with a sickness that was way beyond physical. And, in quick succession, two revolting grabs at the souls of the forest, the gods and every elf. They were what had caused him to vomit. And now he was left with an ache in his head not unlike the aftermath of the taipan venom.

What scared him was that he knew from where each of these events emanated. The grabbing of his soul had been triggered from Aryndeneth and Ysundeneth while the sickness came from every- where. It would unsettle every elf, though many would barely regis- ter it. But he, Takaar, champion of the harmony, the *ula* who once walked with gods, felt it for all of them.

He'd been feeling the unsettling nausea on and off for some time. The events at Aryndeneth and Ysundeneth were something altogether more violent, brutal. Sudden and brief assaults that had fed back through the energy lines that latticed the world.

He'd assumed the power they represented to be benign, latent. Yet the suddenness of his sickness and its violence told of a rippling in those energy lines and a filling of the air with something new that he could neither taste nor touch but could sense with his body and mind.

The energy was not something he could use. Not yet. But it was reminiscent of that he had felt on Hausolis, way back before the beginning of the harmony, when he had discovered the gateway and managed, somehow, to link himself to it. What had awakened the earth? And what did it have to do with the harmony and the anxiety of the elves?

He shouldn't care. Couldn't afford to.

Didn't.

Yes, best you take another edulis leaf, nicely boiled down with a little simarou and crushed beetle wing. Forget it. Forget it.

Takaar nodded. It was not often his tormentor adopted a sym- pathetic tone. Even rarer that he was right. Takaar returned to his shelter. A movement in the brush to his left caught his eye. He had faced every danger the rainforest could throw at a lone *ula*. There was nothing within it that could unnerve him now.

He stopped and stared hard into the undergrowth. A sleek form eased from within it, moving towards him. And it was not alone. He counted three. He should have been scared. He was easy prey. But they were not interested in his flesh.

Takaar crouched and held out a hand. One of them came forward. He felt the panther nuzzle his hand. Her tongue explored his palm and the head withdrew.

'What is it?' asked Takaar. 'What is it that we feel?'

His tears stung the burns on his face. He moved forward on his belly, every excruciating moment punctuated by the feeling of his clothes dragging where they were fused to his body. The skin had blackened on his hands and raw flesh was all that remained of the soles of his feet. Yniss had spared him. Spared his eyes. He did not know why. The last thing he wanted was to live and see what filled his gaze.

He dragged himself the last yard. The stench of burned flesh filled his seared nose. In front of him lay the smoking corpses of Lorius and Jarinn. Olmaat's tears were for them, for the fact he had failed them.

Where the men had gone he had no idea. Olmaat had been forced to suck in his agony, reach down within himself to still his shrieking body. Play dead while they made sure the enemy had killed their targets. They and Hithuur had left then. The *cascarg* and the blink-lives. The poison at the centre of faith.

Killed. That was the word they used. This was not a mere killing. This was destruction visited upon great elves. Inflicted with a hatred that defied understanding and using a power terrifying and incomprehensible. One that had left Olmaat with a lingering taste in his mouth he could not identify. More than that though, whatever it was the men had done, Olmaat had felt through his body.

Even when he had dived across Jarinn, trying to shield him, and been cast aside like a doll by the power of the fire column, he had felt a moment that he could only describe as elevating. Now the pain in every fibre made that a confusing memory.

Olmaat raised himself up on his blistered hands. His palms weren't too awful but the backs were beginning to weep and blackened skin hung off in uneven strips. He gasped, the air over his mouth and down his throat like dragging flesh over broken glass.

What remained of the two bodies was melted together. Neither was recognisable. Parts of limbs had simply been obliterated. One skull had been crushed. No flesh whatever remained. No clothing and no distinguishing marks. It was like some bastard creation, immolated at birth. Something hideous and pitiful, one mouth open in final agony, praying for the end.

And at least that end had been swift. Olmaat prayed to Shorth to comfort the souls of both elves. He prayed to Tual to keep him alive until he warned Katyett and found those responsible. He prayed to Yniss to help him seek them, face them and kill them.

'Olmaat?'

Relief took the strength from Olmaat and he collapsed back onto his stomach.

'Help me, Pakiir.'

Olmaat heard a gasp and the choking back of a sudden sob.

'Tell me that is not our Jarinn.'

'I cannot. All that remains now is reparation and retribution.'

'Yniss preserve us, is there no honour left?' Pakiir knelt in Olmaat's eye line and touched the charred hulk of Jarinn and Lorius to whisper a halting prayer. 'What must I do, Olmaat?'

'Find a temple healer. Find Katyett. The TaiGethen can trust no one. Our own people have turned against us. We must hunt and she must know what men have brought with them.' Olmaat coughed. 'No one else should see this place like it is.'

Olmaat felt a hand on his back. He sucked in the comfort of touch.

'Rest if you can. Don't try and move any more. I'll bring people to you. You'll be all right.'

'How did you escape it?'

'I am shamed, Olmaat. I ran back outside and hid until they were gone.'

Olmaat would have smiled but his lips were too charred for that. 'No shame in common sense. Yniss guides your mind, Pakiir. Go.'

Pakiir's footsteps faded quickly. Olmaat tried to lie absolutely still. The adrenaline was draining from him and the pain was becoming ever more intense. But he lifted his head one more time.

'I am sorry, my priests, I have failed you. I have failed Yniss.'

Nausea swept through him and he surrendered himself to the blissful dark.

It was a rerun of the scene in the Gardaryn though the stakes were immeasurably higher.

'Soak the walls!' roared an Al-Arynaar at the temple workers who had run out when the first torch and oil had struck the timbers. 'Douse the flames and soak the walls. Do it!'

'Weapons!' ordered Katyett.

Twelve TaiGethen and forty Al-Arynaar drew their blades. They advanced a single pace. Each Tai cell formed into its three. Pelyn checked her ranks.

'Double line. Advance on my order. Push them back.'

There were weapons in the crowd. Torches flew. Oil flasks shattered over the steps, over the walls and over the defenders. TaiGethen cells moved to the flanks. Katyett, Grafyrre and Merrat remained central. The mob had reacted to the first torch, howling in pleasure as flames ate briefly at a mural of Yniss giving life to the land. Al-Arynaar had dropped back to organise the temple workers.

'Target the agitators,' called Katyett.

Pelyn's heart raced in her chest. She wiped oil from her face. How close they stood to the brink.

'Move in,' said Pelyn.

She was at their head. The Al-Arynaar marched forward, swords held low but ready. The crowd backed off, but from all parts was being exhorted to hold.

'Remember who you really are,' said Pelyn. 'Ordinary people. You have children, you have lives to lead. Go back to them.'

They moved closer: Al-Arynaar and citizen could almost touch. The rain was coming down harder now but torches bathed in pitch would burn and the oil was resistant enough to do real damage. A torch was thrust through the front rank of the crowd and into the midriff of an Al-Arynaar.

Already covered in oil, she staggered back, flame shooting up her armour, across her hands and into her face. She screamed, pain and fear mingling. Three of her brothers dropped their swords and threw themselves on her, bearing her to the ground. And out of the crowd stormed six *ula*s with more torch-bearers behind.

They rushed the break in the line. Knives and swords rose. Helpless Al-Arynaar were going to be injured or killed. Pelyn had no time to think. She blocked a downward strike with her blade, heaved the *ula*'s arm back across his body and whipped her blade across his chest, a battle cry escaping her lips as she did so.

Blood sprayed into the air to mix with the rain. The *ula* was flung back, stumbling, dropping his knife and grabbing at his body. Pelyn saw it all through a haze. The mouths of elves dropping open. The fingers being raised to point. And the collapse of any semblance of order.

Screams rang out through the crowd. Panicked people ran left, right and back. *ula* and *iad* pushed each other down and aside to escape. More elves threw themselves at the Al-Arynaar. Fists struck down at the burning warrior and her protectors. Fingers raked across faces. Al-Arynaar barrelled into the attackers, sweeping them away.

TaiGethen attacked from left and right. Katyett hurdled the Al-Arynaar line with Grafyrre and Merrat. She bounced on one leg, rose and kicked out flat, driving the blade and arm of her target hard back into his gut. He fell back, sword arm flying out in a futile attempt at balance. The blade struck the face of another standing next to him, taking out an eye.

Pelyn faced a furious knot of elves.

'Murderer! Ynissul slave.'

She could still see the *ula* she had struck moving behind them, stumbling as he tried to escape.

'Go back to your homes. No more need be hurt. You've burned my people and the temple of Yniss. Your shame will live with you in the eyes of Shorth.' Pelyn brought her sword to the ready and moved towards them. 'Any of you want to disagree?'

Four rushed her. Al-Arynaar were either side of her. It was an uncoordinated attack. Two were ahead. One brought an old rusting short sword overhead. She swayed left and it rushed harmlessly past her shoulder. The second flailed out with long fingernails. Pelyn took her blade two-handed and blocked the strike aside with her wrists, leaning in with her right shoulder to connect with her attacker's chest. The elf was spun round and hit the ground hard.

The third found his way blocked by one of her warriors. The fourth made to throw his knife. His wrist was cocked. A hand clamped to it and held him hard. His feet brought him forward and he was dumped on his back. Katyett dropped a knee into his gut and put a blade to his eye.

'Stop this attack or you will be the first to explain yourself to Shorth.'

Pelyn had her blade at the throat of the elf she'd put down. Her other attackers were covered by warriors needing little more goading to push their blades home. On the face of the one staring up at Katyett there was fear and fury.

'It has already been a trying day,' said Katyett. 'And my sword hand aches.'

'Let me up,' he hissed at her.

'I don't think so. I remember you from the chamber. And it was the torch in your hand that has burned my Al-Arynaar sister. You're going nowhere. It's more a question of whether you choose to die now or rot in the Lanyon. Call off the attack.'

The attack was already over. The speed of the TaiGethen and the intent of the Al-Arynaar had scattered the body and will of the crowd. Anyone dragged along by nothing more than inflamed passion had already run. Those with weapons were backing away. Pelyn waved her warriors to move up slowly, pushing the remains of the crowd further from the temple.

The rain began to pound down so hard it stung the unprotected head. Pelyn turned to check on the condition of her burned Al-Arynaar but her eye was caught by a lone TaiGethen running towards the temple having entered the piazza from the east. His body was fluid and in control but Pelyn could see anguish on his face. It was a moment before she recognised Pakiir. Her heart went cold.

Katyett had seen him too and was running to intercept him. The few remaining in the crowd caught a change in the mood. Pelyn watched Katyett. Saw her arms come out to slow Pakiir and grip his shoulders, trying to calm him. Katyett stiffened, kissed Pakiir's forehead and brought him into a brief embrace. When she released him, Pakiir ran into the temple and Katyett turned back. Her face was grey. The rain pouring down it serving only to intensify an expression which would have stolen the thunder from the sky.

'Methian, keep the crowd moving out of the piazza,' Pelyn said to her captain. 'Muster back at the temple when you're done.'

She walked towards Katyett, who had called her Tais to her. As they joined her, they crouched, hands to the earth and heads bowed. Pelyn could hear quiet prayers of melancholy and knew already the magnitude of what had happened.

'Katyett?' she asked quietly

Katyett had tears on her face. Pelyn could see them despite the rain.

'Yniss and Tual have surely turned from us,' she whispered. 'Feel Gyal's tears, feel the anger within them.'

Pelyn was shaking, her breathing fast and her vision tunnelling. 'What has happened? Please.'

Katyett shook her head. 'Jarinn and Lorius. Both dead. Murdered by men and traitors. Burned beyond recognition by something the men brought with them, Pelyn.'

Pelyn's legs had given way and she'd sat down hard, her sword tumbling from her grip to clatter on the stone apron. She put her hands on her face, covering her mouth, eyes and nose. Nausea raged through her. She turned up to the heavens, letting Gyal's tears drum on the backs of her hands.

She was aware Katyett had knelt by her and of the mourning dirge the TaiGethen were beginning to chant.

'We cannot keep this news quiet. We have to be ready for what is to come,' said Katyett. 'You must warn the Al-Arynaar.'

'Who are the traitors?' Pelyn took her hands from her face and looked into Katyett's eyes.

'This is not the time.'

'What will I tell my warriors?' pushed Pelyn.

'Men killed our priests. Men backed by an Ynissul,' said Katyett, the words hard for her to speak.

'Ynissul killed Lorius,' said Pelyn, the sickness deep in her gut and a flash of hate for the temple in front of her impossible to ignore. 'You know how this will play out.'

'Ynissul killed Jarinn too.'

'You and I both know that won't matter,' said Pelyn. 'And Ynissul have brought strangers to these shores.'

'I know,' said Katyett. 'Pelyn, this is a pivotal moment. How the Al-Arynaar react is key. You do understand me?'

Pelyn nodded. Emotions clashed within her. 'It is difficult.'

'Then remember what you're fighting for. What we've fought for. You and I have stood shoulder to shoulder. On the walls of Tul-Kenerit we have faced the Garonin. All because we believe in what Takaar gave us. That has not changed. Criminal elements are taking advantage of the denouncement. We have to stand firm and we have to root out and kill those who would murder our most beloved to bring disorder down on the elves. We will hunt down the rogue Ynissul. Starting now.'

'I want to believe that,' said Pelyn.

Katyett bridled. 'I am TaiGethen.'

'I have warriors who will be seriously conflicted. Tual knows I understand why.'

'You cannot crack. You cannot falter. Flinch and perish, Pelyn. Remember that. But it won't just be your death, it'll be the death of our entire way of life. The waste of a thousand years of effort.'

Pelyn nodded again. 'What will you do?'

Katyett glanced behind her. Pakiir and a group of healers were running out of the piazza.

'I must see to Olmaat. He's still alive and what he has seen is crucial to us. I don't know what's next, Pelyn, I really don't. But no Ynissul will be safe. I am debating taking every Ynissul in Ysundeneth out of the city.'

'You know the message that will send.'

'Do I have another choice?'

Pelyn shrugged and climbed to her feet. Her heart was pained and melancholy ached throughout her whole body. The TaiGethen had completed their dirge and had moved to stand behind Katyett. She was helped up.

'I don't know, Katyett. All I know is that I am empty inside just as you must be. But you have not lost your priest to another thread. This will spread. How long does it take for news to reach Tolt Anoor or Deneth Barine? How can it not consume us?'

'Grieve for Lorius. Hate me if it helps. Just don't turn your back on the harmony. Think, Pelyn. Bring the Al-Arynaar with you or we're all lost.'

'I am thinking, Katyett. And I do not know who to trust.'

Chapter 11

If you pause to regret a killing blow, you will be explaining your regret to Shorth.

Sildaan watched Garan kneel by Haleth and then each mage in turn. She could have told him he was wasting his time. Auum would not have left any of them breathing unless their wounds were mortal. The one he had left alive had lapsed into unconsciousness and was moments from death.

The front of the dome floor was covered in human blood. Ice melted and dripped from the walls and fell like rain from the statue of Yniss. The casting did not appear to have done any damage. Nothing physical. But the effect on the forces which would range against her would be far-reaching.

Sildaan sighed. 'Perhaps you'll listen to my advice next time. I will deal with the TaiGethen.'

'This is dealing with them, is it?'

'You intervened with your magic. You caused this. You do not know what you have antagonised.'

Garan jerked to his feet. 'I think you'll find I know pretty bloody well. That one bastard and his ghost priest killed nineteen of my men. And now he's slaughtered my second in command and four of my mages before the ice has melted from his hair. So you'll excuse me if I don't feel like hearing "I told you so" right now.'

'You've no idea what you've done, have you?' said Sildaan.

'But I'm sure you're going to tell me.'

Sildaan walked towards him. 'Right now, Auum will be organising a muster of the whole TaiGethen order. And their sole focus will be on ripping out your still-beating heart.'

'Well it isn't as if there are that many of them,' said Garan.

'Considering just one has managed to kill twenty-four of your finest, there don't have to be many of them, do there?' Sildaan wondered if she'd slipped her knife into the wrong ally. 'And he's not even the best of them. He's young and his skills aren't complete. Think about it.'

'I'm thinking the rest of the temple Tais did not present too much of a problem.'

'Indeed, but killing the rest with a single casting won't be so easy, will it?'

'My mages will deal with them. Don't worry about it.'

Sildaan gestured at the bodies around the pool. 'I do not share your confidence. What is it that's stopping you understanding just how dangerous the TaiGethen are?'

'I think I've outlined how aware I am.'

'Then you aren't listening to your own words. There are Tai-Gethen cells across the rainforest. A few in each major city too. You don't see them unless they want to be seen. Your damn mages can't cast on something they can't see, can they? Any TaiGethen has the authority to kill any stranger they find in the forest. They are not required to ask you questions.

'They kill without error and without mercy. They are quick and they are silent. They are utterly loyal to Takaar and the harmony of the elves. He is their father as much as Yniss is their god. Not one will waver one iota. That makes them our mortal enemies. And you, Garan, have managed to unite them into a single force with a common goal. Now that may not worry you but, in your language, it scares the shit out of me.'

Garan looked a little uncertain for the first time. 'How many of them are there?'

'It's hard to say at any one time,' said Sildaan, blowing out her cheeks. 'If we assume all are alive barring those we know to be dead, probably around ninety.'

'*Ninety?*'

'Now you're getting it.'

'You've been less than clear about this so far, that's what I'm getting. We need more men. Particularly if your Al-Arynaar side with them too.'

'The Al-Arynaar will be split. We've seen to that. And we don't need more men. We need smarter men, don't you think?'

Garan took on that arrogant air that Sildaan was learning to hate in men.

'You've put me in charge of the muscle and mayhem. And I say we need more men.'

'You've got all you're going to get on the payroll of the new Ynissul, Garan. You need to manage your losses better. You forget that any reinforcements are on Balaia. That's a lot of days of delay. Thirty at least.'

'And you forget that having managed to get rid of your every elven warrior, you're very much alone right now.' Garan's smile was unpleasant. 'Aren't you?'

'It's like the tidal wave that hit Tolt Anoor. You can feel it. You might even be able to hear it. Building and building. And there's nothing you can do about it. The sea has been sucked away from your feet and the wall is about to crash down. That moment of peace and silence. That's now, isn't it?'

Katyett raised her eyebrows. Merrat had put her finger on it. The bizarre atmosphere of peace in Ysundeneth. It had descended after the break-up of the mob at the temple piazza and had left the night-time streets deserted. Haunted only by chanting and shouting.

The news of the deaths of Lorius and Jarinn had spread to every quarter of the city. Messenger birds had been thick in the sky. Dawn had brought crowds to the Gardaryn, the temple piazza and the Hausolis Playhouse. People wanting answers or a place to pour out their grief or anger. Al-Arynaar, the three hundred or so who had turned up for duty, were guarding the key establishments and patrolling as heavily as numbers allowed. Pelyn was visiting those whose consciences troubled them and more would join the ranks as the day progressed.

What struck Katyett was the veneer of normality. The fishing fleets had sailed. Ships were loading and unloading. All the markets were open and visited by members of every thread without apparent animosity. But behind the smiles the eyes gave away the truth.

'Just keep watching,' said Katyett. 'Somewhere, it'll happen. We need to be ready to move.'

Trade was feverish. Gerial should have been happy, but every time he looked down at his credit sheets and coin purse he wondered if it was all about to be rendered pointless. Beneath his stall stacked with fresh fruits and vegetables was his machete. He couldn't raise any shame about bringing it out today.

The central market was heaving. A hundred stalls carrying every type of produce available in Ysundeneth. Two hours into the morning session and some were already running short of stock. It was curious. He didn't see anyone actually panicking but everyone he served from regulars to the occasional was buying that bit more. Preparing for tomorrow, whatever it looked like.

'Father?'

Gerial turned. Nillis and his idiot friend Ulakan were breasting though the crowd, shouting, bargaining, arm-waving and pointing. Tall proud Tualis, the pair of them, but Ulakan was trouble. Never happy with his lot. Jealous of the Ynissul grasp on immortality. He'd been at the temples yesterday. Nillis, thankfully, had stayed away. The difference in their expressions this morning could not have been more stark.

Nillis, anxious but hopeful. Ulakan, angry and disdainful. Gerial watched him push others aside as he came, Gyalans and Beethans shoved from his path. Gerial hadn't seen an Ynissul in the market bar a cell of TaiGethen a little earlier on. He cleared his throat.

'Ulakan, those people are my customers,' said Gerial.

'You shouldn't be serving them,' muttered Ulakan.

Gerial felt his face flush. 'Really? Fancy a mango?'

Gerial held out a fruit. Ulakan reached out his hand, a smirk on his face.

'Tuali food for—' he began.

'Tended by Gyalans, harvested by Apposans and set on this stall by Ixii,' said Gerial. 'Still want it? You're an idiot. Get away from my stall. Nillis, I need you. What did you want anyway?'

Nillis looked briefly at Ulakan, who was staring at Gerial like a slighted child.

'You're being undercut by Heol and old Jasif. You should see the crowds at their stalls.'

'Then they're as stupid as your friend, aren't they? Why would you cut your prices on a day as packed as this?'

'They can feel what's coming,' said Ulakan. 'So they want to sell and get out. Perhaps it's you that's being stupid.'

Gerial shook his head. 'Take your mouth and get away from my stall. You're no longer welcome here or in my home.'

'But—' began Ulakan, gesturing at Nillis.

'Then use your brain before you open your mouth. We don't need your views. Tualis moved on a long time ago. About time you caught up.'

Ulakan made to say something else but thought better of it. Gerial watched him turn. An *ula* looking in another direction collided with him, bouncing off his strong frame.

'Sorry, my friend.'

'I'm not your friend, little-life,' snapped Ulakan, shoving him hard in the chest.

The Gyalan stumbled back off balance and half fell into the back of a group of others buying at a fresh meat stall. Gerial shouted a warning, but in the bustling crowd no one could hear him. One of the buyers sprawled into the display of meat. Trays clattered and fell. The stall shook and a leg cracked. Meat slithered onto the ground.

The group of buyers turned. The stallholder – Kithal, a big, burly Apposan farmer – ran around to try and save his produce. Ulakan was laughing. The Gyalan straightened. The buyers around him grabbed him but he shook them off. He ran straight at Ulakan and threw a punch. Ulakan dodged it and slammed his own fist into the *ula*'s stomach, another into his face.

'Gyalan scum!'

Elves turned. Gerial ran from behind his stall.

'Calm down,' he said, gesturing with his hands. 'Ulakan, shut your stupid mouth.'

Gerial stooped to help the Gyalan up. The *ula* nodded his thanks.

'What are you doing?' Ulakan was beginning to shout, losing his temper. 'He's not one of us.'

Gerial turned on him. 'It's you who isn't one of us. Nillis, get him out of here.'

A fist struck out, taking Nillis on the side of the head. Gerial swore and spun round again. There were people everywhere closing in, or so it seemed. Nillis was sprawled on the ground. Ulakan was bending to help him.

'What did he do?' shouted Gerial. 'Stop this. Now.'

One of the buyers at Kithal's stall pushed Gerial back.

'No one laughs at me,' he said.

'No one was. One idiot child,' said Gerial. 'Calm yourself.'

'Ordering me, are you? Tuali orders Beethan, is that it?'

The Beethan cocked a fist only to have his wrist grabbed by Kithal.

'That *ula* is my friend,' said Kithal. 'As are you.'

'Get your hand off me.'

The Beethan's friends jumped on Kithal, bearing him to the ground. Gerial shouted for them to stop. The Beethan punched Gerial's face. Gerial's head spun and he fell to his knees. He felt hands around him.

'Gerial, are you all right?' Ulakan. Gerial nodded. 'You may hate me but I'll fight for you. For all Tualis.'

'No,' managed Gerial, spitting out a mouthful of blood. 'Leave it.'

But Ulakan was already gone. There was a knife in his hands. Gerial watched him, his heart aching. He felt groggy. Nillis was by his side.

'I'm all right,' said Gerial. 'Stop him. Ulakan.'

Ulakan jumped on the back of the Gyalan *ula*. Gerial saw the knife flash. The Gyalan collapsed. Blood pooled on the cobbles. Kithal's stall was upturned. The farmer roared fury. His fists flew in a flurry. Gerial saw a head snap back. A Beethan slammed a meat tray into the back of Kithal's head. The farmer slumped forward.

Gerial saw red.

Katyett watched the riot spread across the marketplace like a rainstorm across the harbour. She watched the Al-Arynaar try and fail to restore order. She saw murder, looting and destruction. She saw her people begin to split and bunch. Ordinary elves this time. She saw her race begin to fracture.

'The wall has fallen,' she said. 'Come on. Time to act.'

Night in Ysundeneth and the city was on fire.

Katyett had set up a makeshift centre of operations on the roof of the Hausolis Playhouse. It gave her views to all corners of the compass. It was also one of the few flat roofs in the city. It had a gentle camber to channel away rain without upsetting the acoustics of the auditorium.

Riots had blitzed the docks as the sun set. Several coastal merchant ships had been burned at their moorings. Dockside businesses had been wrecked, warehousing looted or destroyed. Ynissul ships, businesses and warehouses. Elves had been chased from their homes moments before the oil and torches fell. Ynissul elves. There had been no killing but it was only a matter of time.

Katyett had put out the word to the TaiGethen remaining in the city of where she was stationed. Tables had been set up and pinned to them were hastily drawn sketches of the city. On each were placed stones representing known flashpoints and the current positions of Al-Arynaar forces, and charcoal marks where any significant destruction had taken place.

'Grafyrre, what's the—' In quick succession, three TaiGethen vaulted onto the roof. 'Yniss preserve us, it doesn't get any quieter, does it? What have you got for me?'

'Significant move towards the spice market. They might be heading here,' said one.

'How many?'

Katyett trotted to the south edge and could see bobbing torches.

'Two hundred at least.'

Grafyrre blew out his cheeks. Katyett looked at the other two.

'What have you got?'

'There's a very big blaze about to be set in the Takaar Gardens. Predictable but it stinks of a diversion to me.'

'All right. Well, it keeps them away from the buildings, I suppose. Al-Arynaar watching them?'

'A good number. Not doing a lot to stop them, mind you.'

'Damn it, Pelyn, where are you?' Katyett rubbed a hand over her face. 'And you?'

The third TaiGethen spread his hands. 'It's more a feeling than fact. A general movement back towards the temple piazza. Small groups here and there.'

'Trying not to attract attention? Tual's balls, who is orchestrating this?' Katyett looked again at the crowd approaching the spice market. They were moving quickly and there were others joining them, the whole spreading out. 'Graf, what's happening your side?'

'Got a lot of torches. Heading this way, I think.'

'They mean to surround us,' said Katyett. 'Something's going to happen at the temples. Who's up there?'

'A good number of Al-Arynaar, a lot of Ynissul inside our temple. I presume the priests and healers have all stayed put except the ones tending Olmaat downstairs,' said Grafyrre. 'What is it?'

'I don't know. It just feels bad. We need to get the TaiGethen to the piazza. All of them.' Katyett stared at her hands. They were trembling very slightly. She shuddered and circled her shoulders, trying to relieve sudden tension. 'Come on. Let's go.'

The faces of eight TaiGethen were turned to her.

'You want us to leave the command post?' asked Merrat. 'What about Olmaat and the healers?'

'When we're done at the temple I want us to leave the city altogether. Olmaat is safe enough. They will not enter the playhouse. They fear what happened here. Tais, we move.'

Katyett led them. She headed for a corner of the roof, swung out and climbed down to the arch above the doorway faster than most could descend a ladder. With a quick glance towards the approaching torches, she jumped the last twenty feet, landing silently and running away towards the piazza, meaning to enter it at the northern end by the temple of Shorth.

Down at street level, Katyett felt blind. She had the eight with her and there were three other cells in the city monitoring trouble. A young TaiGethen came up to her left shoulder.

'I've got the best route to the piazza,' she said. 'We can avoid the mobs and come in between Shorth and Gyal, up the stairs by the western sunken gardens.'

'Thank you, Faleen, lead on. Merrat, Graf, I need you to trace the other cells. Bring them to the piazza as soon as you can.'

'Consider it done.'

Katyett's cell split left and right, sprinting away into the night. She followed Faleen, who darted down a tight alleyway that led south and east between houses and the walls of the Gardens of Appos. She felt more comfortable here. Temporarily, the noise of violence was muted and the high walls leaned in like a blessing from Cefu.

The alley led out onto a quiet street, cobbled and with small businesses and low, domed housing on either side. There were a few lights but most places were dark and silent. Ordinary elves were hiding indoors, frightened and anxious about what was happening in their city, to their way of life.

Here in streets like this was where the anger at what had consumed the city settled most deeply on Katyett. *Ula* and *iad*, young and old, parent and child. Every thread would be represented behind the closed doors and shuttered windows. Scant hours before, they had been going about their normal lives. Secure in the knowledge that Yniss blessed their every step and the harmony was with them, unbreakable. The silent, invisible security blanket that wrapped them all.

And then the denouncement had happened, and those who had determined it to be the moment the world of the elves returned to the days before the War of Bloods held sway in the city. Those who had organised the murder of Jarinn and Lorius had ensured the blood of all threads would be spilled.

Katyett had no idea if there was a way out for the innocents she passed by with her brothers and sisters. She had no idea if the harmony would survive this onslaught, and she couldn't understand why any elf would want to rip it apart. Katyett could recall all too clearly the atrocities of the War of Bloods. They were at the root of her nervousness now. She could still feel the tears.

A TaiGethen warrior ran into the street from the left, sprinting hard, sliding to a stop when he saw them.

'Yniss bless us, we may just be in time,' he said.

'Pakiir. Run with us,' said Katyett. 'Tell me.'

'They're coming from all over. Crowding the temple piazza. Al-Arynaar are trying to hold them but they are too few. They mean to burn the temple of Yniss.'

Katyett's body went cold.

'Not again,' she whispered. 'Tais, run. Run hard.'

The sky towards the piazza was glowing with torchlight. Katyett ran alongside Faleen. The nearer they got the worse Katyett felt. They could hear the noise of the mob. She could almost taste the intent. A chant started. A line of the ancient tongue.

Chilmatta nun kerene.

Immortals die screaming.

She swore and pushed yet harder, forging ahead of Faleen. Still two hundred yards and more, and she could hear fighting. The clash of weapons. Screams of pain above the roar of the mob. An intensification of the mood. Blood was flowing. Elves were dying.

'Up to the roof of Shorth,' she shouted over her shoulder. 'Let's see what we're up against.'

Pakiir was going to be proved wrong. They were not going to get there in time. Katyett heard a roar of triumph that could only mean the defence was broken. Immediately after, there was a whooshing sound and the stink of burning oil filled the air. The roar intensified.

Katyett tore around the back of Shorth's Temple, pounded through the sunken garden with the yelling of the mob all around her, above her and ahead of her. She led the TaiGethen up the side of the temple, using the thick liana that grew there. She ran along the arm and down the body, pulling up at the temple's edge and looking down on mass murder.

Rioters surrounded Yniss. Doorways and windows had been

blocked by heavy drums and upturned wagons. Oil rained down on the building and torches were flicking into the fuel in their hundreds. The temple had caught with a ferocity that surprised even the rioters. Katyett could see those within the temple trying to beat their way out but the barricading was horribly effective. It rocked but did not fall.

Hundreds would be inside, believing themselves safe. But thousands were outside. *Thousands.*

'We've got to get down there,' she said. 'Get those doors open.'

'We'll be overrun,' said Pakiir. 'Look at them. Look at their faces.'

Ugly, twisted fury. Some of them upturned to the TaiGethen. Fingers pointed up while dozens of others added more fuel to the fire, which had already set the roof alight. Paint was blistering. There was screaming from inside. The piazza was choked with elves, safe in their numbers, taunting the TaiGethen. Yelling their hate of the Ynissul.

Down at the edges of the apron a few Al-Arynaar still fought, trying to keep the rioters away. Three broke from the crowd, racing to the barricades to try to pull them away from the main doors. Forty elves engulfed them. She saw fists and feet fly in and the flash of a blade.

A bloodied Al-Arynaar body was lifted aloft and thrown onto the flames. A second was raised, still struggling. Katyett snarled. Pelyn. Fighting hard. The rioters dropped her. More fists and raking fingers went in.

'Yniss save us. Tais, we move.'

Katyett backed up two paces, ran to the temple edge and jumped, her blades in her hands and the will to use them in her heart. Her leap carried her out over the narrow path between Shorth and the Yniss apron, over the heads of the rioters. She wouldn't clear them all, that leap would have been prodigious even for a TaiGethen. She just hoped her arrival would be enough to cause a measure of disruption.

Katyett was coming down from a height of around forty feet. She yelled for space and saw elves begin to scatter. The heat down here was already intense. The screaming and yelling was an assault on the ears. The sheer violence of the atmosphere was a physical shock.

Katyett drew her arms across her chest in an X, her blades resting against her cheeks. She hit the ground immediately behind an *ula* who was pushing forward, desperate to gain himself some space. Katyett absorbed the impact throughout her body, crouching low then standing and bringing her blades back across her body to ready by her sides.

She ran forward while others landed behind her, shouting for space that none wanted to cede. Katyett found her way blocked almost immediately. She lashed out with a foot, catching an *ula* behind the knee. He pitched forward. Katyett ran up his body. She slammed the hilt of one blade into the back of an *iad*'s neck. She dropped unconscious. Katyett hurdled the body, feeling her feet on the temple apron.

The atmosphere was clogged with ash and smoke. The heat was incredible. She'd broken through the main rioter line. Directly ahead was the group of elves fighting the remaining Al-Arynaar. Pelyn struggled on. A big *ula*, a Beethan, had wrapped his arms around her midriff. She struck at him again and again with the back of her head while her feet lashed out, catching another square in the face.

Katyett ran straight into the melee, shoulder-charging an *iad* from in front of Pelyn. TaiGethen ran to either side, heading for the barricades, casting around for something with which to drag them aside.

'Drop her right now,' called Katyett.

The *ula* turned his bloodied face to Katyett. A contemptuous smile twisted his face. He turned instead towards the fire. Pelyn screamed, knowing his intent. So did Katyett. She took a single pace and thrashed a blade through the back of the man's hamstrings. Simultaneously, Pakiir darted across in front of him, snatching Pelyn from his grasp as he opened his mouth to scream. He fell forward, head catching the burning barricade a glancing blow. His hair smoked, caught fire.

Katyett moved left to defend Pakiir. Pelyn was shouting to be let go. Pakiir complied. Pelyn hit the ground and was already turning back to the burning temple. Katyett saw the aching pain in her face, the singeing of her brows and hair. The smudges across her armour. Pelyn ran towards the front doors. TaiGethen who had been trying to break through the flaming obstacle bore her backwards with them as they came, beaten back by the sheer heat.

Rioters on the apron had begun to fall back. A TaiGethen foot whipped out, catching one in the gut, sending him sprawling. A jaqrui whispered away, catching another in the upper arm, forcing her to drop her blade. Al-Arynaar bodies littered the ground. Twenty of them. Katyett blinked away the stinging tears of smoke.

Out in the piazza, the fury was undimmed. Missiles were being hurled towards them and the temple. The building itself and all within it were lost. The roof had begun to collapse and the doors were burned in. Any screaming from within had ceased. TaiGethen still tried to breach the inferno.

Katyett felt tears on her face. The scene took on an echoing, unreal quality for her. Shouts sounded distant. Everything in her vision appeared to slow. She turned her head to see the flames towering into the night sky, pushing clouds of thick black smoke before them. Inside, three hundred and more Ynissul. Innocent elves. Bakers, potters, coopers, priests, healers. Children. Burned to death.

The Arch of the TaiGethen turned back to the crowd, letting the sight of her desecrated temple settle in her memory. She was aware of others joining her – Grafyrre and Merrat with those they had sought elsewhere in the city. Pakiir. Faleen. Standing in a line to stare at those for whom they protected the rainforest, for whom they had sworn to keep the elven people safe.

Wind was getting up. Picking at the clothing of the fallen. Fanning the flames in advance of Gyal's arrival. Her tears would be bitter when they came. The gods would turn from the elves. Angry, betrayed. Their faith insulted, their mercy ignored. The elves would walk alone now. And the path would run with their blood.

A rumbling crack filled the night. Katyett swung round. The front of the temple of Yniss collapsed inwards on a carpet of sparks and threw up clawed hands of fire chasing a wreath of smoke. The symbol of the harmony in Ysundeneth, destroyed by malign hand.

This time when Katyett returned her gaze to the mob, seeing it confused, not knowing what to do next, she felt it. The emotion she reserved for heretics. For thieves and, of course, for murderers. Hate.

And the TaiGethen existed to cleanse Yniss's land of such vermin.

'Tais,' she said. 'We strike.'

Chapter 12

A leader must at all times know the state of the body on which his subordinates gaze when receiving orders to risk their lives.

Takaar recoiled from the guarana as if it was burning hot. He blew on his fingertips before he could stop himself, realising a fraction too late what a ridiculous reaction it was. But he was hot. Burning up like in the worst clutches of a missiata-inspired fever. Sweat had burst out all over his body.

He sat back on the roughly made wooden chair in his bivouac, shivering and breathing hard. Unbidden, an intense sadness swept through him so hard it made him gasp. Like the anguished cry of a god, it reverberated in his mind and body. A shrieking disbelief. A horror from the darkness.

Takaar held his head in his hands, his tears falling onto the ground between his feet. He sobbed and wailed, the emotion uncontrollable, surging within him like flood water over rocks. It flung him back to the days of realisation following his fleeing of the Tul-Kenerit. And further back to the morning he had found his father murdered in his sleep by Tuali rebels.

That day, through the grief, he had sworn to unite the threads so that no other elf should suffer as he suffered. Today, he had no such direction but the pain was of equal intensity. More so because he was lost.

'What do you want of me?'

His cry set birds to flight and silenced for a moment the hoots of monkeys and the rattling of lizards and frogs.

No one wants anything of you barring your death. Why do you ask the gods? They have long since turned from you.

'Then why do I feel this way?'

It is merely your guilt come to remind you of your crimes. Accept it. The leap to your salvation is near.

Takaar shook his head.

'No. Not me. Messages. Messages through the ground and through the air. Calling to me.'

Listen to yourself. Messages coming to you through the ground? Absolutely. And monkeys dress you every morning.

'Get away from me, get away from me!'

Takaar got up and ran. Branches, leaves and thorns caught at his face and arms. He ducked his head and put his arms ahead of him, crashing through the undergrowth. The heat within him was unbearable. The sick pain and intense grief and fury overwhelming. His heart was thrashing. He couldn't drag in a breath deep enough to satisfy him.

He burst through the last of the brush and slid to a desperate stop on the edge of the cliffs down to the roaring River Shorth. He was gasping, shaking and crying, unable to control his emotion. Such a crime, but he didn't know what or where it had happened. His senses were completely deluged, drowning his directional ability.

'What are they doing, what are they doing?'

Takaar clutched at his knees and rocked back and forth, pleading for the heat and sorrow to ease.

A familiar pose. Roll a bit further forward, why don't you? It's merely the entire elven race reminding you of the scale of your betrayal. They will rip themselves apart. Destroy each other. Leave nothing to remember them by. All because of you. All because you ran. All because you are a coward.

Takaar sobbed hard, taking in shuddering breaths and dripping snot from his nose. He knew it was true. And he knew he was helpless to do anything about it.

Run. Run. It is all you have left.

Takaar stared into the forest, tempted to do exactly what his tormentor suggested.

'Shouldn't I just kill myself, as you desire?'

No point now. Too late.

Takaar caught his reflection in a pool of water sitting in a shallow dip in a rock. He laughed and recalled the reflection in his beloved mirror. How could an elf become two such different people? A beard crudely hacked but still long and black, full of lice and insects, dead leaves and pieces of food. Hair he dealt with similarly but that defied his attempts to tame it. It sprang from his head so fast he felt the gods pulling it themselves, just to taunt him. A mass of tangled knots, thick and hot around his skull.

Takaar frowned. He had never thought to try and shave it. He looked at his hands. They shook like they always had on and off since he had arrived here ten years ago. Ah, yes.

'Is that me?'

Yes. Shameful, isn't it?

And it was. Takaar tore his eyes away from his reflection. Still the pain was in his heart but the heat had lessened, giving him some small relief. He stood up and stared away along the glory of the Verendii Tual, where the delta flowed into the ocean.

He had knives that needed sharpening.

Aryndeneth was quiet but for the uncomfortable sounds of men readying for departure. Their smiles of relief did not disguise the ugly promises of violence they uttered. Sildaan had closed the temple doors on the blood that still stained the stone before the statue and pool and on the memory of the expression on Auum's face.

Sildaan walked around to the rear of the temple, ignoring the men stowing the last of their gear into backpacks, sharpening swords and inevitably scratching at their heads and bodies. None of them looked healthy despite the poultices, infusions and balms she had given them.

She carried on into the forest and knelt to pray to Yniss at the Hallows of Reclamation, blessed ground where the dead were laid out to be retaken by the forest. In front of her, already partially hidden by the voracious vegetation and feasted on by Tual's denizens, were her faithful priests and her dear friend Leeth. Nearby lay nine TaiGethen. Flesh blackened by the sick force of human magic and lying on a carpet of bones picked clean and washed white.

'Yniss, hear me. Shorth, hear me. Protect the souls of these recent dead and use them to further your work, your glory. Make them see as I pray you make the living see. Your armies must stand with me. Elves cannot live as one. The threads cannot be compromised, cannot be muddied or mixed. Order must be restored. Order under your glory.

'The lineage of the gods must be reflected in your people. We Ynissul, merciful and kind, will rule the elves again. Peace will be ours. Forgive my actions. I live only to do your work and to see your people flourish in your land. The blood that is spilled will feed the prosperity of the future.

'Your temple will be cleansed. All trace of man will be expunged. All that I do, every choice that I make, I make for you. Bless my hands, bless my eyes and guide me. My soul is yours to take. Hear me.'

Sildaan stayed kneeling for a while, one hand in the earth, the other upturned to the sky. The buzzing of flies around the bodies and the crawling of the undergrowth comforted her. Renewal, revitalisation, reclamation. She bowed her head to the Ynissul dead and rose smoothly to her feet.

Garan was waiting for her and she fell into step beside him as he walked back into the temple village.

'I need to tell you something about your erstwhile TaiGethen friend and his priest. They are travelling in separate and interesting directions.'

Sildaan raised her eyebrows. 'We don't need them muddying our plans any more than they have already. Track them. Kill them if you can. Your men up to that task?'

'I have men particularly expert in that field.'

'Good.' Sildaan cast an eye over her shoulder, back to the recent dead at the Hallows. 'Good.'

'Guilt getting the better of you, is it?' he asked.

'I have no guilt. Only regret that these fine elves could not open their eyes and see the truth.'

'And you call men brutal.' Garan paused in the centre of the clearing. To the right, near the temple's rear doors, stood the group of twenty-five warriors and mages. Garan gestured left. 'And what about these? Wouldn't death be kinder for them?'

Sildaan sighed. A handful of terrified temple workers and three priests who tended them. Priests who believed in Sildaan's way and had not had the misfortune to encounter Sikaant.

'They have committed no crime. They are Yniss's people. There is no suffering and my priests will see to their welfare.'

Garan shook his head. 'Your choice but if it's any help—'

'It isn't. These are my people. Am I not paying you enough to keep your opinions on my business to yourself?'

Garan chuckled. 'You could never pay us enough to fight with you in this hellhole. But that is our negotiation mistake, not yours, eh? Just don't be late with the wages.'

'Oh yes. Alone I may be, but without me you aren't just lost in the rainforest, you're lost and unpaid. Fight well, Garan. Earn your pay. Reassure me we will meet the balance of your force where and when we must?'

Garan began walking towards his men. Their muttering ceased and they looked to him, expectant.

'Shoulder up. We're leaving. I hear Ysundeneth and the coast are blessed with cooler breezes and a glorious lack of biting insects and leeches. Just three days from here too. Are you with me?'

His men cheered, laughed and shrugged packs onto their shoulders, secured weapons belts and tied shoelaces. A few dabbed at sores, blisters and boils.

'You may only have birds, runners and boats to get your messages through this ridiculous country; we have magic. My mages can speak to our ships as if they were standing on deck themselves. Communion we call it, and you will find it a keystone in your precious victory.'

Sildaan raised her eyebrows. 'You can really do this?'

'Care for a demonstration?'

Sildaan stared into Garan's face. There was no hint of malice in his eyes. No hint of a lie. For the first time in days, she felt able to relax a little.

'It will be demonstration enough if your sails are in the harbour when we arrive in the city.'

'Why thank you for your faith in me.'

'Do I have much choice?'

'Not really. But that is no reason for us to feud. One thing, though: while I can guarantee my force's timely arrival, can you assure me your people in the city will have done your bidding?'

Sildaan shrugged. 'You know there can be no certainty. But I have powerful allies in Ysundeneth. What we have set in motion can only have one outcome. Trust me as I must trust you. I know the elven mind.'

'And the TaiGethen?'

'They are your biggest threat. Your mages must be ready for them because your warriors can never be.'

'I see your faith only extends so far.'

Now it was Sildaan's turn to chuckle.

'Faith will not stop a TaiGethen cell. Magic just might.'

*

And they were so stupid that they did not realise what was coming at them. They stood and bayed their hate and waved their cudgels, fists, torches and swords. The TaiGethen, already painted for combat, dropped their heads in brief prayer and swept from the apron down the steps and into the crowd.

'Clear this place,' shouted Katyett. 'Desecrators. Heretics.'

The face of the *ula* in front of her cleared at the last moment and sick realisation slackened his jaw. Katyett knocked the torch from his hand to go sailing back into the mob. She whipped one blade up to sever an ear and chopped the second left to right across his neck. The *ula* clamped his hands to his wound and tried to scream.

Another *ula* fell across Katyett's path, intestines steaming and spilling through his desperate grasp. Katyett took off, glancing right to see Grafyrre bring his bloodied blade to ready. Katyett flicked out a kick into the face of an *iad* carrying a slender blade, landed on the same foot and drove her sword into the elf's unprotected chest.

A torch was pushed towards her face. Katyett snapped up her left leg, blocking the flaming wood and pitch. She kept her foot there, against the *ula*'s wrist, her thigh touching her cheek. She pivoted around with both blades, sweeping them parallel across the elf's midriff.

Katyett bent her left leg at the knee and struck out, clattering her foot into the temple of another rioter, knocking him sideways. She paced forward. Hands and fingers flailed at her. Behind them a face twisted with rage. The mouth lunged, teeth clacking at her face. Katyett swayed beyond the fingers, ducked the teeth. The *iad* screamed and rushed forward. Katyett stabbed straight out. Her victim shrieked.

Katyett paused. There was space around her. With those Grafyrre and Merrat had found, fifteen TaiGethen faced the multiple thousands packed into the piazza. Dozens of bodies littered the ground. The flames of the temple of Yniss cast a hideous glare onto the faces of elves and the bloodied stone.

Pakiir worked with a brother Tai cell. He was deep in the crowd, extracting his vengeance for those murdered behind him in the temple and, no doubt, the burning of Olmaat. Faleen's Tai savaged into a knot of unarmed *ulas* fighting with nails and teeth. A jaqrui chopped deep into the forehead of one rioter. A second lost a leg to a switch sweep of two blades and a third had her neck snapped by a kick to the underside of the chin.

At last, panic began to take hold. The ringleaders had lost the crowd. A certain return to reality melted through the blind spitting fury of the mob. Elves were beginning to run.

'Keep them going back to their filthy hovels!' called Katyett.

She flew back into the action. Her open palm thudded into the chest of an *iad* standing firm, spitting in the direction of the temple. The elf went over backwards. Katyett dropped both knees on her ribs, crushing cage, heart and lungs. Blood flew from her mouth, spattering across Katyett's face.

'Spit your last, *efra*.'

Katyett surged to her feet. The crowd was bunching back. The many fleeing in the face of the few but the unutterably deadly. She brought her blades to ready and advanced. There was a screaming behind her. Screaming her name. Katyett spun round.

Pelyn was coming down the steps, limping heavily. Blood welled from wounds on her face and stained her shirt at the neck. But there was enough strength within her to move and to yell her own rage.

'What are you doing? Stop. Stop!'

Katyett glanced over a shoulder and watched her brothers and sisters moving still, cutting down any that dared stand against them. She turned her gaze back to Pelyn and felt cold.

'I am doing the work of Yniss,' she said.

Pelyn walked right up to her, the pair of them standing a pace apart in the midst of a blood-slick arena of stone strewn with bodies and washed with the flickering glare of the burning temple. The din of the retreating mob echoed against the walls of other temples, which stood in mute judgement over the acts of elves.

'You've done exactly what you told me not to do,' shouted Pelyn, barely able to contain herself.

'I beg your pardon?'

'What is it you said to me?' Pelyn's spittle flew in Katyett's face. ' "Don't let them goad you," wasn't it? "Don't give them a martyr." What by Shorth's teeth do you think you've done?'

'I have carried out sentence on murderers.'

'You've killed those wholly unable to defend themselves against your skills. This is a slaughter.'

Katyett grabbed Pelyn's shoulder and dragged her round to look at the fiery remnants of the temple.

'And what was this, Pelyn? Hundreds of my people, burned in

a place they thought sanctuary. I will not leave such a crime un-punished.'

Pelyn pulled herself from Katyett's grasp. 'I was here. I was here trying to defend them. The most obvious target in the city. I was here. Where were you? Whose people were you defending on top of the playhouse?'

Katyett paused a moment, trying in vain to calm down. 'We are not the police of this city. That is your job. Are you seriously telling me you really thought a mob might actually torch the *temple of Yniss?*'

'You didn't feel the hate,' said Pelyn. 'I did. They would have cast me on too and I guess I have to thank you they did not. They'd have done it because I dared defend the Ynissul. Me, a Tuali. Never mind the temple, it was those inside they wanted.'

'What's done is done,' said Katyett, looking out at the piazza. Fifty bodies lay there. Perhaps more. 'But those who committed this atrocity know they cannot act with impunity.'

Pelyn sighed. 'No, Katyett. For you, it's always so simple, isn't it? And so naive sometimes. Too much time in the rainforest. What it's taught them is that Yniss's elite warriors have no control. That they mete out their version of justice on helpless elves.'

'They have murdered my brothers and sisters by the hundred. They have burned my temple. They have put themselves in front of the TaiGethen blades. I am bound to respond and I am not merely going to shepherd them from the site of their crime.'

Pelyn gestured at the remains of the fleeing crowd. 'And what would you have done if they'd all stood before you, killed them all?'

Katyett said nothing. Just stared into Pelyn's eyes. Pelyn gaped.

'Why so surprised, Pelyn? We exist to remove threats to the harmony. What would you call them?'

'More Ynissul will die because of what has happened here tonight.'

'Not here they won't,' said Katyett. 'We will take them with us. No Ynissul, no elf of any thread, should suffer such a fate as those innocents in my temple.'

Katyett turned away towards her TaiGethen. They were gathering on the temple apron, staring at the ruined timbers, the clouds of embers and coils of smoke rising into the night sky. They began to chant a dirge of grief.

'Take them where?'

Katyett turned. Pelyn looked lost, standing alone in the midst of the carnage. Alone and confused. Scared. Katyett wanted nothing more than to go back and comfort her. But this was not a time for friends. It was a time to do what had to be done to secure the Ynissul and what remained of the harmony. If anything did.

'We will stage them at the Ultan and then move them into the forest.'

'You're *leaving* the city?'

'The Ynissul are being targeted. If we are to hold back the tide of war we must remove the catalyst. I will need the help of the Al-Arynaar. Will I get it?'

But Pelyn appeared not to be listening. 'This place will tear itself apart.'

'I will not shed a tear for those who die trying to destroy the work of a millennium.'

'And the innocents caught in the middle of it all?'

Katyett shrugged. 'The Al-Arynaar are the keepers of the peace. It is why you are drawn from every thread. Looks to me like you'll be very busy.'

'I can't believe you're doing this,' said Pelyn.

'I'm doing what I was born to do. So must you. You said you no longer know who to trust, well you must trust yourself. You're strong, Pelyn. You stood before that crowd and did not back away. You tried to save my people. Our people. Yniss bless you for your courage.

'Somewhere, the minds behind this are working towards their end. The TaiGethen must find them and stop them. And if you truly believe in the harmony and in Takaar's legacy, you will try and keep this city standing so that when the conflict is done, we still have a place, a society and a race of elves of which Yniss can be proud.

'Think on that.'

Katyett walked to join her people in the dirge for their lost.

Chapter 13

Show your enemy his entrails. It is the only negotiation he will understand.

Auum travelled quickly, heading east when he left Serrin. He felt the absence of his mentor and friend more strongly than he had imagined he would. He followed a tributary to the River Shorth and turned north, tracking the great force from just inside the canopy.

He had with him the clothes in which he stood, his twin swords in their back scabbards, three short knives on his belt and his camouflage paints in a pouch next to that which carried six jaqrui throwing crescents. His boots were soft and comfortable, allowing him to feel everything beneath his feet. He would have run barefoot like so often on Hausolis, but so much danger lurked on the forest floor and he could not afford an accident.

Beyond the falls at Shorth's Teeth he had found a small boat with oars, mast and a tattered but serviceable sail. He'd have promised payment to the owner but the village was deserted, bearing the signs of a hasty evacuation. Sildaan's message was already out here.

There was no wind to fill his sail but Gyal was ever present. Rain thundered on the boat, forcing him to stop rowing every time a deluge struck to bail out water. It was a frustrating journey, only tempered by the flow of the river taking him in the direction he wanted to go.

Auum travelled the Shorth for three days. Out here in the middle of the rainforest, he could feel the harm being done to the land and its people. Yniss seemed powerless, or unwilling, to act. Auum rowed or sailed gently past river settlements whose inhabitants stared out at him with suspicion and even betrayal in their faces. He cursed Sildaan for the evil she perpetrated.

Between the deluges and the snatched hours of sleep, Auum thought. Perhaps too much. Out there ahead of him was Takaar. He wondered if there would be anything left of the *ula* he had known only briefly. The hero of the elven race. He who once walked with gods.

Auum wondered what he would say to Takaar. He imagined their conversations, dreamed about them sometimes, and always found his heart beating fast when he awoke. Takaar might not want to be found. He might ignore all Auum's entreaties. He might, of course, be dead.

That was not a thought on which Auum dwelt. Darker moments were banished by a prayer to Yniss or just by lying back and gazing at the glory that was Calaius. The Shorth wound its course through staggering changes of land. Beyond the waterfalls of Shorth's Teeth the banks of the river closed in with swamps making landing all but impossible.

Beyond the swamps hills swept away, covered by trees and scaling high towards cloud and Gyal. A further day's sail north and the land changed abruptly. The river ran between mud walls over a hundred feet high and home to flocks of water birds and a myriad reptile species. The walls were topped by the canopy, and only when the sun was directly overhead was the light anything other than gloomy. And finally, with the Verendii Tual close, rose the great cliffs of the delta. Hundreds of feet up, pocked with caves and crawling with life.

The cliffs ended dramatically, sweeping down to the outflow of the delta's mouth and into the Sea of Gyaam. Auum stowed his boat before he met the brackish waters and difficult tidal flow out there, hoping, praying that Takaar had done the sensible thing and chosen to live high above.

Down here, at the river's edge, Auum felt the full majesty of the cliffs of the Verendii. He had travelled here many times before and never ceased to wonder at the power and strength echoing from every face of stone. Here he could drink in the glory of Yniss's creation like nowhere else and so he sat with his feet in the waters of the western bank and stared up.

Rain was falling, splashing down into the river and painting the rock face dark. At his back the climb was not so steep as opposite. Soon he would head into the forest and leave his mark and direction at the way stones and Yniss shrine. Serrin knew Auum's likely landfall at the Verendii Tual. He would come to the shrine before beginning his search.

Auum looked at his climb. Takaar would be up there on the

eastern cliffs, he was sure of it. They boasted unparalleled views of the forest to the west towards Deneth Barine and Ysundeneth; giving early warning of anything coming into the delta or dropping anchor in the inlet beyond. And, of course, they offered the barrier of the River Shorth between him and most of elven civilisation.

A place where an elf born to the forest could see pretty much everything coming at him and choose whether to be found, to leave or to hide. A place where surprise was the weapon of choice.

Auum could see no sign of habitation up there and did not expect to. So he trotted back into the forest, left his mark at the shrine and rowed across to the opposite bank. There was an easier path up the cliffs a quarter of a mile to the south but he fancied a sheer climb. He found his first handholds, jammed his feet into small cracks up at waist height and began his ascent.

Ysundeneth, dawn, and a shocked quiet hung over the city amidst the palls of smoke and the sounds of grief that echoed from every quarter. Whether it was the crime committed by ordinary elves who by day might open a shop and sell you a loaf of bread, or whether it was news of the extraordinary violence of the TaiGethen response was impossible to tell.

Pelyn stood on the roof of the Hausolis Playhouse and could at least see the sense of Katyett's decision to station herself there. But that was all the sense she could make of this morning. Poor Olmaat was gone from below her, stretchered away in the dead of the night when the rioters had quietened and the streets were the safest they'd been for a day.

Gone to the muster of the warrior elite in the huge bowl of the Ultan, just to the east of the city. Gone to take part in whatever decisions the TaiGethen reached. The Al-Arynaar had helped in the main. Ynissul had been woken from broken sleep, coaxed from hiding places or guarded closely as they strode proudly from their scarred houses to make their way to where their escorts into the rainforest awaited them.

All done swiftly and without error. The TaiGethen way. Pelyn envied them. Not their speed, their strength and their extraordinary skills. But their clarity of vision. The uncluttered nature of their beliefs. You could call it simplistic but there was no confusion for them. No grey in between the black and white.

The growing light, muted beneath lowering clouds, brought with it a feeling of frustrated sadness to the Al-Arynaar clustered on the playhouse roof. Pelyn heard muttering around her. The maps had been wiped of rain so that all the damage could be marked.

Down at the harbour, blackened timbers still bled smoke into the sky and the occasional blaze still burned. The destruction was widespread. Masts jutted from the water. Debris was strewn across the docks. More than half the warehousing was gone and much of the wealth of Ysundeneth with it.

In the wake of the TaiGethen escape from the playhouse last night, the crowd meaning to surround them had returned to the spice market and smashed every frontage. A huge fire had been laid in the centre of the cobbled square and it burned on.

They had reports of three hundred separate houses being attacked and set alight. Timber stores across the city had proved easy targets. Government buildings deemed Ynissul bastions had been assaulted, including the courts and the palace of the priests. This latter was more of a museum now but chambers were maintained for travelling members of the priesthood from any thread. Hazy memory and rumour labelled it a place where pressure was applied to lesser threads and power was brokered beyond the gaze of the public and the Gardaryn.

Pelyn dared not look up towards the temple piazza. Everyone knew what had happened there. Latest word was that some had been to recover bodies, others to just stand and stare. Of the Yniss temple itself and those immolated within, nothing was left but ash, smoulder and a deepening sense of hate and shame.

Since the news of the murders of Jarinn and Lorius had broken, she had seen hide nor hair of any senior member of the government. Helias's house was empty and none of his staff could offer any hint of his whereabouts. The high priests of the rainforest temples had presumably all rushed back to their sanctuaries, and those whose authority covered Ysundeneth were, like Helias, nowhere to be found.

The Gardaryn was due to meet in session this morning. Clearly that would not happen, but priests, administrators and officials should report for their duties. With a feeling of great discomfort and anxiety, Pelyn realised that if they did not, it left her effectively in charge. But in charge of what?

'Pelyn?'

She turned, grateful to be dragged from her thoughts for a

moment. A clay mug brimming with a warm infusion of guarana and sweet leaf was thrust into her hand. She breathed in the invigorating aroma and took a long sip, feeling the liquid fire down her throat.

'Bless you, Methian.'

The ageing Gyalan loyalist smiled at her. He'd been her rock for two hundred years. What she'd do without him, she had no idea.

'You look awful,' said Methian.

Pelyn felt like bursting into tears. Instead she nodded.

'Well, it hasn't been among my better times. Even fighting the Garonin was easier. At least you knew what was coming with them.'

'Had any sleep recently?'

'Guess. And you're not bringing me good news, are you?'

Methian shook his head. 'People are beginning to gather again. Gardaryn this time. The mood isn't ugly like yesterday yet, but then these aren't yesterday's rioters. These are elves wanting answers from their appointed representatives.'

Pelyn rubbed at her face and took another sip of her drink. 'I suppose we had to expect that, but I'd be surprised if any administrators even turned up. This is going to get worse, isn't it?'

Methian raised his eyebrows. 'If there is no law, people will be quick enough to create their own systems of justice.'

'But without the Ynissul in the city, surely tempers will cool.'

'You and I both know that is a vain hope. Lorius may have wanted to maintain the harmony when he denounced Takaar, but he was deceived by those who put him up to it, wasn't he? This isn't about all threads against the Ynissul. They were just the first target. This is about a re-establishment of the old system. Not something with which I'm familiar.' Methian chuckled. 'Not that long-lived, we Gyalans.'

'You think Tualis are behind this?'

Methian shrugged. 'Some, probably. But not all, or you wouldn't be standing here. But it's confused, isn't it? We know an Ynissul murdered your high priest and his. I don't get what that was supposed to achieve. If there's one thread that cannot afford conflict, it is the Ynissul. There just aren't enough of them, not even with the TaiGethen.'

'And why would he kill Jarinn?'

'I expect Jarinn would have got in his way . . .'

'We should head to the Gardaryn, see what's going on. Keep the peace if we can,' said Pelyn.

'So we should,' said Methian, then he paused, conflicting emotions on his face. 'Can I speak honestly?'

'Only if I'm going to like what I hear.'

'Then I shall remain silent.'

Pelyn smiled, though it felt a little grim. 'Go on.'

'We have something in the region of four hundred Al-Arynaar in Ysundeneth. And the city has a population of, what, sixty-five thousand or thereabouts with the Ynissul survivors gone? You've seen it only takes a handful to whip up a mob so it doesn't matter if ninety-five per cent of the population have no wish for violence. Now the Ynissul are gone, the threads have nothing to focus on as one so they'll turn on each other.'

'*Why?*'

'There doesn't have to be a reason unless it is anger without direction.' Methian shook his head. 'Just look at what happened in the market yesterday. So much hate, buried for so long. Yet you and I stand together as friends for two hundred years. The point is that we will no longer know who is enemy and who is friend to us. Four hundred Al-Arynaar will be nowhere near enough and . . .'

Methian trailed off and sighed.

'You've started and so far I'm no more scared than I was before.'

'They won't all stand with you, Pelyn,' he whispered. 'They won't all trust you because you are Tuali, and many of them will see the Tuali as the real aggressors despite what Hithuur did.'

Pelyn was stunned. She'd felt it when she told Katyett she didn't know who to trust but had prayed it wouldn't spread to her warriors. The truth shattered what remained of her confidence.

'So how do we stop this getting out of control?'

Methian leant on the wall beside her and gazed out over the city and the ocean. 'Build a fence round the city and wait in the forest until it's over.'

'That isn't funny.'

'Sorry. I don't really know. Starting at the Gardaryn is as good as anything. But if I was you I'd do what the TaiGethen did and muster your people. You have to know who is with you, Pelyn, or you're going to cause more trouble than you stop.'

'If I do that I remove my people from the streets and therefore all deterrent against trouble.'

'I know.' Methian straightened suddenly. 'That's a whole lot of sails.'

'I beg your pardon?'

'Take a look. Heading this way from the west. Ten. Twelve perhaps. Not merchants. Not elven.'

Pelyn followed Methian's gaze and felt her whole body sag.

'This isn't getting any better, is it?'

Chapter 14

Combat is the simplest of relationships. Your enemy wants to kill you. Stop him.

The rain had beaten down on Auum the whole way up the cliff. An hour's climb at the very least. Every hold had been a study in concentration, every move a risk greater than the last. Every moment had reminded Auum why he loved the rainforest, loved Yniss's creation and loved the blessing of strength and agility that Yniss had bestowed upon him.

He lay on the cliff edge with the first vegetation of the rainforest almost within arm's length and let the rain wash the dirt from his clothes and body. He pulled in great gasps of air and held them, waiting until his temples pounded before exhaling. Here was life. Here was reason enough to desire to save all the elves had built. None should be denied this if they desired it.

Auum sat up with his legs dangling over the drop. Between his feet he could see his boat pulled up on the bank and tipped onto its side against the rainfall. He felt energised but his limbs were tired, like after a three-hour spar with Serrin, the Silent Priest as fast as a TaiGethen. Auum smiled.

A sound to his left and he glanced round. The rain obliterated so much when it fell this heavily. Gyal's tears were the TaiGethen's friend. Hard to be sure what it was. Auum moved smoothly to his feet. It could have been a falling tree branch. It could have been the death fall of an animal. His sense of wrong told him it was neither.

Auum was exposed out here on the cliff edge. He ducked under the canopy, letting the dense foliage hide him. The noise had been quite close. An impact of some kind. He stared into the gloom, trying to pick out anything unusual in the chaos of banyan, fig, balsa, vine and moss-covered branches. A hundred shades of green and brown, the shadows of great leaves and a riot of brightly coloured flowers met his gaze.

This was his land. The land of the TaiGethen. That impact did not belong here. Auum moved silently into the forest, leaving the freshness of the cliffs behind him. He tuned to the natural sounds. Monkeys chittering in the mid-branches, birds calling at every level. The rustling of ground beasts. The singing cacophony of insects. All of Tual's denizens in full cry.

And something else too. A scent, like burned bark but with a bitter edge akin to singed abuta. It came from his right. From where the impact had sounded. Auum crouched. There was movement in the undergrowth and low foliage. The clumsy shaking of leaf and branch. A heavy footfall.

Three men. Presumably one of them had fallen heavily, although the impact had sounded more like something coming down from the branch of a banyan. Auum stilled and tucked into the trunk by which he had stopped. They would come to him and wish that they had not.

Auum could see them. Two were warriors. Leather armour, un-gainly swords and daggers. Tall men, violent. And, just behind them, one standing still and wearing very light armour, no sword. He was one of those Auum had heard called "mage". Dangerous. The mage took a single pace forward and vanished.

Auum blinked, sure the mage must have ducked behind a tree or dropped prone. But if he had, the warriors were ignoring him and moved on slowly, staring beyond Auum or down at their tangled feet. He ignored them, scrutinising instead the foliage at ground level in the mage's predicted path. Nothing moved.

The air seemed to still, suck inwards almost. It was a curious sensation. The next instant Auum felt an awful pressure in his ears. It slammed pain around his skull. He clamped down on his jaw to stop himself screaming but knew something had escaped his throat.

Auum felt disoriented. His eyesight blurred for a moment. He put his hands to his head, trying to ease the shattering pain. He could hear nothing. He sagged to his knees. He blinked furiously, determined to monitor where his enemies moved. He could see blurred shapes. Too close. Whatever had afflicted him had left them apparently un-affected.

They had seen him. Auum's head began to clear. Slowly, but it would be enough. His swords were still in their scabbards, his jaqrui pouch closed. He made no sign that he was capable, remaining with his back hard against the tree and his knees drawn up against his chest. The warriors split to come at him left and right. He still couldn't see the mage.

The warriors closed. Auum saw the set of their bodies and the heft of their blades. They thought him incapacitated. Auum kept his body relaxed and his facial expression pained. He shook his head as if just coming back to his senses. The warriors moved in faster. One slipped on the sodden ground.

Auum drove himself up and forward. He reached over his left shoulder, grabbed a blade and threw it at the right-hand warrior. Immediately, he dropped, rolled left and kicked up, the tips of his toes catching the other warrior in the groin. The man yelled and doubled over, one arm across his stomach. Auum bounced to his feet, grabbed the warrior's head in both hands and twisted savagely.

Auum turned away from the falling corpse. The other warrior was trying to pull the blade from his gut. Blood sluiced from his mouth and washed from around the wound. Auum heard a twig snap. There stood the mage. Behind his dying comrade. He was smiling. His lips were moving and his arms were reaching out.

Auum sprinted at him. He wasn't going to be fast enough to stop him. The mage turned his palms inwards, ready to clap them together. He dropped his head to his chest then raised it to look straight into Auum's eyes. Auum stopped running, choosing instead to send a prayer to Yniss to protect his soul.

The mage jerked forward, almost fell. He made a choking gurgle. He stared at Auum, confusion in his expression, blood running from his mouth. The head of a jaqrui blade protruded from this neck just below his chin. He pitched onto his face.

Not ten yards behind Auum stood an *ula*. His clothes were tattered and roughly mended in a few places. His face was gaunt. He had the remains of a long beard on his chin and cheeks. Where there was skin, it was covered in cuts and scratches as if he'd tried to shave with a blunt knife. His hair was similarly wild, sticking up in clumps, tangled with twig and leaf and hacked shorter in places and left to grow untamed in others.

But he held himself proudly. His arms were by his sides but his hands were moving, fingers rubbing against his thumbs or into the palms of his hands. His eyes darted here and there and there was a twitch in either cheek. When he breathed his nostrils fluted. Auum watched him move smoothly to the mage and work his jaqrui free.

'Lucky I can still use one of these.' He laughed then looked to his right. The humour died. 'I have never forgotten. I trained when you weren't watching me. You don't watch me all the time, do you? No, I thought not. One victory for me.'

Auum watched his saviour walk to the dying human warrior. He knelt by the man, moving his hands away from the hilt of Auum's blade. He took the hilt in one hand, twisted it, rammed it hard into the man's body and drew it out slowly, almost reverently. The man slumped to one side.

The wild *ula* stood up, wiped the blade on the man's clothing and walked to Auum, offering it to him hilt first. Auum took it and nodded his thanks, still unable to frame his question without it sounding horribly sycophantic in his head. The *ula* stared at him and shrugged.

'Well I think he recognises me. Perhaps the hair needs a little attention.'

He growled and the sound made Auum start. Doubt crept into his mind.

'Actually, I recognise *him*. I never forget a face. Particularly when the owner is one of the finer students of the art.' In his eyes there was both warmth and wariness. 'You are Auum.'

Auum's legs almost gave way beneath him. He sheathed his blade. He felt a wash of relief.

'Arch Takaar, I am honoured you know me.'

And then cursed himself for his first words.

'Ha!' Takaar clapped his hands together. 'Told you, told you.'

Takaar gripped Auum's shoulders.

'Good. It will be good to have someone else to talk to.'

Auum just caught himself before he asked the obvious question. Instead he smiled.

'The TaiGethen will bless Yniss that you still live,' he said.

Takaar's face hardened. 'I doubt that.'

Again he glanced to one side. He muttered something Auum couldn't catch before spinning on his heel and striding away into the rainforest. Takaar spoke over his shoulder.

'A good question. A very good question and you utter few enough of those. Why *are* you here, Auum? No one invited you. I detest the unannounced. Not that I have had any visitors these past ten years.'

Takaar stopped and turned.

'Come on, come on, you're here now.'

And off he went again. Auum trotted after him, breasting through the undergrowth, marvelling at how Takaar moved so quickly and left no mark whatever, not even the briefest of prints in the mud underfoot.

'This isn't what I had planned for the day,' said Takaar. 'Very funny. Perhaps you could be quiet for a time. We have a guest, after all. I will not be doing that. At least, not today. So you keep saying.'

Auum kept up easily. After setting off with the skill of the finest TaiGethen, Takaar became erratic in both movement and direction as if he was lost and confused. He muttered and shouted by turn and Auum wondered how he had managed to stalk the mage so effectively. Should anyone else be tracking them closely, their job would be rendered simple.

This was not the Takaar he had hoped to find. Not yet anyway. The question of how he would react when Auum told him the reason for his visit was open to serious debate. Too many of the possibilities were distasteful. Too many of them the elves could not afford. This was not an elf who could possibly unite the threads and restore the harmony.

'Almost there,' called Takaar. 'Come, come to my humble palace.'

He chuckled. Above, Gyal's tears were drying and the sun was edging through the heavy banks of cloud. Auum followed Takaar into his camp and stopped to look at a place that was not the creation of a disturbed mind. A sound mud and thatch hut, a stretched-hide bivouac and what looked to be a peat and stone kiln. Perhaps all was not as bleak as it appeared.

'Such things do I have to show you. A thousand ways to die. A hundred ways to live. All here. Right here under our noses and within the grasp of our fingers.'

Takaar disappeared inside his hut. He was still talking and pinching his index fingers and thumbs together repeatedly to illustrate his latest point. Auum followed him in and came up short, staring at the shelves of pots, the stained and stretched hammock, the stinking wood bucket of vomit and the long table covered in further jars plus a scattering of leaves, flowers, barks and stems.

'This isn't a house, it's a workshop,' he breathed then plucked up his courage. 'I am sorry to disturb your solitude, Takaar.'

Takaar wasn't listening. His full attention was taken with a knife and a thin strip of polished wood, carving symbols into its surface.

'A thousand. A thousand ways and—'

He broke off, swung about and marched to the long table. He slapped both hands on it, upsetting a couple of jars and juddering everything else that lay on it.

'That was never my intent. Always it was for research. My legacy. My . . .'

The anger left him and he nodded, his expression sad as he returned to his work.

'That is true. I have never denied it. Indeed, I deserve it. But a failed elf can still do good. Not by way of recompense, just to do good.'

'Takaar,' said Auum.

Takaar's head snapped round, his face full of ire. Only slowly did it clear.

'Where is my hospitality?' he said. 'I'm not really set up for three.'

'Thr—'

Takaar picked up the knife again. He walked across to his bivouac.

'I have infusions of piedra and cloves. Also some nutmeg if you have a yearning for it,' he said, tapping stoppered jars. 'Cold of course but good, all of them. Nothing to eat. The odd root perhaps. Hunting is at dusk. Care to hunt? It would put his nose out of joint if nothing else.'

Takaar tipped his head at a rough log stool in the corner of the bivouac.

'And that would please you?' asked Auum.

'Enormously,' said Takaar.

'Then it would be a pleasure to learn from a master.'

Takaar's eyes sparkled. He walked to Auum and placed his hands on the young TaiGethen's shoulders. His face was clear, uncluttered, and for the first time Auum saw the focus he remembered in Takaar's eyes.

'And when we are eating our kill, you will tell me why it is you are here and what it is that is about to consume the elven race.'

The clarity and focus disappeared. Takaar rubbed at his face and hair. He jabbed Auum in the chest.

'Good thing you're here. I need a shave. And a haircut. Knife over there, sharpening leather over there. No time to lose. Jump to it.'

Chapter 15

Rarely do gods speak. It is a shame that so often we choose not to listen.

Ultan-in-Caeyin. A name of the ancient tongue, translating as "Where Gods Are Heard".

The Ultan was a huge open grass bowl, U-shaped and bounded by sheer cliffs that provided a barrier to the sea, the rainforest and the River Ix. It had remarkable acoustic qualities and, since the founding of Ysundeneth, had been the place where the elves met in times of celebration and strife. It could hold a quarter of a million, *iad*, *ula* and child. The entire population of Calaius and more.

For hundreds of years it had been left as Yniss had designed it, but recently work had begun to create a lasting monument to the gods. Great stone slabs and pillars were being cut from the quarries to the west of Ysundeneth and moved by barge to form a stage at the northern end of the Ultan where the cliffs met the sea. Carvings were being made to depict the deeds of god and elf, a charting of the often violent history of Hausolis and the trials of life on Calaius.

Talk was that the whole of the open grass area would eventually be set with benches in concentric arcs around the stage. Some wit had suggested a roof might be in order too. Katyett was still able to feel a passing lightness of mood as she gazed up at the vast open space and imagined the timber span that would be required.

This morning, of course, there was no celebratory mood, nor even a common purpose. There was anger, there was frustration, desperation and confusion. And among those whom the TaiGethen now protected, there was fear too and an intense sadness.

The Ynissul evacuation was an open secret by now, and the TaiGethen guarded the approaches and entrance to the Ultan, a good number of them hoping an attack would be mounted. A disappointing reaction in one regard, utterly elven in another. Katyett had complete sympathy and her memories of the temple piazza held no guilt.

Almost three thousand Ynissul sheltered in the Ultan. They had precious little food, just the clothing on their backs and the few possessions they had managed to grab as they were ushered from their houses, places no longer safe for elves of the immortal thread.

They were secured by thirty TaiGethen. Katyett's first act had been to dispatch the birds who would carry the muster message into the rainforest. They would fly to the shrines to Yniss scattered about beneath the canopy, there to wait in secured nesting boxes until any Tai cell checked in to read the message, release the bird and pass the word.

It was necessarily an inefficient method of communication. There was no set check-in routine. Birds were prey to predators above the canopy and, despite the design of the nesting boxes and their entrances, to the attentions of snakes and rodents.

In the vastness of the bowl of the Ultan, the few thousand Ynissul and their guards looked precisely what they were: an insignificant demoralised group of elves soaked by the rain before dawn and huddling under the inadequate shelter the Tai cells had been able to construct. A few fires had been lit and their smoke rose to join the pall that hung over Ysundeneth.

TaiGethen moved among the refugees, offering comfort where they could and giving out what information they had of the immediate future. But rainforest warriors were unused to the roles of counsellors and shoulders on which to cry. However, they missed nothing they were told, and a trend was emerging that was causing a growing fury.

Katyett watched other birds flying over the Ultan. Not those of the Ynissul and the TaiGethen. These would be bound for Tolt Anoor and Deneth Barine. The former a day's sail along the coast east of Ysundeneth. The latter a long journey by sea, river or rainforest trail to the eastern coast of Calaius. She sighed. The conflict was spreading, sped on the wings of Tual's denizens.

Beside her on his stretcher poor Olmaat raised his head a little to see an approaching knot of TaiGethen, led by his Tai, Pakiir. Katyett put a comforting hand on his shoulder.

'Don't strain, Olmaat. Rest.'

'Hothead,' managed Olmaat, his tortured lungs and throat grinding breath and voice. 'Lot to learn.'

Pakiir was with the Tai of Makran, Kilmett and Lymul. They were a relatively new cell, in training only for the last fifty years and with a zeal that needed to be tempered. Their expressions confirmed that their zeal was in control of their emotions.

'We must return to the city. We must clear it. Crimes have been committed that strike to the core of our faith.'

Pakiir's voice echoed about the Ultan. His face was twisted with the anger surging through him. Katyett paused for a deliberately long period, refusing to add fuel to their fires. She chose to speak formally, knowing they had no choice but to respond in kind.

'First, we must lower our voices such that those we seek to comfort are not further scared by the din of our desire for conflict,' she said quietly. 'Second, we must all be in possession of the entirety of information that pertains to this debate. And third, we must retract our demands of the Arch of the TaiGethen and seek instead to recommend and persuade.'

'We cannot just stand here and let—' began Makran.

Katyett silenced her with a glare to wither stone.

'We are TaiGethen,' hissed Katyett. 'Appointed by Yniss and created by Takaar to protect the sanctity of our lands and the harmony against all of those who would destroy it. We do not lash out in hate and revenge. We are here to protect elves of every thread. This day, we protect the Ynissul. Tomorrow it may be Tuali or Beethan or Cefan. We do things as Takaar described. Pakiir. Speak.'

'You led an attack against elves yesterday in the piazza. How is that not lashing out in hate?'

'We all saw the perpetrators of the crimes. Yniss was our witness. We were not lashing out. We removed heretics. What we saw was deliberate desecration and destruction of the harmony of elves. We cannot allow the guilty to escape just punishment.'

'It didn't feel that way to me; it felt like revenge,' said Pakiir.

'There is joy in performing Yniss's work,' said Katyett. 'Makran. Speak.'

The young TaiGethen *iad* nodded. She drew breath. Katyett laid a hand on her arm.

'We are all brothers and sisters here, Makran. We all feel the passions of other elves but we must learn to direct them. Tell me what you have heard. What stoked your anger so much to force you into an outburst unbecoming of the paint you wear on the hunt.'

Makran's eyes were hollow with hate.

'We were too late for some,' she said. 'Not just the ones who have died. The things we have heard. Can you not see it in the faces of the *iads*?'

'What's happened, Makran?'

Katyett could feel her heart beginning to beat hard and more atrocities of the past surface in her memory.

'They knew what we would do. They knew we would go to the temple or deal with major conflict. And all the time they were kicking down the doors of the Ynissul. They blame us because our thread is still pure. No interbreeding. They don't care that our fertility is on a different scale to theirs. So they have raped any *iad* they found, fertile or not. Not to enhance the harmony, to destroy lives. To remove choice. To encourage hate.

'Well they have succeeded.'

Makran was shaking. Katyett felt empty, scoured. She looked across to the refugee Ynissul and every *iad* eye seemed to be on her, imploring her to act. Their *ulas* standing mute beside them, most with bruised and battered faces. Forced to watch, no doubt. Forced to survive to carry the message of their helplessness.

She could see the shock behind their eyes and the grief in the way they held their bodies. She had assumed it to be just the fact of being chased from their homes. How stupid that seemed now. Katyett cleared her throat.

'I understand your anger, Makran—'

'Then we must act. Now. We can identify the guilty.'

Katyett nodded. She breathed deeply.

'Believe me, I am sorely tempted. But we have more pressing concerns. Makran. Silence. I am speaking. The day of judgement for any rapist will come. That is my promise to you. None will escape. But we have to see these people, the innocent, to safety.

'Next, we will gather the TaiGethen from the forest. We will gather the Silent too. Only then we will return to cleanse the city of the filth it harbours.'

Makran made to renew her protest but Olmaat silenced her this time, his voice pained and his lungs wheezing.

'Think, Makran,' he said. 'Preserve what we have now. Stand in judgement later. These people need us here, not stalking the streets of Ysundeneth like vigilantes.'

Olmaat paused to cough violently. His whole body convulsed and an agony he could not hide crossed his face and settled in his eyes. He composed himself, wiping his mouth with the back of a burned, salve-covered hand, before continuing.

'We face a conflict rendered all the more dangerous because we don't know who the enemy really is. It seems to me there are several factions pulling us apart. But these criminals have no escape. If they run to the rainforest, they become our prey. So they will stay in the city, a prison they have built for themselves. And we will pick them off at will. When the time is right.'

Makran nodded. So did Pakiir.

'I hear you, Olmaat,' he said. 'Forgive me.'

'There is nothing to forgive, my brother. We all feel the same. But we must ensure we act as one or we are lost.'

Katyett raised her head at a brief commotion at the head of the Ultan.

'What now?' she said before feeling a wash of pure relief. 'Yniss has not quite deserted us yet.'

Priest Serrin of the Silent had entered the Ultan.

The Gardaryn had been comprehensively ransacked. The treasury vaults had been broken open. Every shop had been looted. Farms ransacked and stripped. Food was stockpiled all over the city and was giving rise to a fierce black market already spilling over into violence.

Any pretence at thread harmony had disappeared like sea mist on a hot day. Individual threads gathered as the unity against the Ynissul broke apart. The Tualis turned their attention on the Beethans for reasons Pelyn could not fathom barring their relative long life. She presided over a city of thread ghettos. Barricades were going up all over the place. Territory was marked. The administrative vacuum was being filled by mob rule. It had been simply stunning how quickly the elves had reverted to type. Without Takaar's law, there seemed nothing to bind them any longer. Priests of most threads had reappeared now but only to stand with their own.

Al-Arynaar were a heavy presence at the temple piazza, where the mood was ugly and where the crimes of two days ago seemed likely to be repeated. The TaiGethen and nearly every Ynissul were gone to the Ultan and were planning their next moves. Everyone knew they were there. No one thought to attack them.

'Good for them,' muttered Pelyn, idly sifting through papers and records in the wrecked offices behind the Gardaryn chamber.

At least the ships had ceased their approach. No doubt they were awaiting a signal but Pelyn had been unable to find out from whom that might be.

'I'm sorry?'

'Just thinking aloud, Methian. Tual's eyes, what a mess. Was there any motive for this beyond the desire for mayhem?'

'Oh yes,' said Methian and his face was grim. 'Addresses. The whole public record is here. Or it was. Details of senior administrators and officials from every thread are missing, as far as we can tell. I mean, we haven't found them so far but it looks to me as if those particular records were picked over with more care than others. That and the treasury information. People have known where to go and what to look for. Some people will be getting very rich on this.'

'And do what with it?' asked Pelyn.

Methian gestured vaguely towards the sea. 'Pay for mercenaries from the north, perhaps?'

'What a cheery thought.'

'I try my best.'

Pelyn looked at Methian. Around them, mainly Gyalan Al-Arynaar were sifting the documents and parchments scattered across the floor and trying to restore some kind of order. Methian looked dreadful. No sleep for two days and the constant struggle to keep the Al-Arynaar a cohesive unit in the face of increasing animosity were terribly draining.

'Thank you for standing with me.'

'I would not dream of doing otherwise.'

A door banged open at the rear of the Gardaryn. Pelyn heard her name called. She sighed and felt her exhaustion sap a little more of her will.

'In here!'

A frightened Cefan Al-Arynaar runner entered. His face was filthy and his hands grimy and bloodstained.

'Down on the harbourside. There's going to be big trouble if it hasn't started already. We've got gangs of Tuali, Beethans and Orrans squaring up over the harbour master's warehouse. Ixii and Apposans too. Plenty of goods still inside. We're between them right now, but if they want to, they can overwhelm us.'

Pelyn nodded. 'Right. Methian, you stay here. Carry on this work. If you get harassed, back off. Get back to the playhouse or the barracks. No fighting if you can avoid it. I'll take the standing guard from the central market. Ready to run back, young Jakyn?'

Jakyn nodded. 'It's bad out there. You can smell it.'

'Trust me,' said Pelyn. 'We'll beat this. Somehow.'

'We could do with a few TaiGethen at the moment.'

'We can always do with a few TaiGethen. But it's just us so let's not fret. We'll stand in line and be strong, all right?'

Jakyn nodded and the two of them ran out of the Gardaryn and onto the hostile streets of Ysundeneth.

Chapter 16

Battles are fought more in the mind than with sword or bow.

Serrin looked for all the world as if he had been for a gentle stroll in the eaves of the rainforest. His white-painted face bore no signs of stress but his eyes were anxious. Ynissul from every group in the Ultan rushed to him, looking for blessing, desperate for hope. He stopped by each in turn, placing his hands on foreheads, shoulders and cupping chins. Katyett stood as he approached, having to restrain Olmaat from trying to do the same.

'Don't be ridiculous, Olmaat. I think he'll understand.'

Katyett opened her arms and blessed the air. The TaiGethen around her followed her lead. Priest Serrin returned her gesture. He walked into her embrace and kissed her mouth and eyes.

'Yniss bless you, Katyett and your TaiGethen.' He nodded his head at the assembled Ynissul in the Ultan. 'Such pain. It is much worse here than I feared.'

'Lead us in prayer and we will talk,' said Katyett. 'I have no good news for you, my priest. And you are travelling alone.'

'Not all news is quite so grim.'

Serrin knelt, placing one hand on the stone of the Ultan and opening his other palm to the sky. Katyett saw Ynissul everywhere mirroring him, though few would hear the words from this quiet elf uncomfortable with speech and completely alien to raising his voice.

'Yniss, lord of gods and father of us all, hear us. Enemies sully our land. The hands of your own would crush the souls of elves. Let Tual guide our hands as we destroy our enemies. Let Shorth embrace those innocents who stand unwillingly before him. Let our faith embrace all those who waver and give them comfort. Let anger and forgiveness, mercy and vengeance guide our hearts. Let us not falter. I, Serrin, ask this of you.'

Serrin stared into Katyett's eyes and she shuddered at the passion she saw within.

'Now we will talk,' he said. 'And I will seek the forgiveness of my god for all the words I must speak.'

'Yniss forgives those who sacrifice themselves in his name.'

Serrin smiled. 'It will not stop the soreness in my throat.'

Serrin switched his gaze at the sound of Olmaat coughing. He moved swiftly to the side of the stricken elf, laying hands on his chest and smoothing the salve that covered his forehead.

'Rest, my brother. Release the pain in your soul. Retain the anger.' Katyett watched Serrin frown and stare deep into Olmaat's eyes, right into his soul. 'You have seen it too, haven't you? What men have brought with them. And you have felt it. Stay with us. We need you.'

Olmaat's eyes were damp and he grabbed one of Serrin's wrists. 'I have no intention of going anywhere. There is vengeance to be delivered.'

Serrin nodded. 'Yet mercy must also exist in your soul, my brother.'

'What I have seen leaves little room for that.'

Serrin kissed Olmaat's eyes. 'Yniss will guide you.'

The Silent Priest stood and gestured Katyett to him. He took her by an elbow and led her away from the ears of others. Katyett felt nervous. There were things Serrin did not know. Terrible things. And she feared the inevitable question. He seemed to sense her anxiety.

'Is Auum still alive?' she asked, hoping to deflect him for a moment.

Serrin released her elbow and instead put an arm about her shoulders.

'It is very difficult to kill Auum. More difficult with each passing day.' He paused. 'Jarinn is dead, is he not? I can see no way in which he could be allowed to live.'

Katyett felt stunned. She stopped and looked briefly away to Ysundeneth, where fresh smoke was rising into the darkening sky

'How can you know that?' she asked. 'He was murdered by men acting for an Ynissul *cascarg*. Hithuur. Olmaat was burned trying to save him.'

Serrin sucked in his lip. 'Hithuur? The betrayal goes high. What I have seen. Katyett . . . Auum was forced to spill the blood of men on the floor of Aryndeneth. They unleashed their magic in the temple. Sildaan has betrayed us too and seeks a return of the Ynissul to dominance over the elves. Throughout the rainforest, villages fear a new War of Bloods. Hope is dying out there.'

Katyett wiped a hand across her mouth. 'Sildaan. Not a name I would have associated with this.'

'I presume Takaar was denounced?'

'And that denouncement unleashed a tide of hatred across Ysundeneth. The temple of Yniss has been burned and hundreds died inside. Ynissul are being targeted for slaughter by every other thread. I had to bring them here or risk more lives. Is Sildaan really the architect of this? It makes no sense. She wants dominance yet it is Ynissul who are dying in their hundreds. There will be too few left. She's just handing power to the Tualis.'

Serrin shook his head. 'It goes higher than Sildaan. It must do. Into the higher echelon of the priesthood. Lorius may have set the denouncement in motion but he would not have wished for this, I'm certain.'

'Indeed not. He died alongside Jarinn.'

Serrin gasped. 'Lorius too? That is a heavy blow. The Tualis are without reason now. Who survived?'

'Lorius and Jarinn are the only two we know have died. We believe the rest of the government is safe but we know little of their whereabouts or plans.'

'Some will be living in fear. Some will be tending to their people. Some will be plotting. We need names. This may not be simply an Ynissul betrayal.'

'What can we do?' asked Katyett. 'Realistically. The TaiGethen numbered just a hundred and seventeen before the trouble began. We are few and this magic seems massively powerful. The Al-Arynaar are struggling to keep themselves cohesive let alone maintain order in Ysundeneth. If the threads truly separate we'll be powerless to stop whoever it is from taking control.'

'There is always hope, Katyett. Save the Ynissul gathered here. Have faith that the harmony is strong in the souls of elves and that it can never truly be broken, only hidden. We can return to peace. But only if we believe.'

Katyett studied Serrin's face. Something was missing from Serrin's plan.

'Where is Auum, my priest?'

'Auum has gone to find Takaar.'

*

Harbourside seethed. Seven different threads were represented by the time Pelyn reached the harbour master's warehouse. Some carried makeshift arms – boathooks, chains and shovels. Most relied on the weapons with which they were born.

She saw them trade insults across decreasing space. The knots of elves were closing slowly on the thin line of Al-Arynaar ranged across the front of the warehouse. Several hundred Tualis and Beethans had taken central positions. Gyalans, Cefans and Orrans were there too in smaller numbers. Ixii and Apposans, in tight knots of twenty or so, looked for opportunity on the flanks.

The Al-Arynaar had withdrawn to secure the building. Pelyn was disappointed to see that they had arranged themselves to minimise the chance of fighting one of their own thread. She shouldn't blame them, but the move, conscious or not, spoke much about the state of mind of her warriors.

So far, the threads had not come to concerted blows amongst themselves, managing to maintain their distance from each other. But the gaps were closing. Each wanted first access to the warehouse. The Al-Arynaar were an impediment. Pelyn's appearance took a little of the boldness from them and she was quick to bolster the confidence of the forty or so of her warriors who stood in crumbling defiance.

'Al-Arynaar, I am proud of each of you. Wear your cloak with pride and remember the reason you took it. We stand to defend the harmony for all elves. I stand with you. I will not desert you. I know what you fear. You fear striking down one of your own. I am Tuali. Tualis stand before us. I will strike them down if I must. A Tuali who attacks me has betrayed both thread and harmony. We all know the sentence for such crimes.'

Pelyn swung round to face the approaching mob. Her voice would not reach them all over the shouting, stamping and clashing, and the chanting of ages-old songs that had no place outside a lesson in the history of the bleakest days.

'I am Pelyn, Arch of the Al-Arynaar. I and my warriors, drawn from every thread, are tasked by Yniss to defend our people, cities, buildings and streets. We defend every cobblestone, every pane of glass and every timber. We will not flinch from our duty. We cannot. Come no further. Return to your homes. Return to peace. The supplies in this warehouse are the property of the city and will be dispensed on the basis of need.'

They paid her no heed. She knew they wouldn't.

'We will strike any who seek to harm us. You are so warned. Al-Arynaar. To ready.'

The swords of the Al-Arynaar, held low until now, were all brought up and forward. Each warrior took a pace to the front to the ready stance. Those with shields moved them into defensive position. Pelyn walked along the thin single line, some fifty yards long. At every pace she spoke for their ears only.

'None of these can fight. Remember your training. Fight for your brothers and sisters. No one before you can beat you.'

'And if they fight among themselves?' asked one.

'Then let them. Those who remove themselves are doing the rest of us a favour. Any of you want any of these to bring up the next generation of elves? Think on it and temper your sympathy.'

The space in front of the Al-Arynaar was disappearing quickly. In the centre the Beethans and Tualis closed on each other, both groups pressing forward into the inadequate space. There was no clear leadership and the formation was chaotic. The inevitable happened. Right at the back the two sides came together. Fighting broke out. Fists and feet. Pushing and shoving. For now.

'Steady,' called Pelyn. 'Hold your positions.'

The advance was immediately distracted. Heads turned. People began to move back. Elves stepped out of line. They collided with their foes. The two threads surged at each other.

'Hold!' shouted Pelyn. 'Hold!'

Bodies were hitting the ground. With a massed roar, Tuali and Beethan let fly at each other. Pelyn saw a boathook buried in the top of a skull and blood fountain into the air. The wielder was engulfed in furious Tualis. Chains whirled and crashed down. Feet stamped on bodies that lay in the dirt of the cobblestones. Fingers raked across faces. Fists ripped out clumps of hair. Knives flashed in the fading light as the rains closed in.

Behind the warring factions another group was on the move. They headed left around the conflict. Running hard. And from the right, others moved to mirror them.

'Flanks, brace for attack. Centre, hold your ground. Facing forward. Jakyn, with me,' said Pelyn.

Pelyn ran to the right. The Apposans and Ixii closing there were well armed and fierce. They moved in an organised unit, ten wide and four deep. Swords and axes to the front and sharpened staffs and javelins to the back. Al-Arynaar turned to face them. They did not flinch in their approach.

Elven blades clashed outside the harbour master's warehouse. The Al-Arynaar line bowed inwards but held. Pelyn ran to its centre. She could feel the reluctance all around her. Jakyn blocked a straight thrust aside, exposing the flank of an attacker. He shoved the *iad* back rather than disembowel her.

At the far right of the line an Al-Arynaar fielded an axe on his shield. Again, he shoved forward when a thrust above the shield would have finished his attacker.

'Bring them down!' shouted Pelyn. 'Fight, don't play.'

She pushed between two of her people. Three Ixii faced her. One ignored her, aiming a blow at the Al-Arynaar on her right. The other two came at her, both meaning to strike overarm. Pelyn swayed inside one blow and blocked the other up and out right. She smashed her left fist into the face of the first Ixii. He staggered back, unbalanced.

Pelyn twisted her blade out from under the hilt of her enemy's, leaving his body entirely open. Pelyn did what she had to do. She rammed her sword into the Ixii's throat. Arterial blood sprayed out. The *ula* clamped his hands to his neck, trying to scream. He collapsed forward.

Pelyn locked eyes with the *iad* behind.

'Flinch and perish,' she said.

She stepped up and thrust her blade into the Ixii's chest. The *iad* stared at her in mute shock. Pelyn was aware of a roaring around her. Fury. Indignation. Pelyn dragged her blade clear.

'I warned you!' she shouted. 'Disperse.'

But it had gone far too far for that. The Apposan and Ixii alliance surged again. An Al-Arynaar Second Reverent lost an arm to a huge chopping blow. Another was stabbed in the midriff and fell forward, taking her attacker down with her. And everything Pelyn's words had failed to stir was brought to the boil in an instant. A third Al-Arynaar deflected a strike to the neck. He riposted, bashing his shield out into the Ixii's face and driving his sword in waist high.

Pelyn ducked a wild swipe, dropping to her haunches. She swept out a foot as Katyett had taught her, tripping the Apposan. He fell sideways, unbalancing another. Pelyn rose, lashing a kick into his face, and disengaged from the fight. She backed into the small space in front of the warehouse doors and looked out over the harbourside.

The fighting Beethans and Tualis battered into the rear of the thread allies attacking the Al-Arynaar. To her right, Apposan and Ixii were simply swept away. To the left it was a little harder going. Out towards the harbour, twenty or more bodies lay on the ground and bloody smears tracked through pools of blood.

'Jakyn!' The lad ran to her. 'I want those doors open. We need a place to go. Quickly now.'

The Tualis and Beethans turned on the Al-Arynaar. The full force of hundreds of enraged elves was focusing on a tenth their number of Al-Arynaar. Pelyn made for the centre of the line. Three boathooks flew in on lengths of one-inch rope. The sharpened ends snagged cloak and armour. Two warriors were simply upended and hauled into the enemy. Fingers tore and teeth ripped. Tualis streamed into the gap.

'Fall back!' shouted Pelyn. 'Fall back to the doors.'

The enemy came at her. She was alone for the moment. Four of them with many more behind though her surviving warriors were closing, narrowing the breach with every heartbeat.

Pelyn drew a dagger with her left hand and moved into a fluid fighting position. Both blades were forward and she bent slightly at the waist to increase her reach while maintaining her balance. The quartet came at her in a rush. None had blades. One had a chain which she circled high over her head. A second carried a pickaxe that appeared too heavy for him. He was young yet, immature.

The chain wielder brought her weapon down overhead. Pelyn leapt back, thudding into the timbers of the gatehouse. She hadn't realised she'd strayed so close. The chain struck sparks from the ground. Pelyn pushed herself off the wall and jabbed her dagger into the pickaxe chain-wielder's gut, leaving it where it lodged. A hand raked in from the right. Pelyn swayed back, feeling nails tear into her cheek and across under her nose.

Pelyn slashed her blade out and right, feeling it glance off the Tuali's skull, ripping his scalp open to the bone. The second unarmed elf hesitated. Pelyn straightened. The *iad* did not know what to do. Pelyn kicked out into her groin and battered the pommel of her blade into the back of the *iad*'s neck, sending her thudding onto the cobblestones, her head bouncing unpleasantly.

Pelyn turned to the pickaxe carrier. The Tuali youth was staring at a blade deep in his stomach right below the breastbone. Jakyn pulled his weapon clear and stared at Pelyn.

'We were at school together,' he said.

'Well he didn't listen well enough.'

'Door's open.'

Pelyn nodded. 'Al-Arynaar. Disengage.'

The Al-Arynaar shoved forward and paced back, buying themselves a yard of space. The Tuali and Beethan alliance of convenience held. They paused for breath.

'Into the warehouse. Now. Jakyn, the door.'

Pelyn and Jakyn rolled the big single door open. Jakyn ran to its other end, ready for his next order. Al-Arynaar sprinted in. The last four came in backwards, swords fencing away at the press of the enemy. One tripped over the rail. Beethan and Tuali ran inside.

'Jakyn, close it.'

The youth pushed hard. The door slid quickly, beating into the body of an unlucky Tuali. The door bounced back a little. Al-Arynaar dragged her inside. Jakyn closed the door.

'Brace it. Seal it. Anyhow.'

Jakyn kept his weight on the door, which juddered with the blows of the enemy without. Al-Arynaar were at work on the inside bolts. Others killed the enemy inside. A moment's respite.

'We won't stop them getting in for long,' said Jakyn.

'Then let's find ourselves a way out,' said Pelyn.

'If there was one, surely they'd have entered through it by now,' said a warrior.

'You're thinking too big.'

Pelyn turned away from the door, which was heaving under blow after blow. Axeheads were already biting through its timbers. The warehouse was huge. Racks stood against each wall and ran away for a hundred yards in six columns. They carried pretty much every conceivable item of any use to the city. Meticulously laid out and organised. Such was the mind of the harbour master.

From ship's masts, anchors, hawsers, sheets and sails, through every kind of pot, plate, mug and server in tin and clay, through a myriad plumbing and guttering joints, through carts, saddles, yokes, barrels, hoops, locks, keys, medical supplies . . . You could wander the shelves, racks and nets for ever.

But the prize lay on shelves to the right, above nets so the mice and rats could not gain access. Tons of it. Food. Dried, sealed and preserved. Meat, fruit, grain and rice for the most part. Barrel after barrel of wine and spirits. Endless pots of dried herbs. Emergency supplies to keep the city alive in the most extreme of times. Times like now.

Pelyn stared at it all and weighed the measure of her failure. Not enough Al-Arynaar to keep the main supplies safe. Supplies they'd all assumed burned in the first hours after the denouncement that were going to be utterly vital in the days to come. Hours when she had focused all her energy on keeping the temple of Yniss safe. Another failure.

The timbers of the door were beginning to weaken. Pelyn's people backed off, bodies tense, hands gripping swords nervously. Those they had protected only yesterday were ready to rip the faces from their skulls. How had it come to this? Pelyn shook her head. The Al-Arynaar were no more than a guerrilla force and the ringleaders of all this knew it. Just like they knew what the TaiGethen would do if the Ynissul were put under threat.

High above, on the gantry built to maintain the roof of the warehouse, were a number of skylights. Pelyn pointed up.

'Get lengths of rope and get climbing. Our way out is not going to come to us.'

Chapter 17

Patience wins more battles than courage and strength combined.

Katyett felt as if she was going to collapse. She sensed a rush of heat across her body and deep in the pit of her stomach. Her feet tingled and her breath gasped in. Of all the things she might have expected the priest to say, that was the most inconceivable.

'What sort of madness is that?' she managed eventually.

She didn't know if she was thrilled or furious. Didn't know what to feel. But whatever it was, it had sent her pulse soaring. Takaar. The prospect of seeing him again made her shiver. Memories of his face fell through her mind so real she could grasp at them.

'It is a chance we have to take.'

'Who made this decision?'

'In the rainforest there are no councils,' said Serrin evenly.

Katyett shook her head, trying to clear the buzzing and fog that encased it.

'You and Auum have taken this massive risk on behalf of us all?'

'Auum is acting on my order.'

'How will he find Takaar, assuming there is anything to find?'

Serrin smiled a little indulgently. 'Takaar spoke to the priesthood before he went into exile.'

Katyett nodded. 'I see.'

'I'm sure you don't.'

'Don't patronise me,' she snapped.

'I am sorry, Katyett. I meant no offence.'

Katyett sighed. 'Me too, my priest. You have taken me completely unawares.'

'It is not often I do that to a TaiGethen, least of all their leader.'

'I just don't understand what good this can possibly do.'

'You say you have no way to revive the harmony if the threads separate. I'm giving you that way.'

Katyett scoffed. 'You think he'll be accepted like he was before? You're out of touch, Serrin. I can't even say all the TaiGethen will embrace him. The populace of Calaius certainly won't. Most of them were born here and have no real knowledge of the influence and charisma he used to wield. And those that do remember, hate him for all the lives he sacrificed. Auum is wasting his time.'

'I'm sorry you feel that way. And I think you are mistaken.'

'Well, we're going to find out, aren't we? Just what exactly did you have in mind? Parading him through the streets of Ysundeneth with an honour guard of TaiGethen and any Al-Arynaar who survive that long? Or perhaps you think he might head an army to sweep the invading men and their magic from our shores. All we need now is an army.'

Serrin made to retort but thought better of it.

'I thought you'd be pleased,' said Serrin instead. 'You of all people.'

Katyett almost laughed but she had no wish to insult Serrin further.

'Takaar literally ran out of my life ten years ago, Priest Serrin. I've spent those ten years trying to get used to the idea that I would never see him again and that the *ula* I swore my loyalty to, that I loved so utterly, had failed our entire race. I had just about reached a place where I could move on, where I could consider a union with another. An Ynissul *ula* because my offspring must have the opportunity to join the TaiGethen.

'I was already confused, Serrin. Proud of what Takaar achieved and hating him because his cowardice triggered all we now face. Now this. You want to bring him back. In the face of all that is sane you want an elf ten years in exile to return and save us all. It cannot work. It cannot.'

'It cannot or you don't want it to?'

'That is an unworthy comment.'

Serrin contemplated her again. There was no apology in his eyes this time.

'We must attempt every means. I do not have to see the streets of Ysundeneth to know how desperate the situation is. I have seen enough of the nature of elves to know the depths to which some will descend.'

'Will? Some already have.'

'Rape will seem insignificant unless we can turn the tide. I have no desire to relive some of the things I witnessed on Hausolis.'

It was easy to forget how old Serrin was. So youthful of face. So at ease in the rainforest.

'I'll do all I can.'

'That has never been in doubt, Katyett.'

'So what's next? The rest will look to you for leadership, you know that.'

'I am uncomfortable with the thought,' said Serrin. 'But I will do my best. We must do as we said. Secure the Ynissul and bring Takaar to the city.'

'I'll bring him,' said Katyett. 'He is my Arch. It is my responsibility.'

'Not this time. I will go. I promised Auum. Don't worry. This will work.'

Serrin kissed Katyett's eyes and moved swiftly out of the Ultan. Katyett stared after him, wondering how in Yniss's name she was going to relate the news to her people. Wondering if her conversation with Serrin could possibly have taken place.

The door to the warehouse was forced open and elves poured in, scattering through the huge space. Pelyn almost felt sorry for them. Still Tuali and Beethan fought each other though they stood amidst plunder that would see both through the next hundred days at least.

The eighteen surviving Al-Arynaar had been quick, taking ship's rope and climbing high into the roof of the warehouse. Ladders to the gantry had been destroyed. They were safe enough up here. Safer than in much of Ysundeneth.

'Look at them,' said Pelyn.

'Just think what it'll be like when the food really does run out,' said Jakyn.

'This conflict won't last that long. And if it does, the TaiGethen will be waiting for them in the eaves of the forest.' Pelyn shuddered at the thought. 'Come on, let's get back to the beetle. Methian was right. We need to muster our people. What's left of them.'

Above their heads, two skylights had been opened and ropes laid from the gantry bars all the way down to the ground at the far end of the warehouse. Even when Pelyn had paused to spit down, none of them below had looked up. So intent were they on their prize and their hate for each other, they had not paused to wonder where their common enemy had gone.

Halfway to the beetle, she could still hear them. Pelyn kept her pace high, trotting much of the way from the packed dockside housing and only slackening off when they reached the first parades of shops and one of the minor fresh goods market squares. From here, the Gardaryn was a short walk and she slowed to listen to the sounds of the city as it grew further into wakefulness.

Rain had begun to fall, but it was light and blown like a fine mist on an onshore breeze. The sight of those sails a day or so out from the harbour entered her mind. Whoever they were, if their intent was invasion or to raid the city, they weren't going to be facing concerted resistance. They couldn't have timed their arrival better if they'd . . .

Pelyn broke into a run.

'Come on. With me, Al-Arynaar.'

She sprinted across the square, down Sailmakers' Row and across the deserted Park of Renewal, in which several fires still smouldered in defiance of the rain, which was falling more heavily now. She tore down Beeth's Crescent and into the southern piazza. The Gardaryn still stood open. Her people still stood guard outside it.

'Yniss bless us, we aren't too late.'

Jakyn fell in beside her. 'Arch Pelyn?'

'Not now, Jakyn. I've just worked this all out. We can win this. We really can. All of you, with me. Come listen to what I have to say inside. Quickly.'

Pelyn ran up the steps and into the Gardaryn. She headed across the chamber and over the stage into the offices behind, her warriors following her. She glanced into every chamber she passed, pulling up short at the central records offices, where Methian and three other Gyalan Al-Arynaar were still sifting through the sea of papers strewn about the floor. Some semblance of order had been returned under the eye of the veteran. He looked up, surprised at her sudden appearance.

'Pelyn? I assume the warehouse has been taken.'

'Aye, but they'll be slaughtering each other over its contents for the rest of the day.'

'Shorth take the lot of them,' said Methian. He looked past her at the faces crowding in behind her. 'Brought me some help?'

'No,' she said and stepped inside the office, turning a circle as she spoke. 'Listen to me, all of you. And get the word out to the Al-Arynaar at every post and station in the city. I want a muster in one hour at the barracks training grounds. If they aren't dead or dying, tell them to be there. If their belief is wavering, tell them to be there and I'll tell them why we are still going to return peace to our city.

'Now listen. We may not have a lot of time. There are a dozen ships heading this way. They'll be landing probably before dawn tomorrow. Whoever is on board has come to fight. To take the city. But think on this. Their arrival cannot possibly be a coincidence. They have been advised when to get here, and that can only be because people here in Ysundeneth have sent them word. I'll bet any of you a hundred days' pay that they were anchored less than two days from here. Probably at the Casolian Inlet.'

'I don't understand how this will help,' said Jakyn. 'Twelve ships full of fighters. If they've really crammed them in, there could be five hundred on board. That's more than enough to take this city. We have less than half that.'

Methian put a finger to his lips. 'Shh now, young reverent. The ships are only one side of this coin.'

Pelyn smiled. 'So they are, Methian. But your question is good, Jakyn. Keep thinking and you'll live through this. Five hundred, you say? Could easily be as many as seven hundred. And they could be bringing the magic with them that killed Jarinn and Lorius and crippled poor Olmaat.

'But this city is sprawling and in chaos. To succeed in cowing the population and beating us, they will have to have inside information on where the threads have gathered, the key areas to take, our likely tactics. People who are here right now will be directing them. No one else can have the right level of knowledge to secure this place.'

'So what can we do?' asked Jakyn.

Pelyn chuckled. 'People will start to believe I've planted these questions with you, young *ula*. We will do two things at once. We will seek those in Ysundeneth who work against us. We won't be looking for mob leaders. We must think higher. Hithuur will be one and there will be others. Kill them and we deal a huge blow. And second, we will seed fear among the threads. Tell them what is coming through those they will still hear. Perhaps let them know of the cargo on those ships. Not the real cargo of course. We can be a little creative, I think.

'Take this out to the Al-Arynaar in the city. Bring them all to muster. We can do this. Believe it as I believe in you. Decide among yourselves which way each of you will go. And be careful. Now go.'

Pelyn laid a hand on Methian's shoulder and raised her other to stop Jakyn running out after his brothers and sisters.

'You two I need with me at the barracks now. We've things to discuss in advance of the muster.'

Jakyn blushed scarlet. 'My Arch Pelyn, I—'

'Methian might die. I might die. I need you too. You might be young but they listen to you. They respect you. Think of this as your training for your next promotion. And stop pretending to be surprised. You know how good you are.'

The three of them headed back out onto the temple piazza. Pelyn could hear the shouts of mobs echoing from all parts. As usual, smoke smudged the skyline. There was the sound of breaking pottery and of clashing metal. Hoots and calls bounced from high walls. The sounds of the collapse of a society so surprisingly fragile, it took the breath away.

'Pelyn, look.'

Methian was pointing towards the temple piazza. Pelyn feared seeing more flames but instead saw four columns of blue smoke funnelling into the air to be dispersed by rain and breeze. She gave a barking laugh.

'The final piece of the plan,' she said.

'Is it?' asked Methian.

'When we have turned back the ships and captured or killed all the traitors, the people of Ysundeneth will want respected authority. It seems to me that Llyron, our blessed High Priest of Shorth, has just applied for that position. We've time to brief her before the muster if we hurry. Come on.'

Chapter 18

Never over-think warfare.

The temple of Shorth was the only building in the piazza that had suffered no damage whatever, though smoke from the destroyed temple of Yniss had stained the walls. Shorth appeared even more magnificent than before, rising from the ashes surrounding it.

Pelyn walked quickly across the piazza, breasting through the groups of elves gathering in front of Shorth. The temple was fashioned in a likeness of Shorth himself lying prone and rose forty feet from the floor of the piazza. Its main entrance was set in the centre of the head and accessed by a colonnaded path across the sunken gardens. A flight of white marble steps led up to the grand wooden doors in front of which twenty torches stood in two rows. Before the doors stood a quartet of Senserii, the hooded Guardians of Shorth.

Dressed in plain grey, they represented the gentle herders of souls whose faces were blank to hide the eternal sorrow of their grim task. Each carried a bladed staff, *ikari* in the ancient tongue. In the scriptures the herders used these to take the heads from the Arakhe, the stealers of elven souls.

The *ikari* were a ceremonial accoutrement but any who had seen the ritual combat of the Senserii knew their capabilities. Katyett rated the Senserii, all of them elves born of mixed blood, as more deadly than the TaiGethen. It was a shame they were so few, numbering no more than fifteen at any time in observance of the scriptures.

Pelyn strode across the moat and nodded at the Senserii, who stepped aside to let her past. She felt her hopes rising. It was so normal inside. So comforting and welcoming. She felt herself relax. Shorth's priests were about their tasks as always. Indeed they would be hard pressed with the number of souls needing succour and prayer for their passage to the halls of the ancients.

The centrepiece of the grand hall of the temple's body was the magnificent raised altar and stairway to the throne of the high priest. The altar was carved from grey-veined marble. It was a circle more than twelve feet in diameter, edged with carvings of entwined hands and resting upon the petrified bole of a mighty banyan tree. Its surface was carved with the scriptures of the dead, which the priests intoned on festival days, and it was reached up a flight of four heavy wooden steps, worn by the footfalls of centuries.

From the opposite side of the altar, a steep stair rose up twenty feet to the intricate wooden throne of the high priest. The throne was carved with a lattice of the limbs and faces of the dead. It was the place from which the high priest led the chants that opened the pathways to Shorth's embrace. His were the last pair of eyes to gaze upon a soul as it rose from the chains of the living earth.

The three Al-Arynaar bowed their heads before the altar and waited for an attendant to come to them. They were not long in waiting.

'Pelyn. Your presence graces us.'

Pelyn turned to the tall thin figure dressed in dark grey robes with a hood over her head. Her hands reached out and Pelyn took them both.

'The grace is all yours, Telian,' said Pelyn. 'And I am glad you are alive and unscathed. So many are not.'

Telian's face was grim. 'We evacuated everyone to the Hallows of Reclamation but could not stay there. We are needed here. Now more than ever. All of us have returned. Llyron too. The pillars of smoke will rise until this trouble is over. All must know they can come to us when their loved ones fall.'

'Shorth's majesty still holds sway but you can call on us if you need more security.'

Telian let go Pelyn's hands and smiled. 'I suspect you are stretched to breaking already. The fifteen are here. Now, is there something we can do for you? Souls needing comfort as they move to the embrace of Shorth?'

'I need an audience with Llyron. If she will see us, we can move more quickly towards a solution to this crisis. We can bring the threads together again under respected authority. Llyron's authority in the absence of so many others.'

Telian hesitated for a fraction. 'Llyron does not normally grant personal audiences outside the days of observance.'

Pelyn spread her hands. 'You know what I am going to say to that. Telian, I must speak with her. The city is torn. There is still a chance we can properly restore order. Surely she will want to hear me.'

Telian smiled. 'I'm sure she will. Come with me. I cannot guarantee you audience but I'll do what I can. So long as you're sure this is what you want.'

'Of course,' said Pelyn, a little confused. 'Why wouldn't I be?'

'Currently, certainty is everything. You should remember that.'

Pelyn chose not to respond. She wasn't sure how to answer such a comment. It barely made sense. Instead, she gestured for Telian to lead on. The priest of Shorth moved off around to the right of the altar, paused to bow at the foot of the throne and headed towards the temple's right arm.

Here, the priests and guests of the temple lived and worked when not required in the hall. They worked on cures for more ills than Pelyn knew existed, on new methods of surgery and of course on scriptures and services to better aid the travelling of souls to Shorth's embrace.

It was the paradox of the Shorth devotee that while their primary role was succour for the dead and comfort for the grieving, the desire of each and every one of them was in prolonging life. Llyron had once joked that her key focus was on rendering herself unemployed. She was the only Ynissul in the order and had been a surprising appointment on the death of the Beethan incumbent four years before. Jarinn had known about her elevation even if he had not known about the many others that had raised the ire of Lorius.

Telian led them past pale-painted walls hung with tapestries depicting the many faces of Shorth's glory, the peace and beauty of death and grand imaginings of the halls of the ancients. The arm of the temple was a far plainer affair. The work of Shorth required no distraction. Timber and stone walls were unadorned and doors to cells, chambers, record rooms and laboratories were simple timber and iron affairs.

The air was cool and the quiet of the temple was intensified by the energy of effort. Pelyn had never been down this arm, only the left, where bodies were brought for blessing and dressed for transport out to the hallows. The Chambers of Stillness would be full today.

Telian led them to a door almost at the end of the arm. A side door back into the piazza was the only other beyond this one.

'Wait here.'

Telian opened the door, on which was carved the embracing symbol of Shorth, and walked inside, closing it behind her. Whatever the tenor of the conversation, it was very brief. The door opened and Telian gestured them inside, closing it to leave the three Al-Arynaar alone with Llyron, high priest of Shorth.

Llyron was seated behind a wide wooden desk covered completely with parchment, book and scripture. She was using a magnifying glass to examine a passage involving delicate, faded images.

'Such magnificent work,' said Llyron. 'You must all examine this text. There'll be plenty of time before you leave, I'm sure.'

She raised her head and favoured them with a broad smile that made her eyes sparkle and warmed the otherwise chill and austere chamber. Llyron was a particularly tall Ynissul, with soft features somewhat at odds with those typical of her thread. Her ears were tiny and flat against her head, her nose slender and long and her eyes less angled. She was beautiful but severe. An artist's ideal of the two faces of Shorth.

Pelyn led Methian and the terribly nervous Jakyn in opening her arms and bowing her head. She spoke while studying the faded rug on which she stood.

'I am honoured and grateful you have agreed to talk to us,' she whispered.

'Come, Pelyn, these are not days for protocol. The Al-Arynaar are revered here. You can look at me when addressing me. Always.'

Pelyn looked up. Llyron was moving from behind her desk, her plain white robes caressing its gentle edge and wafting air beneath a few of the papers on its pocked and scarred surface.

'Thank you,' she said.

'Speak, child of Tual. Tell me of your plans.'

Pelyn took a deep breath to prevent herself from gabbling.

'We still have an opportunity to stop this conflict before damage to the harmony becomes irreparable. There is a fleet heading this way. I'm certain traitors within the city will meet it. I aim to stop them. Find them and kill them. We know Hithuur is one such and we will uncover others if you back us.

'Use your voice. The threads will listen to you and act on your words. You can loosen tongues. Make fingers point. If they do, I can do this. Even with the few Al-Arynaar I have, I can do this. Will you help me? Help us?'

Llyron inclined her head. 'You come to me in the role of saviour of Ysundeneth. But Ysundeneth does not need saving. Nor yet the wider population of our great people. Salvation is all around us.'

Pelyn glanced at Methian to make sure she had heard Llyron's words correctly. Methian's mouth was moving soundlessly as it did when he was confused.

'I don't understand. The threads are disintegrating. They are ripping each other apart out there. Literally in some cases. And they have murdered every Ynissul not taken to safety by the TaiGethen. Forgive me but this is not salvation, it is slaughter.'

Llyron's smile had faded.

'In his heart an elf is still a predatory pack animal. It is in his blood and in the basest of his desires. He only vaguely understands the necessity of a fair and equable society or the need for tolerance of others.'

Pelyn's heart skipped painfully and her body cooled. Beside her, Methian was rigid. Jakyn was trying not to breathe at all. Llyron continued.

'You cannot spread a timber floor upon the crater of an active volcano. Takaar's thousand-year experiment is a failure. There are those of us who prayed fervently for the day he failed. The day the threads turned against him. And now they have. Elves have voted by word and action. They do not need the closeness of other threads. They do not need the abhorrence of inter-thread union. Only Shorth can save those innocents born of such filthy depravity. They need order. They need authority, not idle chatter in the beetle. They need the old order restored. As it was before the War of Bloods. As it was when we enjoyed our longest period of peace. Enter.'

Pelyn glanced behind her at the door. It opened and Telian came in followed by three of the Senserii, by Sildaan the scripture priest from Aryndeneth, Hithuur and six men. Some of the men wore armour. Others did not.

Pelyn felt something inside her give. She snatched out her short blade and rushed at Hithuur.

'Bastard! You murdered my priest. Bastard!'

Pelyn was fast. Hithuur was ahead of the six men and vulnerable. Pelyn slid in, just like Katyett had taught her, keeping her sword in front of her face. Her feet slammed into his ankles, bringing him crashing down. Pelyn drove back to her feet, bringing her sword back to strike.

Every man had drawn a weapon but Pelyn didn't care if she was struck down. She was in the right place for her soul to pass after all. The foot of an *ikari* slapped into the back of her knees, twisted and lifted. Pelyn felt herself tumbling back. A second staff struck her chest, accelerating her fall. She hit the ground heavily, the wind knocked from her body. Before she could take a breath, all three *ikari* blades were at her throat.

'Cease!' Llyron's voice carried complete authority. 'Senserii, hold. Never has an elf been slain within the boundaries of this temple. Men, sheathe your weapons. Your acts are blasphemy. Get up, Pelyn. How stupid.'

Pelyn stormed to her feet, rounding on Llyron. 'He murdered my Lorius. He murdered your Jarinn. How can you stand with him?'

'He was acting on my orders,' said Llyron. 'Who else's do you think?'

'Yours?' Pelyn saw two Senserii ghost to stand by Llyron. 'Then it is you I seek.'

'Well, of course it is,' snapped Llyron. 'Who else can lead the elves now that Jarinn and Lorius are gone? The high priest of Shorth was ever the ruler of the elves. Ever an Ynissul until Takaar meddled. Only within the walls of a temple to Shorth are the threads treated with equality. Only the high priest of the order can correctly govern those whose souls pass through their hands. And only in the Ynissul is the intellect keen and the strength of blood present in order to bestow the correct level of benefit upon each thread.'

Pelyn felt her body sag. Such words should have been buried in history for ever, only hauled out as an example of how unjust the lives of most elves used to be. She stood with her brothers, a Gyalan and a Cefan. She feared for them as she must now fear for herself.

'You have spent your whole life preaching the harmony,' said Pelyn. 'Why do you turn against it?'

'My whole life? Hardly. I have had to pay lip service while Jarinn continued to preach his flawed beliefs.' She turned her attention on Methian and Jakyn. 'You two. Mouths open like piranhas in search of a feed. Nothing to say in support of your lord?'

'What will become of us? Of the Al-Arynaar?' asked Jakyn, his voice admirably calm.

'Have no fear,' said Llyron. 'The Al-Arynaar are perhaps Takaar's greatest creation. A force drawn from every thread, trained to work as one. The perfect army for the defence of Shorth, no? For me. It is a shame the TaiGethen will not have a role but you'll understand that would be difficult.'

'And if we refuse?' said Methian.

Llyron's tone was even. 'That will of course be your choice. And wrapped in your cloak you will be delivered to the feet of those with less mercy than I for the products of Takaar's failure.'

'You will have to kill all of us. None will join you,' said Pelyn.

'Now that is just naive. Many already have. My knowledge of your plans is far more complete than you imagine. As for you three, I will give you time to cool your passion and your hatred. I will return to you at dawn. Just before our fleet docks. Then I will have your answer. Senserii, take them to a contemplation and remembrance chamber. That seems appropriate.'

Chapter 19

I can grieve for those lost in battle. Or I can ensure their sacrifice has worth.

Pelyn was silent for a good long time. The contemplation chamber encouraged as much. It was filled with plants. Natural light flooded in through a skylight grid that covered the entire roof space forty feet above their heads. An ornamental pool fed by hidden pipes trickled happily. Large white and black fish lazed within it.

Pelyn sat in a deep and embracing leather chair. It was one of six making a circle around a low wooden table on which sat beautifully scented cut flowers from the gardens at the rear of the temple. She stared at them until her sight blurred, blinked and did it again. Eventually, the constant movement of Jakyn broke her from her blankness.

'What is it you are doing exactly?' she asked.

'Looking for a way out,' said Jakyn. 'We can't just sit here.'

'You know this isn't like a performance of *The Kidnap of Verendii*,' said Methian.

The old Gyalan had taken the chair opposite Pelyn and had mirrored her mood, probably her actions too. She hadn't noticed him at all.

'I know,' said Jakyn sharply. 'I just don't see the point of sitting there waiting till dawn for an *ikari* blade in the guts.'

'You're expending energy you needn't,' said Methian. 'Come and sit down.'

'I can't,' said Jakyn.

'The impatience of youth,' said Methian. 'And you, Arch Pelyn. Do you have a plan?'

Pelyn stared back at him. Plan. She'd outlined to her warriors how the traitors would be high-ranking priests and officials and then handed herself over to the highest of them all. Some planner she had turned out to be.

'Idiot,' she muttered.

'I'm sorry?' said Methian.

'Not you, Methian. Me. I'm sorry I dragged you two into this. Idiot that I am. I led us right into the jaws of the enemy.'

'You couldn't have known,' said Methian.

'I could have followed my own advice and not trusted anyone. Any senior Ynissul, certainly. I wonder what happened to the muster. Do you think Esseral will have assumed command?'

'She bloody ought to. You gave her the job of second after all.'

'But she's an unhappy Cefan.'

'We're all unhappy,' said Jakyn from a position balanced on the edge of the pool. 'Just got to do your job, haven't you?'

'You'll break an ankle. Can't have you limping to your execution, can we?'

'*Methian!*' hissed Pelyn.

'Get down from there, foolish youth,' admonished Methian with a smile.

Jakyn looked stricken. 'Is that what they'll do to us?'

Pelyn glared at her elder. 'Only if we refuse to cooperate.'

'They won't trust us,' said Jakyn. 'They won't believe we switched sides so easily.'

'Maybe not, but there's one thing I do know,' said Pelyn. 'Being kept in the bowels of the temple doing some menial job gives us more chance of helping our people than if our souls are sent to Shorth.'

Methian cleared his throat. 'Pelyn, I'm going to do something unusual and disagree with you.'

'You really think they'll present you to your enemies for traditional execution, do you? Don't be daft.'

'I'm prepared to take the risk. Look at it this way. If we say we want to join the shiny new path and become Shorth's guardians, I've no doubt at all we'll be manacled to something and given mops, buckets and filthy rags as the first two centuries of our retraining. If Llyron wins, we'll spend the rest of our days as nothing more than slaves. She'll never trust us. We'll be the lowest form of life to her. Not Ynissul and not of mixed blood, though working in her temple.

'Give me a chance to speak, and I'll talk my way out of trouble or die trying. I'd prefer it that way. And if I can persuade whoever it is not to slit my throat, I'll be out there on the street. Back in the fight.'

Pelyn felt a smile tugging at the corners of her mouth.

'And if the Senserii stick you with an *ikari* blade under the eaves of the forest?'

'Then you may berate me when you join me in the halls of the ancients.'

The smile was joined by the faintest flicker of rekindled hope.

'You'd better not be wrong about this,' said Pelyn.

'Am I ever wrong?' asked Methian, his eyes sparkling.

'This would be a bad time for your luck to change,' said Pelyn. 'Jakyn, what do you think?'

Jakyn raised his eyebrows, pursed his lips and shrugged.

'We should probably get some rest. Methian's planning a tough day tomorrow by the sounds of it.'

'Do we follow them?' asked Hithuur.

He stood with Sildaan and twenty human mercenaries at the mouth of Ultan-in-Caeyin. The bowl was deserted. No evidence that anyone had been here earlier in the day remained. Around three thousand Ynissul civilians and a small guard of TaiGethen had disappeared into the rainforest.

'No need,' said Sildaan. 'We know where they're going.'

'And the priests at Aryndeneth? We should try and warn them.'

Sildaan shrugged. 'They're smart. They'll blame me and say they are tending those who I have abandoned. Or they should. I can't help those who won't help themselves.'

'Where's Leeth?'

'Leeth took another path,' said Sildaan, not looking round at him. She began to walk from the Ultan back towards the bridge and the city. 'Come on. The fleet will be in the harbour in two hours. Plenty of Al-Arynaar to round up before then.'

Hithuur didn't move for a moment. He stared after Sildaan. She'd changed. Hardened. Was it really as Llyron said? That elves could never be other than the roots of their race dictated? Sildaan was playing the part all right. Cruel-eyed, chill of soul. Ten years before she had been so honoured to be accepted into the Aryndeneth priesthood and had talked only of spreading the harmony, of forging unbreakable links between the threads.

That was before she had been seconded to Llyron at the temple of Shorth in the forest. That was where it had begun for her. And she'd never lived on Hausolis. Never known the horror of war. She craved it. Hithuur was sick of it. Llyron had given him a path when he was at his most desperate in the days when it became clear his family were gone, lost behind the collapsed gateway. Hithuur believed in the lessons Llyron preached. But not in her method of achieving their aims. What he had led Jarinn into had sickened him. He didn't think he would ever sleep clear of nightmares again. He didn't deserve to.

Sildaan hadn't noticed he'd yet to move. He sighed and trudged after her. The leader of the men, Garan, the ugly big man with sores on his face and blood hate in his eyes, trotted past him and laid a hand on Sildaan's shoulder. She jerked herself free and snapped round to face him, pushing him away.

'Did I not tell you never to touch me, blink-life?'

Garan spread his hands wide. 'Hey. Relax. We're working to-gether, right? I just want to check you're doing the right thing.'

'You're doubting me again?'

Garan's face took on a resigned look. Hithuur watched the exchange with growing interest.

'Without Leeth, who else can be your conscience?'

There was fire in Garan's eyes suddenly. Sildaan hissed through clenched teeth and spared Hithuur a brief glance, unhappy he was obviously listening. She walked away, beckoning Garan to follow. Hithuur smiled. His hearing was particularly acute. It was dry currently and there was little other noise barring the ever-present din from the forest. Nothing to distract him.

'Never mention him. Never use his name to get under my skin like the fly larvae under yours. Remember who pays you. Who keeps you alive.'

'I keep myself alive, Sildaan. That is my job. And I never forget who pays me. That is my livelihood. And you pay me to advise you as well as use my sword. So I want to know why you are letting a significant number of our worst enemy and three thousand Ynissul just wander off into the forest without a care. Out there they are going to have their minds set unshakeably against what you are doing. You say you aren't numerous.' He jerked a thumb over his shoulder. 'That has to represent a significant percentage of the total Ynissul alive today, doesn't it?'

Sildaan pushed her hand through her hair and shook her head slowly. Hithuur watched Garan bridle as she tutted.

'Well, that is why you can't advise me on anything other than how to kill with blade and magic, isn't it? You just don't understand the elven mind at all, do you? And certainly not the Ynissul mind.'

'That surprises you, does it?'

'Not at all.'

'So enlighten me. Help me see the light of your wondrous plan.'

Garan stared down at Sildaan, his aggression barely suppressed. Hithuur wondered for a moment who would win in a single combat. Sildaan was fast and slick with a blade. All the priests were though few chose to carry a weapon. And she had good open-hand skills. Better than Hithuur's certainly. But she was no TaiGethen. She didn't demonstrate the poise, agility or sheer speed of reaction.

Garan on the other hand was simply raw power. He'd find Sildaan surprisingly strong, but Hithuur could imagine that long sword in both of his hands and wondered if any elf could really deflect a well-aimed blow. It would be fascinating to find out. Hithuur wasn't at all sure he knew who he would want to win.

Sildaan pointed into the rainforest and then began walking again, Garan a pace to her left and eyeing her from beneath a heavy frown.

'Out there are three thousand and more ordinary Ynissul. Most of them have lived in the city ever since they arrived here or were born here. And those that lived in the forest have come to live here for a reason. These are not TaiGethen material. They are pampered *iads* and *ulas* who understand a roof over their heads, a mattress on which to lie and a hot meal whenever they choose to eat it, having brought all their lovely fresh food from the market.

'Imagine them now. They've been brutalised by other threads in the city. Beaten, raped. And they are the ones not murdered in the temple. Now they're being forced to run into the rainforest. There's danger in every branch and beneath every step. There's only leaves to shelter them when it rains, and for most a ground covered with crawling and biting insects and reptiles when they sleep, if sleep they can.

'They won't get enough to eat. Thirty TaiGethen cannot feed three thousand. They won't be able to drink until a pure stream is crossed. They left with nothing. A few clothes. The odd book. They are so underprepared it makes you look like a fifty-year veteran of the canopy.

'And, when they get to their sanctuaries, they'll find a few huts, an open fire and a whole lot of elves who don't want to be forced to look after them. They'll be fed roots, berries and monkeys. Given creaking hammocks. What a life, eh?

'So when I go to offer them the hand of friendship . . . One of their own, come to bring them back home, having cleared their city and ensured that none of those who hurt them will do anything more than grovel and serve them from here on in, who do you think they will follow? The TaiGethen, who will despise them for their weakness and lack of faith? Or me and Llyron and Hithuur? Elves who understand them and their true desires. Elves who can offer them a better life than the one they were forced to flee?

'The mathematics are not complex, are they, Garan?'

Hithuur had watched Garan's face unknot slowly and an expression bordering on admiration replace his earlier belligerence.

'And meanwhile, those Ynissul who might oppose you are out of the way and the TaiGethen are kept very busy indeed.'

'Now you're getting it,' said Sildaan, and she allowed herself a small smile. 'I told you I knew the elven mind, but I have to admit even I did not think it would all work as perfectly as it has so far. Pelyn serving herself up has been an unexpected bonus.'

'And what will this mighty warrior decide, do you think?' asked Garan.

Sildaan's hackles rose immediately. 'She could kill you very easily, Garan. Don't mistake her frame for weakness. Takaar didn't choose her to lead the Al-Arynaar for nothing.'

'I meant no offence.'

'But in answer to your question, I think it might be fun to drop in on Shorth on our way to the harbour and find out, don't you? What would you do?'

'Take my chances with Llyron, I think.'

'I thought so. I suspect Pelyn will not be so craven. Want to make a wager?'

'With one who knows the elven mind so well? I think not.'

'You know, I'm not sure if I'm disappointed or not,' said Llyron. 'I commend your beliefs and your courage. And I will of course pray for your souls, which will undoubtedly find mercy and warmth in the arms of Shorth. I just think it's all a bit of a waste.'

Pelyn said nothing. She, Methian and Jakyn had said all they had to in the depths of the night. They had prayed, made plans and spoken the words that needed speaking. Now there was nothing left but silence and a chance to wonder a little at Llyron, whose tone suggested they'd merely decided not to attend a minor function.

The three of them lay on the floor of the hall, just in the shadow of the doors. They had been stripped naked and then sewn into their cloaks such that only their faces were visible inside their hoods. Ropes had then been wound around them to ensure there would be no escape.

'It used to be called "podding", you know,' said Llyron. 'I looked it up last night. The guilty elf was taken into the forest and left lying on the floor much like a seed pod fallen from a tree. Usually, it was the ants that got to work first. Beetles, leeches and flies too, of course. Biting lizards. Snakes were always fun, and then, inevitably, when the scent of blood and fear soaked the air, the panthers and dogs and monkeys would appear.

'It was a very imaginative punishment. An able deterrent. Sort of a live reclamation, don't you think? One I might well reintroduce. Still, the ants and snakes won't concern you. Just the big sentient predators. Now then. Jakyn. You, I think I will give to the Gyalans. That works. They're routinely bitter and you're a strapping young Cefan. Methian, it has to be the Apposans, doesn't it? Why is it that earth and rain never really got on?

'Pelyn, it's the Tuali for you. I understand you slaughtered a few of your own on the harbour yesterday. They are going to be terribly upset with you, don't you think? I did consider the Beethans, but you know, they wouldn't even give you begging-for-your-life time. They'd just butcher you on the spot.'

Llyron paused to shake her head at all three of them.

'I trust you are extremely uncomfortable. Just remember, this is as good as the rest of your lives are going to get. Your carts are waiting for you outside.'

Chapter 20

A general places his army at risk whenever he stops to think again.

Each of them was loaded onto a separate ox-drawn cart and propped in a seated position. Before long, the carts containing Methian and Jakyn peeled away to their destination ghettos. Senior priests were in attendance. Pelyn continued down towards the Park of Tual, where the thread gathered before setting out to raid other parts of the city.

Pelyn supposed she should have been flattered. The grand red carriage carrying Llyron led her cart. The banners, the guard of Senserii and the instantly recognisable figure of Llyron drew two things like flies to a fresh corpse. Deference from every thread and an ever-growing crowd of curious onlookers, some clearly putting their differences aside to find out what was going on.

Public drives by the high priest of Shorth were rare in the extreme. The death of the high priest of Yniss, under normal circumstances, and the Festival of Departed Souls were the only ceremonial appearances. She could of course be seen at the Gardaryn during debates but the myth and aura surrounding Shorth's high priest was the most enduring of the elven psyche.

Iads and *ulas* walked along behind Pelyn's cart. It wasn't long before the more curious moved closer to try and work out who she was and why she was trussed so comprehensively. It was a short step from there to the first volleys of spitting, abuse and threats. Of course they had no idea what faced Pelyn, but her lack of anxiety in the face of their promises only served to further enrage the more determined.

The Senserii and walking priests made no move to deflect the abuse. Indeed they made space for those who wished to get close and only moved to stop the regular attempts to do her physical harm.

From within her pod, Pelyn had plenty of time to stare out at the naked hatred and see their decision for the folly it truly was. After an emotional conversation with Methian and Jakyn, they had convinced each other that they would cow the baying mobs that faced them with reason and reality.

The hard facts of an enemy fleet approaching, an Ynissul betrayal and men walking tall on city streets. Empathy with those who had a common enemy but needed direction to see it. It would be a small miracle if any of them was allowed to open their mouth to do anything other than scream in agony.

Pelyn would have shrugged but there was no room for such an extravagant movement. Her limbs were cramped and the pain in her left calf was constant and deep. Her back was bouncing against a spur of metal in the back of the cart and she had the most excruciating itch in her scalp.

She looked to her left, watching the buildings pass by as she sat, back to the direction of travel. She noted the spires of the Gardaryn away to the right, climbing above the sculpted buildings of the Glade, Ysundeneth's most wealthy residential district. Close now, then.

The Glade thinned into the artisans' district, nicknamed the Mural. Next it was the central fine goods market and that small and beautiful square bordering the Park of Tual. Pelyn could smell ash and burning meat. They mixed with the scent of the sea and the more unpleasant odours of rot and mould. A good downpour would dampen them all but it seemed she was to be murdered before the sun rose on a stultifyingly dry morning.

The carriage and cart rattled across the market square. Senserii and priests closed in around Pelyn. Words were barked. Threats were made by the hooded guards. The following crowd, now numbering well in excess of five hundred, stopped as one. Pelyn watched them fidgeting and looking anew at one another. Beethan moved away from Gyalan. Apposan from Cefan. She almost pitied them but felt instead the stickiness of saliva on her face and wished instead for a riot.

'Shorth take you all,' she muttered.

The cart came to a jarring stop. She felt the driver and his mate jump down. From the park she could hear a good number of voices and the crackling of a fire. The driver and mate appeared at the back of the wagon and unchained the tailgate. They grabbed the bottom of her sewn cloak and pulled. Her head bumped hard against the timbers of the wagon bed and scraped over the iron rivets above its axles.

They stopped short of letting her drop straight to the muddy churned grass and picked her up one side each, marching her upright to where Llyron was standing before a now-silent group of Tualis. The sight of her brought a storm of abuse and a surge forward only curtailed by the mirror move of five Senserii.

Llyron held up her hands for quiet, the only Ynissul who could walk unhindered in Ysundeneth, let alone issue orders that would be obeyed.

'Shorth's blessing be upon you all, denizens and worshippers of Tual. My temple is open and welcoming to all at these times of conflict and anger. I am desolate for the pain unleashed by the denouncement of Takaar and pray hourly for its swift and peaceful resolution. Resolution I feel is close, though I doubt any of you can see it. And I bring to you a gift as night gives way to dawn and Shorth gazes down with relief on those still walking our land. While he rests, I of course may not.

'Shorth blesses every thread, and in his temple all are equal and loved. Shorth takes to his embrace the souls of all who fall, the good and the wicked. It is he who judges the dead. And it is I who must judge those who defy the will of Shorth. Such defiance has been shown by Pelyn, Arch of the Al-Arynaar.

'And, as is allowed under my powers, I hand her back to you, her people, to dispense the justice you see fit for heresy, for traitorous actions against her own thread and for the simple murder of those merely wanting food for the bellies of their children.'

Pelyn barked a laugh. 'She will betray you! She is in the thrall of men. She—'

The foot of a staff slammed into her gut, doubling her over. Her minders kept her standing.

'She ordered Lorius's murder. She is the *cascarg*. Please.'

The driver's fist took her full in the mouth, splitting her lip. The crowd cheered. Llyron raised her arms and cocked a smile at them.

'Defiant to the end, eh? Now, where is the leader among you? Pelyn will be handed only to a recognised authority.'

The crowd quietened. Elves looked over their shoulders. A gap was made and one stepped forwards. Pelyn stared at the face of her executioner.

Helias, Speaker of the Gardaryn.

Less than a mile into the rainforest and the complaints had reached such a pitch that Katyett called a halt to the march, which had only ever been slow to grinding. She tried to sympathise with them. She tried hard. But walking up and down the ridiculously long, straggling column of the unready, the unfit and the frankly unworthy, she could see the damage to her forest increasing and the will of her charges bleeding away like a slash to the jugular.

'Graf. Give the order to make comfortable. Or as far as possible anyway.'

Katyett turned at a muttered curse and saw a couple cling to each other as one stumbled over a root. The *ula*'s face was swollen and deep bruising was coming out across his cheeks and neck. His nose had been comprehensively smashed and had been field-reset by one of the TaiGethen. The *iad* was crying quietly, had bruising all around her neck that looked like an attempted strangulation and a bleak look in her eyes from a memory that would never fade.

She knelt beside them as they flopped to the ground, supporting each other with the desperation of those who know they have absolutely nothing else left. At the sight of her so close, painted and camouflaged, the *iad* flinched away reflexively. Katyett's heart missed a beat.

'You never have to be scared of me,' she whispered. 'I am here to protect you. And I promise you this too. As Yniss is my lord and my life, when this is over, you will never have to fear anyone ever again.'

'But why out here?' asked the *ula*. 'She has suffered so much. Now you're asking us to walk through the rainforest for days. Is there really nowhere else safe other than Aryndeneth?'

'Trust me,' said Katyett. 'All will become clear to you. I am sorry for every reluctant footstep you have to take because it is not your fault. But we have to ensure your safety. We have to ensure no one can get to you again to do you harm.'

Katyett leant towards the *iad* and drew a piece of clean cloth from a pocket. The *iad* took it to dab at her nose, which was bleeding a little.

'Thank you.'

'The TaiGethen hunt those who seek to destroy all we have built. Those who do not belong and those who would take us back to the War of Bloods. This we do in Yniss's name.'

'I don't want you to kill for me,' said the *iad*.

Katyett gazed at her. Humble and ordinary. Dressed in clothes from the rag and make market and with hands that had only ever held a quill, never a spade or a weapon. Inside, though, she was pure-bred Ynissul.

'Yniss guides my soul, Tual my hands. We do what we must.'

'You enjoy it,' said the *iad*. 'Don't you? The TaiGethen way. Killing to make things right.'

Katyett frowned. 'I enjoy the beauty of the rainforest and I enjoy the honour of being TaiGethen. Enjoy killing? No. But our enemies leave us no choice. And they learn that though I might not enjoy it, I am very, very good at it.'

The two *iads* shared a brief smile. Katyett kissed the other's eyes before trotting away to the head of the column, whispering through the dense undergrowth. It began to rain. Hard. Thunder cracked across the sky

'Now that, Gyal, is poor timing.'

Her Tais were trying to help any they could. They fielded questions and begged for patience. Katyett brushed past them all and found Pakiir kneeling next to Olmaat. Merrat was close and Katyett whistled her over. They dropped into the patter of the TaiGethen. Part ancient tongue, part click and chitter borrowed from Tual's finest.

'We've come far enough. Look at the damage they've done,' said Katyett. 'Merrat, what of the Ultan?'

'We aren't followed. All of them returned to the city.'

Katyett nodded. 'Good. And are we sure our mark has slipped away already?'

Pakiir chuckled. 'Barely lasted two hundred yards.'

'Good. And the first *cascarg*? The one asking all the questions at the Ultan?'

Merrat raised her eyebrows. Katyett nodded again.

'Good. All is well. Opinions. Are we clear to turn this walking disaster area around and get it to the staging camp?'

'Absolutely,' said Pakiir.

'I think they've suffered enough,' said Olmaat.

'I agree,' said Merrat.

Katyett smiled. 'Maybe not quite enough. Let's make it a lazy left turn, shall we?'

'You are a cruel mistress,' said Olmaat, coughing violently as he thought to laugh.

'Calm yourself, my brother. And I don't mean it. The *iads* in particular need some sort of security. Let's not waste time. And let's not tell them what's happening. Not just yet. See if anyone else needs flushing out before we get there.'

'How far away are we?' asked Olmaat.

'Well, we've been heading in a nice gentle circle ever since we left the Ultan,' said Merrat. 'We're about four hundred yards away, I should think.'

Olmaat managed a pained smile, it cracked his drying salve.

'Want me to lead the way?'

Helias waited until Llyron and her acolytes had disappeared back across the market and away towards the Mural before so much as looking at Pelyn. She'd been laid on the ground and the Tuali had circled her in almost total silence, like a pack of animals awaiting the pack leader to make the first bite. The silence was unnerving. Pelyn had tried to speak but sharp kicks and jabs with staves and clubs cut short any attempt to get through.

When the last echoes of the wheels had faded, Helias walked into the circle and stood at Pelyn's feet, blade in his hand. He gazed down at her and she met it, unflinching.

To flinch is to die.

Helias had not suffered too badly as a result of the fracturing of elven society in Ysundeneth. His clothing was fine and clean. His chin was shaven and his hair newly washed and tied back in a ponytail that he had draped over his left shoulder. Rumours of shortages of water had clearly not been entirely accurate as far as he was concerned. Or perhaps the Tuali had control of the wells and feeds. Most likely they did.

Pelyn tried to see inside him to the *ula* she knew very well and who had often been vocal in his support for her. The Al-Arynaar had replaced the civil peacekeepers very soon after Takaar's flight and the closure of the gate. They were unpopular in some quarters, naturally. Helias had been right behind them.

But now, of course, the Al-Arynaar were the created arm of a discredited hero. The police of a society that no longer existed. And Helias was nothing if not a fine judge of mood and the direction of the wind. What Pelyn saw in his eyes was contempt because that was what his new-found acolytes expected to see. Pelyn wondered if there was something more behind that.

'Well, this is a rather interesting surprise. Pelyn. *Cascarg* of Shorth.

Apparently. Not sure I believe that. But there are things I do believe. Fervently.'

Helias edged his blade under the first of the ropes binding her. The rope was neither particularly thick nor particularly strong. Helias jerked his blade up. The rope sheared to cheers from the assembled Tuali.

'I believe in the right of the Tuali to be the masters of their own fate within the race of elves. Not to touch earth to the Ynissul.'

His blade snagged the second band. Cut it.

'I believe that those who supported the Ynissul in their efforts to regain dominion of the elves deserve nothing but the eternal hatred of the thread into which they were born.'

And then to the third band. Cut it.

'I believe that Takaar's harmony was a millennium-long sham. An apology for the subjugation of every other thread by the Ynissul and a cloak for its continuance under the murderous iron fist of the TaiGethen and Al-Arynaar.'

And so to the final band. Cut.

'And I believe that those Tualis who would carry Ynissul children are not merely *efra*. They are unfit for life.'

The mob around Helias howled their agreement. Elves closed in, shutting out the pale light of dawn that had just begun to edge out the night. Helias crouched down next to Pelyn's head and put his face very close to hers. She could smell the sweat on his clothes and the coarse alcohol on his breath. She was baking hot inside the cloak and Helias's sour breath wasn't helping her growing feeling of nausea. She found she wasn't scared. Frustrated. The only thing she feared was not being allowed to speak. That would be a disaster for all those who stood about her, baying for her blood.

'I know what you are,' he hissed into her ear. 'And I know what you believe I am. But I am not so ignorant. And what you would tell us, I do not wish my brothers and sisters to hear.'

Pelyn could barely focus on his face but she could see the unpleasant grin on it.

'What?' he said. 'You think an *ula* should not look after himself first? Please.'

'You always were a snake, Helias.'

'I can live with it. I can't say the same for you.'

Pelyn was going to die. The certainty pained her and she let her head fall back to the ground. Helias got to his knees, sheathed his short blade and took out a knife.

'Let us see, shall we, what is inside this pod. Let us feast on the Al-Arynaar uncloaked.' Helias's leered down at her. 'I know the rules of the pod. And you always hid yourself from me. Such a shame, my pretty. Such a shame.'

Helias drew the knife down the length of her cloak. The stitching sliced easily and her covering fell aside.

Pelyn smiled. 'Oops,' she said. 'You really should be more careful what you expose.'

Pelyn sat up fast and her left fist made an intensely satisfying connection with his chin.

Chapter 21

The general you serve cannot save your life in battle. Only those who stand beside you can do that.

Takaar felt at his smooth scalp again. There were a few scratches. And his chin. That was smooth too. And now his head was cold. He wondered if his hair would regrow. Meanwhile, he might have to fashion a hat from something. The rain hurt his head when it was very hard. Lucky he had the forest to cover him. It was in the mornings he might suffer though. Out there on the cliff edge. Talking with his tormentor. There the rain could be very hard indeed.

Troubling. All very troubling.

Auum was nearby. Auum would help him. Like he'd helped him shave. Like he was helping him hunt. He was good, this Auum. Very quiet. Very accurate. Had a lot to learn, mind you. And he was very rude. Wouldn't speak to the tormentor at all when they were in the camp.

Troubling.

And why was he here, that was something else. Takaar feared what he might ask. What he might want of Takaar. Takaar wanted to remain here. Here he could live. Here he could hide.

Here you can wallow in your guilt and make excuses for your continued existence.

'What are you doing here?' hissed Takaar. 'You aren't invited.'

I go where I please. I watch what I want.

'Don't get in the way of the javelin.'

I'll be right behind you.

Takaar glanced across at Auum, who was all but invisible, crouched by the trunk of a fig tree. Takaar raised his eyebrows and spread his hands. Auum frowned and went to put a finger to his lips. Stopped himself but Takaar saw the gesture anyway. The student teaching the teacher. Time to see how much he really knew.

The jao deer they had been tracking was a tasty prize. Small, quick and well camouflaged it was a night walker, preferring to keep hidden during the day, when the risk of attack from panthers was higher in this part of the forest. Takaar and Auum had tracked it to a bubbling stream fed by a beautiful cascade falling from an ivy-covered crag about forty feet high. The splash pool was small but deep and a favourite of many of Tual's denizens.

Safe too. Neither panther nor elf killed there. Muddying the poolside with the blood of a kill kept others away for days on end. This time, though, Takaar could indulge in the luxury of flushing the deer towards his hunting partner. Risky. He did not know Auum's skill with a javelin, and the one he had given the TaiGethen was a little rough and didn't fly so true. They might go hungry if there was too much Auum didn't understand.

Takaar indicated to Auum to be ready and set off towards the pool. It was an idyllic sight. The water splashing down, the deer, long elegant neck extended so it could drink its fill. Its ears twitched continually, hunting for any sound of a predator. Takaar, though, was silent. He moved to the edge of the small clearing. The soft brown and red markings on the deer's flanks rippled as it breathed and swallowed.

Takaar edged slightly to his left. He felt the ground beneath him give slightly and he rocked back. He moved his foot and replaced it. Firm and noiseless. He glanced at Auum. He had not moved. The javelin was still held tip down in his right hand. Takaar wondered if he had understood the plan.

Oh, another disappointment looms.

Takaar did not respond. Something about Auum and the set of his body, the penetrating gaze, suggested competence and confidence in equal measure. So be it. Takaar circled round a little more. The deer raised its head. Its small bob tail flicked a warning. It had sensed but not heard.

Takaar could take it right here. His throw would be unimpeded. Jao deer roasting over a fire would taste sweet. But this was a lesson, was it not? And he had outlined the deer's movement on the run at some length earlier in the night. Theory over. Practice separated a good ear from a good aim.

Takaar stepped from cover and clapped his hands sharply. The deer looked down the length of its back, startled. It set off. Its first bound high to escape the jaws of a panther. It hit the ground and darted left. Past a single tree it switched right, its agility improbable if described rather than seen. It ran low. Another high bound. Another change of direction.

Auum had cocked and thrown his javelin in the smoothest movement Takaar had ever seen. He did not throw with too much force, keeping his shape compact and holding his follow-through for a heartbeat. The javelin's flight was flat and fast, the slightly uneven shaft wobbling. The deer switched direction again, twisting its body back on itself and planting its feet to spring.

The javelin struck it at the base of the neck, burrowing deep to pierce its heart. The animal sprawled to the ground, still and dead. Auum moved swiftly from cover to crouch by the deer. Takaar remained where he was. He felt a lightness in his heart that he had not experienced in a long time and never on Calaius.

Auum removed the javelin and propped it against a tree. He picked up the deer and slung it across his shoulders. He retrieved the javelin and looked over at Takaar.

'Hungry?' he said and could not keep the smile from his face.

Takaar glanced over his shoulder.

'Disappointment? Wrong again and another victory for me.'

But it won't end here, will it? Has he come here to treat with you or to kill you?

'You're hoping I'll let down my guard.'

Since you are too craven to kill yourself, I'm left with little else. Think you can beat him if he comes at you?

'I am Takaar.'

You were.

'I'm sorry?'

Auum was walking towards him. Takaar flapped a hand.

'It is nothing. A private conversation. Well done. A clean kill. You've hunted the jao before?'

'Never like this. Thank you.'

Takaar wobbled on his feet. Something was coming. Through the ground and through the air. It grabbed his brain and squeezed. It clutched his gut and twisted. It lay on his chest and grew heavy. Takaar blinked. Dawn was here. Why was it so dark?

Pelyn was on her feet before Helias had hit the ground. She lashed a kick into the side of his face and another into his kidney before the mob engulfed her. She was borne backwards, rough hands and arms

about her waist, chest, neck and head. She was hurled to the ground
and rolled in the mud. She bounced quickly to her feet. She was
surrounded. Weapons were held out. The mob began to close,
trampling her cloak. A couple of *ulas* helped Helias to his feet. He
spat blood from his mouth and advanced on her. This time, though,
he had armed help.

'Listen to me,' she said, trying to catch the eye of any she could.
'Helias will deliver you all to the Ynissul. He is with them. Men are
coming. Landing at the harbour. Please.'

How much they heard was impossible to know. The howls of
abuse reached a new crescendo as soon as she opened her mouth.
Two spears were levelled at her, their points clean and sharp. One
was to her gut, the other to her neck. She backed away and felt hands
on her back. Elves gripped her arms and held her at a gesture from
Helias. He waved for quiet.

'I'm disappointed,' he said. 'Desperate lies from a mouth so
beautiful atop a body so perfect.'

Helias wiped at his mouth and nose. Pelyn was suddenly acutely
aware of her nakedness but made no attempt to jerk her hands free to
cover herself. Instead, she stood taller, prouder.

'Come and take a closer look,' she said.

'I'll have as much time for that as I need,' said Helias. 'So will
every other *ula* with a mind to do so.'

There was cheering in the mob. Pelyn spat on the ground at
Helias's feet.

'And every *iad* will be delighted their leader is a common rapist.'

Helias walked forward and crashed his fist into her nose. Pelyn felt
bone crack and a wave of pain shudder through her head. Blood
began to flow. The cut she had sustained yesterday reopened too,
stinging her face.

'Oh dear,' said Helias. 'I appear to have spoiled the view.'

'Llyron was right,' said Pelyn, the salt taste of blood in her mouth.
'Elves are no more than animals.'

She found her strength renewed. Her death seemed inevitable. The
brutalisation of her body equally so. But there was a chink. She could
try to exploit it. Force it wide. Her last retort, though, she knew that
to be an error the moment she uttered it.

'Oh!' Helias stepped back and spread his arms wide, turning in
a circle to encompass the hundreds who stood around them. *Ula*
and *iad*, the enraged and the anxious. 'Hear that from our former

protector? We are all animals. Let us disperse back to our hides and holes and think on the error of our ways.'

The rhythmic cheering and chanting, growing in volume, reminded Pelyn of a distorted version of the chamber of the Gardaryn. Helias was its bastard Speaker and, surrounding him, government and public were one.

'We are mistaken, all of us! Berate yourselves. You aren't here to ensure the security of the Tualis. You aren't here to make sure there is food and water for your families. You aren't here to fight for a better tomorrow for your thread. I have misled you all. You are nothing more than a pack of dogs. O Arch of the Al-Arynaar, thank you for taking the veil from our eyes.'

The laughter from the mob was hard, aggressive. Faces took on manic looks. Pelyn felt her heart skip.

'You are better than this,' she shouted into the gale of noise. 'Remember who you are. This is none of us. Please. Face the real enemy. It isn't me. It isn't me!'

Helias turned on Pelyn again. He stalked up and grabbed her chin, forcing her head back. He pressed himself against her, and those behind her made sure she couldn't push away. His body reeked of lust and was puffed with his power. Pelyn tried to turn her face away but his grip was strong. His fingers and thumb dug into her cheeks. Blood dripped down onto his hand.

'You are no enemy; you are nothing more than a common murderer. A *cascarg*, *efra*. And you are wasting our time. There is a fight going on here which your meddling will not distract us from any longer. You fail to understand what is truly happening. Why the threads ripped apart so quickly. The old order must not be re-established. We must battle for the ground we want, as must every thread.'

'I understand that you are about to betray all of these people to the Ynissul.'

But her words were thick and muffled by his grip on her chin.

'I know the law on a podding. Many here know it. You have no status. You no longer belong to any thread. You are meat. Animals feast on meat before the inevitable kill. We are animals. So you said yourself.'

Helias made a beckoning gesture.

'Take her. Restrain her. Do with her what you will, any of you. Remember she killed her own on the docks just yesterday. Remember she opened her legs to Takaar. It must have been his last thought of sanity that bade him turn her away. She may not wish to give herself to you so willingly. Perhaps I should show you how it is done. Lie her down. Pin her. Spread her.'

Pelyn thrashed wildly but too many arms were about her. She was dumped on her back. Her shoulders were pressed to the earth. She bucked her hips and kicked her legs. More *ula* forced her buttocks into the mud. More dragged her legs apart. Helias smiled down at her. She stared back at him.

'Tual will turn from you. Shorth will take you to eternal torment.'

'That is tomorrow. This is now.'

Two *ulas* appeared above her. They stood together, their backs to her, straddling her legs, pushing the restraining elves away. Both carried clean, sharp, short blades.

'The law also states that such acts may not take place until dawn,' said one.

Pelyn took in a shuddering breath. She recognised that voice. Tulan. One of her own. Though without his Al-Arynaar cloak, he was a deserter.

'Stand aside,' grated Helias.

'No,' said the other, and Pelyn recognised his voice too. Tulan's brother, Ephran. 'Those who lead must uphold the laws they expect their charges to follow. Or how can they lead?'

'Don't quote Takaar's filth at me,' said Helias. 'Must I question your loyalty to the thread? To Tual himself? Protect this meat and you make yourselves *cascarg*.'

The mob had quietened completely. Pelyn was sure they'd be able to hear her heart drumming against her ribs. Pressure on her body had slackened but she didn't move.

'This is not about her,' said Tulan. 'We shed the cloak for a reason and that reason hasn't changed. But laws, repealed or active, have to be followed or crimes now will go unpunished. That has never been the elven way. Not even before the War of Bloods. Dawn is close. Save carrying out your sentence until then. What harm can it do?'

If she craned her neck, Pelyn could just see the expression on Helias's face. She fought hard to keep hers straight. His eyes were wide and his cheeks pinched and reddening. Only she and he knew the implications of waiting until dawn and the arrival of the human invasion force. He had trapped himself most effectively.

Slowly, Helias dragged a carefree smile onto his face. He shrugged and opened his palms upwards.

'Dawn it is. Why not? Perhaps thought of sentence will make some of us more creative, no?'

Disappointment flew around the mob. The hands on Pelyn released. She drew in her arms and legs but did not get up. Tulan stooped and picked up her cloak. He shook it out. Mud tumbled from it. It was torn and misshapen. He threw it down at her, not looking her in the eye.

'Cover yourself up.'

Pelyn grabbed it greedily and pulled her knees right up to her chest, where she hugged them and wrapped the cloak around herself. She found herself shuddering and unable to control the tremors that flooded her body. She felt no relief. This was not salvation, merely a stay of execution. She wondered how Methian and Jakyn were faring. Could their captors be any more vile then hers? Mercy would have been to make it quick if murder was their intent. Helias had no such release in mind.

'She is now in your charge.' Helias jabbed a finger at the two former Al-Arynaar soldiers. 'Don't think to flee or release her. Keep her here. Others, more loyal others, will be watching you. Understand?'

Tulan and Ephran nodded. Helias spun on his heel and pushed his way through the mob. Two *iads* fell into step beside him. The manner of their gestures and his in response were not encouraging for Pelyn nor her new protectors. Without immediate direction, the mob wandered off after Helias in dribs and drabs. Whatever their plan for the hour, whatever diversion Helias had planned before his betrayal, was forgotten now. Few even gave her a backward glance but one or two came close. Spittle flew; abuse came with it and the comments to Tulan and Ephran were little better.

'It's going to be a lonely place for you two,' she said.

Ephran turned. He reached down a hand.

'Get up,' he said.

Pelyn slapped the hand away and pushed herself to her feet. She was full of aches, her nose and mouth throbbed and her muscles screamed for a moment's relaxation. She threw her cloak around her shoulders and held the edges together in front of her stomach.

'Helias will have you killed, you know,' said Pelyn. 'I suppose I ought to thank you, but it doesn't seem right.'

'Then don't,' said Tulan. 'This isn't for you. Anyone could have been podded and left here and we would have done the same. This way. And don't run. You know what we'll do.'

Pelyn felt a moment of disappointment but knew it should have been no surprise.

'I don't have the strength to run.'

'Or any place to go. Believe me,' said Tulan.

The two brothers walked a little way in front of her, unable to bring themselves to look at her. But before she said what she must, there was no harm in seeing where they really stood.

'So you think I should just stay with you until dawn breaks and Helias comes back to complete his rape and then offer me up to whoever else wants a go? I'll take my chances with the Beethans, thanks.'

Tulan cringed. 'No. No, that isn't what I meant. And I don't want that, for what it's worth.'

'Not much.'

'I meant—'

'I know what you meant. I get it. Nowhere is safe. Not for the Al-Arynaar. And where are they, my loyal brothers and sisters, so far as you know? Still at their posts, still walking their beats or lying slit open in a gutter in the Salt or the Orchard?'

'Holed up in the barracks mostly, from what I've heard,' said Ephran.

'Shut your mouth,' snapped Tulan.

'What odds does it make? None, that's what,' said Ephran. He turned to Pelyn. 'Not so many wear the cloak. Your disappearance led to a lot of desertion.'

'How many are left?' asked Pelyn, trying to sound calm even at this latest blow.

'He doesn't know,' said Tulan firmly.

They were walking across a corner of the park towards a square of wealthy town houses which had the park as their open side. Pelyn recognised it well. The Ash, the area was called after being rebuilt following a damaging fire not more than forty years ago. Helias had a house there, as did others in high office. A couple of houses showed the odd lantern light but it was mostly quiet. No doubt any non-Tualis had been hounded out.

Tulan led the way to the nearest house. A two-storey property boasting private gardens. The house was dark and empty. The domed roof held balconies to all sides. He walked into a large entrance hall and went through the first door on the left-hand side. It was a large dining room with a single window and no other door. He pointed to a chair at the head of the table, furthest from door and window. Pelyn sat in it. Her guards, her former brothers not just in god but in service and belief, stood at the end of the room. Both of them looked steadfastly out of the window.

'So,' she said. 'Tell me we're just waiting for the mass of hidden Al-Arynaar to come down the stairs.'

'You're joking, right?' said Tulan.

'Not totally.'

'Then you'll be disappointed.'

Pelyn sagged. She hadn't realised she'd been clinging on to such a fanciful notion.

'But you will release me to do my work. I'll see to it that you're treated properly, you know that. You can trust me.'

Tulan looked at her for the first time. He didn't look as if he'd slept since the denouncement.

'Don't you understand? That's all gone. No one will ever know how it happened so fast but it has. Helias is right. There is going to be a fight for territory and resources. Then there'll be talking and an order will be established. A new order.'

'Oh, Tulan. Ephran, you believe this too? Helias is a traitor. *Cascarg*, like he called me. But he's worse than that. There isn't even a word to describe him. He's—'

'Pelyn,' said Tulan sharply. 'No. You can't talk like that.'

'I want to hear,' said Ephran.

'Who's upstairs, Eph?'

'Well, I don't know. Probably—'

'Exactly. You don't know. Helias has loyals everywhere already. He works fast.'

'No, he doesn't,' said Pelyn. 'This has been in the plot for years. Probably a decade.'

'Pelyn . . .'

'If you want to shut me up, come over here and do it. Otherwise let me tell you that Helias is in with the rogue Ynissul and they are led by Llyron. Yes, Ephran, Llyron. Believe it or don't, I hardly care. A fleet of mercenary ships is about to land. Helias is going to hand over the Tuali aggressors just to save his own rotten skin.

'But you know what? I don't think I'll bother saying any more.

Why don't we all just sit back, relax and watch the sun come up amidst the deluge of man's magic. Hey, if we go upstairs we'll get an even better view of the last dawn of the elves.

'What do you think?'

Chapter 22

The shame of a coward lies in the eyes of the innocents he condemns.

The staging camp had been abandoned and forgotten for over nine years, ever since the last of the refugees from Hausolis had been housed elsewhere. Nine years was a long time in the rainforest. Beeth had been hard at work. Growth had been voracious but the canopy above was still thin.

The camp lay an hour into the forest beyond the southern wall of the Ultan. It had been fashioned in a natural clearing, expanded to house twelve long low dormitory buildings made of mud, timber and thatch and one large covered area for eating, resting and sheltering. The latrines and baths had been located inside buildings attached to each dormitory.

At its busiest, the camp had housed over fifteen hundred people. Katyett walked in with more than twice that number and found the camp in worse repair than her scout had intimated. From a quick glance, she knew that four dormitory roofs had collapsed, that the open-sided covered area was unsafe with the sheer weight of ivy, vine, lichen and mould swamping it, and that the four-foot-high grass and undergrowth would be a happy hunting ground for every predator in the forest.

But it was the best they were able to provide beyond a forced march to Taanepol, which, at the pace of the Ynissul civilians, would have taken at least six days. The attrition rate among those they'd saved would have been appalling. It might be dangerous here for a while but at least it was manageable.

Katyett looked back at the column and closed her eyes at the numbers she saw. She sent TaiGethen into the camp to beat the grass and scare off whatever they could before bringing them all in and making them find their own spots. TaiGethen then patrolled through them while others searched every building, trying to identify where the civilians could go.

Olmaat was set down among the civilians and was immediately fussed over by Ynissul *iads*, who produced cloth and salve from seemingly nowhere. Katyett saw a smile on his face that touched his eyes for the first time since he'd left the Gardaryn with Jarinn and Lorius.

'Graf, Merrat, Pakiir, Faleen.' The four TaiGethen trotted over. 'We need to work fast. We're lucky because the rain isn't coming back for an hour or two. Not until dawn has broken anyway. I need you to find every willing *iad* and *ula* you can and divide them, one group to each spare Tai. By spare I mean all those not engaged protecting the rest.

'I need working parties to clear vegetation from the dormitories that are viable and, if you're feeling brave, from the bivouac roof. If we can make that safe, we can billet a lot of people there.

'I want others to start collecting food. Yniss knows we need Beeth to provide us a bounty beyond imagining. So berries, roots, herbs. Not just for food, medicine too. Let's not be naive. We're here with people who will get bitten, scratched, stung and infested. We'll need pots of the critical stuff. Tea tree, vismia, verbena and pareira as a minimum.

'I want others to get down to the river. We've got spears with us so we can attach vines and fish. I need traps for meat. Tual save me, I don't need to tell you. As much as you can as often as you can. Pass your knowledge as you need to. We have to keep the camp smoke- and flame-free, so teach steaming and how to build a rock oven, clay stoves, anything. Get them involved in their own survival. Let them sit and fester and they'll get desperate and difficult. Inspire and survive, as Takaar would have said. We're only three miles from the Ultan. We don't need wanderers and we don't need attention.

'Anything else?'

Merrat chuckled. 'No, we understand. And that just leaves you to do the talk, right?'

'Which talk?'

Merrat spread her hands. 'Rainforest survival, naturally. Just a pity you haven't got all your skins, shells and paintings, isn't it?'

Katyett thinned her lips and glowered at Merrat, though there was a little warmth of humour in her gut.

'And you, Merrat, can take your party to do the most important job in the camp.'

Merrat's mirth dissipated. 'I don't want to ask, do I?'

Katyett shook her head. 'No, but I am ordering you to ask just the same.'

Merrat laughed. 'My Arch Katyett, leader of the TaiGethen. Which is the most important job in the camp?'

'Latrines,' said Katyett. 'Latrines for three thousand elves unused to trail food and exposure to heat and rain. And you'll be close enough to hear my talk too. How lucky you are. Sorry, Merrat, I didn't catch that.'

'I said Yniss blesses me with the tasks he sets.'

'He does, my Tai. He really does.'

Pelyn hadn't persuaded them to go upstairs. In the end it didn't matter. If there was one thing for which Sildaan could be relied on, it was punctuality. The skies had remained clear for her too. The sun was banishing shadows from the top of the canopy behind them. It rose to sparkle against the tall spire of the Gardaryn.

Down on the approaches to the harbour, in the quarters of the city the Cefans and Orrans had cornered for their own in a loose alliance, or so Tulan had grudgingly revealed, it didn't matter that the skies were clear. It rained anyway. Teardrops of pure, beautiful and terrifying dark yellow. They fell dense and heavy like Gyal's grief, trailing smoke.

Behind them, orbs of brown and green traced up high into the sky, crashing down on buildings or disappearing from sight, their impacts told by the rumbles and echoes of detonation. The rain set alight everything it touched. Quickly, the whole of Harbour Side and Salt were ablaze. Thick smoke fled into the heavens.

Pelyn had stood and walked to the window to get a closer look. The three of them had belatedly moved onto a balcony, their unfettered view all the more terrifying. Pelyn thought she could hear screams and the clash of weapons. It was hard to be sure. But she knew what she felt.

Yniss had turned from them. Tual had retreated to his fastness in the forest. Shorth's arms would have to be wide indeed to embrace all the souls heading his way. Men and magic were rampaging through the elven first city. She watched their castings rise and fall. She felt heat from the fire and cold from the ice.

She felt a terror so deep it reached through her and back into history. It chilled the souls of the ancients in the halls of the dead. It rooted her where she stood and meant she cared little that her cloak was hanging open or that her erstwhile guards were standing at her shoulders. Not as captors, as Al-Arynaar behind their Arch.

Pelyn stared while the echoes of light danced on the backs of her eyes. She stood as the skies began to darken for the first rains of the day and the streets drummed already with the sound of the footsteps of elves fleeing they knew not where. And then she turned from the raw power battering her streets and stared straight into Tulan's stupefied eyes.

'So do you still think you should serve me up to be raped by every Tuali *ula* in Ysundeneth, or are you going to go and find me some clothes and a sword?'

Katyett and the TaiGethen had been drawn to the north end of the camp some time before dawn as if in response to a growing threat. The nose for danger was, Takaar said, the single biggest difference between a Tai warrior and any other elf. Katyett disagreed, preferring to think of her speed and reactions as her greatest assets.

Whoever was right, there was no doubting the feeling that they all shared. It was going to be a beautiful morning in one respect only. And while the skies lightened to a glorious blue sluggishly filling with cloud, the scent on the air was bitter and cloying. Calaius smelled wrong.

The more curious of the Ynissul refugees had begun to join them, looking towards the coast, over the Ultan's walls and down towards Ysundeneth, the highest spires of which were just about visible on a clear morning such as this. Katyett looked to her left. The *iad* she had spoken to on the trail yesterday was standing between her and Merrat, his partner behind her. She was called Onelle, and if Katyett could save one elf in all this, it would be her.

'I don't think you'll want to see this,' she said.

'What is it?' asked Onelle.

'Awful power unleashed indiscriminately,' said Katyett, feeling a sense of helplessness with which she was unfamiliar.

'Tualis grasping power,' said Onelle.

Katyett shook her head. 'You're looking in the wrong place for your enemy. This is the hand of man under the eye of the *cascarg*

Ynissul. Rogue Tualis are being opportunistic in their atrocities and the grasping of influence.'

Onelle wanted to say more but a bloom of green light, tinged brown, grew above the city, casting lurid shadows across the ocean. Myriad flashes of deep yellow light appeared in the sky, falling like blossom. Deep-coloured flashes low to the ground, throwing spikes of light up the spires. Flames, yellow and hungry, ate at helpless timbers.

Katyett swallowed, her throat dry. A cold rage sank deep into her body and soul. Ynissul at the heart of this evil. Ynissul possessed by greed, distorted self-importance and a curious revisionism regarding Takaar. It was not the way of the Ynissul to have such short memories. But then, recognising the truth would be inconvenient.

'What are we going to do?' whispered Merrat.

'Wait,' said Katyett. 'Do nothing different to the plan. Ta— Auum and Serrin will return soon. We'll have our answers then and perhaps a banner to walk beneath.'

'I don't understand,' said Onelle, then blushed. 'I'm sorry, I don't mean to intrude on your conversation.'

'This concerns you as much as it does us,' said Katyett. 'What don't you understand?'

There had to be fifty fires in the city. And more of the deviant power the men had brought with them in evidence. Olmaat had warned them what they'd see. But he didn't mention how it squeezed at the soul. How the very air felt tainted and the land beneath their feet poisoned.

'Why won't we go back when the Ynissul have forced order on the city?'

'Order?' said Merrat. 'Sorry.'

Katyett shook her head. 'They are not restoring the harmony. They have no interest in its maintenance. If you believe in the Ynissul right to rule, then you will find friends there. If not, you should stay with us.'

'How can the harmony be restored after what has happened to us?' asked Onelle.

'Because even after the War of Bloods, we learned to live together. To forgive in time. But we can't think that far ahead yet because it assumes a resolution that leaves the Ynissul in control.'

'You think they might not beat the threads with the power they have at their right hands?' asked Rydd, Onelle's partner.

'Oh I have no doubt whatever that Ysundeneth will be cowed by the magic of man. What I fear is the next step.'

'Why?' asked Onelle.

Katyett shrugged. 'Because if I was a man, I would know I wielded all the power and I would have no desire to remain in the pay of any elf.'

Takaar roared his agony and Auum feared for the fallen hero's life. His collapse had been dramatic, his head striking a rock on the way down. Auum had picked him up, still with the deer around his neck, and run back to the camp. At first he had no idea what had afflicted Takaar. A bite, a sting. A disease he had been fighting. It could have been anything.

But there were no physical signs of any of those things. When he could, when Takaar's body was calm enough, Auum checked for bite marks, the tiny sharp red pinpoints that might mean a sting. He looked for discoloured skin, for boils, sores, foam at the mouth, cracks on the scalp, split skin on the feet. Nothing. Nothing at all.

Whatever raged within Takaar seemed to be confined to his mind, but the pain it brought him, the desperate look in his eyes whenever he forced them open to plead with Auum for help, was excruciating to witness. Feeling utterly helpless, Auum tried to make him comfortable, tried to get water into him and warmth too. He was shivering as if cold, though this dawn was glorious.

Auum had lit a fire. Had skinned the deer and hung joints above it to roast. The scent was magnificent. Perhaps it would help. Takaar's torment had been going on for an hour as the sun rose and the clouds gathered. Periodically, he pawed at the ground only to snatch his hands away as if he'd touched hot embers.

Takaar's eyes flickered open. They steadied but were not focused on Auum. They looked beyond him, away over the rainforest to the west.

'Gnawing fires,' he said. 'Globes puking brown power. Eating everything.'

'Takaar?' Auum tried to get into his eye line, to get him to come back to himself. 'Are you bitten? Are you poisoned?'

'It rages through the lines. They run but their footprints turn to ash. Wickedness walks the streets. Feeding on the helpless. There is no defence. Why does the rain not fall?'

'It's coming,' said Auum. 'Soon.'

Takaar made no sign that he had heard Auum. 'Separation. Cowering. The spire is lit up. They don't believe. Hope is only scattered splinters.'

'Please,' said Auum. 'Talk to me.'

Takaar's voice dropped to a low mumble and nothing he said was distinct. His body had stilled now; only his eyes moved. He was blinking very rapidly. Abruptly, he relaxed completely. Tension flooded from him and he took in a deep and even breath.

'They are killing us,' he said. 'And we have ushered them in.'

'Who?' asked Auum. 'Men?'

Takaar's eyes rested on Auum.

'I know why you came here. I am not stupid.'

Auum fought to meet Takaar's gaze. It sliced straight through to his soul.

'We need you,' he said. 'Not just the TaiGethen. All the elves. They are unpicking all you have done. We're going back to the War of Bloods unless you agree to stand with us. Unite us again.'

Takaar sat up and pushed himself back to sit against the bole of a tree in his bivouac. His head was shaking side to side, a small and rapid movement. He glanced to one side.

'I know *I* caused it. You have no need to remind me of that again. You have been reminding me of my failing every day for ten years. Let me think.'

Auum found a vision in his head of walking into Ysundeneth with Takaar, only for him to gibber and argue with the voice in his head. Some saviour. Doubt swept him yet again.

'Come back with me. Talk to the TaiGethen and the Silent at least. They are waiting for you.' Auum took a breath, knowing what he was about to say was a gamble in Takaar's fraught emotional state. 'Katyett is waiting for you.'

Takaar didn't react at once. His eyes searched the ground to his left. A hand rubbed idly at the earth.

'She is alive?' Takaar nodded to himself and tears began to fall down his cheeks. 'She is the core of my betrayal. My cowardice. I was never worthy of her attentions and her love. I proved that, didn't I?'

Auum said nothing in response. Takaar seemed to be searching inside himself. Auum prayed it was to seek the strength he would need in the days to come.

'Takaar? I am TaiGethen. You are my brother and my Arch. Still to this day. Nothing has changed. We exist to serve Yniss in the ways you taught us. So I ask this of you. Come back to lead us. Come back to unite the threads. Come back to repair the harmony and bring us back into the grace of Yniss.'

Takaar stared at him for a long time. Fat from the deer hissed and spat into the fire.

'What happened?' he asked. 'What happened when I ran?'

Chapter 23

The last refuge of he who has lost his courage is warm water and a sharp blade.

The silence of Tul-Kenerit, the last bastion on Hausolis. Even the din of the approaching Garonin had not been able to mask it. Alone across the courtyard ran Takaar and the eye of every TaiGethen and Al-Arynaar followed him. Every pace he took bled will, belief and courage still further. Auum, like them all, refused to believe what he was witnessing.

Takaar did not pause, nor look over his shoulder. His hands slapped into the metal of the keep door. He bent his strength to it and slid it wide. He ran into the gloom and was lost to sight. The elves stared after him. Auum felt a desolation sweep him, like he was the only one left standing. He dragged his gaze from the keep, the still-open door, and looked along the rampart to Katyett and Pelyn, standing above the gates.

A whistling and whining.

The tumult of the approaching Garonin flooded his senses once more.

'Brace!' he yelled.

His shout was taken up across the bastion. Auum looked over the parapet. A hundred barrels had spat smoke and flame. A second volley was incoming and the first was yet to strike.

'Yniss preserve us.'

Projectiles thundered into the upper section of the walls or flew overhead to drop in the courtyard. Heavy bow emplacements were obliterated. Timber shattered, splinters thrummed away, ripping into face, body and legs. Elves screamed. Impact after impact drove into the rampart wall. Steel bent and split. Stone was shattered. Bodies were flung backwards.

Auum crouched low behind the walls, his hands over his ears. If any orders were coming, no one could hear them. A great pall of smoke was rising from the gatehouse. He could see his brothers and sisters, ripped open and dismembered, lying on the parapet. Blood smeared every surface.

Another volley struck home. A projectile slammed into the wall right in front of Auum. Steel bent inwards, stone was shoved back. Auum was thrown from the rampart. He tried to orient his body as it spun helplessly under the force of the blow. The pitted ground of the courtyard rushed to meet him. He managed to turn into the impact, rolling over one shoulder, absorbing much of it. But his legs were not under control and they took him into a bruising tumble before he came to a stop fully seventy feet from where he had been crouched.

Auum pushed himself to his feet, staggering under sudden pain. He looked down. A thick splinter of wood jutted from his left boot. Blood seeped. He tested his weight on it. Not good. His hands were scraped raw and his leggings torn to shreds. His body armour had saved his torso from major damage.

Auum looked up at the rampart. Projectiles were dropping onto it and down into the courtyard. He kept staring as he moved towards whatever shelter he could find in the lee of the walls. There was no order up there. Elves were turning from the enemy, running to stair and ladder. Bodies were thick on the ground around him. Most were not moving. Others were already running for the keep.

The barrage ceased. Smoke wreathed the bastion, clearing slowly. Into the quiet came the cries of the injured and wails of the dying. Prayers were uttered to Yniss and Shorth. Those still largely unhurt were regrouping in the centre of the courtyard. A drumming sound came from without. Garonin infantry. Running.

'Form up!' Auum spun round. Fresh pain raced up his leg from the impaled foot. It was Katyett. Standing with Pelyn. 'To me, brothers and sisters. Defend the keep.'

Auum hobbled towards them. A TaiGethen came to his shoulder, took some weight for him.

'Thank you, Olmaat,' he said.

'Can you still hold a blade?' asked Olmaat.

'Both of them. Just don't ask me to fight open hand.'

'That time is past, I think.'

They hurried to the lines of elves at the door of the keep. It still stood open against what they knew was to come but which had to be delayed for every possible moment. Perhaps three hundred stood before the keep. Al-Arynaar and TaiGethen. Lines eight deep. Weapons ready.

Katyett stood front and centre. Her Tai was gone, Jaleea injured and surely unable to survive. Takaar fled. So Pelyn was next to her. Arch of the Al-Arynaar with the new Arch of the TaiGethen. Some strength still remained. Elves stood with them. Courage endured.

There was a metallic rattle, rhythmic. The steel plating on the walls of the bastion was shaking. The eyes of most elves were on the gates. They shouldn't have been; the Garonin were climbing the walls. Gauntleted hands grasped the ruined rampart. Helmeted heads and armoured bodies appeared. Legs thumped down onto the parapet. Without pause, they jumped down into the courtyard and the flood of enemy stormed in like a wave breaching a dam.

'Steady,' called Katyett. 'Steady. On my order, front four ranks move up to engage.'

The Garonin covered the ground with frightening speed. Weapons were level. Barrels spat short tongues of flame. Defenceless elves were cut down.

'Engage!'

TaiGethen and Al-Arynaar ran forward. Unable to fight on the move, Auum stood with Olmaat in front of the door of the keep. TaiGethen, sprinting ahead of their Al-Arynaar comrades, flew at the Garonin soldiers. Blades flashed. Enemies fell. A roar rose among the defenders. A release of anger, an expression of frustration and shock.

Katyett slammed both feet into the face plate of a Garonin soldier, bearing him to the ground. One of her blades sliced across his throat. The other swept low, chopping into the ankles of another enemy. Katyett powered up, her first blade chopping into the gut of a third. Her second blade came down on the neck of the one she had crippled.

The Garonin could not track her movements. Her speed confused them. Her strength surprised them and her will baffled them. But the elves were so few, the TaiGethen fewer still amongst them. Weapons fire intensified. Garonin and elf alike were cut down in the blizzard. The Al-Arynaar in front of the keep made to move up.

'No.' Olmaat's voice was strong. 'Withdraw. Get inside the keep. This battle is done.'

And it was. But Katyett was deep in the fight. Pelyn, with ten Al-Arynaar, was forcing a path towards her. There was a shouted exchange. The elves disengaged, those that could.

'Back!' shouted Olmaat. 'Back into the keep. Defend the bore.'

The gates crashed in. The Tul-Kenerit was truly laid open. The machines began to roll in. Weapons fire skipped and cracked off the walls of the keep. There were screams from within. The keep was full of elves waiting to leave.

'We need someone down at the gate. We just need people through. As many as can travel,' said Auum.

'Go,' said Olmaat.

'Not me. Ferille?' The door guard turned. 'Get down to the gate. Do everything you can to get as many through as you can. Try to avoid panic. Hard, I know. Tell them we will give them as much time as we can. And Ferille. Don't leave yourself behind. When the time comes don't hesitate. Go through.'

The last of the TaiGethen ran in on a hail of fire. Inside, waiting to descend, ordinary elves were already falling prey to the panic Auum had sought to avoid. Katyett dived through the door, Garonin after her.

'Close the door!' called Olmaat.

He ducked a swinging fist and thumped a blade into a Garonin gut. The soldier staggered back, colliding with the closing door. Auum threw a jaqrui, the blade cutting deep into the top of his helmet. The enemy sagged down. The door clanged shut. Elves surged over the marooned Garonin. Brief silence in the entrance hall was punctuated by hard breathing echoing into the rafters.

Lantern light illuminated a cold steel room, circular and with a wide spiral staircase leading down into a brightly lit space, noisy with the voices of ordinary elves desperate to escape. They were packed in tight and the tunnels through which they had arrived would be crowded with more. Below them, the bore. A three hundred foot deep hole at the bottom of which was the gateway to Calaius. It was this that the Garonin desired and which the elves dare not let them take or Calaius would also be laid waste.

The gate was maintained by forces none but Takaar understood and which would collapse should he pass through it. And while a collapse would stall the Garonin, it would maroon a huge number of elves too.

The moment's calm was undermined by the fear of the civilians below. What was coming was as inevitable as it was unstoppable. The Garonin machines began to pound the door of the keep. Auum spun round at the sound of running feet below them, at the base of the spiral stair.

'No! Katyett, they're trying to get back down the tunnels.' Auum leaned over to shout his warning. 'You're going the wrong way. Take the ladder down the bore!'

'Al-Arynaar. Twenty detail. Get down there. Keep the people going down the ladder,' ordered Pelyn. 'Methian. You're leading. Move!'

The barrage on the door reached a deafening clamour. From below, the shrieks of terrified elves echoed up. It sounded like a stampede down there. No one who faced the door spoke. Huge dents had been beaten in the four-inch-thick steel. Like great fists were striking again and again. The fists of gods. The first tear appeared dead centre of the door. Daylight streamed in. Immediately, the barrage focused on the weak point.

'Not long now,' said Olmaat.

Behind them, panic deepened. A sheet of light fled up the bore. A second followed it and lastly a series of sharp flickers. Auum's heart skipped a beat. An Al-Arynaar appeared in front of Katyett and Pelyn.

'The gateway is failing. Takaar ran through and now it's coming apart.'

Katyett stared at Pelyn and at her warriors. Auum could see it in her eyes. They had lost. Projectiles fell like an avalanche on the door. The tear had become a hole an elf could walk through upright. A large missile flew through and slammed into the far wall, smashing stone and causing a fall of beams and rubble.

Katyett swallowed. She nodded.

'It is done,' she said. 'Warriors of Hausolis. We can do no more than sacrifice our lives to no avail. The Garonin machines will kill us at distance. Your choice. Go to your peoples and stand until they come for you. Or go through the gateway now and live to fight the day the Garonin find us again. Travel to Calaius and help the elves of Hausolis build anew. My advice: live today. Orderly descent. Go.'

Olmaat wrapped an arm around Auum's shoulder.

'I will not leave you behind,' he said.

Auum and Olmaat ran together. Down the spiral stairs and onto the floor around the bore. Other Tai and Al-Arynaar ran to the panicking, fleeing elves to try and turn them around, to guide them to safety. Auum stared at them while the light from the gateway flickered and faded.

'Run! Go!'

Warrior elves, many with civilians in tow, swarmed down the ladder. More crowded the head, desperate for a foot on the first rung. Elves urged those on the ladder to move faster. More and more crowded on, pushing down on those below.

'Ease the pressure!' shouted Katyett.

With a rending wail, the great steel door gave way. A torrent of heavy footsteps could be heard. Garonin in the keep. All pretence at order dissolved. Elves surged onto the rungs. They climbed over each other or packed into the tunnels to escape back into the forests of Hausolis.

Auum released himself from Olmaat.

'We have to buy more time,' he said and trotted back towards the spiral stair. 'TaiGethen!'

A hundred elves turned and packed back towards the Garonin. The first enemy soldiers were descending. Weapons fire rattled down the stairs. Olmaat raced past Auum, clubbing his sword into the lower leg of an enemy. The Garonin pitched down the stairs. TaiGethen finished him. More filled the space. The density of fire increased. TaiGethen were blown aside. Garonin jumped down from the hall, feet slamming onto the ground by the bore.

Auum ducked. A Garonin weapon butt missed him by a hair. Auum threw himself forward, grappling the Garonin's legs. The soldier fell back. Auum crawled up his body and plunged a short blade through his eye slit. A weapon rang out. Something smashed into Auum's side spinning him over. Olmaat was by him. His blades whispered in the air above Auum's head. A Garonin body pitched over the balustrade and dropped onto the packed floor, hitting friend and foe alike.

'Time for you to leave, my friend.'

Olmaat grabbed his left arm and pulled. Pain filled Auum's body. He gasped but did not let go. TaiGethen blades were all around them. Weapons fire clanged and sparked against metal, thumped into defenceless bodies and ripped away limb and head.

'Go!' yelled Olmaat. 'All of you. Go!'

The TaiGethen disengaged. Down on the ladder, elves fought to descend. The weak and unlucky fell. All around the edge of the bore, TaiGethen shunned the ladder and climbed down the walls.

'Can you do that?' asked Olmaat.

His free hand whipped out, his blade ran through a Garonin side and up under his ribs. Olmaat kicked him aside. They reached the edge of the bore. Garonin were everywhere.

'I'll be fine,' said Auum.

Olmaat released him. He almost fell. He took a shuddering breath and hauled himself into the bore. TaiGethen were pouring down the walls now. Garonin fire chased down after them, raked the ladder. Elves juddered and fell. The survivors pressed harder. Al-Arynaar and TaiGethen fought around the lip. Garonin fell, tumbling to smash into the floor of the gateway chamber. Too many warriors joined them.

All the while, the light of the gateway guttered and spat, sending lurid shadows up the bore. Like all the Tais, Auum went head first. The bore was rough cut. Handholds were easy. He kept his body flat against the rock, letting his clothes supply friction to slow his descent. His side ached. Blood flowed from both of his wounds.

Auum began to feel light-headed. He resisted the temptation to speed up. Two TaiGethen came to his sides. Another dropped in front of him.

'Just keep moving, brother,' said one.

Moments later, weapons fire took her from the walls and thrust her to the ground. Auum cried out. His arms shook and his mind clouded.

'Go on,' he said. 'Leave me, save yourselves.'

The other two ignored him and he was too relieved to thank them. He followed the hand- and footholds of the Tai in front of him all the way to the ground. Ahead the gateway wavered violently, steadied and then shimmered.

'Run! Run! Get inside.'

Auum was half carried across the floor. It was full of running elves. At the face, a line stood to keep back the Garonin.

'Let me stand,' he said. 'I can still fight.'

'Don't be ridiculous,' said Olmaat, next to him once more.

He took Auum from his charges and ran him through the gate. The last thing he heard was the sound of weapons fire, the shrieks of elves and the calm orders of warriors facing certain death.

'Shorth, embrace your souls.'

*

Auum knew what Takaar was thinking. Or what a sane Takaar would have been thinking. There was no dodging who had triggered the rout.

'With me standing, we might have stood for hours more,' Takaar whispered eventually. 'Think how many more thousands might have been saved.'

'Maybe,' said Auum.

But he knew the whole truth.

Takaar's eyes narrowed and he gestured angrily over his shoulder.

'I might have known you'd chirp up about now. Don't you ever tire of reminding me?'

'Takaar,' said Auum.

'No, I thought not. And I will not do it. You think if I haven't found the courage in ten years I might suddenly do so now? Your wheedling voice cannot make me do anything I don't care to do. We'll need to bring some poisons I've been perfecting.'

Takaar stared at Auum. The young TaiGethen blinked.

'What's he saying?' he hedged.

Takaar's shoulders drooped.

'It's as if you can't hear him at all,' he chided. 'And perhaps you can't hear me either. I said, we'll need to bring some poisons I've been working on. Some of the better burn salves too. So I'll be needing your help.'

What cascaded through Auum then fell nothing short of pure joy.

'You're coming!' he said, the sound of his voice setting animals to flight in the nearby brush.

'I would have thought that was obvious.'

Auum nodded. 'Of course, of course. Thank you. The whole elven race will thank you.'

'Hardly,' said Takaar. 'And *you* just need to give it up. I am not going to throw myself from the cliffs. I have dreamed up another and more satisfying way to die. Care to join us?'

'I . . .' began Auum before realising to whom Takaar was speaking.

'You know this has nothing to do with redemption or regaining my position or anything. You've known me ten years and you still don't realise I don't care for such things.'

Auum paused before speaking, waiting for clarification. None appeared forthcoming. Takaar strode away to his hut and began selecting various pots. The conversation was clearly over.

'Could I ask why you are doing this?'

Takaar stared at Auum. It was disconcerting. It unpicked him from the inside out. Takaar thrust some pots and a net bag fashioned from old strong liana at him.

'Pack these. I'll explain how they work on the way.' He moved to his hammock and picked up a cloth-covered bundle. He unwrapped it, exposing back scabbards. One still retained its blade. 'It should be obvious why I am going. It's because *he* said that I would lack the courage to do so.'

Auum was having trouble getting used to the constant raising and deflating of his hopes.

'Not for your brothers and sisters? Not for Katyett?'

Takaar snorted. 'Hardly. I have worked out these years gone that I know nothing. But I am irritated that my life's work is being undone. And I am most certainly selfish enough, and brave enough, though he would say otherwise, to see it un-undone.'

It would have to do. Auum set about making the camp tidy and checking his meagre gear. He found Takaar staring at him again when he was about to kick earth over the fire.

'What are you doing?'

'Readying to leave,' said Auum.

'Don't be in such a rush.'

'But—'

'There is food to eat and no elf should set about a task with an empty stomach. No elf should decide to eat on the move when there is comfort to be had. Sit. We shall eat. And then I shall show you the best way to pack our meat, the raw and the cooked, to keep it at its best. Then we shall leave.'

Auum shrugged his shoulders, blew out his cheeks and sat down.

Chapter 24

There is no easier enemy than the intransigent general on indefensible ground.

The clothes were too big and made of a cloth far finer than Pelyn had ever worn. They were for an *ula* too and had space in all the wrong places. There was no armour. She slung her cloak about her shoulders and grimaced at the ruin that had been made of it. At least the sword on her hip was sharp – Tulan's second blade, and he always kept his edges keen.

'What do we do?' asked Ephran.

He was staring out of the upstairs window at the fires that completely encircled the harbour. Salt and Sail Maker were ablaze street by street. The Park of Tual was in the path of the human advance. Already, hundreds of Cefans and Orrans had fled their ghetto, not caring that they were running into enemy territory. Most had been chased off, away towards the Glade, to the Gardaryn and the Chambers quarter.

The more persistent, those urging the Tualis to flee before it was too late, were beaten. Worse, some had been strung up against trees in the old Tuali ritual execution of *tua-mossa*. Sliced and spit, was the common slang. Pelyn had watched desperate elves pleading to be heard. The only response was evisceration followed by a spear driven up through the body.

'Still glad you deserted the Al-Arynaar, my brothers?' asked Pelyn.

Both had the decency to remain silent.

There was no organisation. Just this pointless, hideous and brutal defence of small pockets of Ysundeneth by the disparate threads. Llyron and Sildaan had been relying on just that. The Tualis still couldn't see what was coming, though every fire, every casting must have screamed at them to run. Their misplaced belief in the traitor Helias was about to cost them very dear. They were waiting for orders but hadn't worked out that when he came back he'd be bringing hundreds of men with him.

'We have to find what's left of the Al-Arynaar. But I've got business to attend to on the way to the barracks, if there's anything left of it.'

'We're with you,' said Tulan.

'Forgive me if I don't turn my back on you just yet.'

'We had to protect our own,' said Ephran quietly.

'Dammit, that's just what you haven't done, isn't it?' Pelyn stalked towards him. 'We all had our doubts but those of us with any strength knew that the only thing, the *only thing* that mattered was preservation of the harmony. Look what you've done. You've turned Tualis into ravening animals prepared to murder those they prayed with two days ago. And I have no doubt that elsewhere in this city Tualis are suffering the same fate. Congratulations on sticking a sword in the gut of the elven race.'

The two of them were staring at her with the pained expression of a wronged child.

'What? You thought I'd fall over myself to bring you back to the bosom of the Al-Arynaar? Let's get something straight so we don't misunderstand each other out there on the burning streets. You two are deserters. The fact you saved my life means you have enough sense and decency to know you've made a big mistake. But I can't trust you like brothers, can I? I can't simply forget what you did. Nor what other deserters have done. So it's up to you. Stand with me and try to win this fight and we'll see where we are when it's done. Or run into the rainforest now and throw yourselves on the mercy of Tual's denizens, the Silent and the TaiGethen.'

Tulan nodded. 'I don't think we'll be running.'

Pelyn smiled. 'Good. I thought not. Now let's go. Tell me where the Apposans have made their stand. I'm guessing south side. Probably at the Grans or maybe Old Millers.'

'Creatures of habit,' said Tulan. 'Why them?'

'Methian was podded and given to them.'

Tulan hissed in a breath. 'Pelyn . . .'

'I know. But I have to try.'

'We'll go out the back. Avoid the Tuali mob.'

'We do need them,' said Pelyn. 'Whoever survives. It doesn't matter what they would have done to me. Not for now.'

Tulan nodded. 'But first things first, right?'

'Right. And put on your cloaks, though Yniss knows you don't deserve to wear them. I don't want us looking like a Tuali snatch squad or whatever the hell you've been playing at.'

They trotted down the stairs and out of a rear door, across a small private garden and through a back gate into a narrow alley. Tulan led. Ephran followed. Pelyn kept them both where she could see them. The sun was rising and hot but the sky was burnished with the foul colours of human magical fire mixed with the yellow of burning wood. The stench of ash was heavy in the air.

Away from the immediate fighting, the city was strangely silent. The streets were deserted. Thread mobs were keeping their heads down. The majority, the shocked civilians wanting no part of it, would be in their homes – those that still had them. Or hiding wherever their thread was strongest, forced to seek refuge among those they despised for their actions.

Pelyn sighed as she ran. It was so hard to see how there could be any resolution to this that would hold. You could glue a smashed pot back together but the cracks would always be visible, the pieces always prone to fall apart.

The Grans was a densely populated area, favourite of forest workers and home to a warren of houses and winding streets as well as logging yards and a few construction businesses. The Apposans, followers of the oldest earth god, had always been the largest-represented thread there and had a long history of excellence in farming the forest and working the wood.

But they were an aggressive thread, historically. Intolerant. They were also the shortest-lived, barring the Gyalans, with whom they had fought across the millennia over triviality after triviality. Coming out of a side street onto Yanner's Approach, which led into the Grans, Tulan slowed.

'They were in Orsan's Yard last night, most of them,' he said, pointing away over pitched roofs to where a thick column of smoke rose. 'They may not be there now of course.'

'Why not?' asked Pelyn.

'We raided there last night, early on,' said Ephran. 'Retaliation for an attack earlier in the day near the Gardaryn.'

'Terrific,' said Pelyn. 'So they'll be particularly welcoming this morning.'

Tulan moved quickly away into the Grans. Elves were in evidence here. Scuttling about, collecting water. Some children even played.

Others made play of a normal life, but those that didn't stop and stare at the cloaks were more concerned with the pall of smoke hanging over the docks. Surely some in the thread knew what was coming.

Towards Orsan's Yard, Tulan headed off the main avenue and wove deep into the warren. The yard fence stood tall beyond the end of the last row of houses and across a small patch of open ground where children were playing or watching the fires. There was a burst of laughter from within. It was genuine and heartfelt, accompanied by a smattering of applause and shouts of 'Another.' Pelyn drew up, surprised.

'You'd think storytelling would be the least of their desires right now,' she said.

They crossed the open ground and hugged the fence around to the right towards the gate. There was a good deal of traffic in and out and the gate was guarded by blade carriers. They were spotted quickly.

'Al-Arynaar. You are not welcome here,' said a guard, a short Apposan with thickly muscled forearms and powerful fists gripping axe and sword.

Pelyn walked in front of the brothers now. She hitched her cloak back to reveal her sword but did not make a move to touch it.

'You have one of my people. I've come to get him back. I want no fight with you. The Apposans are my friends.'

The guard beckoned to two others, both powerful, stocky *ulas*, and sauntered towards her. He spat to the side.

'Tuali? And you don't want a fight? Should have told that to your brothers and sisters last night. We've eight dead and twenty injured. Still. Only three of you this time.'

He hefted his blades and moved up. Tulan and Ephran moved to her flanks. She made a calming gesture and walked a pace ahead of them.

'Your fight is not with the Al-Arynaar,' she said.

'Wrong,' said the Apposan.

He ran the last couple of paces and swept both his blades out to in, chopping towards her neck. Pelyn stepped inside the strikes, blocked both his arms with hers, and straight-kicked with her left leg into his gut. The Apposan doubled over. Pelyn smacked the heel of her palm into his forehead as he came up, knocking him onto his back. She dropped to his side, her sword from her scabbard and at his throat.

'I have had a very bad night,' she said. 'I am tired and my temper is short. Give me Methian. Alive.'

The Apposan's hands were off his weapons and in front of his face, palms out to her, pleading. Tulan and Ephran were in front of the other two guards. All other action had stopped. Children stared, their games forgotten. Pelyn bounced to her feet and held a hand out to him.

'I am not your enemy.'

After a pause, the guard took her hand and allowed himself to be pulled upright.

'Methian?' he said, almost bleeding gratitude. 'He's inside. He's very much alive, I promise you.'

'Good. Then lead on.'

Pelyn tried and failed to hide her relief. The guard, with Pelyn uncomfortably close to him, led them inside the yard. It was busy. A big central fire was burning and various pots and trays hung on tripods or on Y-staves over the embers at its edge. *Ula* and *iad* were busy making spears and crude arrows.

With Tulan and Ephran walking with the other two gate guards, the small party approached a ring of around forty Apposans, standing and seated, listening to a single voice. Their arrival brought an abrupt end to the story. Faces turned, weapons were drawn and the ring opened.

There sat Methian on a log with his cloak for a cushion and a steaming mug in his hand. He wore leather trousers, a thick wool shirt and a short leather coat. Tree farmer's clothing. He was barefoot, but a pair of battered boots stood next to the log on which he sat.

Pelyn smiled and shook her head.

'They were supposed to murder you,' she said.

'Ah, but Llyron doesn't know as much as she thinks she does. Three of my daughters partnered Apposans. One of my grandchildren made me this infusion. Guarana and clove. Lovely, it is.'

'Only you could be that lucky,' said Pelyn. 'You could have told me last night.'

'Shorth has ears everywhere,' said Methian.

Around them the Apposans were relaxing. Methian helped them out.

'My friends, this is Pelyn, Arch of the Al-Arynaar and defender of

us all from ourselves. And these are Tulan and Ephran.' Methian
stared at them but chose to say nothing more. 'Lower your weapons,
please. This is cause for celebration. What happened to you, by the
way? The Tuali weren't there or something? Or did you escape by
hopping very quickly?'

The Apposans laughed. Weapons were lowered. Pelyn sheathed
her sword. The gate guard pushed past her and marched back
towards his post.

'They have other things on their minds right now,' she said.
'And anyway, unlooked-for help came my way.' Pelyn raised her
eyebrows.

Methian nodded. 'Nice clothes,' he said.

'You too. What have you told them?'

'The truth. We know men are coming. The Apposans are heading
into the forest.'

'Good,' said Pelyn. 'Who's in charge?'

'I am, for what it's worth. I am Boltha. '

An old *ula* stepped forward. His face was a mass of wrinkles and
his eyes sagged along with the tips of his large ears. His hair was
thick and grey except at the crown, where it was thinning. Pelyn
had seen him around the city. He was a financier or a banker, she
thought. He probably owned half the yards here.

'I'm honoured to meet you,' she said. 'Everything Methian will
have told you is true. Men are rampaging through the city and are in
the pay of Llyron and Aryndeneth priests. They'll pick this city apart
bit by bit. Stay in the forest. Don't be tempted back until I or the
TaiGethen come for you. You're heading to Katura Falls?'

Boltha shook his head. 'Not so far as that. We aren't running;
we're waiting on opportunity, if you see what I mean. We'll hole up
at the Olbeck Rise.'

'Good. And can we call upon you if we need to?'

Boltha smiled. 'An axe can fell a man easier than a tree.'

'Appos and Yniss protect you. I won't forget this.' Pelyn turned
back to Methian. 'Jakyn.'

Methian nodded. 'He'll be fine. He's smart and the Gyalans are
less embittered than Llyron believes.'

'We need him.'

'I know where they'll be,' said Methian.

He stooped to put on his boots.

*

But Jakyn wasn't fine.

The entrance to the museum of Hausolis was characterised by an ornate wooden arch, under which a stone footpath ran to the wide stairs that led up to the doors of the building built in the likeness of the keep of Tul-Kenerit. The Gyalans had chosen it as their base, standing as it did in the heart of their district.

Jakyn was bound to the arch by his arms. Above him hung crossed flags depicting rainfall on upturned palms. Jakyn's naked body glistened with his blood. Gyalan guards stood either side of him, paying him no heed. But Jakyn was long past begging if indeed he ever had. Pelyn could see the method of his torture and murder.

Cuts. Hundreds of them. Covering every part of his body. From mere scratches to deep gashes. His nose had been cut off, as had both of his ears. His lips had been slit along their lengths. He had been castrated. His nipples and eyelids had been removed. Every humiliation had been visited upon his body. His eyes being put out would have been the last abuse.

The Gyalan way. Or it had been. As they approached, Methian walked ahead. He strode up to the two guards.

'Welcome, brother,' said one. 'Though I can't extend the same greeting to your others.'

'That won't be necessary,' said Methian. 'A true ceremonial *klosil*. Proud of it, are you?'

The guard smiled up at Jakyn's body.

'Pity you weren't here. He squirmed and screamed. Called for his god. Not loud enough, eh? I put that one across his forehead. A second smile, right?'

'Mind if I add my own?' asked Methian.

Pelyn tensed. The guard grinned.

'Always room for more.'

Methian drew the Apposan blade on his left hip with his right hand. In the same movement, he carved it up through the guard's body, the tip tearing through his shirt, slicing up through his chest and thudding up to split his lower jaw and tear his throat apart.

The guard stared at Methian for one stunned moment before clutching at his neck and falling back to writhe until death. Methian had his blade at the other guard's neck before he could bring his makeshift spear to the ready.

'Gyal wreaks revenge on such as you. Shorth hears her and your soul is already promised purgatory. This elf. This fine young Cefan *ula* that you murdered in agony, was a friend of mine. Cut him down. Gently and with respect and reverence. And if you drop him, I'll drop you.'

Chapter 25

There is beauty in a kill worked by the hands of the TaiGethen warrior.

'Enough fire,' said Sildaan, coming to Garan's shoulder.

The man looked round at her, a smile on his face. The attack on Ysundeneth had advanced incredibly fast. Not a blow had been struck by steel. Elves ran in fear of the magic of men. Over five hundred mercenary soldiers and mages had disembarked. They were well organised, powerful and ruthless.

They were advancing on three fronts, spreading in a wide arc across the north of the city and tracking south. Some of the mages were flying – in defiance of all Sildaan knew or could readily accept – and they provided a simply massive advantage. Able to overfly every thread base, every pocket of potential resistance and direct mage fire with stunning accuracy.

'They need to know we can't be stopped. We want them to run before us, don't we?'

'I want them subdued not panicked. And I want enough of the city left standing to reallocate. Call off the mage attack. Round up prisoners. We need this quarter sealed then move on to the Gardaryn. When we take that, we all but have the city in our grasp.'

'Whatever you say, boss.'

Garan raised his eyebrows, a measure of dissent Sildaan just about tolerated. The man shouted orders in the ugly speech of the north. Mages started falling back behind the line of mercenary blades. A unit of a hundred, led by a bilious lieutenant with a massive scar right down the centre of his face, ran on ahead of the main force. Mages flew above them.

Sildaan shook her head. 'And what did you order them to do?'

'Exactly what you asked. We'll force those seeking shelter ahead left, back onto the dockside and into one of the least damaged warehouses. I'm sending archers and swordsmen ahead to do house to house up in the . . . What do you call it? Never mind, anyway up the Path of Yniss a way. And we have our right flank moving in on your friend's group. We just need his confirmation.'

'Helias is not my friend.'

'Tell him that. That's him, isn't it?'

A small group of elves had walked into the Path of Yniss, the wide and winding tree-lined avenue that crossed the city north to south, broken by buildings and monuments in places but nevertheless the spine of Ysundeneth. Helias led them, five in all.

'Let them approach,' called Sildaan. Garan repeated the order in his own language. 'Helias. You've brought guests.'

Helias spread his arms. 'A little personal security, my priest. The streets are dangerous.'

'But getting less so by the moment. Who are these?'

'Advisers, guards.'

'Fine, and not necessary now.' She waved a hand at Garan. 'Move them somewhere, would you?'

'Helias, I must protest,' said one, a haughty *iad* with a long knife pushed through her belt. 'This Ynissul cannot—'

'I think you'll find I can do anything I want, Tuali.'

The *iad* snatched her knife out. Garan stepped up and cracked a fist into her chin, knocking her cold.

'The rest of you be quiet,' he said. 'Where do you want them?'

'Do I look like I care overmuch? You're in charge of holding pens.'

Garan signalled and six of his warriors came over. A few more words and they moved to Helias's people.

'You won't be hurt,' said Helias. 'It's for your own safety.'

They were led away muttering curses at him and Sildaan.

'You know that might not actually be a lie,' said Sildaan.

'What should I do?' asked Helias.

'Your people are in the agreed location?' she asked.

'Naturally.'

'And Llyron's athletic little gift?'

Helias smiled, a thoroughly unpleasant event for any *iad* to witness. 'She awaits my pleasure. Just tell your muscle to leave the houses around the park undamaged.'

'Good, then you can go where you please. Go back and do what you want to her or, if I were you, I'd save that for another day and get to Shorth. Llyron will keep you safe enough.'

Helias blustered. 'I'm not walking alone that sort of distance.'

'Then walk with us. Just keep out of my way; I have work to do.'

'Don't treat me as some sort of lower-thread minion.'

'How else would you have an Ynissul priest treat a Tuali?' returned Sildaan. 'Don't worry, you'll get your rewards and your position. Until then, I'd . . .' Sildaan touched a finger to her lips.

'You need me,' Helias said. 'Don't forget that.'

'You are as inevitable and irritating as blisters in new boots. Run along.'

Helias shot her a glance that Garan noted with raised eyebrows before shouldering his way through the mercenaries on his way to the gods knew where and cared even less.

'Someone else to keep your eye on,' Garan said.

'He is nothing. Alone, he has no strength to fight. No courage. Let's move on. I want to set one particularly large fire before the rains come back.'

Pelyn watched the men flying in the sky on what looked like wings made of nothing but smoke and shadow. She'd seen them dive and climb. They could fly at some speed too. Very agile and yet totally corrupt by all the laws of every elven god. And they presented a huge problem.

They'd returned to the house at the side of the Park of Tual. Hundreds of Tualis were gathered in the park. They stood in groups, talking, sharpening weapons and waiting, she presumed, for Helias. They were going to get something quite different, and Pelyn wanted to be there to witness it. Tulan had planned an escape route and he and Ephran were waiting downstairs.

Pelyn turned to Methian. The old Gyalan's face still held the anger from Jakyn and the museum arch.

'You did exactly the right thing,' she said.

He looked up, his eyes boring into her face. 'It isn't that. Those two Gyalan animals deserved to die like the dogs they were. I just wish we'd fired the museum. None of them deserve life. Not after what they did.'

'I understand, but you can't afford to think that way. Eventually, there will have to be forgiveness. Yniss save me, I'm probably going to have to forgive Helias. That *ula* is elusive as a taipan and has more life than an Ynissul, I swear it.'

Once the Gyalan guard had laid poor Jakyn on the ground, Pelyn had seen something she never thought to see. Methian lost control of himself. Pelyn had half expected him to slap the guard on the rump with the flat of his blade, tell him to take a warning back to the others. But he had punched the guard in the stomach as he straightened, slammed the pommel of his sword into the Gyalan's neck to knock him down, kicked him over onto his back and buried his blade in his chest.

Only then had he broken down in tears. Tulan and Ephran had moved Jakyn's body into shade and Tulan had laid his cloak across the boy's ruined body. They planned to collect him later and take him into the rainforest. The temple of Shorth was out of bounds.

'I'll think on it. But I'm old, Pelyn. Getting old, anyway. And I never thought to see this. The violence is frightening. My violence frightens me.' Methian's hands were shaking. 'I should have gone into the forest with the Apposans.'

'You still can. That's not desertion, it's retirement.'

Methian managed a smile. 'Thank you, Pelyn. But I think I have to see this through. Find out who we are as a race of people. I don't want to turn my back and not know what I've left behind.'

Pelyn looked away across the Park of Tual. There was movement all around its periphery. More further up the Ash too.

'Tulan. Men are coming.'

'We're ready,' said Tulan's voice from the bottom of the stairs.

Pelyn took a pace away from the window, hiding herself more firmly in shadow.

'I think we've been foolhardy coming back here,' she said

'We needed to get a picture of the city. Something to plan by.'

Pelyn chuckled. 'I saw the look on your face when you heard me suggest it, old *ula*. And I saw you look over towards the Hausolis Playhouse.'

Methian got up from the end of the bed he'd been sitting on and joined her.

'Well, I did wonder. No thought of a little malicious enjoyment watching the Tuali run?'

'You know me too well. But still, be ready to run yourself. No doubt Helias told them to leave the houses untouched, but these are men we're talking about here. Paid thugs. Trust them?'

'Like I trust a piranha.'

*

Nillis saw the movement, thought it had to be the perimeter guard, looked again and was equally certain that it was not. He tightened his grip on the sharpened stave he'd fashioned while sitting about waiting for Helias to come back, then tapped Ulakan on the shoulder.

'What is it?'

Ulakan was bored. Nillis could see it in his eyes. Privately, he thought Ulakan had gone too far, got too violent in the raids last night. But the *ula*, barely out of education like himself, seemed to revel in it. Like his parents, who were also here, he was not slow in saying that this had been coming for a long, long time.

Plenty of other Tuali had seen what were presumably enemies gathering on the borders of the park, still mainly hidden by fence, wall and tree. Voices were raised in warning and the group, maybe three hundred strong, began to spread in anticipation of combat.

'Come on, cowards!' called Ulakan. 'Show yourselves. Take us on if you think you're able.'

Ulakan's taunts were picked up across the crowd. Laughter followed. Fists and weapons punched the air. But what emerged from the brush and climbed over or broke down the ornamental fencing were not Ixii or Beethans or Cefans. Voices quietened. Tualis started backing anyway though the enemy was coming in from all sides.

Bravado died in throats. Weapon tips dropped. Nervous elves glanced around, their eyes flickering over the faces of those beside them, looking for comfort. There was none to be had. Nillis guessed there had to be a hundred of them. Most armed but some of them not. Men.

Fear spread through the Tuali. They were just civilians in the main. Big and brave when running and fighting other civilians. But coming at them now were professional soldiers walking with cool purpose, keen edges drawn and ready. They wore stiff leather and steel-capped boots. They were tall, powerful and brutal. Scarred and bearded. Cold-eyed.

Walking just ahead of them were unarmoured men. They'd all heard men were here and that something called magic had been used to murder Lorius. Nillis knew that those men in common clothes were the wielders of it, whatever it really was. Nillis felt Ulakan near him.

'We've got to get out of here,' Ulakan said. 'Make a break for it or we'll be trapped.'

Nillis's heart was beating fast. 'It's too late for that, isn't it?'

'No. Follow me. Any others who come, good luck to them.'

'What about your parents?'

'It's now or never. Come on!'

And Ulakan ran. He ran hard towards the north end of the park where the line of men looked a little thin. Nillis took off after him. He heard the shouts of some and the footsteps of others follow them. Ulakan was laughing, excited by the sprint. From the line, two of the unarmed men stepped forward. They raised their hands, palms out. Nillis could see them talking. They made a pushing motion.

Ulakan collided head on with something and bounced off, falling back. Just like he'd run headlong into a wall. Two paces later, Nillis suffered the same fate. He bloodied his nose on the invisible barrier, jarred one wrist and snapped his stave. He sat down hard on his backside and looked over at Ulakan. His friend was staring at him, disbelieving. Ulakan got up. A single pace this time and the barrier was there.

Ulakan reached out to touch it. Nillis did likewise. It felt like nothing. Not metal, nor wood. He couldn't describe it. But it was moving as the men moved. Nillis backed off fast. He turned, ran back to the crowd. Men were closing in all around them. A dozen of them, all with their arms outstretched, pushing the barriers before them.

More and more Tuali tried their luck only to bounce off the implacable blockades. Elves were screaming. In their panic, Tuali *iad* and *ula* flung themselves at the invisible barriers again and again. Blood smeared faces and hands. Knuckles were raw. Nillis and Ulakan stood shoulder to shoulder. Ulakan's parents were behind them. All of them backed off pace by pace as the walls closed in.

Nillis fought to believe what was happening. He knew it was real. He could feel the barrier right in front of his nose but still it confused him and part of him felt his mind was playing tricks.

'We're in big trouble here,' said Ulakan, his confidence gone and real fear in his eyes. 'What if they don't stop pressing?'

There was no space. Tuali were crammed hard against each other. The heat inside was rising. Nillis's arms were down by his sides and he had no way of raising them. Bit by bit, they were being squeezed. The screams and cries to stop grew louder in the confined space. Prayers to Yniss and Tual were chanted.

Nillis tried to turn his body and found he could not. Ulakan next to him was being crushed back and front. His breathing was coming in short gasps. Behind Nillis, someone passed out, their body leaning against his, unable to fall.

Abruptly, the movement ceased. Indeed the pressure eased just a fraction. People could breathe again. Literally. Nillis watched the warrior men move to stand in a ring just behind the others. One took a single pace forwards. His speech, heavily accented, was in reasonable common elvish.

'You will drop any weapons you hold. Then we will give you more space. You will then lose any weapons you carry in scabbards, belts, boots. We will then release the barrier and you will be our prisoners.'

Iad and *ula* hurried to obey. Weapons hit the ground with thuds and clatters. The man shouted in his own language and was answered by several others, all with what sounded like an affirmative. The unarmed men drew back their arms a little, giving the Tuali glorious space. Nillis flexed his arms and rolled his shoulders. The *ula* who had fainted behind him was helped to the ground and tended. At least six others that Nillis could count were in similar states.

'Good,' said the man. 'Now, any other weapons. We are watching you.'

Nillis took both of his knives from his belt and dropped them to the ground to join the thickening carpet of weapons. Ulakan hesitated.

'Don't be stupid, Ulak,' said Nillis. 'Now is not the time for your sort of bravery.'

'We can't just surrender. It's just giving ourselves up to the Ynissul.'

'Live today, fight tomorrow,' said Nillis. 'You won't help anyone by getting stuck by a human blade because you tried to take them on all by yourself.'

Ulakan glared at him then unbuckled his sword belt, on which hung three daggers. He brought a short knife from his boot too and threw it down. He made a show of empty hands to the men outside the barrier.

The one who was apparently their leader, a big heavyset human with a thick beard and a nose squashed over his face, strutted to and fro, nodding and laughing.

'Fucking sharp-ears,' he said. 'You don't get any smarter, do you?'

Nillis felt cold as the laughter spread around the circle. The man barked another order. The barriers were gone. Warriors charged them.

'NO!' screamed Ulakan.

He dropped to his haunches and snatched up his sword. He held it to ready. Nillis, too terrified even to scream, felt warm and wet down his legs and tried to back away to nowhere. The men crashed into the helpless elves. He saw one bat Ulakan's sword aside and then plunge his blade straight through his chest. Blood fountained into the air.

Bloodied blades rose and fell, chopped and hacked. Elves tried to run in every direction. Men howled in brutal pleasure. Nillis turned around. A blade covered in slimy gore ripped into the neck of an *ula* standing right in front of him. The elf crashed back on top of him, trapping him.

He stared out at the carnage. Shrieks filled his ears. Laughter too. Prayers turned to sobs and then to nothing. The sick thud of metal on flesh and bone. The desperate pleading, the screams cut off. The awful wounds. Jaws smashed to fragments. Skulls cracked open. Bodies split, entrails pouring on to the ground. The splash of boot through blood. The hot sour stench of shit mixed with innards. Steam rising.

Blood slapped at Nillis's ear like the gentle incoming tide. The elf lying atop him was still shuddering with the last of his life. A blade came down and hacked deep into his skull and the shuddering stopped. The body slid to one side.

Nillis stared straight into the cruel eyes of a human swordsman.

The man grunted a laugh. His teeth were broken and rotten when he grinned.

His blade rose.

Nillis watched it all the way down.

Chapter 26

Courage lies in the willingness to die for those who are yet to be born.

Pelyn had her hands over her mouth to stop herself from screaming. Tulan and Ephran had run upstairs to confirm by sight what they had heard. Methian was standing in front of the bedroom door, stopping them from running out to fight.

The slaughter was done. Hundreds of Tualis butchered by men in the service of the Ynissul. Pelyn felt sick. The spray of blood when swords were raised to hack down another youth or helpless *ula* or *iad* would remain in her nightmares for eternity. As would the sight of men walking through the charnel, kicking the bodies to make sure all were dead. Chopping down on those still in the final throes.

Others knelt to clean their blades as best they could on blood-soaked clothes before searching pockets and picking up the best of the weapons. Daggers smothered in gore. Short swords kicked from the hands of those who had tried to defend themselves at the last.

'We can't just stand here!' shouted Ephran.

'And what will you do, the pair of you?' snapped Methian, shoving them back yet again. 'Rush out there and take on a hundred men and their bastard magic?'

'We have to do *something*,' said Tulan, weeping his words.

'We can keep quiet for a start,' hissed Pelyn, dragging her gaze from the park. 'And we will do something. We'll take news of this to any who will hear. And we will strike back, I promise you.'

Pelyn felt empty. Never mind that many of those murdered would have visited equal cruelty on her. This they did not deserve. No elf did. She glanced back outside. Men were gathering, talking and pointing. Immediately, they began to move towards the houses of the Ash. Others were already most of the way to the street.

'And they don't want any witnesses,' said Pelyn. 'Time to leave.'

The four Al-Arynaar ran down the stairs and headed for the back entrance across the garden. The men were already at the front door, crashing through it. She heard shouts behind her. They'd been seen.

'Move!' shouted Pelyn.

They headed across the broad communal gardens, breasting through the thick bamboo edging into the back alley. Pelyn looked left and right. Men appeared right and sprinted towards them. She pushed Methian ahead of her. Their escape route would lead them back down towards the Glade and into the face of the men advancing up the Path of Yniss, heading for the centre of the city.

Six or seven men were behind them, losing ground but shouting for others to join the chase. Tulan led the way down the narrow passage between garden borders. Pelyn glanced up on instinct. Mages above them were directing the enemy.

'We've got to find cover!' she shouted. 'Tulan, head for the fish market. We can lose them in there if we can make it.'

Tulan made the end of the alley and turned right, the others close behind him. They'd exited onto Keeper's Row. It ran parallel with the Path of Yniss for a time before angling in to join it at the head of the Glade. From there a run north halfway back towards the harbour, and they'd find the fish market.

Pelyn glanced behind her. A mage hovered overhead. He was calling and gesturing. Men spilled out of the alley fifty yards behind them. The mage flew overhead, tracking their route. She saw him looking to his left and making another beckoning gesture.

'Tulan. Watch left. More coming your way.'

She needn't have warned him. Six more men ran from another alley to block their escape. Tulan slithered to a stop and drew his sword; Ephran came to his right to stand by him. Pelyn turned and drew her own blade, Methian to her left. Four against twelve with more undoubtedly coming. It didn't look good. The mage circled overhead. At least it seemed he couldn't do any other damage while he was in the air.

'Keep talking,' said Pelyn. 'Keep moving. Don't break the circle.'

The men ran at them in line abreast. They carried long swords; some had daggers in their free hands where others preferred to go two-handed.

'Time for your revenge, Tulan,' said Methian.

'I hear you,' said Tulan.

A shadow flashed across the facade of the houses to Pelyn's right.

She heard a mourning wail. Light sparkled on metal. The mage screamed. All eyes looked up. A jaqrui crescent jutted from his chest. His wings flickered and disappeared and he plunged to the ground.

Pelyn smiled at the hesitating humans.

'Oh dear,' she said. 'You're in trouble now.'

Seizing the moment, Pelyn ran forward, slashing her blade across chest high. Her target saw her late, his guard only half formed. Pelyn's sword dashed his from his hand. She balanced quickly and reversed the blade high across the man's face, the edge biting deep.

Next to him, a second man dropped soundlessly, falling forward. A third followed, blood spurting from his mouth, the elven blade plunging into lung and heart. Behind them, Grafyrre spared Pelyn the briefest of smiles before launching a fresh attack.

'Methian, help Tulan. We've got this lot,' said Pelyn.

The men were in disarray, not knowing which way to turn. One came at Pelyn though his attention seemed elsewhere. Pelyn blocked the half-hearted strike to her face easily, stepped forward and punched her enemy square on the nose. He staggered back. One of his comrades called a warning. Another man fell forward, blood sheeting down the front of his armour.

Grafyrre bounced into the air, turned a somersault and landed legs wrapped around the neck of his next victim. He jammed daggers into either temple. The man collapsed. Grafyrre rolled backwards, landed on his hands and sprang back to his feet. Pelyn drove her blade into the last man's gut, just above the waist where leather met leggings.

The man gasped and fell to his knees. Grafyrre wrapped an arm around his head and broke his neck. Pelyn turned. Three more men lay dead. Grafyrre swept up his weapons but made no further move to join the fight.

'Leave them,' he said to Pelyn. 'It is under control.'

And so it was. Tulan battered his blade into the side of one, putting him down on the ground. One of two short blades held in Merrat's hands finished him. The other stabbed up into the groin of a human knowing his time was done. Ephran took the sword hand from the last man. He whimpered, clamped his other hand across the stump and stared at the six elves.

Merrat ghosted up beside him. She spoke in common elvish.

'Do you understand me?'

The man nodded.

'Good. Then listen. This land is ours. This city is ours. We shall not yield it. Go back to your army. They will leave or they will all perish.'

The man started, amazed he was to be allowed to live. He mouthed words but no sound came. Ephran poked him with the blade that already carried his blood.

'Run,' he said. 'Before we change our minds.'

Howling fear, relief and agony, he ran away, back the way he had come.

Pelyn turned to Grafyrre. 'Where did you come from all of a sudden? Thank you, by the way. We were in a spot of trouble there.'

'We saw the magic and the fires,' said Grafyrre. 'Katyett was concerned for your safety.'

'This is the same Katyett who left the city a couple of days ago, is it?'

'There is only one Katyett,' said Grafyrre evenly. 'And we have come to get you out too. We need all the Al-Arynaar out. Others are at the barracks. Let the city go.'

Grafyrre and Merrat began to move.

'Let it go?' Pelyn fell in beside them, beckoning the others to follow. 'Why? What about the entire population? Men are slaughtering them. I've just seen it.'

'We have plans,' said Grafyrre. 'And we cannot think to mount an attack any time other than the night. Not with mages able to fly.'

They ran across the Path of Yniss and turned west, heading out of the city in the direction of the Ultan.

'What difference does the night make?' asked Pelyn.

'Men cannot see in the dark.'

'Can't they?' Pelyn checked to make sure that Grafyrre wasn't having her on. 'Well. That'll help.'

'Best way to deliver poison. Are you sure no one else has worked this out?'

'Why would they? Thousands of years of bow skills have adapted well here on Calaius,' said Auum.

Takaar shrugged. 'We must adapt to our surroundings.'

'And we haven't employed animal poison either.'

'Hard to believe.'

'Not really. You can't hunt with poison, can you?'

'Lucky I had the time to investigate it then. Give this a go, anyway. And don't breathe in through your mouth. Not a good way to die.'

Auum tied off the tiller and took the bamboo stem from Takaar. He looked down its length. Takaar had polished the rough inside smooth. The tube was about three feet long. Perhaps a little more. Takaar handed him a dart. It was made from the thick thorns of an elsander, which were particularly dense and sharp with small barbs on one edge.

Auum pushed the dart into the tube and put the tube to his mouth. He breathed through his nose and puffed the air out sharply through his mouth as Takaar had demonstrated. The dart flew fast and straight for about fifteen feet before dropping into the coastal waters of the Sea of Gyaam.

'Hmm.' Auum passed the blowpipe back. 'Let down by its range.'

'Let down by its user,' said Takaar.

He loaded a dart in the pipe and blew it three times the distance Auum had managed. Auum raised his eyebrows.

'I'll keep practising.'

'And imagine it tipped with yellow-back poison. Or a larger dose of taipan venom is very effective if you can pierce neck or eye, say.'

Auum tried not to look too hard at Takaar lest he slip out of this period of lucidity into one of the more negative and destructive moods to which he was prey at any given breath. Takaar had spent increasing amounts of time in what Auum had come to consider to be silent introspection. That wasn't worrying in itself as it didn't threaten the small boat. Other moods were not so passive.

'How much frog poison do you need for a barb or arrow tip?' Auum asked.

'The scarcest molecule.' Takaar rubbed thumb and forefinger together. 'An amount vanishingly small. What I have in that one pot is enough to kill hundreds, maybe thousands. Contact is all that you need.'

Takaar's expression was fierce.

'The rainforest has bounties we still know nothing about. Man thinks he can rule the lands of the elves. He is sorely mistaken.'

'With your help, we can send them back across the ocean, never to return.'

'Back?' said Takaar. 'None are going back.'

Just at the moment Auum began to believe, he saw Takaar's eyes dart left then right and his body tense. 'You're alone, aren't you?' he said, demanded.

'You know I am,' said Auum.

'I see.' Takaar nodded to himself. 'Does anyone know you came to get me?'

'What? Yes, of course. In fact I was ordered to come and find you.'

Takaar made a dismissive noise. 'I doubt that. A TaiGethen never travels alone. It is an insult.'

Auum didn't want to ask but felt he had to.

'What is?'

Takaar's eye blazed. 'I am Takaar! I have the ear of the gods. I break bread with Yniss. I am the first Arch of the TaiGethen and saviour of elvenkind. And in our hour of greatest need, I am sought by a lone warrior.'

Takaar held up one finger.

'One. Am I really so unimportant that I am granted but one guard? Was that the decision of the Ynissul wise? The priesthood? Katyett? Or perhaps I am merely to be thrown at the enemy should I be fortunate enough to make it alive.'

'That wasn't how the decision was taken,' said Auum and instantly regretted his words.

'Oh? And how was it taken?'

Auum considered fabricating something but Takaar was waiting for falsehood. He heard the truth unfold with increasing incredulity.

'I am bodyguard to Priest Serrin of the Silent. We witnessed desecration at Aryndeneth. I was forced to spill the blood of men within its dome. Senior Ynissul in the priesthood have betrayed us. We had no time to seek the advice of Katyett or Jarinn or Llyron. So Serrin journeyed alone to Ysundeneth to make a report and warn the TaiGethen. I travelled here. To find you.'

Takaar settled back against the gunwale about halfway towards the bow.

'So you two sat in the forest and decided it all by yourselves?'

'It was and is the right decision,' said Auum carefully, hanging on tight to his temper. 'And one Katyett will embrace when she hears of it.'

'You don't know much about the history between us, do you?'

'Does it really matter? The elven race, or at least the civilised elven race, is at risk.'

'What matters is that I am summoned on a whim by two elves who've seen a couple of bad things in the forest. This is not a home-coming that is going to inspire a reignition of the harmony, is it?'

'I'm bringing you back to help save lives, not to pander to your ego,' muttered Auum. And then he shrugged. 'The Takaar of Haus-olis didn't care for glory or for worship. Just to win. Maybe you've changed even more than you and I think you have. So if you don't like it, if it's too low for you to stoop, you can always leave and go home. I'm not dragging you to Ysundeneth against your will.'

Takaar nodded. He turned his head as if listening to something else before, quite calmly, rolling backwards out of the boat. Auum cursed.

'Just couldn't quite keep your mouth shut, could you?' he said to himself. 'Fool.'

The boat sailed on under the favourable wind. Auum put hard about, heading to the shore some hundred and fifty yards distant. The beach looked sandy and easy. Thirty yards beyond it was the rainforest. They were about midway between Tolt Anoor and Ysundeneth. Still a long way from where they needed to be.

Takaar was a very strong and graceful swimmer. The incoming tide helped his pace and his strokes were smooth, his kick light and rapid. While Auum had to make continual adjustments on this leeward tack to avoid spilling too much wind from the tatty sail, Takaar powered straight in. He beat Auum to the beach com-fortably.

The fishing boat ground up the sand and Auum leapt out of the prow, pausing only to drag the craft above the high-tide mark. Takaar had run straight into the forest and disappeared from sight. Auum knew only where he had entered and followed him in, his sight adjusting fast to the dim light beneath the canopy.

Five paces in and Auum knew he had lost his quarry. The sounds of the sea were already eclipsed and the scent of the ocean had been submerged under the rich strong smells of earth and leaf. Takaar was the most light-footed elf Auum had ever seen. There was no trace of where he had gone.

Auum stopped, choosing to listen instead. This was an alien part of the forest to him. It was quieter than the deeps around Aryndeneth. Few of the larger predators patrolled this close and the warning buzz of reptile and rodent was muted. As for the sounds of a TaiGethen master moving through the forest, there was nothing at all.

'We think your motives to be impure.'

Takaar's voice came from the right and high. Auum moved softly, scanning the trees for any sign.

'We think you would serve us up for slaughter.'

From the right and low. Impossible. No one moved that fast. Auum paused. He had his back to a tree and was facing thick undergrowth that grew head high. To his left, a slope ran down back towards the sand. To his right, the land rose gently, the vegetation thinning slightly.

'I am TaiGethen,' said Auum. 'Incapable of betraying my own.'

'But I am not your own any more, am I?' Takaar's voice echoed from rock and tree. 'I am a thorn in the side of progress by dint of my survival.'

'Only a very few know you're still alive.'

Auum turned at a rustling just to his right. Tapir.

'Idiot. A few is all you need when they are traitor priests. And the TaiGethen are the bodyguard of the priesthood, are they not?'

'Some.'

'Like you. And those must die.'

Auum frowned. Even for Takaar this was not a logical direction.

'Without a hearing? That is not the elven way.'

'The elven way is gone. Swept away by the few who wish all power for themselves.'

Takaar was closer now. Auum prepared himself, mouthing a silent prayer to Yniss.

'I am not among them,' said Auum. 'I desire what every TaiGethen desires.'

'And that is?'

Left. He was coming from the left. Did he really mean to attack?

'The harmony enduring. Faith unwavering.'

'Serve up Takaar and all will be well, won't it?'

And that was barely the voice of Takaar. It was lower, malicious.

'No,' said Auum. 'All will be in ruins.'

Auum didn't draw a blade.

'I thought you said you were not here to pander to my ego.'

'I'm not.'

'Good.'

Takaar's foot caught Auum squarely on the right side of his head. Auum knew it was coming less than a heartbeat before and managed to balance himself enough not to be knocked unconscious. He landed on one shoulder, rolled with legs tucked to absorb the force of the blow and came up facing the direction of the attack.

Takaar was already on him. The heel of the master's palm slammed into Auum's sternum, knocking the wind from his body and sending him sprawling down a short slope and into a brackish stream. The chill of the water was revitalising, clearing his head. Auum moved up the opposite slope, looking to put a little distance between himself and Takaar. He scrambled up the bank, rolled right and came up to his haunches, his right-hand side nestling against the trunk of a balsa tree.

Takaar leapt the stream and ran around to his left. He was soundless, his feet the merest kiss on the forest floor.

'Only a coward refuses to let his opponent stand and fight.'

'Only a fool allows his enemy a sight of victory,' said Takaar. 'Though I am glad you remember my words.'

Auum pushed himself upright. He was groggy from the head kick and his breath was pained. Takaar had bruised a rib or two.

'I am not your enemy,' said Auum. 'You are my Arch, my general.'

'Was, Auum. Was.' Takaar paced in, his stride easy, his body relaxed. 'We were talking, on the swim to shore.'

'I'm sure it was a fascinating conversation.'

Takaar ignored the jibe.

'And we decided that no one comes to take a fallen hero to glory, only to his doom.'

'That can be one and the same thing,' said Auum.

Takaar glanced left. 'I told you he'd say something like that. Tell me, Auum, are you afraid to die?'

'Only a fool is not when life is blessed by Yniss himself.'

Takaar clapped his hands slowly, four times. 'It appears you have ingested my every word.'

'Only the ones that made any sort of sense.'

Takaar was close. Within ten feet. Close enough to strike without warning. Auum tried to remain relaxed. He was clinging to the belief that Takaar did not actually want to kill him. If he had wanted to, a jaqrui would have done the job before he planted his first kick.

The trouble was, of course, that Takaar was several places removed from sanity most of the time. His perception of the situation was not knowable. Another of Takaar's maxims came to mind.

To know the enemy mind is to beat him before he stands before you.

To know Takaar's mind was to know crushing guilt, a decade of solitude and an unhealthy focus on how to die in the rainforest while being extremely careful not to actually do so. Incomprehensible.

Takaar struck.

Auum was ready because he had studied under the master.

Takaar ran straight at him, planted his left leg and kicked out with his right. First kick a feint to the gut, second full force to the throat. *Blocked with crossed wrists. Foot deflected left.* Follow up left punch, straight and full. *Sway right. Riposte. Forearm smash blocked easily.* Foot sweep. *Jump. Crouch. Left leg to right kneecap. Target gone.* Blow to the head. *Unblocked.*

Auum went down flat on his back. He rolled right. He heard the sound of a punch striking the earth. Auum was on his haunches. Very quickly. Takaar came again. Two feet, head high.

Sway left. Elbow into side ribs. Strike connected.

Takaar tumbled sideways, rolling against a thick stand of bamboo at the stream's edge. Auum ran at him. Takaar pushed off the ground with his hands. His feet whipped into Auum's body left then right. Takaar's momentum carried him to a crouch. Auum steadied. Both elves moved to a standing position. Takaar's words rolled around Auum's head.

Instinct gets you through the first blow. Anticipation gets you through the rest.

Auum smiled. Takaar glared. He didn't mean to but he felt his ribs where Auum had struck the only blow he'd landed so far. Auum sprang forward, unleashing a multiple strike. Straight punch, head. Triple jab, body. Straight finger jab, neck. Straight kick, gut. Roundhouse, left temple.

He didn't land a single one of them. Takaar's defence was quicker than Auum could follow. His ripostes just predictable enough to evade. The two TaiGethen bounced away from each other, sizing up the space around them and each other's weaknesses.

'Takaar. I am not here to kill you or lead you to your death. As Yniss is my witness and Shorth owns my soul. I am TaiGethen. You can believe me without fear of betrayal.'

Takaar was staring to his right.

'He is who he says he is. I never forget a face.'

'I shouldn't have come, you're right. Best on the cliff top, rocking over the drop. Perhaps tomorrow I will tumble.'

'I am not here to prove myself to you. I do not have to prove myself to anyone. I am Takaar. I—'

Takaar's expression darkened.

'I did. I killed them. All of them. Blood is on my hands. But I can wash it.'

Takaar scrambled back down to the stream and plunged his hands into it, scraping at his palms with his nails.

'See? It fades. It fades. And one day it will all be gone.'

Takaar stood up and jabbed a finger at Auum.

'You are a spy. You would steal all my secrets.' Takaar ran up the slope towards him. 'I want them back. Where is all my work?'

'It's in the boat,' said Auum. 'Completely safe and completely untouched.'

Takaar planted his left foot on level ground and leapt at Auum. His right leg outstretched, fists balled and covering his face. Auum swivelled his torso, putting his weight into a two-handed block. Takaar tumbled in the air, came down and rolled to his haunches, springing up in the next movement.

Auum took up a crouched defence, legs wide, centre of gravity low. Takaar's fists blurred. Auum defended on instinct. Left high, *block right*. Right torso, *block down*. *Riposte palm to chest*. Blocked. Straight kick groin, *block right foot*. *Riposte right fist to head*. Evaded. Roundhouse right temple. Landed. One, two, three.

Auum sprawled on the ground, rolling over and on to his haunches. Takaar was on him. Left fist cracking into his jaw, sending him down again. Auum tumbled, bounced back to his feet, ran three paces up a tree trunk and grasped a branch ten feet from the ground. He spun around and dropped, both feet flat. Takaar dodged. Auum landed, ducked low. Takaar's foot washed over his head. Auum straightened, powered into a standing jump and kicked out first left, then right foot.

Takaar caught his right foot and twisted. Auum followed the movement with his body to avoid his ankle being snapped. Takaar pulled his foot in and smashed a kick at Auum's groin. Auum blocked with his left thigh. Auum landed on his back, twisted his foot from Takaar's grasp.

Takaar hurdled him. Auum scrambled to turn round. Not fast enough. Takaar kicked out backwards, catching Auum in the kidney. Pain blossomed up his back. He pitched forwards. Auum rolled onto his back. Takaar's fist was at his face. He knocked it aside but not the second blow which slammed into his nose, bloodying but not breaking it.

Auum's head thudded against the ground. He brought his knees up sharply and twisted, catching Takaar's side and unbalancing him. Auum's fists licked out, the left catching Takaar in the side of the jaw. Takaar pushed himself away back to his feet. Auum ran at him, steadied and kicked out to the knee. Takaar moved easily aside.

Auum blocked a punch to his throat. The second and third were too quick though. One made more of a mess of his nose, the last, an elbow caught him in the side of the neck. He hit the ground again. Takaar pounced on him, cocked his hand for a straight fingered jab to the throat.

'No one should look for me,' said Takaar. 'I am not to be found. Not ever. And you. Came here alone and you will die alone. We see it and we agree.'

Ghost white loomed overhead. Fingers with cruelly sharpened nails closed around Takaar's throat and a knife point came to rest at his temple.

'You of all people should know that a TaiGethen is never alone.'

Chapter 27

Speed is nothing without the wit to use it.

'Why did you authorise this? What purpose was there? We are here to subdue not slaughter! We want to keep them divided. You are forcing them to reunite.'

Sildaan was incandescent. Screaming her rage. She kept rubbing her hands over her face and walking round in tight circles. Garan let her exhaust her dismay, keeping his expression neutral and his lieutenants elsewhere entirely. Here, in the middle of the Park of Tual, with the stacked bodies beginning to stink in the heat of a day which had yielded little rain, they could be quite alone.

'I cannot believe what you have *done* here!'

Sildaan pointed at the bodies. Carts and oxen were being found to take them out to the rainforest for reclamation. Garan found the idea repellent. Apparently, elves drew great comfort in knowing their bodies would be torn apart by a thousand different species of animal and bug when they died. All it did to Garan was make him itch more.

'Llyron wanted to rule these people, not pray for their souls in a mass service of Shorth's embrace.' Her face cleared just about enough. 'Why did you do it?'

'Right,' said Garan, taking a breath. 'There are two reasons, but first let me apologise for not squaring this with you. That was an error.'

'An *error*? Oh, sorry, I made a little *error* of judgement. Rather than herd these Tuali into the harbour master's warehouse, I accidentally ordered a total butchering. Silly me. Such an easy mistake though, don't you think?'

Garan took it. Just. 'Sarcasm doesn't become you, Sildaan.'

'False apology doesn't become you, blink-life.'

Garan felt his anger rising. 'The fact that you pay me does not give you the right to insult me. Sharp-ears. I am trying to subdue this city as quickly as I can. Your interruptions and lack of knowledge regarding proper tactics are undermining your own operation. You should just let me do the job you are underpaying me to do.'

Sildaan shook her head. 'I'm interrupting to stop you doing two things I expressly ordered you not to do. Razing the city to the ground and throwing every elven body on the fire. Your way, you get submission by having no one left to rebel. And because I pay you, I get to interfere any time I like and change my mind as often as I like. Is that completely clear or must I spell it out further to your slow human brain?'

Garan almost snapped. Only the thought of the near future stayed him from breaking her neck right then and there. He grabbed the collars of her coat in one gloved hand and hauled her towards him. He knew what she'd do and made no attempt to move the knife blade he felt pressing against his shirt over his stomach.

'You will let me go or I will kill you,' said Sildaan.

'I have no doubt that you will. Just ask yourself how long you will last with my blood on your blade and four hundred of my men waiting for my next order. So you will listen to me and then we will move on.'

The knife did not withdraw. Nor did it push in further. Good enough. Neither of them would look away. Garan stared into eyes full of indignation and contempt. He trusted his were as cold as others told him they were. He let her coat go.

'You don't believe me but this needed to happen,' said Garan. 'Firstly because every elf in this city needs to understand the price of resistance or rebellion. And your message will be about how these elves set an ambush and would not lay down their arms, leaving us with no choice. Secondly, these are Tuali. This is the warlike thread you warned me needed shocking into submission. Let me ask you something. Which is more desirable? To have all these Tuali just waiting their opportunity to strike – not now perhaps, not even tomorrow or the next day. But one day. Or to have them gone and to have every other Tuali, maybe every other elf, too scared to dare oppose you in the street.

'This has happened in Balaia too. You cannot afford to have elves like this in your new society. You can't. You need order and obedience from day one. Damn me if you like, and I'll take my chances with your god Shorth. Or wait to see the wisdom of my slow human brain.'

Garan stepped away and opened his shirt.

'Take me down now or move to the Gardaryn. We can have this city in our control by sundown.'

Sildaan considered stabbing him. He could see it in her eyes. Fascinating, these elves. The veneer of sophistication was so easily scraped away to reveal the bestial nature so close to the surface. Garan hadn't seen them fighting each other. He'd heard how it went and wasn't at all sure he wanted to. Eventually, Sildaan gave a fractional nod of the head.

'No more killing unless you're attacked. We cannot afford it,' said Sildaan.

'You have my word,' said Garan, smiling as warmly as he could manage.

Sildaan's expression did not change. 'Your word is worthless. Your actions say everything. You are a long way from home.'

'And you have none of your own to defend you.' Garan beckoned his lead mage over. 'We really should get on much better than we do.'

'The day you sail away is the day I get on with you as well as I ever will.'

'Promise me you'll write,' said Garan.

Sildaan tried very hard to hide the smile. 'Only if you leave me enough of your blood for the letter.'

Garan laughed loud. 'Good for you. Let's get on. I mean to send my soldiers up the Path of Yniss and across the Gardens of Cefu. We'll also come to the Gardaryn from the south across that market the name of which I've forgotten. We'll seal off the approaches and clear the building. Then we'll wait for you. How's that?'

Sildaan considered briefly and then nodded. 'And prisoners?'

'The balance of a hundred men are tasked with prisoner duties. The harbour master's warehouse is secure and empty of anything useful to an elf with a mind for trouble. We've established a safe corridor to bring in more prisoners from the south and west of the city. We've laid alarm wards where we can't physically cover areas of ground.'

'What is an alarm ward, exactly?'

'Simple casting that when someone walks near it, makes an unholy row. Quite invisible to the naked eye.'

Another nod. 'Just remember to stick to what you've just told me. I'll be with Hithuur and Helias.'

Garan watched her go. She paused at the bodies and carts and dropped her head in brief prayer. Garan didn't get it, not really. These were enemies. A waste of prayer, surely?

'Garan, you wanted me?' said Keller.

Excluded briefly from Triverne, the city and college of magic, for conduct unbecoming a mage, Keller was the perfect man for this job. He had forty-three others with him. Sildaan had no idea of the power they represented.

'What's the situation over the city?'

'We've had one setback. I'll take you to the scene in a moment. Otherwise, the west is very quiet. No thread mobs on the streets. The temple piazza is very busy, as we assumed. Llyron is in great demand.' Keller raised his eyebrows.

'I'm more concerned about the south. Apposans and Beethans in particular. I want to avoid trouble there if I can.'

'Last reports, the Apposans have gone into the forest and we don't know where they are. The Beethans are numerous and have their quarter well defended but they are not venturing out.'

'Can we take it?'

'Swords and wards, my friend. Swords and wards.'

Garan grinned. 'How many swords do you need?'

'Thirty will do it. Ten mages too.'

'You've got them. Quick Hand is free now this work is done. Take him and thirty of his team and secure the Beethans. Let me know when it's done.' He laughed. 'Gods drowning, and the elves think we're the slow wits in this city. Now where's this setback you were talking about?'

Garan had called for Sildaan when he reached the side street. Twelve dead. A mage and eleven swordsmen. That meant one soldier was missing. No trace of elven blood.

'TaiGethen,' said Sildaan.

'I told you we should have followed them. Clearly they haven't all run away to Aryndeneth.'

'One thing we've always known is that they would be back. One thing I always knew was that they would evacuate the Ynissul. All you have to do is deal with them when they come back with purpose.'

Garan chuckled. 'Your sense of humour is keener than you know. You don't call this slaughter, "purpose" then?'

'No,' said Sildaan. 'Just one cell, I'd say. Here for a look around, but you said your people were tracking some Al-Arynaar away from the park. From the position of your forces, I'd guess this is where they trapped them. Shame for them that the Tai were here too.'

Garan saw Sildaan was smiling. It was a wry expression and there was a minute shake of the head that he had come to associate with grudging respect.

'What is it?'

'Well, we didn't find Pelyn among the dead in the park, did we? I wonder if she talked her way out of their clutches when Helias deserted them?'

A door opened a little further down the street. Garan drew his blade. A lone man came gingerly into the light, his expression when he saw Garan only just short of euphoric. He was terribly pale and clutched a blood-soaked cloth over his other hand. He half ran, half stumbled over, bringing with him the stench of excrement and urine. Garan saw the stains on his trousers and held up his hands.

'I think that's close enough. What's your name, son?'

'I'm Naril, sir.' He had stopped and was staring about him at the bodies in the street. Unpleasant memories played out, his face a mirror of his earlier fear. 'They fell on us so quickly. I never saw them until they spoke to me.'

'They spoke to you?' said Garan.

'What did they say?' asked Sildaan.

Garan loved hearing her talk the Balaian language. All her accents were wrong but it stirred something in his loins that he was a little conflicted to be feeling.

'They warned me that we'd all die,' said Naril.

'Ah yes,' said Garan. 'One left standing to tell the tale. That's something you and I have in common, young Naril. How many were they?'

'Just two of the quick ones. Four others. Al-Arynaar but a bit shabby.'

'Two?' Garan turned to Sildaan. 'Thoughts on who it might be?'

'Not really. They only work in threes when they're hunting. This was just a look about, I'm sure.'

'It doesn't affect our plans. Don't worry about it, Naril. Get back to your ship. Find a mage to deal with your injury. Clean yourself up and get some rest.'

Naril bobbed his head and ran off in the direction of the docks.

'Plans?' said Sildaan.

'Yep.'

'I'm looking forward to hearing them at the Shorth temple this evening. I'm sure Llyron is too.'

'Let's hope I don't disappoint you.'

'Again.'

'Sildaan?'

'Yes.'

'Your humour. I was wrong about it.'

Pelyn was shaking like she had a fever. The shivers had settled on her not long after she ran into the staging camp. On her instruction, Tulan and Ephran had been disarmed and taken into custody by loyal Al-Arynaar. Similarly on her instruction, Methian was sleeping in one of the long dormitories. Pelyn herself had been sitting with Katyett when the shakes had come on. She'd been sure Katyett had something important to tell her but it had been forgotten when Pelyn's teeth began to chatter.

Katyett brought her a hot drink from one of the tree-trunk steamers the TaiGethen and Ynissul had built. Clever pieces that boiled water for washing and drinking but which gave out almost no smoke or flame due to the dispersal of the former through hollowed roots into a nearby stream and the shielding of the latter by an ingenious bamboo system for feeding air into a small clay dome placed under the trunk.

'What's wrong with me?' she asked.

'Nothing that won't fix,' said Katyett. 'You've been through a lot. Just take your time. Feeling cold?'

'No.' Pelyn looked out into the darkening sky. 'Just not very clean. And why is everyone looking at me?'

'Probably because your face is a bit of a mess. We'll see to it,' said Katyett. 'And what do you mean, everyone?'

'All the TaiGethen for a start.'

'You're imagining things,' said Katyett, who wouldn't catch her eye.

'I'm shaking; I haven't gone blind,' said Pelyn. 'What's going on?'

'Later. Let's get you straight first. Let's talk about something else and try and bring this shock out.'

'So there is something going on.'

'Pelyn!'

'All right, all right. What do you want to know?'

'Well, we could start with the state of Ysundeneth.'

'All right, but you can start by telling me why you didn't mention you were going to hide here? It would have been useful information.'

'For Llyron too,' said Katyett. 'Anyway, we didn't know who we could trust.'

'Well you could trust me,' said Pelyn, knowing she was whining.

'Come on, Pelyn. You're smarter than this. You, I would trust with my life. Others in your organisation—' Katyett nodded at Tulan and Ephran, apart from everyone else and under guard '—were not so worthy. Besides, we needed to leak the information deliberately to some Ynissul we knew had to be plants.'

'How did you know?'

'Not enough bruising. Not enough trauma. Too calm and too measured. There were five of them that we took to the Ultan. All of them have reported back on our apparent direction.'

'And you're sure there are no more?'

Katyett shrugged. 'We can never be completely sure. We've a couple of suspects but they aren't going anywhere. This place is easy to defend from absconders and we've let it slip that anyone who leaves without permission will be in front of Shorth to explain themselves, not me. So, the city?'

'You know almost as much as me. Merrat and Graf will have told you how many men are on the streets. They've set the place up brilliantly, you have to hand it to Sildaan and her ilk. There is no concerted defence. They knew the Al-Arynaar would be torn every which way. They probably thought we'd run with you. I wish we had. How many did we get out? A hundred and three? Pathetic. That means there are three hundred lost in there. Dead, captured or deserted. So many friends.'

'How long before the city is under Llyron's control.'

'They're moving very fast. The men are brutal and they have a coherent plan. They're going from ghetto to ghetto, as far as we could make out. We think most elves are being confined in their homes or taken somewhere near the docks to makeshift prisons. I've no doubt the city's prisons will be similarly employed when they're captured. They'll be in control by tonight. Tomorrow dawn at most.'

Pelyn took a long draught of the guarana and clove infusion. She understood why Methian enjoyed it so. It smelled wonderful. Each swallow brought her renewed energy.

'Llyron,' said Katyett through a sigh. 'Do you really believe it?'

Pelyn laughed and shook her head. 'Well I do now. Seriously, it gives you a lot of problems after this is over. The Ynissul are split from top to bottom. Who knows which other priests out there are of the same mind as the high priest of Shorth. Who are you going to appoint to the seat at Aryndeneth?'

Katyett blew out her cheeks. 'There's no point wondering about that right now. If they win, we'll find Hithuur or Sildaan in the chair, I've no doubt.'

'How can we win? There are so few of us. How many TaiGethen and Silent do you think will come?'

'I don't know. A hundred if everyone reads the call to muster. We'll know in about eight days.'

'*Eight days?*' Pelyn's shakes had gone completely now only to be replaced by a gnawing desperation in her gut. 'By that time, Llyron will have the city sewn up completely. What chance will there be for a small force with none of this magic to call on and no defence against it? Tual's tongue, they can even fly.'

'Eight days will seem a long time to them too. Every night we'll be mounting raids. We'll kill men and leave their bodies laid out in their most secure places as warnings. We'll undermine their moves to subdue the population. We'll make sure there is no security for anyone in that city.'

'I hope you're right,' said Pelyn. 'I hope there is the will in the people to follow you, to go back to peace knowing their neighbours would have killed them the day before.'

'But there is reason to hope. Or I think there is. And it isn't me we want them to follow. I have to tell you something. It'll come as another shock. It did me.'

And Pelyn knew. With total certainty she knew, and the shudders came back so strongly she dropped the rough wooden cup onto the ground. A return to the past. To the pain and the confusion. That was why the TaiGethen were staring at her with all that sympathy. Her and Katyett both. Old wounds to be opened. Old memories to be scraped raw. And she had only just finished waking up without the pain of rejection in her heart.

'It's Takaar, isn't it? He's coming back, isn't he?'

Chapter 28

Keep your enemy turning. That way, when you come to strike, he will not know from where you have come.

'Would he have killed you?' Serrin had returned to his gruff-voiced terse self. Auum found that most comforting. 'His mind is not strong.'

'That, my priest, is a major understatement. He moves from lucid teacher to muttering introspection to this new thing of allying with the voice in his head. He hates himself and then there are flashes of the sort of ridiculous pride he never ever fell prey to when he was at his height on Hausolis. What sort of good can he possibly do? And yes, I have no doubt he would have killed me. You should have seen him. He is so *fast*.'

Serrin frowned. 'I did see him.'

'Watching the show, were you?'

Serrin smiled.

'How long were you tracking us?'

'From Verendii Tual.'

'Good. And how is the muster?'

'Most know. All who know are travelling.'

'We need to move on,' said Auum. 'The boat is up on the beach.'

Serrin looked at Takaar. He was sitting on a rock at the side of the stream. Serrin's appearance seemed to have knocked him back into introspection. He had been conversing with his tormentor for an hour, only looking at them to unleash another stream of expletives in their direction.

'Takaar is less dangerous on foot.'

Auum nodded. 'I know, but we could be horribly slow. I don't understand this. When I met him, he hated this other voice. Did everything he could to antagonise it.'

'Ten years is a long time to live with such guilt alone.'

'We're giving him the chance to redeem himself.'

'He may not see it that way.'

Takaar was staring at them. His face was pale. He was chewing at his top lip and frowning as if trying to recall something. He pointed at Auum.

'Your left guard is fractionally low. It leaves your temple vulnerable.'

Auum opened his mouth to protest. 'Thank you,' he said instead.

Takaar nodded at Serrin. 'Your stance was in error. Though you may have killed me with the knife, it is possible I could have jabbed back with an elbow and burst a testicle. Your left foot was in too close, your stance was too open. Your neck grip was sound but approach sideways. Don't give me a target next time.'

Serrin nodded his thanks.

'We should move on,' said Auum. 'The boat is—'

Takaar was shaking his head.

'Not the boat. Never again. I'm scared of water.' Takaar dissolved into helpless laughter. Eventually, he regained control enough to speak again. 'He has been trying to get me to kill myself by jumping into a river, and he never knew I was so terrified of the water, not the drop, that I would never do it if I lived to be ten thousand.'

Takaar snorted and snot blew from his nose. Auum jerked a thumb back to the ocean.

'But you just swam a hundred and fifty yards. I watched you. You are an excellent swimmer.'

Takaar was clutching his gut against the pain of his laughter.

'Why do you think I was so fast? Think what might be below the surface. Ready to snap at my toes. Ready to drag me under.' Takaar's mirth dried up as quickly as it had come. 'To drown. To have no option but to open your mouth and let the water flood your lungs. To feel your life ebbing away and all you can do is claw at the sunlight just out of reach.'

Takaar was staring at his hand, opening and closing his fist. Serrin and Auum exchanged a glance.

'I'll go and bring the gear from the boat.'

Serrin nodded. Both elves rose. Auum saw Serrin walk over to Takaar, heard him speak.

'A prayer?' he asked.

'The gods no longer listen to my prayers,' said Takaar.

Auum passed out of earshot. Breaking out of the rainforest and into the sea breeze, Auum took several huge breaths, letting the freshness suffuse him. The sea lapping on the beach was a pure and beautiful sound and the smells carried on the water invigorated him.

Auum paused on his way to the boat, turning back to the forest. He replayed the events of the last two hours, which had already taken on an unreal quality. He felt his nose. It was swollen and crusted with blood. It itched like mad.

'Real enough.'

He shuddered as he plucked Takaar's bags and blowpipe from the boat. He was lucky to be alive, not standing before Shorth, pleading his case to be admitted to the halls of the ancients. Auum shrugged his shoulders to dispel the thought. Under the aft bench was a leather bag for storing the catch. It wasn't big, suggesting the confidence of the owner of the boat. But it was of a size and quality perfect for Auum's needs. He transferred the packages of meat to it along with the net sack of Takaar's herbs, poultices and poisons.

Auum hefted the sack onto his right shoulder and trotted back under the canopy. He came upon Serrin and Takaar close together, hands in the dirt. Serrin was praying silently. What Takaar was doing was anyone's guess. Auum liked to think he was praying too but for the one who once walked with gods, that might have been a step too far.

The TaiGethen waited for them to finish.

'How far to Ysundeneth?' he asked of Serrin.

'Six, seven days. We're heading for the old staging camp.'

Auum nodded. 'A good place to strike from. Takaar, are you ready?'

'That is yet to be determined.'

A hundred men surrounded the Gardaryn. Behind them stood curious fearful elves of every thread. Ordinary elves too scared to leave their homes until now were emerging as the city quietened, cowed under the iron fist of human mercenaries. Twenty mages stood with the men.

Cloud was thickening overhead. The first real rains of the day were imminent. Sildaan stood with Garan, Hithuur and Helias. Mages overflew the building. The doors were all closed, the windows shuttered. The turrets were empty.

'Who's in there, do you think?' asked Garan. 'TaiGethen?'

'No,' said Sildaan. 'Maybe Al-Arynaar, but without Pelyn they're unlikely to stand and defend anything. No. I'm guessing our Orran friends might be holed up here. Good strong building, lots of space, plentiful supplies. Go easy. We need the place cleared and the records moved up to Shorth.'

'You want paperwork. Why by all the gods drowning would you want all that?'

'Records equal control. It's a mess in there of course, but nothing much is missing. It gives us the name, address and thread identity of every elf in Ysundeneth and in the Ysun rainforest zone. Once we take Tolt Anoor and Deneth Barine, that extends to every elf on Calaius.'

'You seriously think that every elf born in the depths of that green hell is reported to you faithfully? Or that every move is told you? Get real.'

Sildaan smiled. 'As I will never tire of saying, you don't understand us, do you? There is such pride in the birth of every child. Such importance is attached to bringing the young to the thread temple to feel the touch of the gods and the blessing of the priest. Communities are so close that any move is first unusual and second a matter for sorrow and celebration in equal measure. This is our way.'

'Or it was,' said Garan. 'Fine. I don't get you. And my people will be only too happy to become pack animals for all your papers and parchments.'

'Just get on with your job,' said Sildaan.

'Keller!' called Garan. 'Are you set?'

Keller was in the air, directing his mages into a ring around the Gardaryn. He glided down to land next to Garan. Sildaan shuddered. Of all the things she had seen, the fire and the ice, this was the most unsettling. Neither man nor elf should fly. It was against faith and against nature.

'Just say the word and we'll secure your advance.'

'Good.' Garan turned to his men. 'Squads three and four ready to approach the doors. No other access. Subdue escapees. Maintain the cordon. Keller, if you please.'

Keller shot back into the sky. 'Shields!'

'Shields up,' came the call from around the Gardaryn.

'Advance!' ordered Garan.

Twelve warriors with two mages behind them moved quickly towards the doors. Shutters opened all around the building. Arrows flew thickly. Every shaft bounced from the invisible shields that surrounded the soldiers, the barriers spiking briefly with colour as they repelled each impact.

Voices rose in shock and surprise. Sildaan glanced round at the growing crowd filling the piazza. The humans moved on, ignoring the shafts that continued to bounce harmlessly from the magical shields. The two squads reached the doors. One man stepped forward and tested the great iron rings. He shook his head and withdrew. One of the mages moved up and began to make small gestures in the air in front of his face.

Garan called out another order. Men advanced on the open shutters, forcing them to close and the arrows to cease. Another order. Half of his men on the piazza side turned to face the crowd. Other men were running in to bolster the defence. Sildaan felt a little exposed. She gestured to Hithuur, and the two of them walked a little way closer to the Gardaryn. Helias copied their move.

The mage finished his preparation. He held his hands in front of his face, palms forward, and made a shoving motion. The doors, designed to open out, groaned against their hinges. Sildaan could see them bowing inward at the centre. The mage, his body rigid, his arms shaking, dropped his head to his chest and pushed again, deliberately and slowly.

The doors shuddered. Rivets on the hinges popped. The top of the lintel cracked. Timbers in the doors bent and shattered. The mage cried out with the effort, withdrew his hands and shoved again, hard. The doors blew in on a cloud of splinters. Iron and timber tumbled into the hallway and through into the main chamber. Sildaan saw elves diving for cover. The shutters in the front of the building rattled. One threw its fastening and cracked a hinge, falling open and hanging broken.

The two squads of men ran inside, their mages behind them once again. From within, Sildaan heard shouts and the clash of metal, brief and final. From behind her she heard the shouts of elves angry at the damage to this cornerstone of their city. Glancing behind she saw a concerted move forward. Next to her, Garan saw it too and barked orders to warriors and mages.

'Don't worry,' he said. 'They can't get to you.'

'Let's get inside,' said Sildaan. 'Hithuur, get to records as quickly as you can. Helias, this is your building. Let's not leave things behind we don't want to.'

The four of them marched up to the shattered doors, Garan

moving inside first. His men had subdued about twenty elves in the
main chamber. The place was a mess. Blankets, discarded clothing
and food, waterskins and rubbish were scattered across the floor.
Sildaan picked her way towards the stage.

'Don't get too far ahead,' said Garan. He turned and shouted
outside. 'Squads ten, eleven, twelve. Room to room. Move.'

More men ran inside, mages in the wake of swordsmen. Arrows
flicked down from above, from the rafters where the TaiGethen used
to hide. Garan did not flinch where Sildaan ducked reflexively, hands
over her face. Garan stared up. There were multiple shapes of elves
up there. He crooked a finger at them, speaking in clear common
elvish.

'Best come down before we shoot you down. You cannot harm us
but we can certainly harm you. It's your choice.' He waved a mage to
him. 'Keep this chamber shielded. I don't care if they make a stand
up there or not. It doesn't go well for them whichever way it works.'

'Yes, sir.'

Sildaan looked up to the rafters. Those staring down at her did so
with eyes that hated, eyes that found it hard to accept their betrayal.
Desperate, hopeless eyes.

'Do as he says,' she called. 'It's too late to resist.'

Hithuur was at her shoulder. He was looking at the partially
scorched tapestries.

'We should keep these,' he said.

'Whatever for?' asked Sildaan.

'They are part of our history.'

Sildaan made a dismissive noise and pointed towards the adminis-
tration and records offices through the back of the stage. She could
hear a little fighting and a great deal of shouting and pleading.

'Through there, that's our history. At the museums, that's our
history. These . . . these are lies, the invention of a romantic story-
teller. They will burn.'

Sildaan sat alone on the steps of the Gardaryn. Through the long
hours of sunshine and torrential rain, the records of a nation had
been removed box by box from the building, loaded onto requisi-
tioned carts and driven away under guard to the temple of Shorth.
And during a day that was declining towards an angry, clouded dusk,
the crowds had thickened on the piazza and all approaches to the
Gardaryn. Word had travelled quickly. Elves of all threads thronged

to see the emptying of their most loved building. They'd tried storming the magical barriers. They'd tried deputations of protest and reason. She had refused to treat with any of them.

Most of them now stood silent or in prayer. Occasionally, a chant would grow, one of the old chants denouncing the Ynissul, demanding freedom and equality of power. Loud, emotional chants from the mouths of what had to be fifteen to twenty thousand elves. But futile.

Garan sat down beside her. His men were moving the last of the records from front and rear, each box making a further statement to the mass before them.

'Where were they all hiding?'

Sildaan shrugged. 'At home, I guess. Funny, isn't it? Hithuur said it felt like the whole city had taken up arms and joined the mobs when Takaar was denounced, but it was hardly any of them really, was it? Most of them stayed home, unless they were forced to move, and hoped it would all blow over.'

'Why did they think that?'

Garan appeared genuinely interested. Sildaan shrugged again.

'We've had troubles before. We're complex in some ways and ever so simple in others. But there's always been a minority prepared to riot or march any time anything goes astray. We've had trouble with food shortages – unbelievable you'd think with the ocean here and the rainforest there – but it's true. We've had very unpopular building and tax laws and we've had stringent preservation laws passed too. That's to name but a few.

'But there's always been the Al-Arynaar to restore order and the Gardaryn in which to protest and hold the government and the priesthood to account. Now there isn't, and they're just beginning to understand that things are changing for good. This strikes so deep at the elven soul that I'm surprised so many didn't feel it more plainly. But that's elves for you. Close their eyes, most of them, and pray the nightmare is gone by the morning.'

'Not this time,' said Garan.

'No indeed,' said Sildaan. 'How much longer?'

'We're almost done.'

'Good. I don't want the rain to spoil the show.'

Garan laughed. 'Mage fire cares not if it rains or shines, my priest.'

Sildaan was worried by that statement and wasn't completely sure why. Behind her, Keller sauntered out of the Gardaryn. He nodded at her.

'Empty,' he said. 'What's next.'

'Fireworks,' said Garan, getting up and brushing himself down. 'Sildaan, is the order given?'

Sildaan stood too. She gazed up at the beauty of the Gardaryn, the beetle. A thousand years of debate and, yes, she supposed, history. Obsolete now and a dangerous symbol of a way of life that had to change. She breathed deeply and closed her eyes briefly.

'It is.'

'Right. Keller, over to you. Set inside and out. I want this inferno seen from Balaia.'

'Consider it done.'

Sildaan stood. 'You're sure they'll hear me? You're sure I'll be safe?'

'This is going to be something no one will ever forget.'

And so it was that Sildaan stood on the steps of the Gardaryn a short while later. Above her, Gyal's tears fell with outraged ferocity. Behind her, the flames of the Gardaryn, tinged with the brown colour of human magic, roared into the dark sky. In front of her, twenty thousand elves howled their fury, impotent to act, helpless to save their most beloved building. And when she opened her mouth, with spell shields behind her keeping back the fires and more spells cast to amplify her every word, her voice echoed across the piazza and out into the city.

'Elves of Ysundeneth, hear me. Those of you in front of me now and locked terrified in your homes or cast out onto the streets. Hear me. I am Sildaan, scripture priest of Aryndeneth. I am the mouth-piece of Llyron, high priest of Shorth, who is, from this moment on, ruler of the elven nation of Calaius.'

The statement stilled the howling of the crowd more surely than Yniss appearing before them and putting a finger to his lips. The drumming of the rain and the hissing and roaring of the Gardaryn as it burned were thundering background to Sildaan's oration.

'The harmony is dead. The fragile belief held by many against the true nature of the elf has been torn to shreds. The true nature of Takaar, he who once walked with gods, has been revealed, and he has rightly been denounced along with his laws. We have all seen in the past days the real soul of the elf. It is in separation. It is in every thread to their own community. It is in power based on longevity.

'The Ynissul were put here by Yniss himself to rule. Wisdom can only be built by the immortal. Wisdom that can bring genuine peace to our race can only be handed down by those who have lived long enough to understand it. Elves have lived for a thousand years with the knowledge that those of other threads who deal with them do so through a thin veneer of brotherhood.

'Order, from this moment forth, will be restored. There will be no further violence between the threads. Know this. Those working for the Ynissul have the authority to act with any force necessary to keep the peace in our streets.

'Go back to your homes and wait for instructions. Know this. Until we re-establish the markets, your food and clothing and other essential needs will be serviced centrally by the harbour master. The operation of black markets and other measures of extortion amongst threads will be dealt with severely. Expect announcements on the living quarters for each thread. Some of you will be relocated. I suggest you gather all that is valuable to you or risk losing it.

'Assets no longer in your gift if your thread is short-lived will be returned to the Ynissul for correct distribution as status demands. Other announcements will follow regarding employment and access to areas of the city, the temples and the rainforest. Any of you living in a mixed-thread partnership will be separated and your bastard offspring given to the temple of Shorth for education.

'You have all read the history of our race. You have all heard the stories. Yniss created this earth and the lesser gods to serve him. He created the Ynissul to rule the elves and the lesser threads to serve them. So shall it be again. So it is from this day forward.

'In the name of Yniss and his servant on this earth, Llyron, I make this statement. Peace and your god be with you.'

Sildaan walked from the steps, and before the dam of emotion burst, all she could hear was the sound of Ysundeneth weeping quietly.

Chapter 29

Strike the earth where your enemy lays his head. Defeat lies in the absence of certainty and security.

The music of loss played on unchanged in the temple of Shorth. The musicians set in their dozen acoustic alcoves caressed their bamboo pipes with lips and fingers. The beauty of death filled the air. The priests and temple keepers, the Senserii and the scripture readers continued as they had done for millennia. For Shorth, there was no society, no pecking order of threads, no misery or joy. There was only life or death.

In Llyron's chambers, change was complete and total. A banquet was laid out on her dining table. White wine and wheat beer stood in flagons on tables around the edges of the room. Conversation was focused on the immediate problems of ruling Ysundeneth and wider Calaius.

'How long before we receive messages back from Tolt Anoor and Deneth Barine?' asked Llyron.

She was standing with what had become, for now, her inner circle. There were however many more senior priests in the rainforests making the necessary announcements and changes who would sit higher up the table than any of Sildaan, Hithuur and most certainly Helias.

'We can expect early indications in perhaps five days. Most likely it'll be ten and above before we'll know anything certain about the success or otherwise of our plans.' Sildaan took a sip of wine. Llyron had noticed that she imbibed very little, keeping her eyes on Garan and his mage Keller. 'We have no humans in either city to do what we did today so there will be a far longer period of ghettoisation and conflict among the threads.'

'All well and good so long as the faithful Ynissul are removed to safety,' said Llyron.

'It is the central strand of everything we are doing,' said Sildaan. 'All the faithful priests running the rainforest will make stops at both cities. The Tuali sympathisers we seeded in the Al-Arynaar forces ten years ago are ready. But there will inevitably be more bloodshed before order is resolved in the right way.'

Llyron nodded. 'Much work for Shorth to do. And interesting experiments in anarchy and a chasm in leadership giving rise to a clutching at any new hope by ordinary elves.'

'You sound like a textbook,' said Garan.

His mouth was full of food and a large wooden cup of wine was in his hand. Keller moved with him like his shadow.

'I am a student of history,' said Llyron evenly, moving away fractionally towards her three Senserii. 'I am also a student of warfare. Perhaps you could tell me how it is that you plan to keep this city as quiet as it currently is and, perhaps more importantly, how you intend to deal with our TaiGethen problem.'

Garan smiled. 'Both are, of course, inextricably linked. We expect and are ready for attacks by the TaiGethen at any time. We've been caught out once today but my people will shortly begin to lay magic-based traps and set up observation posts to warn of incoming enemies.

'I have had personal experience of exactly how skilled these Ynissul are. So don't worry that I'm being naive. But they have no defence against magical attack, and their numbers are small.

'We will kill from long range any who approach or enter the city. We will continually seek out their hiding places and kill them where they rest. And we will do the same with any remaining Al-Arynaar siding with them.

'As to the city, well, removal of the TaiGethen threat will serve to dampen any hope your somewhat reluctant subjects have of a turn-around in their fortunes. Even so, I have a little over five hundred swordsmen, archers and mages at my disposal. Not enough to maintain the peace if there is a concerted effort to rebel. Certainly not enough to help subdue populations in other cities.'

'And so?' said Llyron, shooting a sharp glance at Sildaan.

'We had the budget for the numbers we have and no more,' said Sildaan.

'Or your negotiation skills are not as honed as you led me to believe,' said Llyron.

Garan cleared his throat. 'I have to defend Sildaan here. Her price is ruinous, her bargaining severe. I would not have agreed had it not been for other factors.'

'Which include?' pressed Llyron. 'And will this answer our security question?'

'Yes, in a manner of speaking. Your money is only one way of paying a mercenary. To the man who sees it, the treasure is his when its owner no longer controls it. So my men are happy enough, and I think you expect that. But we need more men or the job will not be completed. So more are coming. Quite a lot more.'

'I beg your pardon?' said Sildaan. 'There is no agreement for this.'

'No, but it is happening anyway.'

'And there is no budget either.'

Garan laughed but his eyes were cold. 'Like I said, to the man who sees it, the treasure is his when its owner no longer controls it.'

The city was almost silent but for the violence flaring between the multiple threads locked together in the harbour master's warehouse. The guards outside did nothing to stop any trouble inside. Little did they care. Moving into full night, the sounds echoed out over the harbour, beyond the walls and out across the Ocean of Gyaam.

Katyett, Merrat and Grafyrre had scouted the harbour quarter and approaches. The area had been all but burned out barring key buildings occupied by the humans. Few could see what the Tai-Gethen could see from their perch on the roof of the warehouse. Even fewer could do anything about it.

'Should we not free all these beneath our feet? Cause some mayhem at the very least.'

'Not tonight, Graf. We have some brief time. Releasing them now would not achieve what we want. Most would be recaptured before the real problem hits, and that helps no one. And the humans would be alerted to the fact that their perimeter security is poor. We need to pick ourselves a time between now and the moment the humans burn this place to the ground.'

'When will that be, Katyett?'

Katyett stared out into the ocean. The moonlight was strong but she didn't really need it to see. A lot of sails were coming. Fifty at least. Perhaps two thousand more men from the north with their muscle and their magic.

'The wind has backed. It's offshore now and likely to remain so for days,' said Katyett. 'They'll be in the harbour in two days, maybe three. It is then that captives like all those beneath us will become mere irritation. Make no mistake. Men have come here to conquer.'

'So what now?' asked Merrat.

'Now we go and do some damage to a guard post or two and relate what we've seen to Pelyn. But more than all of that, we pray Takaar is not dead and that when he arrives, he has all the answers.'

Chapter 30

A more numerous enemy is wasteful and complacent. There is nothing to be despised more than waste.

Takaar's unpredictable state had led them to rush. To ignore just one of the central rules of travelling the rainforest at speed. So basic and so important. Look where you are treading. Auum did not and he stepped on a branch which moved beneath him. Serrin did not and the branch snapped under him.

The Silent Priest's weight was thrown forward but his left leg was trapped in a mesh of undergrowth and root. He twisted as he fell, his knee wrenching sideways, his calf and foot locked in place for a heartbeat too long. His cry was akin to the howl of one of Tual's denizens in distress. He tumbled partway down a rise, sliding to a stop, screaming once again before regaining control of himself.

When Takaar and Auum reached him, he was sitting up. Serrin's breathing was deliberate, deep and slow. His eyes were closed and his mouth was moving, his words of prayer private. His hands were on his knee, probing gently. He winced with almost every touch.

Auum felt an immediate relief that there was no obvious break. The leg was not twisted; there were no lumps beneath the skin indicative of broken bone pressing against the surface. But the damage was obviously severe enough. Swelling had already begun all around the joint. Tendon, ligament, muscle – all would have been torn. It only remained a question of how much delay the injury meant to their journey.

Takaar was already burrowing into the fisherman's bag. The stench of previous contents would attract scavengers from all directions. He fetched out a large pot, untied the lid and scooped a soft green paste onto his fingers.

'Escobilla,' he said by way of explanation and began to rub it gently into the knee. Serrin sighed as the salve penetrated his skin.

'Normally best as a tea you can use to bathe wounds, but you know that already. I've found you can make a paste with careful reduction and endless pounding of leaves. Works better. Gets to the pain faster and it's better at reducing swelling.'

'It works,' managed Serrin. 'Leave it with me.'

'Sorry, my priest. Nice try but we're not leaving you here,' said Auum. 'You can't run and you can't fight. Every predator within five miles will have heard your pain. We'll make you a crutch or a stretcher.'

'No time,' said Serrin.

'A TaiGethen may not leave the helpless to die,' said Auum.

'O paradox,' said Takaar, his expression mischievous and gleeful. 'Leave him helpless to die or delay your journey to our people and so consign how many more of the helpless to death?'

'The Silent are friends of Tual's denizens.' Serrin gasped a breath as he dared to move his damaged leg. 'I will be safe.'

Auum had heard the stories. Silent Priests defended from attack by panthers. Snakes that didn't inject venom when they struck. Scorpions relaxing their tails. He didn't believe them but it was hard not to be swayed by the sheer force of Serrin's faith.

'Strap him to immobilise the knee. Make him a crutch and we must go,' said Takaar. 'He knows. Others' needs are greater than his.'

Auum stared at Takaar, hating his perverse enjoyment of the situation.

'Look at me,' said Serrin.

Auum hesitated, knowing what Serrin was about to say. But he didn't make the Silent Priest repeat himself.

'You know he's right, don't you?' said Serrin.

The forest seemed to have quietened around them and Serrin's quiet voice sounded over-loud in Auum's ears.

'I know he finds my discomfort amusing and presumably feels the same way about your pain.'

'But you know he's right, don't you?' Auum nodded his head fractionally. 'So do as he suggests. I will survive.'

'You understand why I find this difficult,' said Auum.

'I would feel slighted if you didn't. Auum, come closer. I have no desire to exercise my voice any more than I must.'

Auum crouched right in front of his mentor. 'You're going to release me from my duties.'

'I am not so formal,' said Serrin. 'Or stupid. Just listen to me. I believe this accident has happened for a reason.'

Auum couldn't help it. He rolled his eyes and made to turn his head away. Serrin's long-fingered hands caught his cheeks, his fingernails caressing his ears.

'Listen. Yniss is not as passive as you believe and Beeth's root gave beneath me, not you. I feel the hand of Yniss guiding that of Beeth. Change is here. Such change as we have not felt since the end of the War of Bloods. The Silent have felt it most deeply. We have always been uneasy in the company of others, and though I was prepared to travel with you, the pain of what was to come was growing within me.

'And now here I sit, unable to walk, unable to help. For me the decision has been made. For others of my calling, minds are in turmoil and desires clash with obligation. Free them if you find them as I find myself free now.'

Auum shook his head. 'I don't understand.'

'The Silent are changed. I am changed. The rainforest is my home. It is my soul. The place where I will serve Yniss and tend to Tual's creatures and Beeth's root and branch. No longer will I leave the canopy. Not to enter a settlement, not to enter a temple. Not even Aryndeneth. I belong alone. Let me go.'

Auum felt tears edging his eyes. 'If it is what you truly desire.'

Serrin smiled and smoothed Auum's cheeks as he let them go. 'It is. And it is what we all desire if we look within ourselves. Help those you meet to make the choice.'

'Of course.'

'Bless you in your work, Auum. The harmony will prosper while such as you are among its champions. And remember, whatever happens in the cities, the forest belongs to elves who understand harmony, balance and the intertwining of all things.'

Auum leant in and kissed Serrin's lips and eyes. He stood. 'I'd best set about that crutch.'

He turned away before his tears began to spill.

Katyett brought her Tai to the city perimeter for a third night and to a third entry point. Makran's cell ran ahead of them, heading for the guard posts either end of the Ultan bridge before moving onto the farmland before the city proper to clear scout targets for the following night.

Katyett could see them moving along the bamboo shroud that marked the banks of the treacherous piranha- and crocodile-haunted River Ix. She brought Merrat and Grafyrre to a position deep in the long grass to the left of the trodden path to the Ultan.

'We'll run in straight after them. Take the marsh path in.' She turned. 'Pakiir, Faleen, Marack. Wait for us to clear the bridge. Stay hidden. Scout your targets. No combat.'

So far, they had kept their incursions quiet. Killing guards and mages in small numbers to keep the invasion force on edge. Keeping themselves out of sight. Tonight, it all had to change. The wind had backed again, aiding the approaching ships. They would make land some time during the next day. Enemies of the harmony or not, Katyett would not leave elves helpless against humans.

Two guards stood at the near end of the bridge, leaning against one of the main support piles. Great banyan timbers, sunk deep into the ground and carved with vines and leaves climbing the trunk of a tree. Their swords were in their hands and they tested their heft occasionally, swinging the blades from side to side.

They were talking, gesturing and laughing, but their eyes remained fixed on the night beyond the torches and lanterns hung from the bridge. The twittering of night birds and the rasp of myriad insects drowned out their voices. They were keen to show off their nonchalance to each other but there was fear in their bodies.

At the far end of the bridge three guards and a mage were gathered around a cook fire just to the left of the piles. Two, one of them the mage, were seated on logs. The other two stood, looking alternately out along the bridge and into the conversation.

Makran turned and made a hand signal. Katyett gestured back. Makran's Tai broke from cover, three shadows flowing through the grass, graceful as panthers. Heading for the light and the men who had no idea they were about to die. Makran led her Tai towards the mouth of the bridge.

The men had sensed something, perhaps seen slight movements in the grass beyond the circle of light. They came together, swords gripped tighter, staring out. Makran burst onto the path a couple of paces before the first timbers of the bridge. The men backed off. One smiled.

And Makran was engulfed in flame.

The sound of her screams and those of her Tai would live with Katyett for ever. A wall of fire climbed into the air, catching the three

TaiGethen, immolating them in moments. Fire ate into their flesh, scorched the clothes from their backs and melted the iron of their belts and scabbard harnesses.

They staggered on, their momentum carrying them a few dreadful agonised and dying steps forward. Nothing but walking skeletons, screaming their agony, calling for Shorth to give them succour. They collapsed on the bridge. Makran, Katyett thought it was Makran, raised a hand towards them. Katyett thought she heard her sister say 'please'. The men just watched. Offering nothing. Not even a blade to end the torment.

The flames roared unchecked into the sky. Katyett stared at them. No mage had cast this. It was as if it had been waiting in the earth for Makran to trigger. Like a tripwire in the forest to snare a tapir. Death invisible.

'What do we do?' asked Grafyrre.

Katyett turned to her Tai, both with eyes wide with shock. 'Walk only where they walk. Run on the edges. And make the humans pay for what they did to Makran. Marack, your orders stand. Tai, with me.'

Katyett was up and sprinting the next instant. She headed for the bamboo shroud running perpendicular to the end of the bridge, her eyes on the flames, her prayers to Yniss keen with every step she took. Katyett leapt, feet first and horizontal.

She caught a corner of the carved pile and pivoted around it and over the rail, her boots slamming into the back of the nearest guard, propelling him off the bridge to tumble down the slope. He rolled straight into the flames to be consumed like the TaiGethen he had refused to help.

Behind Katyett, Merrat hurdled the rail. She ran the width of the bridge and delivered a left hook to the second guard's jaw. The man's head snapped back. He fell back against the rail and toppled down into the river.

Grafyrre landed on the rail, turned and began to run down its length. Merrat mirrored him. Katyett took the centre. The three remaining guards moved to block the exit, the mage behind them already gesturing in the air. Katyett took a jaqrui from her belt pouch and threw it on the run. The sickle-shaped blade mourned away. It sliced into the sword arm of the centremost guard. He cried out and dropped his weapon, clutching at the blood flowing from the deep clean cut.

At a command from the mage, the guards dropped to a crouch. The air chilled. The mage pushed out his hands. Katyett yelled a warning and fell prone, her momentum setting her rolling, her arms tucked into her chest, fists either side of her neck. Merrat and Grafyrre leapt high as they ran, turning rolls into the sky before flattening their bodies horizontal, arms stretched out to the sides.

The casting howled over Katyett's body. She gasped freezing air. Behind her, wood became thick with ice. She heard the cracking of timbers as moisture froze and expanded within them. She rolled on another turn before slapping her left palm down to push herself up. She came up, still turning, found her feet and strode on. Merrat and Grafyrre landed either side.

Ahead, the guards swallowed, not believing what they had just seen. It was not something they would tell friends or lovers. Katyett pulled out a short blade and swung it two-handed, chopping into the neck of the injured man, feeling the edge grind against bone.

She leapt over his falling body, leaving the sword where it had stuck and closing on the mage. He was trying to form another casting but the fear in him was too great. He held out his hands in supplication. Katyett knocked them aside with her left arm and crashed her right fist into the point of his jaw. He crumpled down and back.

Katyett turned. Merrat and Grafyrre were walking past their victims. Blood dripped from blades. Merrat paused to work Katyett's sword from the neck of her kill. He wiped it on the grass and handed it to her. Katyett glanced back down the bridge. Marack was kneeling by the bodies of Makran and her Tai, praying.

'We need to move. This won't have gone unnoticed,' said Katyett. She nodded at the mage. 'Bring him. He has a lot to answer. Let's go.'

The main road into the city from the bridge drove straight through cleared and cultivated land and passed the river fishing fleet, their jetties, marina and a ramshackle assortment of huts and shelters. They wound their way deep into the maze of buildings and businesses that served the fleet. Boatbuilding and repair yards, sail and oar makers, crab catchers, eateries, inns and the local marketplace.

The humans hadn't been here. It was deserted anyway. Few elves lived here for long and those that did had long run into the forest to seek sanctuary. The maze led on to the Kirith Marsh. Treacherous to any who blundered into it unknowing, but perfect access to the beaches and harbourside if you knew where to tread.

Katyett, her Tai and the groggy mage moved on, their trail already cooling like the blood of their kills.

Chapter 31

If I stand by you in battle, I will die before I let you die. That is my pledge. If we all pledge this, we cannot be defeated.

They saw the western sky light up. The windows of the panorama room on the upper floor of the left arm of Shorth's temple looked directly towards the Ultan. They had been granted the freedom of the upper floor, but this chamber, light and warm, decorated for joy and furnished in luxury, was where they spent almost all of their time.

They were not, Garan said, prisoners. They had the run of the temple, just not the wider city, which remained under total curfew. Indeed he had insisted that the business of the temple carry on as normal, or as close to normal as anything could in the city. It was a partnership for control of Calaius, he said. Balaia's college of magic at Triverne wanted to forge a long-term alliance with the elves of Calaius for mutual benefit. But in the short term that meant control of the country had to pass to the military and magical power of Balaia.

He said.

'TaiGethen,' said Sildaan, feeling a sadness she had not expected. 'I hope they survived that.'

'Why?' said Llyron. 'We're as good as dead anyway.'

'I'd rather die on the blade of an elf than of a human,' said Sildaan. 'At least then we'd know our land was free of man.'

'Such sentiments sound hollow coming from your mouth,' said Llyron. 'And Shorth will be unimpressed.'

'Why are you talking this way?'

Both turned from the window to see Helias wringing his hands as he paced up and down. A performance of cringing anxiety that would not have looked out of place in the Hausolis Playhouse.

'Because, Helias, we have been betrayed by men and I suppose we should have guarded against it,' said Hithuur from a seat as far from the Tuali former Speaker as it was possible to get.

'How could we have done that?' asked Llyron, her face angry at the implied slur.

Sildaan was interested in the answer too, although she was in silent agreement with her fellow priest. Besides the fifteen Senserii, who were elsewhere in the temple and perhaps no longer alive, no professional elven fighters had been approached by the conspirators, let alone recruited.

'You trusted the fact that money would buy loyalty.'

'As it has in the past, yes. What is your point?'

'This place is too rich for human mercenaries to leave with nothing but a few coins to show for the job,' said Hithuur. 'I hate to say it but we should have bought the loyalty of Helias's Tuali reserve militia. A hundred or so angry farmers and sailors would have been handy right now.'

'It doesn't matter,' said Helias. 'None of you are getting it. It just doesn't matter.'

Llyron favoured Helias with a withering glare. 'Because?'

'Because we are where we are, and because we are still in the best negotiating position of any group on Calaius.'

'And I thought by your rather painful display of fear that you, like us, felt us to be prisoners on death row for knowing too much,' said Llyron.

Sildaan, though, was thinking. 'This is a tough country, my priest. I think we should hear the Tuali out.'

Llyron waved a hand and went to recline on a long cushion-covered couch.

'You understand, Sildaan, I knew you would. I'm pacing up and down looking for an angle while you're all talking of certain death and facing the unbound fury of Shorth. And I think I have one.' Helias paused and massaged the sides of his nose with his index fingers. 'Calaius is an impossible country to rule unless by consent. It is too big, too complex and too dangerous outside the cities. I don't believe for one moment that the humans want to rule us for any longer than is absolutely necessary.'

'They've sent another two thousand men. The mercenaries we hired were clearly given to us by this city-of-magic place,' said Sildaan. 'It is an invasion.'

'It is a statement of intent and power,' countered Helias. 'With magic and muscle, we now know they can take our cities as and when they choose. And they can also back any future government with this power. Look at it logically. If you're a Balaian, do you want to live here fighting every day to stay alive, or do you want to enjoy the massive wealth of Calaius using a puppet government?'

Sildaan exchanged glances with Llyron, whose mask of disgust had slipped to one of contempt.

'You want to tithe this whole country to *men*?' she said.

'For now, yes. Look, right now . . . right *now* this is about saving our lives. Tut and look as shocked as you want. Call me a coward. I've no problem with that; I'm just telling the truth. The reason we are alive is that we are useful. The moment that stops, we are dead. The moment we become a threat? Dead.

'So yes, let them set the taxes. Agree to run the economy to deliver. Govern. We already have the system in place to keep the threads working at what we want for how much we want. The thread segregation system is perfect for that. For a few years they'll leave a heavy presence, but when they think they have us in their pockets, they'll reduce and reduce because men are expensive to keep here.

'And all the time we can work to increase our fighting strength. Over time, we can train a whole new army. Men will lose focus on us if we keep sending them their taxes. And as the old ones die and new ones take over, that focus will get ever more blurred. And us? Well, you are immortal; I've got a couple of thousand years left if I'm careful.

'It doesn't matter if it takes a hundred years. Two hundred. We have time. They do not. And when we are strong enough, we simply stop sending them their coin. By that time the elves will be behind us. Their hatred of man will be at such a pitch that they will be baying for conflict. And we will preside over victory. Hate turns to love when slavery turns to freedom.'

Sildaan knew Helias was talking complete sense. She could see both Llyron and Hithuur knew it too, distasteful as it was.

'But before you start there's one big problem out there,' said Hithuur. 'The forest is untameable by us or by man. Never mind what we've been trying to do, it is too vast to police and it is where rebellion will inevitably arise. And then of course there are the TaiGethen and the Silent Priesthood. How do you deal with them?'

Helias spread his arms. 'Hey, I'm a negotiator, not a soldier.

Garan and his people can sort it out. After all, if you want to own the jungle, you have to deal with the predators.'

Katyett pushed the mage in front of them. They were closing on the warehouse. Burned buildings were all around them. Few sounds other than wails and angry shouts could be heard beyond the restless noise of the ocean.

'Shout for help if you want. Run if you desire. Just know that you will die and we will escape and your death will have been a complete waste.'

'What I want is you tell me what you want,' said the mage. He was called Palant. It was at least the tenth time he had rephrased the question. 'Then will I help.'

His elvish was passable. A bit confused but mostly comprehensible. He had a broad bruise growing across his chin and lower jaw and he had several chipped teeth. A headache too, probably, and he kept on working his jaw from side to side to relieve the aching and stiffness.

'You plant those traps of magic – what did you say they are called?'

'Wards.'

'Wards.' The Balaian word sat uncomfortably on Katyett's tongue. 'We need access to the harbour master's warehouse and we don't want to explode before we get there. You will dig them up, or whatever you do.'

'Dis-spell,' said Palant.

'That's why you're in front. You hit the bad stuff first.'

'A fire or ice ward will kill us all,' said Palant.

'You first,' said Merrat. 'Fancy it much?'

Palant shook his head. 'Wards are thick approach south. In buildings walls high.'

'You di – dis – spell them.'

'Why? You me kill any ways.'

'That remains possible,' said Katyett. 'But not as certain as if you don't.'

'No need dis-spell to them,' said Palant. 'No wards on sea side approaches.'

'Oh,' said Katyett, surprised. She took out a knife, clamped a hand over Palant's mouth and slid the blade between his ribs and into his heart. 'Thank you.'

The Tai ran, turning right at the next junction, heading back towards the harbourside. Palant might have been lying but Katyett did not think so. It made partial sense if you thought about it. She supposed there had to be a safe corridor to get people in and out of the area. But to leave every harbour approach clear was careless.

They picked their way through the wreckage of Ynissul businesses that had crammed the docks with life and commerce less than ten days ago. From a vantage point inside a partially collapsed shop, they could see a guard of eighteen soldiers and three mages spread across the front of the warehouse.

Most were gathered around a large timber fire about midway between water and warehouse. Others patrolled in front. The warehouse doors, damaged when Pelyn had made her escape, had been competently patched up. Guards walked up and down the sides of the warehouse. Their attention was not keen. The warehouse had been built for strength and security.

'No one is going near the door,' said Merrat. 'Look.'

She was right. In fact, now they looked, a semicircle of barrels Katyett had assumed were makeshift seats marked a no-go area. The door must have had wards placed on it.

'There goes our first plan,' said Katyett. 'Any ideas?'

'Can a ward be so delicate it triggers by just walking too close?' asked Grafyrre.

'I'd ask Palant but I'm afraid he's a little under the weather,' said Katyett a little sharply. 'We don't know so we don't risk.'

'You misunderstand. I think we need to brief everyone inside before we liberate them. I just want some idea what would trigger whatever it is on the doors. They'll have spun them some story inside. But what's the truth?'

Katyett smiled. 'Fair enough. Well, we can't ask the humans and I still say there's too many to take on in this much space, so let's go and ask our friends, shall we? But let's be careful. We don't know how far up the roof that ward spreads.'

The three TaiGethen moved in cover towards the rear of the warehouse. Palant's information on wards focused their attention. They watched guards approach, stop, turn and head back. Counting paces, marking exact distances and moving with caution.

When they were agreed on a strategy, Katyett led them closer. Precious little noise came from within. Most would be asleep. Katyett was gambling that each thread would have marked its own area and set guards against attack by others. She had no idea how many were within but it had to number thousands.

Cramped. And revolting by now.

The guard was almost at the end of his patrol. He stopped, looked towards the end of the warehouse and turned on his heel. Katyett waited until he had moved away five paces. She beckoned her Tai to follow her. They moved quickly and silently, beginning to climb immediately. The warehouse was made of sturdy timbers strengthened with iron bands and with a pitched roof of slate. It had withstood hurricanes, arson and attempted robbery. The harbour master was proud of his store and maintained it in superb condition.

It all made for an easy climb. Not a rivet was out of place, not a timber was loose. The TaiGethen had swarmed up the wall and onto the roof well before the guard returned. They crawled along to the skylight left partially open by Pelyn. Katyett stuck her head through the opening and withdrew it in the same movement. Her eyes were watering.

'Dear Yniss save us, it reeks in there.'

She took a deep breath and took a second look. The warehouse had been stripped of everything down to the last shelf and rack. The floor space was covered in sleeping bodies. Elves walked to and fro. As she expected, there were distinct gaps between various groups indicating division along thread lines.

At the southern end, with what looked like the less numerous Cefans nearest, were what passed for latrines. A few boxes had been set in a row and had holes knocked in the tops to sit over. The boxes sat on sailcloth which had been tied around them. It was woefully inadequate. Katyett could see pools of urine and excrement at the base of every box. Other pools indicated where some had not bothered to wait for a box to be free, or perhaps could not face sitting where they were supposed to.

Down by the doors there was a single length of rope laid in a semicircle, matching the barrels without. The floor was clear inside this boundary. Katyett scanned the floor quickly. The threads were in rough thread longevity order from door to latrines. To the left of the doors was a small group. No guards. Katyett looked more closely. She counted them. Thirty-four. Covered in sheets.

Katyett withdrew her head. Her expletives surprised even Graf and Merrat.

'They haven't even let them move their dead,' she said and felt sick in the pit of her soul. 'We need to end this. Right now.'

'Can we get down?' asked Merrat.

'It's a couple of jumps but nothing as tricky as crossing the Ix at Taanepol. I'll lead.'

Katyett dropped through the skylight, her hands gripping its edge and hanging briefly before dropping down to the gantry. She scanned its length and the spurs that led off to maintenance points and other skylights around the roof. She cursed quietly. Merrat and Grafyrre joined her.

'Problem?' asked Grafyrre.

'You could say. The ladders are gone.'

The Tai cell looked down on the crowded, stinking warehouse floor.

'How far to the floor – a hundred feet?' said Grafyrre.

'Something like that,' said Katyett. 'But getting down isn't the problem. We can use the roof beams and eaves to get us to the top of the walls and we can drop from there. But look at the walls. That damned blue paint the master's so attached to. Glossy and slippery. You might be TaiGethen but try and climb those.'

'We can speak to them from here,' said Merrat.

'We need to be on the floor with them. Standing aloof is exactly what they hate about us, isn't it?'

'So?'

'So, Graf, I go down to the floor. I talk to them. Then we act. Me from in here, you from outside.'

'You're at high risk down there,' said Grafyrre.

Katyett shrugged. 'I can't help that. But look at them. Who's going to take the first step to attack me, do you think? Tai, we pray.'

They dropped their heads, murmuring two prayers to bless the actions the split cell must take. Katyett prayed for understanding. Grafyrre and Merrat prayed for strength, speed, the darkening of the night and a storm of Gyal's tears. Thunder cracked across the sky.

'Gyal has heard you,' said Katyett.

'You don't believe that,' said Merrat.

'Makes good scripture, doesn't it?'

Katyett laid a hand on each of her friend's heads and then moved off along a spur of the gantry. She reached the end and swung onto the nearest roof timber, moving quickly along it towards the eaves. She dropped to the timber below and made the top of the walls. She eyed the blue paint with distaste. Below her, the thread guards were unaware of the TaiGethen above them.

With a nod to Merrat and Grafyrre, Katyett hung underneath the beam. She swung her legs to give her some pace, let go her hands and dropped. Her feet slapped against the wall and she began to run along the sheer surface, angling sharply down. When her weight overcame her speed, she pushed away, twisted in the air, dropped sixty feet and landed on the balls of her feet, turning a quick roll to absorb the impact.

She came to a stand between the Beethan and Gyalan threads. Guards snapped round. Katyett raised her hands in peace, placed a finger to her lips and walked quickly towards the door of the warehouse. The guards, all unarmed of course, came towards her from all angles. Sense prevailed and they kept silent. Katyett stopped close to the rope barrier. She allowed herself to be surrounded by elves with hate in their eyes and violence in the set of their bodies.

'You can do one of two things,' said Katyett. 'You can kill me right here and now and I will not raise a defence against you. Or you can listen to me and I will save all of your lives. Which is it to be?'

Chapter 32

I do not require you to die for me. I do not want you to die for me. I merely want you to be prepared to die for me.

'They are giving us neither food nor water. They are weakening us. The only thing free here is sleep and we spend most of the time sleeping. What else is there but despair?'

The Beethan *iad* looked exhausted and sick. None of those standing before Katyett looked capable of fighting. The thirst would be maddening, the hunger painful and the boredom dangerous.

'And what of the dead?' asked Katyett, gesturing at the covered bodies. 'How did they die?'

'We had a riot here in the first hours after the doors were closed,' said a Gyalan with bruising across his face and a long cut on his right hand, presumably from fingernails or raking teeth. 'Twenty died. It was over thread hate and rumours about who had what food and water. The others died when they tried to rush the doors to knock them down. It was horrible.'

'What do you mean?'

'Come,' said the Gyalan.

He led Katyett to the bodies. The other guards, five of them, followed at a short distance. The Gyalan stooped and drew the cloak from a body. Katyett took an involuntary step back and glanced up to the gantry where Graf and Merrat looked on. She forced herself to look down again.

It was hard to tell if she was looking at *iad* or *ula*, Gyalan. Cefan, Beethan or Ixii. The corpse had no hair. The scalp was blackened. The face looked as if it had been lashed by a whip of fire. It was slashed and cauterised in twenty places. Ugly, burned scars that had taken both eyes, ripped through lips and nose and pared through to the jawbone.

Though the clothes were largely undamaged, the right hand was burned so deep that Katyett could see the white of finger bones. The left hand was gone entirely. This body had bare feet too. They were blackened and melted. The pain must have been terrible. Katyett knelt and spoke a prayer for the soul to find peace, rest and comfort.

'What did this?' she asked, replacing the cloak and straightening.

'Human magic,' said the Cefan guard, an *ula* with oozing patches in his scalp where his hair had been ripped out. 'Placed on the door. It was like the lightning of Gyal's worst storm of rage. It came from the wood and covered them, jabbing into them, flaying them and setting their flesh on fire. Since then, we haven't fought amongst ourselves and we haven't tried to escape again. There is such fear in here. Most are waiting to die.'

'And you have brought this on us,' said the Beethan. 'The Ynissul invited men to our shores. Here is the result.'

'So take out your fury on me if you really believe that I, Katyett of the TaiGethen, invited those enemies into our homes. The truth is that all of you who cheered the denouncement of Takaar and the shattering of the harmony have rendered us helpless. Standing together, the threads would defeat this enemy. Fighting amongst ourselves makes us weak.

'Ynissul heretics have brought this plague to our shores. The rest of us have allowed it to spread unchecked.'

'You're blaming us?' The Gyalan's voice was raised.

'Voice down!' hissed Katyett. 'I blame all of us, including myself. I did not see betrayal in those I served and loved and I am shamed for that. I blame you because you chose the route of hate of all threads but your own. Because you sought to protect only your own and damn the rest. Because you made it so easy for men to take charge. And do not doubt that they are now in charge of this city.'

'Really?' The Beethan gestured around the warehouse. 'I see no Ynissul here. Nor do I see Apposans and nor do I see Tuali.'

Katyett moved a half-pace towards the Beethan, menacing for the first time since she had dropped amongst them. The Beethan took a full pace back.

'The Ynissul are not here because after they were victimised, brutalised, raped and beaten by elves from every other thread, I had to take them from the city. I wonder how many in here are guilty of crimes, yet I still wish to save you. The Apposans are not here because they were fortunate enough to be warned away and are now in hiding under the canopy.

'The jails are full of Orrans and Ixii, and of your brothers and sisters too. All other elves are subject to curfew and are prisoners in their own homes. And the Tuali are not here because men surrounded them in the Park of Tual and slaughtered four hundred of them while Helias walked with the *cascarg* in another part of the city.

'We are all expendable to humans. We are all suffering. And your hate has made the situation so much worse. And still I wish to save all of you.'

Katyett pointed back into the warehouse. 'Every *ula* and *iad* in here deserves freedom. I have to have your help or most will die. There are more ships coming. Thousands more men will be here tomorrow and it is our belief that they will murder everyone in here when they arrive. You are trouble and they cannot afford to let you live.

'So I stand with you. If you are with me, when the time comes, most of us will breathe fresh air once more. If you are with me, you will go and wake those of you in each thread who command authority and respect and I will tell you what must be done.'

Katyett drew both blades from her scabbards and flipped them, holding them out hilts first.

'If you are not with me, take these blades and end my life now because I have no wish to live among elves with no courage, no belief and no will to survive. And I do not wish to burn.'

There was the most fractional hesitation before the guards exchanged glances and trotted off back to their own peoples. Katyett looked up at Grafyrre and Merrat. She made quick hand signals.

Get Pakiir, Marack, Faleen and Ekuurt. We await you.

Katyett was a powerful force. One elf among thousands should have been swallowed, but the sheer strength of her will had turned a divided mass of desperate elves into a single entity for the moment. And a moment was all she hoped they would need.

Grafyrre and Merrat were in the burned-out shop again. With them were the TaiGethen Katyett had requested, brought back from scouting duties deep in Ysundeneth. All six assessed the dockside. Eighteen soldiers, three mages. The numbers were the same but the atmosphere had changed.

Grafyrre smiled to himself. The humans could feel something and it was making them anxious. They were staring into the night beyond their fire but could see nothing. They were glancing at the doors to the warehouse too, and it was there that their poor senses told them all was not well.

Right on cue the chanting began, and it sent shivers through Grafyrre. Rhythmic clapping accompanied the voices. They sang prayers to Cefu, Gyal, Beeth and even Yniss. Humans flew to their feet or ran back from where they had been standing to gather by the line of barrels. Anxious glances were exchanged. Swords were drawn. The mages came together, standing behind the line of warriors. Orders were barked. A pair of swordsmen ran off down either side of the warehouse.

The volume of the singing grew steadily. Above, the clouds were deep and dark. Lightning flashed in their depths. Rain began to fall, hard and heavy.

'Let us not waste this blessing,' said Grafyrre. 'We'll take the mages. Marack, take Pakiir and Ekuurt as your Tai. Target the swords. Don't move inside the line of barrels. And we need something to batter down the doors from distance. There has to be a mast on the dock somewhere. The master used to keep a dozen in the warehouse. Faleen. Find one. TaiGethen, we move.'

Grafyrre and Merrat tore out onto the harbourside. A moment later, Marack's Tai followed them, moving directly at the warriors. The noise of chant and rain masked their approach. Only belatedly did the men sense their peril. They turned and shouted warnings. Mages began to move, gesturing and muttering as they went.

Running towards the fire, Grafyrre saw Marack's Tai begin their assault. Jaqruis flew out. The soldiers reacted fast. One missed high, a second man deflected his away with his blade and a third man ducked. A jaqrui thudded into the warehouse doors. Sharp white light encased the weapon in a lattice of flashing, spitting energy.

Marack drew both her blades. She raced in towards the line of men. To their right, the mages were still, heads bowed in concentration. Grafyrre powered towards the fire, Merrat by his side. They leapt, turning triple somersaults high over the hissing flames, feet slapping down in a deep puddle right in front of the mage trio.

To a man they flinched and backed off. Grafyrre bared his teeth. His left hand drew the blade from his right-side back scabbard and he chopped the edge through the shoulder of the first mage, crashing through his collar bone and into top of his ribcage. His right hand speared out, straight-fingered, crushing the windpipe of the second.

Merrat kicked the third mage in the gut. He fell back. Merrat turned her body sideways and struck with the base of her left foot, catching the mage under the chin. He lifted from the ground and smacked head first into the stone. Merrat drew a blade and ripped open his throat.

Turning, Grafyrre saw four bodies already on the ground. He saw Pakiir drop and sweep the legs from a swordsman. Ekuurt leapt over Pakiir and landed on the man's chest, driving a blade into his heart. Pakiir jabbed up from his crouched position, his blade slicing into the waist of another. Ekuurt lashed around two-handed, embedding his sword into the gut of a third.

Marack fenced with a skilled swordsman, who launched a swift attack, feinting to strike down and left but reversing his angle and coming in right. Marack blocked the blow and leapt back. The man came on. Marack ducked a blow to the neck and another to the stomach. A third strike came low at her legs. Marack leapt above it, her right foot snapping out and catching the man in the chest. He was knocked back. Marack landed and spun, unwinding a high kick that slammed into the side of her opponent's head. He reeled sideways. Marack stepped in and lodged her blade in his heart.

Ekuurt swayed away from a flailing sword. He balanced instantly and lunged with his right-hand blade. The human deflected it with the dagger in his off hand. Another came to join him. Ekuurt backed away a pace. The two warriors attacked together, blades flashing in left and right. Ekuurt blocked both strikes with his blades. A dagger drove deep into his chest. Blood gushed from his mouth. He fell.

Grafyrre and Merrat joined the fight. Grafyrre dragged his blade across the back of a warrior's thighs. He collapsed in a heap. Grafyrre side-kicked into the face of another. The blade of a third whipped in neck high. Merrat's block deflected it and she followed up with her second blade, opening a deep gash on her enemy's face.

Still the chanting rang out and the rain drummed down. On the doors of the warehouse, though the wood was untouched, the jaqrui had melted and dripped to the stone flags of the harbour, where it spat and cooled in the rain. Grafyrre noted it, ducked a wild sweep and thrust up into the groin of his attacker. The man fell back.

Grafyrre drop-kicked him, both feet slamming into his chest. The man was thrust backwards through the barrel line, his body striking the door. He screamed. White lightning speared to his face, hands, mouth and eyes. It burned the hair from his head and ripped the flesh from his cheeks. His eyes smoked and his last shriek ended in a gout of flame from his throat.

Grafyrre swallowed and turned. One man remained. Brave. He faced the four TaiGethen with his sword ready. He beckoned them on with his free hand. From all around the warehouse the clanging of bells and the flat blare of trumpets erupted. Alarms calling the enemy to the dockside. The man grinned.

'Too late for me. Too late for you as well. Open those doors and bring the whole place down.'

Marack stepped in from the side and sliced his throat with the tip of her blade.

'Bleed,' she said.

'More will be coming,' said Grafyrre. 'We have to get those doors open. Faleen?'

'Over here!' she called, stripping sail cloth from three masts, loose rigging, barrels and crates. Grafyrre was heading towards her when he realised the singing had stopped. He skidded to a halt and ran back to the line of barrels. The rain was still falling in spears, rattling off tile and spatting high off stone, but he thought he could hear a voice.

'Katyett, is that you?' he shouted. 'Katyett!'

Grafyrre edged closer. His eye was distracted by the smouldering corpse slumped in front of the doors. He definitely heard a voice this time. It sounded like a demand to know what was happening.

'Katyett. If you can hear me. The guards are down. We have to break down the doors. Stand well back. Be ready to run. More enemies coming.'

He repeated the message three times. Turning, he saw his brothers and sisters heading his way with the mast of a coastal cutter slung between them. It was rigged for carrying with leather bands nailed to it in four places from which hung leather loops. Grafyrre ran to join them. They had the base of the mast forward.

'Pakiir, Marack. Move back. That set of handles is too close when we hit the doors. Let's hurry. I've asked those inside to stand back.'

'Did they hear you?' asked Merrat.

'We'll find out.'

Grafyrre joined Merrat at the second band. Faleen was on her own on the third with Pakiir and Marack on the last. The mast was heavy and awkward despite the carrying handles. The TaiGethen moved as smoothly as they could towards the doors. The rain had slackened a little but the alarms were still sounding their discordant summons. Time was short.

'Straight in,' said Grafyrre. 'Push hard!'

They upped their pace. The mast knocked against their thighs, the leather handles bit into the palms of their hands. Ten feet of the fifty-foot length of mast was between them and the impact point. Grafyrre put his head down. Three paces later, the mast struck the doors. Timbers creaked. Lightning chased itself across the face of the doors. Splinters flew out and there was a deep dent. But no break.

'Again!'

They backed up ten paces and ran in, slamming the mast base in as near to the original impact as possible. The splinters were bigger and the dent deeper. The flashes of lightning a shade darker.

'Keep it going.'

The alarms all ceased as they prepared to make their third run. The silence was curious, expectant.

'What does that mean?' asked Pakiir.

'Nothing good,' said Merrat. 'Let's go again.'

They ran forward. The mast struck a third time. Door timbers screeched. There was a resounding crack and two of them bent sharply inwards. A splinter as tall as the doors was stripped away. The human magic embedded in the doors spat and lightning writhed around the mast base. When they withdrew, the light kept on spitting and flashing.

'Almost there, Katyett!' called Grafyrre. 'Keep back.'

'Last time?' said Marack.

'Let's hope so.'

They backed up. Lights were approaching, bouncing along in the hands of men running down the sides of the warehouse. Faleen dropped her loop and reached for a sword.

'No,' said Marack. 'We have to get this door open.'

'I can defend you,' said Faleen. 'It's the right thing.'

'Stay close,' said Marack.

The four of them ran hard, Faleen's absence making a considerable difference to the strength and speed they could bring to bear. The mast struck the door firmly. The first men appeared from the left. Faleen ran to intercept. The mast did not break through.

'This is going to take too long!' called Pakiir.

Faleen chopped the sword hand from one warrior, grabbed the lantern from another and dashed it into his face. Flames leapt over the man's face and head. Faleen turned a back flip away as swords came in from left and right. Fourteen had come around the left-hand side of the warehouse.

'Just break it,' said Grafyrre. 'It's all we have to do.'

'How do you know?'

'A feeling. Can't you sense the hold of the magic on the door? It needs the door to be smooth and whole. Back up. Quickly.'

The four TaiGethen moved. Grafyrre glanced left. Faleen ran in, leapt and turned a roll over the front line of warriors, landing behind them and in front of two mages. Her swords rose and fell. Men turned. The shouts were angry and ugly.

'Run, Faleen!' called Merrat.

More men came from the right. Another seven. A mage stepped to one side and began to cast. The swordsmen came at the elves and their battering ram. The TaiGethen began to run again. Merrat was looking right.

'Concentrate,' said Grafyrre.

Merrat punched out with her right hand. A man fell. She didn't break stride.

'Casting!' shouted Pakiir.

The mage had clapped his hands together and opened them with a shout. The men had scattered. A ball of fire rushed across the space. Grafyrre could feel the heat.

'Away!' he shouted. 'Pakiir. Marack!'

The back of the ram hit the ground as the two elves dived out of the path of the circle of fire, brown swept with angry red. Grafyrre and Merrat had some momentum. They ran the last three paces and shoved the ram at the door as hard as they could. It gave a little more and nothing else.

The magical flame struck the tip of the mast and chased along its length. Grafyrre turned.

'Yniss preserve us,' he breathed. 'Merrat, away. Away!'

Grafyrre dropped the mast, ran two paces and threw himself full length away to the left. He saw that Faleen still evaded her enemies, leaping high, sprinting, trying to get them to follow her from the dockside. Grafyrre landed and rolled. The flame touched the doors. Magic collided with magic. The air was sucked past him. In the periphery of his vision, he saw Pakiir stand up.

'NO! Pakiir. Down!'

The door to the warehouse exploded. Grafyrre was picked up by the force of the blast and hurled out and right. He saw Pakiir engulfed by flames. Someone else lying on the ground was immolated in a heartbeat. He prayed it was a man and not Marack.

Flames, ash and wood scoured across the dockside and high into the night sky. Fire rolled out like a wave across the sand, licking down into the sea over the harbour's edge and setting it to steam. Grafyrre landed and rolled, barely under control. The noise of the detonation had deafened him. He drove to his feet. He was fifty yards from where the doors had once been.

And they were gone. Nothing was left of them or the entire front of the warehouse. Flames ate up the frame and were licking back thirty feet along the roof and sides already. The stone flags in front of the warehouse were a carpet of fire, white, orange and brown. Great clouds of smoke billowed out from the doors. An orange and brown glow covered the entrance.

'Katyett,' breathed Grafyrre.

Ignoring the pains in his shoulders, hips, elbows and knees from his landing, Grafyrre sprinted back towards the warehouse. The group of men trying to catch Faleen had been cast all over the stone of the docks. Of Faleen herself there was no sign.

On the other side of the warehouse the men had not been hit by the blast. They were grouped just away from the magical fires etching away at the dock and backing away from Merrat, who had a murderous set to her body and was advancing, her eyes only for the mage.

In front of the warehouse, Grafyrre had to stop. The heat was extraordinary. With every moment, the unquenchable fires consumed more of the building. Flames and smoke were burrowing in under the roof timbers. He could barely see the ruined ground right in front, the place where he wanted Katyett to be able to run to freedom. All she had in there were two short swords and a few jaqrui. Nothing that would trouble the walls enough to make them an emergency exit before the whole place came crashing down. She was trapped.

Grafyrre was short on options. He stood, staring at the inferno covering warehouse, stone and sky. It was two things. A clarion call to every enemy warrior and mage in the city. And it was death to all who were within it, praying to Yniss for a miracle. Grafyrre wondered if they were shouting, whether any of them could hear him. But his ears were ringing and useless and his vision was nothing but glare when he tried to see in.

Grafyrre took a deep breath, trying to calm a sudden racing in his body. The fires were not dying down on the apron, they were gathering force. It had begun to rain again but the only result was the hissing of steam as water collided with fire.

He stepped back, the sheer heat a barrier shoving at him. Part of the side of the warehouse gave way, falling in a shower of burning timbers but revealing nothing more than the gathering firestorm within. Grafyrre looked left. Nothing moved but one shape, hopping from body to body. Faleen.

Grafyrre looked right. Merrat had drawn both blades and was advancing. The enemy wouldn't have seen it but she was favouring her right foot. There was a dark stain on her left thigh. There were four warriors in front of a mage. The latter was doing something. It was he she would target and they knew it.

And the answer, the faintest hope anyway, was right before him. Grafyrre began running and shouting, yelling for Merrat's attention. The roar of the conflagration made a mockery of his efforts. He tore across the space, the fire licking at his feet, his pace keeping him from the worst of the pain. He didn't bother with blades. One way or another, he wouldn't need them.

Merrat attacked and Grafyrre knew the course it would take. The men, of course, did not. She ran for the centre of the quartet, letting them assume she intended to take them head on. Dutifully, they prepared and shifted their positions to strike. A pace before they could land a blow, she fell to the left, rolling around her lower back and hips.

In the same movement she rose to the left of the rightmost soldier, taking the other three out of the game. Merrat backhanded her right-hand blade into the neck of her target. She was already spinning right and her left blade slammed round and down into the shoulder of the next man. Two down.

The others had barely registered her change of angle. The first blocked her straight kick with an arm but it sent him wildly off balance. Her left blade pierced his heart. The fourth and last faced her full on. She dropped to the ground, swept his feet from under him, crabbed forward and buried her right blade in his gut, her left in his chest.

Merrat rose and turned to the mage, who had ceased creating whatever casting had been in his mind. He backed off.

Grafyrre upped his pace. He was screaming Merrat's name but she wasn't hearing him. The word sounded loud inside his own deafened skull, booming and reverberating.

Merrat advanced. She took two quick steps. Grafyrre knew what was coming. Merrat cocked her left-hand blade at her waist and her right-hand blade at her neck. She took the final pace. Grafyrre took off. He stretched out his arms, his right fingers snagging Merrat's jerkin. His left hand caught her waist and spun her. One of her blades still struck out and he heard the mage yelp and grab at his head.

The two TaiGethen tumbled away right in a heap. Merrat was the quicker to react. She balanced on one knee and had a sword ready to strike through his throat until she saw who it was.

'Graf!' she shouted, the word indistinct. 'What are you doing?'

'Trust me,' shouted Grafyrre. 'We need him.'

Merrat scowled. The mage had realised he had been reprieved. He was staring at them, one hand clamped to the side of his face. It looked as if his ear was gone. He was backing away. Merrat pounced on him, bearing him to the ground. Behind them, the roar of the flames intensified. Another part of the warehouse collapsed. Grafyrre could hear screams behind him now. He got to his feet and scrambled over to the mage. The heat was stifling, sucking the air from the sky.

'Put it out,' he shouted into the mage's face. 'Put the fire out.'

The mage stared at him, his face blank and terrified. Grafyrre and Merrat hauled the mage to his feet.

'I know you can understand me. Put this fire out. And I promise I will spare your life.'

'Graf . . .'

'Not now, Merrat. Too much to lose.'

'You will slaughter me like a pig,' said the mage.

'I promise that I will if you don't put this fire out now.'

'I cannot.'

'You use fire,' said Grafyrre. 'Use ice. Try.'

The mage looked past him to the inferno. 'It will not work.'

'Try and I will spare you,' said Grafyrre. 'Don't try and you will burn in your own fire.'

'I—'

'No time. My friends are dying within. Is this why you are here?

To supervise the murder of thousands of helpless elves? Are their crimes worthy of this death? You have a soul as do they. Study it. But do it quickly.' Grafyrre held the mage's gaze. 'I am TaiGethen. You can trust my word. I will spare your life.'

The mage was alone. He might have more help coming but it would not arrive in time. He shook off the elves' hands and stepped forward.

'I will do my best.'

Grafyrre and Merrat stood very close behind him while he prepared. Merrat made a small hand gesture. Grafyrre nodded and Merrat drew a knife and kept it a hair's breadth from the mage's back. The man breathed deeply and held his palms together in front of his face. He whispered a word and opened his palms, fingers pointing down towards the fire.

Just like on the bridge, the air froze. Grafyrre felt the air rushing by him. The mage channelled it out over the fire in front of the warehouse. Ice met fire. A dense fog erupted into the air. Within it, brown and orange sputtered and died. But the warehouse still burned, its timbers still fell and its slates cracked and tumbled.

The mage held his arms out, pushing the freezing wind over the stone apron. Grafyrre twitched his hand. Merrat put her knife away. The fog tattered and dispersed on the breeze and under the pressure of the rainfall. In places, the fire roared back to life but at least there was a path. Grafyrre touched the mage on the shoulder, breaking his concentration.

'Go,' he said. 'Others will not share my mercy.'

The mage took off. Grafyrre ran towards the warehouse.

'Katyett! Come on. Bring them out now. The warehouse won't last!' He ran into the mouth of the ruin. 'Katyett!'

The warehouse was a pit of night choked with smoke. He could make out shapes all over the floor. Roof supports had come down over the first forty feet. Many still burned. The fires along the walls had reached to the last twenty feet or so. Bodies were strewn by the entrance, buried under collapsed wood or burned in the first explosion.

'Katyett!' screamed Grafyrre.

Movement. He could see movement. People approaching at a run. There was a thundering crash from deep within. Fire fell from the roof. Tons of slates slumped down. Elves screamed. Some were engulfed. Those still standing ran. Beethans, Cefans, Orrans and

Gyalans ran past him and out into the open air. Some drew up the moment they felt safe. Others just carried on running away from their prison and back into the city.

Grafyrre searched the crowd for Katyett. His heart tolled in anguish, his breathing was too rapid. He fought to calm himself. The mass was thinning. Those still inside were the wounded, some being helped, most just left to help themselves.

'Come on, come on.'

Right at the back, he saw her. An elf had his arm slung around her shoulder and was leaning hard into her. He was struggling to walk at all. There were burns on his face. Other elves were with them, lending support. Grafyrre ran inside.

'Yniss bless you. Come on. This building is coming down.'

Katyett managed a smile. 'You noticed? What kept you, by the way?'

'I'll tell you later. Pakiir is gone. Eaten by the fire. Faleen is here but I can't see Marack.'

Grafyrre choked.

Katyett released her charge to another and came to his side. She spoke to the thread elves first.

'You know what to do. Hide, run, anything. Don't get in the way of the humans. We will deal with them.'

'Thank you, Katyett,' said one. 'I—'

'No matter. Thank Yniss. And thank the harmony that means I remain in your service.' She turned to Grafyrre and the two of them trotted away from the warehouse entrance to where they met Merrat and Faleen. 'Graf?'

Grafyrre squeezed his eyes shut and tried to remain calm. 'The flame was so hot. Pakiir, he . . . It just consumed him. How can a soul survive such a scourge? We will find nothing of him. He is ash on the wind. Gone.'

'The soul cannot suffer such harm,' said Katyett. 'Shorth will embrace him. The halls of the ancients will welcome him. He will be waiting for us.'

'And Marack?'

Merrat shook her head. The three walked to the harbourside and looked back at the warehouse, seeing its final demise. Thread elves made their way to wherever they wanted to go. Grafyrre could see the lights of torches all over the city.

'We need to go,' said Katyett.

'Before you do, can you help me up?' Grafyrre spun round trying to pick up the direction of the voice. 'Down here.'

'Marack.' Grafyrre dropped to his knees and reached down into the harbour. The relief he felt sent a thrill of cold through his body. 'Odd time for a swim.'

'It wasn't by choice. I was blown so far I thought I'd land on Balaia. Just get me out. It's cold in here and I don't have the energy to float any more.'

'We lost Pakiir and Ekuurt,' said Grafyrre, hauling her up, Faleen and Katyett reaching down to help.

'We'll pray and grieve later,' said Katyett. 'The humans will want revenge. Let's be sure we are ready.'

Chapter 33

If you do one thing for yourself, let it be this. Never let your blade's edge dull.

Garan and Keller watched the boats come in. After last night it had been decided to anchor the fleet offshore. Even the most prodigious leap of the TaiGethen would get only one per cent of the way. Even so, every crewman had been given a bow for his watch.

Behind them, Garan's men picked at the ruins of the warehouse. Most of the bodies were charred beyond recognition. Elves and men were no different when reduced to blackened bone and ash. It was impossible to say how many elves had died around or inside the collapsed building, which was still too hot to check. Garan had lost forty men and his one eyewitness claimed to have seen only five elves fighting.

'How many are coming ashore, did you say?' he asked.

'Two thousand, two hundred and seventeen,' said Keller. 'Think it'll be enough?'

'I was going to ask you the same question.'

'Ystormun is with them.'

'Oh, great. Come to give us the blessing of the One College or just the usual advice on how to conduct an offensive.'

'You're talking about a lord of Triverne,' said Keller sharply.

'Don't get all loyal-to-the-lords with me, Keller. Gods burning, you weren't sent here with me because you're in favour, were you? All the favourites are either disembarking now or safely at home drinking in the beauty of the Blackthorne Mountains and the Triverne Valley.'

'And you knew it was likely one of them would come. This is a significant investment.'

'They're dangerous. Him and his cadre have way too much power and are way too careless with how they go about securing more.'

'There will always be conflict in the ring of towers,' said Keller.

'I was glad to get away from there,' said Garan. 'Couldn't you feel it? Like a poorly shielded fire ward waiting to explode. I worry about what might happen, I really do.'

'Well, you can ask him all about it yourself,' said Keller. 'He's in the first boat.'

And so he was. A tall thin figure in a deep-blue cloak with hood thrown back to reveal a bald pate and hawkish features. His nose was so thin it looked likely to break if he sneezed too hard. His eyes were tiny and set close. His cheekbones were high and prominent like an Ynissul's and his mouth had almost bloodless thin lips set in a perpetual line of contempt.

Garan considered that, in all honesty, he was the best of them. The most liberal. It really could have been much worse. Pamun, for instance. Now there was a real bastard.

'You should remain a few paces back,' said Keller. 'I'll welcome him.'

'If you insist.'

Garan watched the boat approach. Keller walked to the relevant jetty and waited with his arms held across his waist, his fingers linked together. Ystormun stood as the boat approached, his guards and attendants with him. The three pairs of oarsmen slowed their pace and kept the boat level on the placid water. Keller was standing by the steps. Ystormun took one look at him and lifted gently off the deck, his mistwings moving him serenely to the jetty.

'Bloody show-off,' muttered Garan.

The wings were dispelled when his feet touched the ground and he marched past Keller without a second glance. Keller hurried after his master. Garan took a deep breath and felt a shiver pass through him.

'Here we go,' he said.

Ystormun strode up to him, his thin lips pursed so hard they were practically invisible. The frown above his eyes almost closed them.

'My Lord Ystormun,' Garan said. 'Welcome to Calaius.'

'They have put a soldier in charge of our conquest,' said Ystormun, gaze arrowing down past his nose. 'And hence, when the benefactor arrives, he is greeted not by bunting but by smoke, ash and flame and the quite extraordinary odour of burning human flesh. I had heard this city was firmly under your control.'

'We suffered a small attack last night. It has been repelled.'

'An interesting choice of adjective.' Ystormun's voice, at odds with the depth of his chest, was sonorous and powerful, carrying to echo from building and ruin alike. 'I could see the flames from my ship. My Communions suggest a significant problem with a group called the TaiGethen. Is this true?'

Garan stared at Keller, whose eyes were elsewhere.

'I'm not in the business of fabrication. In the context of the city and our control of it, this was a small attack. Successful in that prisoners were released. But these are all ordinary elves broken by internal conflict. They are no danger to our venture. Your informant is right. The TaiGethen are a significant problem.'

Ystormun glanced up at the sky, which was filling with dense, dark cloud.

'It rains a lot here,' said Garan.

'Then we shall seek cover. Where's my carriage?'

'Keller, can you help with that one?' asked Garan. 'Carriages?'

Keller shot Garan a venomous look. Ystormun swung around, his eyebrows already on the rise.

'This is a hot, uncomfortable country,' he said. 'I do not expect to walk or fly when I can sit in comfort. I presume these savages do have carriages, do they?'

'Yes,' said Keller. 'Ornate state carriages in some cases. We had a second attack in the main compound at the temple of Shorth last night. There was significant damage to carriages, oxen and stabling.'

Soldiers and mages were beginning to mass on the docks as boat after boat landed at the many jetties that ran their length. Ystormun watched them for a moment before gesturing Keller and Garan together so that he could address them both.

'How many TaiGethen attacks were there last night?'

'Eight.'

Ystormun paused, the answer clearly not anticipated. 'Eight.'

'They are a persistent thorn,' said Garan.

'And where do they hide?'

'The rainforest is vast.'

'But they cannot fly unless I am mistaken. So they are not deep within it if they can strike here seemingly at will.'

Ystormun looked meaningfully at Garan.

'We are looking for them and we will find them,' said Garan.

'That should reassure me, should it?' snapped Ystormun. 'Which way must I walk through this ludicrous architecture? While I am listening to your incompetence, I feel I should do something useful.'

Keller gestured and they began walking towards the temple piazza. Thunder was rumbling and the first lightning flashed as prelude to a heavy downpour. Garan grimaced and prayed the rain held off. He knew his prayer would be ignored.

'What I want,' said Ystormun, 'is for you to tell me that you know where they are and that you will kill them.'

'And that will come,' said Garan. 'They are not numerous, but they are masters of stealth and concealment. It will take time.'

'Not numerous? Really. How many of them do you estimate are mounting these attacks.'

Garan thought to lie but Keller was already speaking.

'They are a particularly skilled class of warrior. Far better than anything we have seen on Balaia. Assuming our information is accurate, the total number of these people is in the region of ninety. At the moment we believe around thirty are in the vicinity of the city.'

Ystormun closed his eyes and walked on though he had clearly thought to stop. His cheeks had reddened and his fingers, laced in front of him, had tensed. A knuckle cracked.

'How many did you kill last night?' he asked quietly.

'Two definite fatalities on the dock,' said Garan.

'And how many of our people did they kill?'

'In all attacks, fifty-seven.'

'Fifty-seven!' Ystormun's hold on his temper expired. 'That is ten per cent of the advance force. In one night. Bloody hell, Garan, what are you doing here?'

'Securing the city and hunting down our enemies,' said Garan carefully.

'No need to hunt, is there? Apparently. They're coming to us. Seems to me they are doing the hunting. And therefore you are not securing the city. In fact, after last night, are there not more potential problems on the streets not less?'

'We have been holding. Waiting for the main force. Another two thousand soldiers and a hundred-plus mages will make our stranglehold complete.'

'And why should I have confidence in that statement? By my calculations, they'll have killed the lot of us in about fifty days and there'll still be a quarter of them left. Whatever your plans are, they are not good enough. My information suggests your methods are, in the main, weak. You are negotiating with elves, not dominating them. You have made examples of a few in one park one early morning. Where is your strategy for the demonstration of our power?'

Garan moved up alongside Ystormun. Keller stayed a pace or so behind. Meek fool. Garan determined to keep any sense of complaint from his voice.

'I accept that conditions and enemies here have surprised us and that our erstwhile elven allies did not deliver on their promises to hand us the TaiGethen before we had to remove them from authority. But we have doubled our guard on approaches to the city and we have a comprehensive system of wards, both alarm and explosive, as a first line of defence.'

'It isn't working!' screamed Ystormun and now he stopped. 'You're telling me these elves are a different class of fighter to anything we've seen, yet you've set up a defensive perimeter to keep back Wesmen and Rache barbarians. Ridiculous. Must I point out to you that differing enemies require differing tactics?'

'We could lay more wards,' suggested Keller.

Ystormun's gaze drilled so hard into Keller he backed up a pace towards the lord mage's guards, who were trying very hard not to show their amusement at the tormenting of their seniors.

'Did I really pick you for your perceptive qualities? If so I resign my place in the ring. *Differing*. It means other, not the same. You have to stop these bastards *wanting* to get in because it is already clear you won't stop them getting in if they so choose. And once you have done that, you have to go out and drive them away. How are you searching? A couple of mages in the sky and a few scared soldiers in the fringes of the forest?'

Neither Garan nor Keller said anything.

'Then listen,' said Ystormun. 'Here is how you deal with these people.'

And they listened. And when Ystormun was finished he walked away with just his guards for company, the spires of the temple piazza his guide. Keller looked at Garan.

'Do we have any choice?' he asked.

'Not if we want to stay alive,' said Garan.

'It's just going to make them angrier,' said Keller. 'He doesn't understand.'

'He will. Probably by the end of the night, or if not tonight, then tomorrow night, when their rage has had a chance to bake.'

'We have to tell him his error.'

Garan looked askance at Keller. 'Right. Well. I'll buy you a drink when you get back.'

The guards were all gone. There were X-frames hammered into the earth at regular intervals and hanging from each one was an elf. Ordinary civilians. It was this way at the Ultan bridge, at the Apposan crossing, the Ix south bridge and every other entry point.

Forty elves in all, slashed at the gut to let their intestines trail on the ground for animals to feast on while they still lived. Their eyelids removed so that they faced the fierce heat of the sun and the stinging lash of the rain. Their limbs bound tight against the frames, bloodied at wrist and ankle from their desperate, futile struggles to escape. Each had a parchment pinned to the chest. Each parchment carried identical wording.

Katyett led prayers at the Ix bridge before sending her elves to remove all the bodies. They were to be laid out for reclamation. Prayers were to be spoken throughout the night. There would be no attacks. Before she read the parchment she knew that to be the intent of the demonstration. It could be nothing else.

Katyett read the words to Merrat and Grafyrre as they walked back towards the forest and disappeared within, their elven dead dragged behind them until they were beneath the canopy proper. They paused like every night to ensure they weren't being followed.

'This is the hand of an elf,' said Katyett. 'Their betrayal is complete. No mercy for the *cascarg* when this is done. These words are evil.'

'Do we want to hear them?' asked Merrat.

'No but you must. This is what we are up against.' Katyett cleared her throat and read. ' "Elves of the TaiGethen, the fight for Ysundeneth is over, and with it the fight for Calaius. You will make no further incursions into the city. The blood of these forty dead is on your hands. Set foot in the city again and forty times forty will suffer their fate. Kill another soldier or mage and forty times forty times forty will suffer their fate. The life of every elf in this city is yours to save or sacrifice.

' "Furthermore, you will surrender the Ynissul civilians you are protecting and the Al-Arynaar in your midst. Lastly you will surrender yourselves. You have two days. If you have not presented yourselves at Ultan-in-Caeyin at dawn on the third day, we will kill forty elves at every bell and at every fresh drop of rain that falls. Executions will take place outside the temple of Shorth. We are not without mercy. The souls of the dead will have just a short distance to find embrace.

'"There will be no negotiation entered into. You are so warned."'

'Is it signed?' asked Merrat.

'What do you think? And they call us uncivilised. Come on.'

Dawn had come but it was bloodied and sick. Hithuur had barely slept. The sounds of the innocent being dragged from their homes and eviscerated at the borders of the city would haunt him the rest of his life. It was not so much the screams of pain. It was the pleading. And they hadn't been pleading with men for their lives. They had been calling out to Llyron.

Hithuur put on his clothes with deliberate care, hoping to still the nausea he felt throughout his body. He had committed crimes. But they had been for the good of elves. To advance the nation by returning to the way of life they all knew instinctively was the best one. Yes, it had inequality but it had certainty and security. It worked. Yniss knew it worked. But this. This was hideous. And he had helped perpetrate it. It had to stop. It had to.

Hithuur walked from his room and walked the short distance to the panoramic chamber where he hoped to find Llyron and Sildaan. He could hear Llyron's voice before he put his hand on the latch. He paused to listen. Helias was in there. Sildaan too. So were men. Garan. And the gaunt mage lord who despised them all and who smelled so very dangerous. Hithuur took his hand from the latch.

'. . . but you could not give me the TaiGethen,' said Garan.

'I needed time,' said Llyron. 'And I would have delivered them to you.'

'Time is irrelevant. Action produces results, as I have proved,' hissed the mage lord, Ystormun. His elvish was very accurate, if a little accented. 'I have removed their capacity to strike.'

Sildaan choked back a laugh.

'You have done no such thing. They will not surrender, as you believe. They will worry about how to get to you without you murdering thousands of their people, but if they have to sacrifice every elven soul in Ysundeneth to get to you, that is exactly what they will do. The only difference now is that they won't just kill you, they'll rip out your heart and show it to you while it still beats.'

The room fell silent. Hithuur fancied he could feel the chill through the closed door. Fear oozed through the timbers and into his heart. He shuddered, forcing himself not to back away.

'You exaggerate,' said Ystormun eventually, his voice cold and malevolent. 'And your melodrama does you no credit. The TaiGethen will be eliminated. No elf, however quick, is immune to magic. And I am very, very good at magic.'

'I merely wanted to warn you that they will come for you,' said Sildaan.

'Then let them come,' snapped Ystormun. 'And let them burn. Enough. Why am I wasting my breath talking to you? Now then, Helias, isn't it?'

'My lord Ystormun,' said Helias. 'What is your wish?'

Hithuur shook his head. 'Snake,' he whispered.

'Your proposals have merit and we will discuss them at greater length. The fewer the moments I must remain here, the better my mood will be. But there are more pressing matters. Tell me, Helias, which of your . . . threads, is it? Threads, yes. Which of your threads are of use to me and which are not?'

'I beg your pardon, my lord?' asked Helias.

'It is a simple process,' said Ystormun.

Outside in the corridor, Hithuur felt a slick of cold sweat over his body.

'I don't—' began Llyron.

'I am addressing another,' said Ystormun. 'Be seated. One by one, Helias. Let's begin with the, ummm, Ynissul, they call themselves. Priests and warriors, I understand. What about the rest? Do they work? Can they create wealth and produce resources for Balaia? For me?'

There was a silence. Helias weighing up his words. Hithuur prayed he spoke wisely. He did not.

'They are traditionally the ruling class. Most are business owners. Employers. Not labourers. A very strong priesthood and warrior ethic.'

'See? Easy,' said Ystormun, his voice laden with judgement. 'There is a new ruling class. And I am at its head. The Ynissul are super-fluous, barring their priests. Worse, they provide bodies for the TaiGethen order. It seems to me their existence causes more trouble than it solves. Garan. Eliminate them.'

'You cannot do that!' stormed Llyron.

There was the sound of a hand slapping a face.

'You will discover, *Ynissul*, that I can do whatever I choose.'

Sildaan snorted. 'You don't even know where they are.'

'Wrong again,' said Ystormun. 'How stupid you truly are. Moving on. There's a long list of threads, isn't there? So let's get down to business. Who lives and who dies?'

Outside, Hithuur fought down a rising panic.

'What have I done?' he whispered.

He listened further and his soul cried.

Chapter 34

A warrior with a clear mind lives longer than one remembering the glories of yesterday.

Over the course of a day they emerged from the deep shadow of the canopy and into the dappled sunlight that fell on the staging camp when the rain clouds parted. The Ynissul shouted welcome and broke into spontaneous applause that clearly unsettled the Tai-Gethen and Silent, who were wholly unused to anything beyond the solitude of the rainforest.

Katyett stood at the edge of the covered area, where her makeshift command post was set up, and prayed with each cell, kissing eyes and lips, kneeling in silence and blessing Yniss for the meeting. Her heart swelled at sight of them. Tall, graceful Ynissul, swords across their backs, light leathers and shirts of green and brown, soft boots, close-cropped or shaven heads and camouflaged faces.

She knew each TaiGethen by name, each cell leader by touch and scent too. Out in the forest they had left their work, leaving the sanctity of the canopy vulnerable to attack. But they were here to stop the rape of their land by a plague of men, and all accepted this new task from Yniss with stoicism and determination.

There was little talk beyond the words of welcome and the low voices of those gladdened to see brothers and sisters after long periods separated by the vastness of the forest. Katyett felt the warmth of the gathering and the sadness of its inadequacy. In the finer days of Hausolis three thousand and more TaiGethen had swelled the order. Now, if everybody not assumed lost or known to have fallen attended the muster, eighty-one, making up twenty-seven cells, would stand here. And out there somewhere were twenty of the Silent with their bodyguards.

Still, there was formidable skill and experience among those standing uncomfortably under the glare of the Ynissul civilians' concerted gaze. Quillar, Thrynn, Acclan, Oryaal, Illast, Kerryn, Dravyn, Corsaar, Estok. All veterans of the war against the Garonin. Tai cell leaders she would trust with her life.

With the muster past sixty, making twenty full TaiGethen cells, the first of the Silent Priests entered the camp with his TaiGethen body-guard. The Ynissul packing the camp stared in mute respect. None would have ever seen a Silent, the arm of the priesthood that never entered a city, never left the canopy. Face and body painted white, he wore just a loincloth and had bare feet and sharpened teeth and nails. Frightening to the young, awe-inspiring to the adult.

It was Sikaant with Ulysan. Sikaant moved as if he was gliding. Knots of Ynissul parted like the grass before him as he made his way to Katyett. She came forward to meet him. Sikaant laid a hand on either cheek and drew her head forward, kissing her brow and the lids of her eyes.

'We are blessed by your presence, Priest Sikaant.'

Sikaant nodded. Katyett met his gaze and shuddered.

'What have you seen?' she asked.

'Too much,' he said. 'Prayer.'

Every TaiGethen knelt, one hand to the earth, one crabbed to-wards the sky. The Ynissul followed their lead. Silence swept the camp. Sikaant's voice, broken and rough, echoed through the trees and from the walls of the dormitories.

'Shorth embraces our souls. Evil walks the forest. With your bless-ing, Yniss, we will destroy it. Guide our hands, smooth our path. Prepare us. Sikaant asks this.'

'Thank you, Sikaant. Any word on the rest of the Silent?'

Sikaant shook his head.

'Few will come,' said Ulysan, a young TaiGethen, reserved and deadly. 'You know what happened at Aryndeneth?'

Katyett nodded. 'Priest Serrin has been here.'

'Priest Sikaant was there when the temple was attacked.'

Katyett sighed and offered her hands to Sikaant. The Silent Priest took them.

'Then you've seen what we have. I'm sorry.'

'Our temple is defiled,' he said.

'Yes, and we will scour it. I promise you that.' Katyett turned back to Ulysan. 'Tell me, what else have you seen as you travelled here?'

Ulysan wiped a hand over his chin, smearing his camouflage. 'Stories have spread. Trust in the TaiGethen and the Silent has gone.

Most won't talk to us. Some wouldn't even let us sit at their fires. There is much to do to restore the forest to balance.'

Katyett turned to her warriors. 'The forest is failing. But before we restore it, we must sweep away the disease that besets our capital city. *Cascarg* Ynissul and men from the north. The betrayal goes to the highest level of the priesthood and government of our land. To Llyron and Helias. We can trust only ourselves and the Silent. But we must be careful. The men have brought with them a power that we cannot defend against. I have seen it. Sikaant has seen it. It is more deadly than the blade of a TaiGethen.'

Katyett held up a hand to still the murmurs.

'And there is one thing more. Priest Serrin and Auum are searching for Takaar. If he is alive, he is coming.'

'No, no, no, no.'

Auum stopped again. Takaar was crouching, leaning his head against a tree wrapped in strangler vine. The closer they had come to the staging camp, the more Takaar had drawn into himself. His other voice spoke to him with increasing frequency and increasing authority. Doubt reigned.

'If I step up there, I will be cast down. Stoned. Murdered. I don't care what you say. I am what you say I am. What you've always said I am. I will not die that way. I will choose. You will not push me.'

'Takaar,' said Auum quietly, kneeling beside him. 'He poisons you. Look into your heart and your soul. Your people need you. I need you.'

Takaar stared at him. 'Of course you would say that. And he says you poison me. I'm travelling with two people and neither of you is speaking the truth.'

'The difference is that I am not forcing you to go anywhere. What you do is your choice, what you believe. One of us appears to be encouraging your suicide. Why would someone do that unless they wanted to do you harm?'

'But I deserve to die,' said Takaar, his face earnest, his hands pressed hard together. 'I am a betrayer, a coward.'

Auum fought for the right words. 'You spent your whole life in the service of Yniss and the elves of every thread. You saved countless lives. The peace of a millennium is your doing. You are no betrayer.'

'But I am a coward. I ran. Tens of thousands died. You know. You were there.'

'I know that, without you, the death toll would have been far greater. I know that, without you, we would have cracked and run twenty years before we did.'

Takaar put a hand to Auum's cheek. 'You are kind. But I can hear them from here. And they hate me. All of them. Why do the other TaiGethen not come close?'

Auum paused. They were less than five miles from the camp but certainly not within earshot. Other TaiGethen were moving towards the muster but Auum had chosen a path that would avoid all of them.

'The TaiGethen respect your need for peace as you travel. As do I. None will approach unless you ask it. And the Ynissul await you. They hold hate but it is not for you. It is for those who have committed crimes against them in Ysundeneth these past days. Your coming will give them faith that they can return to their lives.'

Takaar shook his head. 'I cannot carry that burden. I don't want their faith. Yes, you're right. Hate is easier to face. Hate does not require courage and broad shoulders. I know. I shouldn't have come. I will not lead.'

Auum filtered Takaar's words for those he assumed to be directed at him. 'No one will expect you to lead. But come. See the plight of your people. Advise us. Then go if you want to. Surely you still love those who live under the guidance of Yniss? Even if they do profess hate, which the Ynissul do not.'

'I cannot face so many. The smell of people that close. The crying of their souls. It will hurt my ears.'

Auum held out a hand. 'I am TaiGethen. And I will protect you, Takaar. In your heart you know you can trust me. Please. Come and look. Do that for your brothers and sisters.'

'He doesn't force me. His hand is held out to aid me. It is not to bind me. Stop. Your words are meaningless. There is no cliff from which to jump. I will go a little further. Then we shall see.'

Takaar reached out and grasped Auum's hand, pulling himself upright.

'I will not let you down.'

'I used to say that too,' said Takaar.

Auum trotted off in a northerly direction, looking to come to the camp via the old western trail. There would be none of it left now of course, but the ground was sure and it was unlikely they'd be seen by any but the outward scouts until they were close to their destination.

The first of the morning rains began to fall. A sharp downpour that rattled and cascaded off the canopy. Tual's denizens were in full voice above. Birds and mammals, lizards and frogs providing a stunning backing to Gyal's tears. Auum knew he should have been proud to have brought Takaar this far but he couldn't shake the feeling that he had not done enough work on the fallen hero's fragile emotional state. He found himself anxious when he imagined their entrance into the camp. Funny thing. In the time before he found Takaar, he had seen faces full of hope, cheering and smiles. Strength and purpose and determination. Too often in the latter days, his visions were of disdain, disappointment and sadness. Shrugged shoulders, tears of desperation and the fading of last hope.

Auum shook his head. The rain helped to clear his mind and he upped his pace. Takaar was in his shadow, moving with that effortlessness that Auum did not understand. It had something to do with his closeness to the lines of energy he could sense in the earth. Auum wondered if all the TaiGethen shouldn't spend a decade alone with nothing but the clothes on their backs, their weapons and the bounty of the rainforest. To survive, to learn and to become genuinely one with the land they were sworn to protect. A thrill swept through him. To be alone. No priest, no Tai cell.

Takaar heard the voices of the Ynissul before Auum. His hearing was extraordinary. Auum doubted there was a beast in the forest with a keener sense. Takaar had put his hand on Auum's shoulder and the two of them stopped, crouching in deep undergrowth along the banks of a stream that bordered the camp on two sides.

'Some are bathing,' said Takaar. 'And there is much chatter in the camp. Plainly they are not pressed by our enemies.'

'Men are scared of the forest,' said Auum. 'They cannot pierce it and they don't understand it.'

'Don't be so sure. If what I felt from the city is an extension of their power, they might come into the canopy with fresh impetus and powerful weapons. We cannot afford to be taken by surprise.'

'With Katyett leading us, that won't happen. And now you're here too.'

Auum looked across at Takaar and his heart fell. He had been worried that the sound of voices might trigger the perverse response that had followed his swim from the boat. This was almost as bad. Takaar's hands were fidgeting. He scratched at his palms, rubbed his hands together, cleaned under his nails, laced and unlaced his fingers. His eyes were hooded and his face was crawling with nervousness.

'Of course I can't go in there. It isn't fear of what they will say. It isn't. I knew you'd imply that. I need to prepare. To be ready to face so many after so long alone.' He looked at Auum, the relief of a reason on his face. 'That's it. I need to prepare.'

'Takaar, I don't think we have time for—'

'Get down,' hissed Takaar

Takaar grabbed Auum's shoulder and the two of them lay prone. Not far to their right, a matter of a few yards, a mage melted into view. Other humans moved up around him. There were nine in all, moving with impressive quiet and with an easy stride. These were not ordinary soldiers nor yet like those Auum had met near Takaar's hiding place. They were headed towards the stream and the sounds of bathing, thence to the camp.

Auum made to move after them but found Takaar's hand keeping him still. Auum looked at Takaar. The nervousness was gone and in his eyes was all the focus of old combat back on Hausolis.

'They are too many, too well spread and too skilled. Follow but do not strike yet. They mean to uncover the whereabouts of the Ynissul. We can't allow them to escape with that knowledge.'

'They'll kill those at the stream,' whispered Auum.

'In all things there is a price. Don't quiz me on why I know that so well.'

One of them managed to scream but it was cut off abruptly. Katyett flew to her feet, her blades in her hands, and tore through the camp, hurdling Ynissul civilians. Every head had turned towards the desperate terrified sound.

'Tai, with me. Pelyn bring ten. Spread a line across the edge of the canopy. Marack, Faleen, guard our rear. We're attacked.'

Katyett raced past the last of the dormitories. Behind her, her TaiGethen were ringing the camp and spreading through the fearful civilians. Eighty stood with her now. And fifteen Silent Priests. The muster was all but complete.

She entered the canopy and slowed. Merrat and Grafyrre were at her shoulders. She indicated: spread out. Her eyes adjusted instantly to the light conditions and she searched the undergrowth for signs of disturbance. The scream had come from the stream. Either the bathing area or a little upstream where water was gathered. A look right and back told her Marack and Faleen were on station. Pelyn would already have set her line. Hers was the blade most itching for fresh action. It was why Katyett had not allowed her back into the city. Pelyn was prey to thoughts of revenge and, good as she was, she didn't have the speed or the skill of a TaiGethen.

The foliage here was not as dense as in much of the forest. The stream wound a slow course east to west and had gentle sides where vegetation grew and overhung the water, giving cover to any of Tual's denizens who chose to use it. But on the water's edge there was a silt bank, wide from countless years of deposits as the stream rounded a wide bend.

Anyone who stood there was exposed. Katyett cursed herself that she had been too trusting of human incompetence. Either that or someone had been followed back from the city when they had cut down the murdered forty.

Movement. Directly ahead. Katyett held up a hand, fingers straight. Merrat and Grafyrre stilled. None wore camouflage paint on their faces. It frightened people in the camp and there had been no time when the scream sounded. Katyett felt naked without it. Exposed and vulnerable. She tucked into a broad-leaved plant.

Two men moved up, their footfalls careful and all but silent. They breasted through the foliage, their blades held down, not used for hacking a path. They were about thirty yards distant. Further right, there were two more. Left, two more. Hard to see. Their cloaks were dark green and their hands covered with black gloves. Their faces were dark with beards and long hair.

'Pairs,' whispered Grafyrre, crouched at her side. 'That is a weakness.'

'And they are walking too far apart to defend one another. They appear competent but that is a basic error. We'll take the middle pair. Mop up the rest if they run away. Pelyn and Marack can have them otherwise. Tai, we move.'

Katyett had identified the strike point. A tapir trail led through dying brush leaving the slightest of openings and plenty of room. She moved silently forward, her eyes never wavering from her target. Merrat was two yards to her right, Grafyrre very close on her left. The men had not seen their approach.

Katyett broke cover five yards from the first warrior. He reacted quickly, calling out and bringing his sword to ready. A jaqrui whined past his head, thudding into a tree just behind him. He twitched reflexively. Katyett leapt, bringing her knees to her chest and moving her blades out, tucking her elbows in. The man recovered, tried to raise a guard.

Katyett sliced down with her left blade, beating his sword aside. She slashed the right blade across his face. He ducked but the edge caught the top of his head, thudding into his skull above his ear. He fell sideways. Katyett landed, levering the blade clear. Merrat was sprinting at the other man. A third blinked into view from absolutely nowhere. He was ten paces away, his back to a tree. His arms and mouth were moving.

'Mage!' shouted Katyett.

She ran at him. He cast. Katyett felt as if she had been hit with a tree trunk. An invisible force caught her in the chest, spinning her aside to tumble into a thorn bush. Birds scattered. The mage moved his arms in sweeping motions. Brush and branch were bent and broken, flattened and crushed in the path of the casting. Trees shuddered.

'Get beside him,' Katyett called, moving again. 'Graf, move behind trees.'

Merrat and the other warrior had squared up. He was a quick swordsman but he would not be quick enough. Blade and dagger were held in either hand. Merrat chose two short blades. She fenced easily. The man would not know of course that her deadliest weapons were her feet.

Grafyrre was tracking left. The mage drew in his arms, trying to watch them both. From the right, more movement. Another pair of warriors coming in. Presumably there was another mage with them. The movement was mirrored the other side, behind Grafyrre.

'Watch your rear, Graf. Left flank pair on the way too.'

The mage in front of her punched out his arms again. Katyett was ready, ducking behind a thick banyan trunk. The mage repeated the move, thrusting out towards Grafyrre this time. Katyett moved in.

'Keep him guessing,' said Grafyrre. 'I—'

Grafyrre was projected forward to slam into the ground not three yards from their target mage. Katyett stared left. Two warriors flanking another mage. Advancing fast. Grafyrre was stunned, unable to get up.

'Merrat, to me. Quickly.'

Katyett dodged behind another tree. The casting rattled its branches and dislodged leaf, twig and Tual's denizens by the dozen.

Katyett dived right. The mage tried to track her movement. The trio of enemies were nearly on Grafyrre. Katyett dropped a blade, took out a jaqrui and threw it. The blade whispered through the air, carving into the gut of one of the soldiers.

Grafyrre was moving but groggy. The mage drew in his arms, meaning to crush Graf with his casting. He smiled at Katyett. He died with the smile still stamped on his face, Merrat's blade tearing out his throat.

'Merrat, behind. Take the others.'

Katyett checked Grafyrre and stood in front of him, facing the two humans. Mage and soldier. The mage held his casting close. The soldier moved warily, sword held out, gripped in both hands. Neither of them wanted to die. Both knew Grafyrre was vulnerable and she couldn't take them both at once.

The humans split, the mage to the left, warrior to the right. The mage was looking for clear space to push out his casting again. Around the next tree and he would have clear line of sight. Katyett followed him with her eyes while keeping a blade pointing at the swordsman. She could hear fighting from close behind her. Merrat had found the others. Katyett made her choice.

She passed her blade to her right hand. In the same move Katyett grabbed a jaqrui and threw it at the soldier. She dived over the prone form of Grafyrre, rolled to her feet and stabbed up. The mage gasped as the blade split his groin and buried in his gut.

Katyett turned and dived back, leaving her blade where it was. The jaqrui had missed. The soldier was running at Grafyrre. Katyett dragged a knife from her belt. She was going to be a heartbeat too late. The warrior raised his blade to strike down. Katyett dived across Grafyrre, meaning to take the blow. It never came.

Katyett heard a thud. She turned her head. It was the sound of the warrior slumping to his knees. His weapon fell from his hands. He stared at nothing, blood flooding from his mouth and over his chest. He reached towards his back and fell to his side.

Behind him, another figure stood. Katyett stared at him. He reached out a hand and she took it, allowing him to help her stand. Katyett took her hand back. She swallowed.

'Hello, Katyett,' said Takaar.

Chapter 35

Grieving for time lost is a task with no end. Do not begin it in the first place.

Katyett had to get her mind and body into some form of order. She turned away from Takaar, from her shock at seeing him standing there and the shock of his appearance. Dishevelled, hollow-eyed but still him. Still so powerful and beautiful. She looked down at Grafyrre and helped him to a sitting position.

'Ummm. Graf. Anything broken?' she asked, a tremor in her voice. She was desperate to turn to check if Takaar was a mirage but forced herself to focus on her Tai. 'Anything twisted?'

Grafyrre shook his head. 'Just a few bruises.'

'Good. Take your time getting up. He is here.'

'He?' asked Grafyrre. He looked at Katyett and knew.

Katyett turned. Auum handed her two blades and a jaqrui. All hastily cleaned. Katyett nodded her thanks and stowed her weapons, studiously avoiding Takaar's gaze. She had no idea what to say or what to do. But she couldn't just ignore him where he stood, waiting for her.

'Your skill and bravery are even finer than I remember,' said Takaar, his face solemn, his stance awkward. He handed his blade to Auum, who cleaned it on the cloak of a dead human. 'I'm glad Yniss has spared you to lead the TaiGethen.'

Katyett flew at Takaar, cannoning into him and bearing him to the ground, where she knelt astride him, shaking him by the collars of his tatty leather.

'I shouldn't have had to, should I?' she screamed into his face. 'Where were you? Ten years you left me alone. Ten years with the harmony fading and hate growing. Didn't you feel it? Stuck out there with nothing to do but sense the fading all around you? You, who said you held the harmony in your body as surely as you did your own heart? Well? Or were you so drowned by your own remorse that you had no room for anyone or anything else? We followed you. We believed in you. We loved you.'

Katyett let him go and sat back so he could get up if he wanted.

'We still do,' she whispered.

Katyett felt Grafyrre's hands on her shoulders, so tense they seemed like rocks. Takaar scuttled away, his face a picture of confusion and fear. Auum shook his head at her and went over to him, tried to calm him.

'Told me it was wrong and I didn't listen,' said Takaar. His hands writhed across one another.

'Did you hear her?' asked Auum. 'She still believes in you. Still loves you.'

'Not. No,' said Takaar. 'I will not do it! Don't try to push me. You think me weak. Ten years and still you can't see my strength has never cracked under your constant wheedling. Let me be. Auum, why do they test me? Why do they stare? I have no place to see out. I can't. Where are the humans?'

'All are dead,' said Auum. 'And you saved a life. Katyett's life.'

Takaar frowned and muttered to himself. Katyett couldn't make out the words. Auum sighed and leant back, waiting. Katyett had her hand over her mouth. Takaar's words made no sense. His reaction was that of a frightened child retreating from a violent parent. He was hugging himself now, his knees drawn up hard against his chest.

Katyett stood, feeling the companionship of her Tai around her. She could not calm her heart or her breathing. She felt a little faint and nauseous. Both Merrat and Grafyrre put arms around her, steadying her.

'No one needs me,' said Takaar and he looked to his left at nothing but rainforest vegetation. 'You know full well why I came here. It was to prove to you that I was not under your control. That I could act on my own. It has hurt you, hasn't it? Not having me on the edge of the cliff with your hands on my back ready to push. I would laugh in your face but laughter eludes me.'

'Who—' began Katyett.

'Later,' said Auum. 'It's complicated.'

'It's not complicated at all,' said Takaar. 'Auum ignores our companion. I hope you won't be so rude.'

Katyett was reprieved from the necessity of a response by Pelyn breasting into the small clearing. She didn't notice Takaar or Auum.

'We've got a problem,' she said.

'How right you are,' said Katyett.

'What?'

Katyett pointed across. Pelyn looked over at Takaar. She caught her breath and tensed. Katyett watched emotions she recognised very well pass across her face. She swallowed and turned back to Katyett. Her eyes were dry but there was a tautness in her face and a tremble in her voice.

'Um. Faleen's tai have taken down another three men across the camp. They're getting closer, quartering the forest. It's only a matter of time before we are overflown.'

'Yniss, spare me. We don't need this,' said Katyett, reaching out a hand of comfort, which Pelyn took and squeezed briefly before dropping.

'They'll have found our base before nightfall at this rate. We need to be ready. We're due to surrender at dawn as it is.'

'Surrender. Right. I'll eat my own jaqrui pouch first. As for ready, I'm not sure that's possible. How close are the flyers? We can take out the land scouts but those damned flying mages are the real problem.'

Pelyn considered. 'It's not as if they can see much through the canopy. They're looking for partial clearings like this. They won't see it until they come over the hills south or around the tall slopes north. And they are close to those, but they have to keep changing scouts, like they get tired or something, or have done their spell. If our luck turns, the next one could find us before we eat again. Time to get bows up to the canopy roof?'

'Don't ever speak to me like that! You don't even know these people. How can you judge them?'

Takaar's voice split the relative calm. Pelyn flinched violently, her concentration on her task broken. She made to walk to Takaar but seemed unable to decide if it was a good idea.

'Maybe you can calm him. I didn't do a very good job,' said Katyett.

'What did you do, punch him?'

'No, I shouted at him while banging his head against the ground.'

Pelyn snorted back a laugh. Takaar's head snapped up and he scrambled to his feet. He shook off Auum's hand and walked forward a couple of paces.

'Pelyn, your laughter has been lost to me for too long.'

Katyett watched Pelyn and saw a mirror of herself. Loss, confusion. Fury. Exhilaration.

'I can't think of a single thing to say,' said Pelyn. 'After all this time. Pathetic, isn't it? And I replayed this moment so many times. But I thought you dead. Sometimes I wanted you dead. I was ready for you to be dead.'

'There are a thousand ways to die in this rainforest, did you know that?'

'What does that – ?'

'I investigated many of them, you know.' Takaar turned and beckoned Auum to him. 'Here are some. Ways to kill a thousand men. But we need to be close. Yes, as close as that, and we may smell their sweat, but that is a price worth paying to smell their mouldering corpses the day after, is it not? Hmm. I win again.'

Pelyn turned to Katyett, shaking her head in confusion.

'I think he has voices in his head, ' Katyett said.

'Right.'

'And we don't have time to pander to him. Say something. Just don't bang his head on the ground.'

Pelyn made a face. 'I'll try not to.'

'And be tactful,' said Katyett. 'He's fragile. Odd.'

Pelyn nodded. 'Takaar, a moment, please?'

Takaar was searching through a stitched leather bag from which the strong odour of fish billowed out. He made a triumphant sound and pulled out a clay pot with a wooden stopper in it. He bounced it from hand to hand.

'Be careful with that,' said Auum.

'In here is the death of thousands. Thousands upon thousands more, if we go harvesting.' Takaar's eyes gleamed with something akin to zeal. 'You don't think I'm right in the head, do you, Pelyn?'

'That wasn't what I wanted to talk to you about,' said Pelyn carefully. 'Takaar, we have little time.'

'The men are coming. They will unleash a storm on this forest that we may not survive. And I may not lead. Do not ask that of me. There, satisfied that my pride is under control?'

'I'm not asking you to lead us,' said Pelyn. Takaar looked crestfallen, as if he were about to burst into tears. 'But we do need your help. Will you help us?'

Takaar clicked his tongue in his mouth. He sucked in air over his teeth and shook his head rapidly. Katyett felt sorry for him. Sorry for all of them. She'd placed so much hope on Takaar and here he was, barely clinging on to sanity if he was actually clinging on at all.

'A cloak with a hood,' he said abruptly.

'You want one?'

'Evidently. We cannot encumber ourselves further with my being recognised by others, can we?'

There was relief in Pelyn's posture. 'No, no, of course not. Perhaps one of the dead humans . . .'

'Ideal.'

Katyett frowned. They were taking a huge risk involving him. Merrat was already unhooking one of the light traveller's cloaks from a dead mage. She handed it to Pelyn, who passed it on to Takaar.

'Good.' Takaar set off towards the camp, the TaiGethen and Pelyn trailing in his wake. Auum fell in beside Katyett. 'Now then. You mentioned being overflown. How is that possible? I must see this for myself. Auum, put this away.'

The clay pot was tossed casually over his head. Auum snapped out a hand and caught it. He held it carefully for a while before returning it to the sack slung over his shoulder.

'What's in there?' asked Katyett.

'The pot or the sack?'

'Well both, but let's start with the pot.'

'Yellow-backed-frog poison. Takaar says they secrete it from their skin. Touch it and die. Put it on the end of an arrow or something and kill your enemies very quickly.'

Katyett raised her eyebrows. 'He's *harvested* the stuff? Aren't we taught just never to touch one?'

'That was the guts of my training on the subject. But Takaar, as he is very fond of saying, has had ten years with little else to do but study his guilt and all the ways to end his life should he be brave enough to do so.'

Katyett smiled. 'I expect you've had quite a journey. What's he like, really? Like he is now?'

Auum's voice dropped to a whisper. 'Truly I never know from one moment to the next. He's utterly unreliable in his mood and attitude. I'm not sure he really knows why he is here. Sometimes on the journey he appeared so calm and lucid that I forgot he was ever other than that. The next instant, raging and jabbering to the voice he can hear or withdrawing so far I can get nothing from him. Not even a pace in the right direction.'

'He's a serious risk, isn't he?' said Katyett, lowering her voice too.

Up ahead, Takaar and Pelyn were talking. Pelyn was clearly ill at ease. Auum touched Katyett's arm and gestured they fall back a little way. Katyett had not realised she was trembling all over.

'Takaar could win us this fight or he could bring disaster down on us. But he has all his old strengths in there somewhere. I pity the rogue Ynissul who mistakes his oddness for weakness. His combat skills are undiminished.'

'Had a fight, did you?'

'He tried to kill me. Serrin stopped him. Serrin is safe, by the way. I'll tell you about him later.'

'As you wish. Listen to me. Things have been getting much worse here. The rogue Ynissul are not what you need to worry about. Takaar has guessed it but not the scale.'

'I'm listening.'

Katyett related the recent history of Ysundeneth, watching the dismay deepen on Auum's face.

He was silent for a while. 'It's after some big use of this magic that he's most vulnerable. That's what worries me if the mages start making a lot of castings.'

Katyett frowned. 'How can that be? He's never been anywhere near any of it, has he? Certainly not near Ysundeneth.'

'He's different from us,' said Auum.

'I can see that,' said Katyett, surprised at the bitterness in her tone.

'No, I don't meant that. He feels everything that happens to a greater or lesser extent. It's to do with the energy lines he found here. He picks up on changes and violence in the earth's energy. Like the Apposans and Orrans say they do. But more. What you told me about the playhouse and the warehouse? All makes sense. He felt those things happen as if they were personal attacks.'

'There's something inside him waking up and he says we all have it. I think it causes half of the problems in his head. If he was still truly feeling the guilt and remorse of the Tul-Kenerit, do you think he'd really still be alive? I don't.'

Katyett couldn't find a reply. Not long after, they walked back into the camp. The eyes of every Ynissul civilian and warrior were on them, as were those of the Al-Arynaar. The more astute paid particular attention to Auum and the hooded newcomer. TaiGethen were signalling to each other across the camp. Some began to move towards the corner of the covered area where Katyett had set up what passed for a command centre.

'Merrat. There are Ynissul out there who need to prepare their people for reclamation. Help them but do it quickly. We need to plan.'

The answer to Takaar's question was in view from the camp. About a mile to the south and high in the sky. Katyett shuddered again. It still wasn't an easy sight to ingest. She saw Pelyn point towards the mage. Takaar stopped just beneath the covered area and stared out. Katyett began to hurry when she saw him stretch out his arms and to run when he started to make motions like he was reeling in a rope.

Takaar's movements were so theatrical and dramatic that those nearest to him who could see him began to laugh, assuming a joke. But then his hood fell back and the effort on his face and the fury in his eyes stilled some of the laughter. And those with long memories, those who had escaped from Hausolis, began to wonder who it was in their midst. Some were putting the pieces together.

'Tual's balls,' snapped Katyett. 'Pelyn, get him away from the crowd.'

Word was spreading faster than wind over long grass. People were standing, pointing, beginning to move. TaiGethen, at a signal from Katyett, got in the way. They formed a cordon, moving swiftly through their charges and obscuring Takaar from sight. Katyett stood square in front of him.

'Is this your idea of a subtle entrance? What are you doing?'

Takaar had dropped his arms to his sides but his eyes were alight with passion.

'I can see what tethers him to the earth. It's like a net of energy and he sits atop it. It's what keeps him in the sky at the same time. It is so clear I can touch it. But I can't drag him down. Some other power stops me.'

Katyett glanced at Auum, who raised his eyebrows.

'What can you see?' she asked Takaar.

'Colour and energy. The shape of the wings that balance him. It is beautiful.'

'But you can't break it. Can't make him fall.'

Takaar shook his head.

'Shame,' said Katyett. 'And a shame that you've stirred up so much attention. I think your cover might be blown.'

Takaar looked out past the cordon of TaiGethen at the sea of faces pushing towards them. His name was being bounced around. Questions were being asked. Katyett sensed confusion and aggression.

'What do we do, announce him?' asked Grafyrre. 'This isn't going to die down and we need to organise ourselves.'

'Let me talk to them,' said Takaar.

His eyes were bright and fierce, just like at the Tul-Kenerit before . . .

Katyett paused. 'Are you sure?' she asked.

Takaar shook his head. 'No. But it'll irritate him if I stand up and speak to those I betrayed. He doesn't think I possess the courage.'

Katyett found herself looking at Auum for encouragement again. The young TaiGethen shrugged and cocked his head to the side. Why not? It was as good a reason as any on this strangest of days. Katyett dispersed the TaiGethen back into the crowd to spread word of an announcement.

It was quickly done and almost every face was turned to the small party, expecting Katyett to speak. But it was not she who stepped forward. It was the most famous of them all. An *ula* from the pages of history.

Chapter 36

Do not follow me. Believe in me and then follow your heart.

'Ynissul of Ysundeneth. Al-Arynaar of the threads of elves. Tai-Gethen, my brothers and sisters. Among you are those who have heard of me but not seen me. There are those who have seen me but do not know me. And there are those who fought by me and thought never to see me again. I failed you all as I failed the elven race.

'I am Takaar.'

Katyett had always felt that the phrase 'heart in mouth' was melodramatic and ridiculous. No longer. Her pulse thudded so hard in the back of her throat it was painful. The lump could not be swallowed and she thought to choke at every breath. She felt giddy and leant on Grafyrre for support, muttering prayer after prayer that this would not all go horribly wrong. Not for her sake. For him. Takaar. She found that she wanted him to be accepted. To be heard. Understood. Respected even. But not ridiculed. Not that, she prayed to Yniss. Anything but that.

If Takaar had expected adulation or abhorrence at his unveiling, he was disappointed. There was a murmur through the crowd but nothing more. Takaar let it subside. Standing a pace behind him, Auum turned to Katyett and nodded his confidence. Takaar continued.

'I am not here to ask for forgiveness or to seek redemption. Those things are rightly denied me. The blood of every elf of every thread who died when I fled the walls of the Tul-Kenerit is on my hands. Through ten years of exile it has not scrubbed away. It will remain there for ever. As it should.

'So I am standing here not as a general or a leader but as an ordinary *ula* asking for your help in the fight to rid our country of men, to restore the harmony of the elves and to return us all to the lives we love. I wonder if you'll listen to me.'

Out in the crowd many nodded their heads. A few said 'Yes' and fewer still applauded, demanding more. Takaar inclined his head deferentially.

'Thank you.' He pointed up at the mage. 'Up there, against all nature and Yniss himself, the eyes of man search for us. Beneath the canopy, they seek us. And in the city thousands of men of violence await the word to attack. Just as they await the word to slaughter helpless elves imprisoned in their own homes.

'Inevitably, they will find this hiding place and then they will send out their mages with their castings and they will attempt to burn us and to flush us out onto the swords of their warriors. They want us all dead. You, me and the TaiGethen, who they rightly fear.'

Consternation ran through the crowd. Katyett closed her eyes. Grafyrre drew in a sharp breath. But Takaar merely walked another pace forward and held up his hands.

'Yes, we're in trouble. But if we work together, we can get out of trouble. Some of us will die. Others will be wounded. Some will panic and flee. Such is the way. I know. But be assured, I do not expect you to take up swords against these men and their magic. That is the work of TaiGethen and Al-Arynaar. All I want you to do is this.

'Listen to instructions. Question nothing. Move where you are asked as quickly as you are asked. Help those less able to help themselves. Carry wounded. Move water and food. Give courage to those who need it. Stand with your people against whatever comes at you. Because if you do, the TaiGethen and Al-Arynaar will be able to face the enemy with strength and focus.

'I—'

Takaar stopped and stared out and up at the mage in the southern sky. He pointed vaguely and began to shake his head.

'Oh no,' breathed Auum. 'He's going to lose it right in front of them.'

The crowd began to stir, many looking up at the mage, who was some way distant and no threat whatever. Others were pointing at Takaar, and more than one called for him to be helped. Auum ran over, stood in front of Takaar and looked at him. He paled visibly.

'He needs help,' said Auum. 'Quickly.'

Pelyn and Katyett both moved. Takaar pushed Auum away.

'No.' He turned and Katyett pulled up short, seeing the pallor of his face, the tremble in his lower lip and the red filling the whites of his eyes. Sweat covered his features and a vein pulsed in his temple. 'It's coming. The magic is coming. That mage is not searching. He's watching.'

'He's—' began Katyett.

A deep-brown magical orb arced across the sky, trailing steam behind it. It hung at its apex for a moment, beguiling the crowd, which stared up, entranced. The orb began to fall.

'Scatter!' yelled Katyett. 'Get under the canopy.'

Iad and *ula*, screaming and shouting, scattered, looking for shelter, a way out, anything. The orb crashed through the broad leaves of trees high above them. It ploughed into the branch of a mighty banyan that acted as the outer stay of the bivouac and exploded into a thousand tears of fire as big as a fist. They showered down across the camp.

Order disintegrated. Undergrowth, grass, leaf and branch were set ablaze. Elves were thrown to the ground, their flesh eaten in heart-beats by the voracious magical flames. Screams rose with the smoke and stench of burning. Ynissul ran blindly, pushing aside any who got in their path.

Katyett turned to her people inside the bivouac. 'Illast, see Olmaat to safety. Head for the river and go south. TaiGethen, to the hunt. Sikaant, you'll be needed by the lost out there in the forest. Pelyn, run the flanks of the Ynissul – you're the last defence they have. Find the men. Kill them.'

TaiGethen and Al-Arynaar flowed out from under the bivouac, muttering prayers as they went, smearing their faces with brown and green paint. Katyett watched them help Ynissul from the ground, those that could be helped. She heard cries of fear and shouts for help. Dozens lay out there, dead or dying. Nothing to do for them now but pray for their souls to find the embrace of Shorth.

More orbs filled the sky alongside the rain Katyett had seen falling over the city a few nights ago.

'Yniss preserve us,' said Grafyrre.

An orb detonated on the roof of the bivouac. It ripped skin, timber and palm apart. Blew the moss of years to dust and sent the whole lot crashing down to the forest floor. To the rear of the bivouac, Katyett saw Illast and his Tai dive out with Olmaat on his stretcher, clinging on as he bumped and slid along the ground.

Auum grabbed Katyett's arm and dragged her out into the blazing camp. Roof supports thundered down in their wake. Fire fell around them. Orbs smashed through the thin canopy, splattering across the roofs of dormitories, immolating brush and torching the carpet of grass. Bodies were consumed where they fell.

Katyett stared about her, desperate for sight of Takaar. Auum held her steady, weaving a path through the fire deluging the ruined haven. An orb battered into a small stand of trees to their right, sending fire lashing out across the camp in head-high sheets. Auum dived, taking Katyett down with him. She landed and rolled, waking from her trance. She came to her feet. Auum was staring at her. She nodded and the two of them sprinted under the canopy.

South and east, the shouts of panicked civilians were a beacon for the enemy. The shrieks and cries sounded muffled through the canopy. Countless animals, startled at the sounds of elves and terrified by the smell of burning and the sight of fire, set up a deafening cacophony all around the camp. The human attack had been expertly laid. The Ynissul were scattered from their protectors, easy prey. But the king predators of the forest had been set loose: TaiGethen were thick on the ground.

Katyett came to a halt and turned. Grafyrre and Merrat were right behind her. Marack and Takaar in their wake. Takaar had vomit on his chin and down the front of his shirt. He looked groggy, on the verge of passing out. The flames were gorging on the land immediately behind, roaring and hissing. Smoke and steam billowed up to skies darkening for the next rains.

'You're enjoying this, aren't you?' said Takaar.

Katyett made to reply but Auum touched her on the arm and shook his head.

'Hoping that one of those things falls on my head and I die screaming. *Chilmatta nun kerene*. You can stop chanting it. I've heard it all before.' He stared at Katyett. 'I've lost my blowpipe.'

'Takaar,' said Katyett firmly. 'Listen to me.'

More orbs fell on the camp, blasting little more than ash now. The fires were beginning to eat into the dense canopy. Fires that rain would struggle to extinguish. Takaar dragged his head around and fixed Katyett with a gaze full of pain and fury. Katyett flinched.

'I know where they lie,' he said and moved off at startling speed.

Katyett ran after him, seeing how his feet made barely an impression on the forest floor and his body hardly touched the thick vegetation around him.

'Marack, Auum, make a cell with Takaar. Marack, you're leader. Graf, Merrat, to me. Let's do some damage.'

Onelle had lost Rydd. The surge out of the camp, the blooming heat from the castings and the confusion of the dark beneath the heavy canopy had generated such panic. The shouts of lost and injured *iad* and *ula* echoed hollowly through the thick, grasping vegetation. The stench of burned flesh followed her through the hanging branches and tangled vine and liana. There was noise everywhere yet she found herself alone.

She ran left, then straight ahead and then right. Chasing the fading sounds of other Ynissul. Onelle called out for Rydd twice but heard nothing other than the calls of animals. She couldn't understand how she had lost them all. She thought she'd been heading towards the stream, but perhaps she hadn't left the camp that way after all. So hard to remember in all the confusion.

Eventually, she stopped and rested against the bole of a tree. She checked the ground for anything dangerous before letting her back slide down the bark till she was squatting, mainly hidden by ferns. She remembered one thing Katyett told her. That she wouldn't hear TaiGethen, that only civilians and enemies made noise in the forest. So she decided to wait and listen while she tried to orient herself.

Onelle looked up to find the sun but there was only the green and black of the canopy. Full of life and death. She knew she should be able to see flames from the camp still, but turning around in her hiding place, she could see nothing in any direction. A haze of smoke drifted around her. It didn't help.

The screaming began then. Faint at first but growing louder and closer very quickly. Six Ynissul came past her. Two hanging on to each other. Another four trying to push them along more quickly. They kept looking over their shoulders. They needed to look ahead, Onelle wanted to shout but didn't.

A human stepped into their path. He swung a sword and carved into the front pair at the waist. Blood slapped into broad leaves. The elves tumbled sideways together. The other four stopped, split and ran. A man came up from behind and swept his blade through the back of one. A second fetched up against a tree and begged for mercy. The blade was driven straight through her unprotected heart.

Onelle put a hand to her mouth to stop herself crying out. She was shaking. The tears were streaming down her face. She didn't want to see what happened to the other two but someone had to be able to report it.

The surviving Ynissul had both stopped running and were backing away, holding out their hands but saying nothing. Three swordsmen moved towards them. Smiling. How she would have liked to smear those smiles from their ugly faces and turn them into blood. She took her hand from her mouth and made it into a claw. Her nails were good and sharp. Perhaps she should.

A shadow whipped by her right-hand side. A man began to turn. Twin blades took him in the neck and across the midriff. A keening sound grew. A jaqrui lodged in the face of another man, biting deep into the bridge of his nose and slicing into both eyes. The third was felled by a flurry of punches and kicks too fast to follow. None was shouting his agony for long.

Onelle found herself terrified all over again. The violence of man had been brutal but the speed of the TaiGethen was truly shocking. She wanted to stand and show herself but something stopped her from moving. A feeling, nothing more. She watched the TaiGethen check the elven bodies and comfort the survivors before pointing them on their way.

One turned and walked directly towards her, stopping a few paces away and crouching. Onelle didn't recognise her. She held out a hand. Onelle shook her head.

'It's safe now,' she said. 'You can come out.'

'It isn't. Please,' said Onelle.

A terrible aching cold howled through the space in front of her. Frost deepened on leaf and branch, blackening everything it touched. The storm of ice and wind raged past her, forcing her to clutch herself tight and close her eyes. And as quickly as it had come, it blew out, leaving her nauseous but alive. Though when she opened her eyes, of the TaiGethen, fallen men and elf, there was nothing left at all.

A cloaked human crunched onto the ice-rimed ground and looked about him, his expression one of satisfaction, of revenge complete. Onelle had no idea what possessed her then. She stood from her cover and walked in front of him. She was still chilled to the bone, though the frost was beginning to melt from the leaves around her, leaving them blackened and dead.

The man stopped and backed off a pace before smiling when he saw her for the lone lost *iad* she was. He chuckled and muttered under his breath. Onelle hated everything about the man. Hated the eyes that looked on her as nothing more than an animal. Hated the smell of him, and hated what he carried within him. She could sense it. Energy forged to evil.

Onelle ran across the gap. She was quick. Very quick. She cocked her arm and lashed her fingers across his throat. She felt her nails catch, dig in and rip at his flesh. She should have recoiled but it didn't feel revolting. It felt right. Deep they went, the tips of her fingers snagging sinew and her nails catching on his windpipe. She dug in her thumb and closed her hand. Blood was pouring over her wrist and forearm. The mage gurgled, his face gone from contempt to shock.

'Do not dare kill my people,' said Onelle.

She jerked her hand back hard.

Takaar was a heartbeat too late. The mage pushed out his hands. The *ula* in his sights was plucked from the ground and crushed against a tree, his head making a horrible cracking sound as it struck. The body slumped. Takaar hurdled a low branch, kept his left leg straight and caught the mage in the side of the head.

The casting failed and the *ula* fell to the ground. Takaar landed and spun. Auum had run to his left. Warriors were on them. Beside him the mage still moved. His body was jerking and his eyelids fluttered. Takaar dropped to his knees and jabbed straight-fingered into his throat. Death for him would be full of desperate fear.

Takaar leaned to one side and vomited bile. Castings were still falling all over this region of the forest, making his head spin and his stomach turn over. He squeezed his eyes shut, searching for a way to contain his reactions. He stared down at the mage, who still clung on to life, choking and making feeble grabs at his throat.

'What you have,' whispered Takaar, 'I can take from you.'

Everyone and everything had this energy to a greater or lesser extent. It was an element as common as air. But this body before him had more. Like he was able to hold it, focus it in to something far more dense than any ordinary man, elf or beast.

'What you have learned, I will learn,' said Takaar.

This to be your grand new project, is it?

'Don't start on me.'

I'd work on living right now if you really must.

'Takaar! Roll!'

Takaar twisted left. A blade bit the ground where he had been kneeling. Marack leapt over him, landed and round-housed the human soldier in the side of the head. Off balance, Katyett's blades saw him to the wrath of Shorth.

Marack turned and held out a hand. Takaar took it and stood.

'We're clear here,' said Auum. 'We've got them running back towards the Ultan.'

'Keep them turned,' said Takaar. 'Katyett. Don't let them regroup.'

'Normally I'd agree with you, but right now we have more pressing concerns. Pelyn! Pelyn, I need you.'

An Al-Arynaar came into view from their left. Takaar recognised him but couldn't place him.

'Methian,' said Katyett. 'You'll do just as well.'

Methian. That was it. Pelyn's confidant. No wonder he didn't look at Takaar with any warmth.

'She's close,' said Methian. 'She'll have heard you.'

'We have to round the survivors up. Get them away from here. Olbeck Rise would be ideal. Think you can square it with the Apposans?'

'I reckon,' said Methian.

'How many did we lose, do you think?' asked Merrat.

'Hundreds,' said Methian. 'Hundreds. No exaggeration.'

'TaiGethen will track for you. Follow the stream. We'll secure the route and send them on as we find them.'

'Katyett?'

Pelyn appeared from the undergrowth along with two other Al-Arynaar. Brothers. Deserters but perhaps forgiven by now. She glanced at Takaar, bit her lip and focused on Katyett instead.

'Are you clear?'

Pelyn nodded. 'The last we chased are either dead or running for the Ultan bridge.'

'Good,' said Katyett. 'We're clearing towards Olbeck Rise. Methian will fill you in.'

Pelyn shook her head.

'No. We can't just gather ourselves and leave. It's night in a few hours.'

Katyett was looking at her blankly. 'I'm not with you.'

'And the TaiGethen surrender at dawn or the humans will start slaughtering innocents, remember? Hanging them out on the edge of the city.'

Katyett drew in a sharp breath. 'Damn me for a fool. How could I forget that?'

'It doesn't matter,' said Pelyn.

'It does,' said Katyett. She couldn't stop herself glancing at Takaar. 'Mind elsewhere. Hardly the right quality in a leader.'

'If it makes you feel better, I'll question you about it later,' said Pelyn. 'What I don't understand is, why did they attack us in the first place?'

'They are trying to provoke you. Make sure you enter the city,' said Takaar. 'They won't be expecting meek surrender. Llyron will tell them that much, I'm sure. They will have hoped to spread confusion, kill a few . . . lessen you.'

'They've succeeded,' said Katyett. 'To a point. The question is, how do we stop them killing our people? Because we aren't going to surrender and we are going to attack. We have no choice. They will know that, won't they? They'll be ready.'

Takaar nodded. 'This will test us.'

'A head-on assault won't get us anywhere,' said Marack. 'We are too few. We have to do something that will stop them carrying out their threat.'

Katyett smiled and Takaar saw her confidence in herself return in small part.

'We need a hostage,' she said. 'Graf. Marack. Call the TaiGethen. We'll meet in the lee of the Ultan at dusk. That leaves us the day to find as many of our people as we can.'

'Is Olbeck far enough from the city?' asked Auum.

Takaar saw Methian and Pelyn both shake their heads.

'Pelyn, I need you to go with Methian,' said Katyett. 'Clear Olbeck too. Make for Katura Falls.'

Pelyn didn't respond. Takaar watched her weighing up her response. He knew what she was thinking. She was being kept from the attack on the city. Marginalised.

'The Al-Arynaar are the police of Ysundeneth. You need us there.'

'There are not enough of you to fulfil that function.'

Pelyn raised her eyebrows. 'You have fewer people than I do. You need us.'

'Yes, I need you to save the Apposans and Ynissul, get them away from here. Lead them. All of them are citizens of Ysundeneth.'

Pelyn shook her head. 'The fact is that you think us not good enough to run with you.'

Katyett's face was stone. 'Yourself excepted, you are not good enough to do the work that must be done tonight. Methian is a worthy fighter and a great asset, but he has not the speed. He knows that and so do you. Please, Pelyn. This is the right way.'

'Pelyn,' said Takaar, and he remembered the tone that made her listen to him. 'Will you hear me.'

'You know I will, Takaar,' she said quietly.

'Don't chase glory in battle. This task Katyett has set is steeped in honour. If she is unsuccessful. If she should fall, the elves who survive will need a leader of your quality. You have the gift of bringing threads together. It's why I made you Arch of the Al-Arynaar. No one is better suited. And when we're done, we will find you at Katura.'

Pelyn inclined her head. 'I'll go. For the harmony, not for you. And Katyett. Don't die, all right?'

Katyett smiled 'Yniss bless you, Pelyn, I'll try not to.'

Chapter 37

A hero never needs a second chance because he has not erred in the first place.

Seventy-four TaiGethen. If Takaar was counted among their number. None spoke to him. None would stand near him. His presence was both inspiration and anxiety. Takaar stood apart, unwilling or unable to be among them while they planned and talked.

Marack and Auum had agreed to run with him into the city. Katyett had no idea whether he would remain with them or not. He had fought well in the forest but only when the mages had stopped casting so much of their magic. Until then he had been weak as a newborn.

Katyett looked at her people. So few. They had gathered at the mouth of the Ultan. The night was full and dark. Gyal had spread her shroud across the stars and the eyes of men could not see them. They had prayed together, applying their face paints and blessing their weapons, both flesh and steel.

Seventy-four against thousands. In a city where magic was scattered like dust underfoot. Any step could be the one that took *iad* or *ula* to Shorth's embrace. An invisible killer surer than anything the rainforest had to offer. Yet there was no fear in the eyes of her people. Yniss blessed their bodies. Tual guided their hands and their feet.

'Men are everywhere in Ysundeneth. They have occupied the temple of Shorth, the barracks of the Al-Arynaar and taken homes from elves, putting them on the street or to the sword. Their magic is terribly dangerous and their weapon skills decent. They fight heavy and wear armour to make up for their shortcomings. They have some skills with bows too. But they are slow.

'Do not underestimate them. Their numbers are high and their fear of their master will drive them on. Do not be tempted away from the paths I have laid out for you. You are all aware of what we must achieve. Show no mercy. Expect no mercy.

'They know we will come. They can't place their ward castings where they themselves might stand but they will place them where we might travel. If anything smells or feels wrong, go another way. I can't afford to lose any of you. I love you. You are my brothers and sisters. My family.

'Questions.'

There was silence for a time. Katyett saw unease sweep them. She saw the glances too.

'Estok,' she said. 'Speak. Unlike you to be silent.'

Estok nodded and gestured at Takaar, who was close enough to hear.

'What is he doing here?' he hissed. 'We can't trust him. And you've yoked him with Marack and Auum.'

'We need him,' said Katyett.

Estok's expression was like a slap in the face.

'*We?* We've followed you for ten years and you have never led us along the wrong path. He walks in from nowhere, and every time you want to make a decision, you look at him like you need his assent. We don't need him. We don't need the invisible presence he mutters to half the time, either. Perhaps you do, though.'

Katyett felt stung and had to force herself to face Estok and not glance to her left where Takaar stood.

'My past with Takaar is my past,' said Katyett carefully. 'And you are not seeing this situation clearly. Yes, he is a risk. He will tell you that. But think. Whatever the outcome of tonight and the days to come, we face a struggle to unite our people. And to rid Calaius of man. The reputation of the priesthood is in ruins. At the moment we needed them most, priests did not stand together in harmony. They divided. Some betrayed us all. Elves will need a figurehead. Who else can you think of?'

'He's been denounced!' Estok's voice bounced from the walls of the Ultan. He hushed himself. 'Who will follow him? What of his reputation? You saw him speak to the Ynissul. Did they embrace him or were they suspicious? He cannot hope to wield the influence he once did. This is ridiculous.'

Estok looked square at Takaar.

'It's madness,' he said. Takaar was not paying them any attention whatever. He was rubbing at his chin and muttering under his breath. 'Is that really the salvation of the elves?'

Katyett stared at Takaar, and Estok's words sank true into her belly. Takaar was at war with himself again. Every eye was on him but he did not notice. She caught snatches of what he was saying. His responses to what he heard in his head were those of someone desperately trying not to be undermined, and failing.

'I would speak.'

Katyett felt blessed relief.

'Auum. Yes, of course.'

'Estok, I hear you,' said Auum, choosing to speak formally. 'And it seems that Estok speaks for most of you. I hear you too. Now you hear me. Takaar has saved my life. He has also tried to take it. He is not the *ula* who stood with many of us on the walls of the Tul-Kenerit.

'Takaar has faced what he did and what he is. He lives with it every moment, waking or asleep. You do not trust him. He does not expect your trust. You do not love him. He does not expect your love. Nor your forgiveness. But think on this. Takaar once walked with gods and now he is reduced to the most vilified of elves.

'Yet still he returned. Ask yourself about the scale of strength and resolve it takes to come and face the judgement of your people. Ask yourself why he has chosen to do this. Not for himself. Not for redemption. Ask him. He doesn't believe he deserves that either. But from his exile at the Verendii Tual he *felt* the shivering of the harmony. And his belief in its endurance overcame any fear he kept for himself.

'Takaar is here for you. For every *ula* and *iad* that wants to drag us back from the nightmare into which we are descending. He might fail. So might we all. But does not every elf deserve a second chance?'

Katyett waited for Auum's words to settle before she spoke.

'Tais. We hunt.'

Silent Priest Sikaant saw her sitting with her back to a tree and hugging her knees to her. He saw the blood on her hands and on her face. The body of the man was close. His throat was ripped open, a gory, bloody mess. He had died in terror and agony. Shorth would see his torment continued for eternity.

Sikaant crouched in front of her.

'I've lost my Rydd,' she said.

Sikaant held out a hand. 'Let us find him together.'

The *iad* took his hand and he felt an energy surge through her fingers and encase his body. Brief like a spear of lightning.

'Something has happened to me,' she said.

'Yniss blesses you,' said Sikaant.

He had felt this energy before but through his feet, never from within another elf. The *iad* shrank back, something behind him making her fearful. Sikaant turned where he crouched. It was another of the Silent. Resserrak. He had been a long while hidden in the rainforest and Sikaant could see why Onelle would fear him.

Only half of his face was white. The other half was covered in tattoos, as was much of his body. Words from the Aryn Hiil that he would never speak. His nose and ears were pierced with bone. His eyes were wide and wild. Resserrak had always been closer to Tual's denizens than any other of the Silent. Now it appeared the transition was almost complete. Sikaant rose and the two priests kissed each other's eyes and foreheads. Behind Sikaant, the *iad* had summoned the courage to stand.

'I am Onelle. Please. I want to find my Rydd. Will you help me?'

Resserrak looked at her and Sikaant knew he could see it too.

'We are changing,' said Resserrak, his voice hoarse and quiet. 'Serrin knows.'

Sikaant smiled. 'Growing. Come, Onelle. We will find Rydd. We will find all the lost.'

There were guards on the Ultan bridge. Ten of them and three mages. The bridge was a beacon of light. Lanterns hung from every hook. Torches burned at each main pile. The guards and their mages seemed relaxed. No doubt they were basking in the success of their raid on the staging camp. No doubt they felt their wards would save them from the TaiGethen gathering just beyond the light.

Takaar surveyed what the mages had done. Pale grey globes of essence sitting on the ground. Shifting and swirling, occasionally sending out sparks of brown and green light that connected one to another. There were eight of them in front of the bridge. Placed such that no one could possibly approach without stepping on at least one and so triggering all of them. He didn't know what the casting would be but walls of fire had been favoured, so he'd been told.

There were others too. Placed along the rails of the bridge. The humans were not keen to repeat the error of a few nights past.

Unfortunately for them, they had no knowledge of Takaar's gift. And they would die having none.

'We can avoid them,' said Takaar. 'They are laid across the width of the bridge and ten paces towards us. They are on the rails for the first fifteen paces.'

'Good. Tais to me. Now is the time for any last questions. Speak freely.'

Takaar approved of the targets and the number of cells at each. Five cells led by Estok would attack the harbourside, where the humans stockpiled their supplies and where a diversion would have the greatest effect. Ten cells would move to encircle the temple piazza. Five, led by Katyett and including Takaar, would raid Shorth, where it was believed Garan, leader of the human soldiers, was stationed. There were four other cells and two single TaiGethen whose cells had perished in the attack at the camp. These were to keep the barracks under observation and run messages between Estok and Katyett.

'You're sure this Garan is big enough bait?' Marack addressed herself to Auum.

Auum nodded 'He's the leader of the men. Of the soldiers at any rate. He was the only one Sildaan spoke to and he was the one leading the men Serrin and I killed in the forest. We don't know who came in on the second wave of ships. He's the only target we know.'

'Good enough,' said Katyett. 'Marack, he's yours, but you can always take more than one hostage should others present themselves to you. Anything more?'

Marack shook her head.

'We're clear. We're keeping it simple. No one takes down Llyron or any *cascarg*. This is in and out.' She looked meaningfully at Estok. 'None of us can afford to stay too long.'

'We shouldn't leave innocents locked up and vulnerable,' said Estok.

'Estok,' said Katyett, and Auum felt the chill in her voice. 'We have been through this. The balance is right. Keep in mind what we are trying to do, what we must do. Hit your target and get out. We need negotiating power and proof we can attack at will.'

Estok nodded, but Auum could see he was not satisfied. Takaar looked at him, his eyes dark, his brow deep with a frown.

'We must all follow the orders of our leaders. Else all we have is chaos. And when chaos leads, elves die.'

Estok's eyes flashed anger and he opened his mouth to retort. Auum tensed. Takaar merely smiled, though Auum saw the slight tremble in his hands.

'That you care is what makes you TaiGethen. I am proud of your anger.'

All the wind was taken from Estok's sails. He sagged visibly.

'It shames me,' he said.

'There is only one of us here who need carry shame,' whispered Takaar.

An uneasy atmosphere grew in the wake of his words. He could feel it like he could feel the pull of the magic laid in front of them at the bridge

Let them sweat. Let them see the real you. Indecisive. Reluctant. Craven.

'There is beauty in this magic,' said Takaar, screwing his eyes shut to banish his tormentor. 'A perfect, pure way to die. Like there is beauty in the taipan strike and the sweat of a yellow back.'

'But can you tame it?' whispered Marack.

'Oh no,' said Takaar. 'Not yet, anyway. I have too much to learn.'

'We should make a statement,' said Katyett.

'I agree,' said Takaar.

He stared at Katyett like he found himself doing a good deal when his tormentor was quiet. Strong, beautiful, faithful. She felt his gaze and turned. He didn't flinch though her eyes held all the regret of a decade gone by.

'What?' she asked. 'That look always has some dreadful words of wisdom in close pursuit.'

'I'm sorry,' he said quietly.

'That doesn't scratch the surface of the last ten years,' said Katyett.

'I was talking about you.'

'So was I. Thank you for trying, anyway.'

'What does that mean?' *Never could understand her, could you? Always one step behind. Poor Takaar.* 'No I'm not. I don't feel sorry for myself.'

'What?' Katyett's eyes rose and her expression hardened. 'We don't have time for this. Let's move. All of us. Forward. If a mage makes to cast, scatter back. Follow Takaar. Do not step in front of him. Do not tread where he does not. Watch. Copy. Live.'

*

'This is some of my best work, actually,' said Poradz, feigning a hurt tone. 'Ystormun himself could do no better.'

'Since your best work so far has been fixing that rodent problem out in the Triverne slums, that doesn't necessarily fill me with confidence.'

'The trouble with you, Dagesh, is that you don't know artistry when you see it.'

'I don't see bloody anything. Can't see the wards can I? Not a mage, am I?'

Poradz smiled. Dagesh was funny when he was in this mood. The mock belligerence. Any luck and they'd be treated to his impersonation of Garan before long.

'Ah, my poor blind friend. Such a world is forever closed to you and you are left having to trust me, the poor feeble mage.'

'Where the fuck did they all come from?' Dagesh was pointing out towards the rainforest and its diabolical noise. 'Gather round, lads, we've got company. Get some shields up, would you, Adzo?'

Poradz followed Dagesh's outstretched arm and flinched like he'd seen a ghost. Standing just inside the cast of the lanterns and torches, not close enough to trip his wards, were those damned painted elves. They made him shudder. He'd not seen them fight but he'd heard what others said. Nasty.

'Jylan, a shield, please.'

'Yes, boss.'

The guards gathered around Dagesh a few yards from the end of the bridge. The elves clustered behind one of their number who looked a bit of a mess in all honesty. Like someone had shaved him with the jaw of a dog. There was something about him though, something knowing that Poradz didn't like at all.

They just stared, not making a sound or a gesture. Their eyes didn't blink. Poradz could feel the cold aggression rising from them. An intent that was hard to deny even though he knew they'd never get across the bridge.

'What *are* they doing?' asked Hadran, booming voice echoing off the river rapids underneath them.

'I'm thinking they're not so clever,' said Dagesh. He wandered down a couple of paces and beckoned to them. 'Come and join us. Plenty of room up here. Bit early for you to be surrendering. Perhaps your timekeeping is lacking, eh? Dawn's that bit when the sun comes up. Fucking sharp-eared savages. Not a fucking clue.'

Behind him they all laughed. Dagesh spat towards them and turned, a broad smile on his face. Unseen by him, the elves melted back into the night, silent and smooth.

'What was all that about?' asked Poradz.

'Buggered if I know,' said Dagesh. He came and stood beside Poradz and the two of them looked out into the night. 'Who's to know the mind of a—'

The scruffy-looking one was coming through the air. Poradz watched him bring his body into a tight tuck and turn two somersaults before landing on the balls of his feet not a yard from them. His blade was out in the next breath and before Dagesh's shouts had registered on the rest. Before Dagesh's blade was drawn, the elf had stuck him straight in the heart and torn a big gash in his chin.

Poradz felt hot blood spray on his face. He cried out and staggered back. More and more of them were leaping onto the bridge. Huge jumps. Clearing his wards easily. Part of him admired the grace with which they moved. Most of him was too terrified to pull the shape of a spell together to help himself or anyone.

He could already hear some of his comrades running. Poradz backed away. One of the elves approached him, quick, like he was gliding. Poradz felt an impact to his temple. Another to his gut. And one of exquisite pain that broke his left knee. He screamed and fell, tried to scrabble away.

The rest were all running but the elves were so *fast*. Poradz saw his comrades engulfed. Cut down. The sheer speed of the elves' limbs when they struck registered in his agonised mind. They barely paused in their stride either. Like a dance. Poradz stopped trying to move. His knee was a sheet of pain and he thought he was going to throw up.

A hand grabbed his shoulder and threw him over onto his back. The scruffy one was looking down at him, curious, like a predator seeing new prey for the first time. Poradz shuddered at the gaze. There was intelligence there but something else too. Like bits of his mind were elsewhere and he couldn't stare with the whole of both eyes.

The elf spoke. Poradz hadn't bothered learning elvish and didn't catch a word of it. The elf put a hand on his head, the other on his chest. The elf breathed in deep and nodded. He said something more, nodded again and walked away. Another elf took his place.

This one had blood-slick blades in her hands.

Estok took his cells left to head away through the yards and round the marsh, meaning to track the coast all the way to the dockside. With him went two of the reserve cells. The other reserve cells moved along the main road before disappearing into the back streets to come to their starting positions.

Katyett led the main force across the dark fields, where the grain grew tall and dense. Takaar was ahead of them all, ensuring their path was safe. Where the stems thinned before the first buildings of Frey-Ultan, the district dominated by farmers and farm workers, they could see the four columns of smoke that signified the occupation of Shorth by its high priest.

Katyett wondered if Llyron remained free or was languishing in one of the cells below the temple. Those reserved for the elves of mixed thread for assessment of their suitability or otherwise for service. Maybe she was dead. Somehow Katyett doubted that. Llyron would not have been slow to point out that, without a high priest of Shorth, no order would remain among the elves. Humans didn't want riots; they wanted subservience.

The temple piazza bordered the rainforest at the south-eastern edge of the city. It was protected from the forest's lust for expansion by the River Ix, which plunged through a sheer cleft in the earth that ran for two miles, upstream to the borders of the Olbeck Rise and downstream to the rapids at the Ultan bridge. It had a crossing, known as the Senserii Approach. This was a grand wooden structure, beloved of pilgrims because it was the most direct route to the piazza from the canopy.

Myth held that the first Senserii, or those who became the first Senserii, had used it to escape persecution in their villages and towns deep inside the forest, taking sanctuary in Shorth as was their right. It made a good story, but Katyett preferred to believe that the first Senserii had been the results of mixed unions in the slums of Banyan and Valemire in the west of the city and been dumped at Shorth unwanted and unloved.

'I wonder what's happened to them?' she said.

'Who?' asked Grafyrre.

'The Senserii,' she said.

They were moving through the fringes of the grain fields, their passage barely moving a stalk. Takaar had slowed dramatically.

Katyett trilled a warning, using the sound of a common swift. Behind her, the TaiGethen stopped.

'We could do with them right now,' said Grafyrre.

'Not if they remain loyal to Llyron,' said Katyett.

'They will have had little choice despite what Pelyn thinks,' said Merrat.

They moved up to Takaar's shoulder where he was crouched with Marack and Auum. Katyett could almost taste the unease of her people behind her. The mistrust of their former Arch. But this time Takaar wasn't muttering. Katyett waved her Tai to crouch. The walls of the temple of Orra were close. Twenty paces across open ground and a drainage channel. Takaar spoke.

'They have set their castings right along the boundary and across the entire span of the bridge on the outside of the rails. They are all over the walls and probably on the roofs of Appos, Orra and Gyal. Cefu too. I can't see anything around Shorth. We're too distant.'

'Can we jump them? Weave through them?' asked Katyett.

'Not this time. They're too well placed. I suspect they've withdrawn any guard to the central lawns and are using the castings as early warnings.'

'So where's our way in?' asked Katyett.

'We're going to have to go straight up the Path of Yniss,' said Takaar.

'That's going to make silent approach a little tricky. Why not the other side of the piazza?'

'You think it'll be any different?'

Katyett stared at Takaar. 'Wait for Estok to get going. Then we move.'

Chapter 38

Move yourself away from the ula *who tells you he is not frightened of battle.*

Corsaar peered over the apex of a pitched roof directly opposite the Al-Arynaar barracks. His heart was racing. It had led him to send his two spare TaiGethen to warn Estok to stall his attack if they could get to him in time.

'This can't be right,' he whispered. 'What are they doing?'

Hundreds of men crowded the barracks training grounds. Lights burned in every window. Corsaar could see warriors drilling and mages working with small squads of swordsmen, practising. Looking down the hill, along the Path of Yniss, he could see lines of lights. Hundreds, thousands of torches.

The lights stretched right down to the harbour and turned corners into every quarter of the city. Corsaar could see the glow of lights rising above the rooftops. And there were soldiers lining the roads under the torches. The elves had known the city would be under curfew but this was something more.

'It's like a prison,' said Everash, Corsaar's second.

'It's worse than that. Looks to me like none of them are asleep. It's the middle of the night.'

'Katyett said they'd be expecting us.'

'But not to this extent,' said Corsaar. 'They're ready aren't they? All of them.'

Thrynn moved up the steep roof with his Tai. Corsaar saw the expression on his face before he shook his head.

'It's bad, Corsaar. We've been on the ground and on the roofs. They're everywhere. Areas of the city are cordoned off. We assume there's magic along some boundaries, and everywhere else there are men and mages. We haven't seen a single elf. There are no lights bar those the humans have lit. It's so silent down there. What's going on?'

'I don't know. But we could get in big trouble very fast. We need to warn Katyett. They've—'

Light blossomed down on the dockside. Orders were barked in the barracks yard. At least a hundred men and mages ran out, heading for the harbour. Corsaar cursed.

'Thrynn, get to Estok. Get him out of there. Get back to the forest. I'm going to the piazza. This isn't going to end well.'

The light of a spell bloomed to the north. Katyett signalled they move up. Behind them came the noise of marching and shouting from the direction of the barracks away down the street. Ahead of them was the double entrance to the temple piazza. The Path of Yniss split around the tower temple of Cefu, running left past the low dark-painted walls of Appos, and right past the spectacular murals and living stone of Tual.

Men guarded both entrances and more were gathered on the lawns around fires and cook pots. Mages and swordsmen. There was no way to get to Shorth without a fight and the plan had changed from one of stealth to one of speed. If they could defeat the guard before the alarm was raised, they might get in and out without too much trouble.

Forty-five TaiGethen split left and right. They crept up to the walls of the temples, hidden by shadows, invisible to their enemies. Jaqrui pouches were unclipped. Swords were drawn from scabbards. Limbs were flexed and joints rotated. Prayers were spoken and new camouflage applied.

'Quick and low,' whispered Katyett. 'Don't give the mages a target. Marack, don't hesitate here. You know what you have to do.'

The rasping sound of a cicada came from across the road. The left-hand side was ready. Katyett chirruped an acknowledging call. She waited a few moments. There was no new sound from the humans. Katyett made the hoot of a spider monkey and TaiGethen flowed into the temple piazza.

Ahead of them, swordsmen straightened in surprise, spread out and shouted warnings. Twenty-five jaqruis whispered away. The lethal blades flashed across the short space. Metal carved into leather, flesh and sparked off blade. Men screamed.

One ducked, not fast enough, the jaqrui lodging in his forehead.

Three more were killed outright, blades striking face and neck. Crescents struck sparks from the walls, sheared off metal armour, slammed into midriff, chest and arm.

Auum powered ahead. He leapt, Marack and Takaar in his wake, twisting as he cleared the fractured human line. He hacked down with his blade, cleaving into the neck of a hapless enemy warrior. Auum landed, spun and ran, hearing the TaiGethen overwhelming the defenders behind him while he led the charge to the lawns, their fires and their mages.

Men were running towards him, away from him, across him. Orders were called. He could see mages gathering behind their defenders, dropping their heads to begin casting. Auum upped his speed. Takaar went past him like he was walking. His speed was ridiculous, unearthly. He was heading for the mages. He hurdled a fire and was lost to sight.

Auum moved up to support, tearing around the left side of the blaze. Takaar leapt, spun in the air and delivered a vicious kick to the side of a mage's head. The man crumpled. Takaar landed. His fists blurred. A second one went down, his face slashed and his chest punctured.

Auum slid into the legs of a mage who had raised his head to cast. Auum bounced up, kicking down hard at the same man's face, cracking his fist into a second enemy's jaw and lashing his blade through his unprotected gut. Warriors ran around a fire to his right.

'Bows,' said Auum.

There were more mages too. The cells to the left had them in their sights. More swordsmen were running across the lawns from defensive points around the piazza. Marack touched Auum on the shoulder.

'The temple.'

Auum followed her. Behind them, the bulk of the TaiGethen force was on the lawns, running to engage man and mage. More jaqruis flew. Ahead of Auum, a crescent blade sheared through a bow, and sliced in under the chin of the archer. From the flanks, more TaiGethen surged in.

To the left, a mage cast. Three TaiGethen were hurled from their feet, slamming hard into the walls of Orra across the lawns. The mage moved his hands. Not fast enough. A TaiGethen blade swept down and up, taking one hand and reversing into his chest.

Auum followed Marack and Takaar towards Shorth. The doors

were deep in shadow, almost certainly shut and barred. Guards stood there, ready but nervous. Marack had no intention of going that way. Others would take them. She jumped down into the sunken gardens and swarmed up the vines that encased side and rear walls, almost eclipsing the stone of the body and arms in places.

Auum had always wanted to be able to look down upon it. To see the sculpted head lying face up, the top of its skull home to the temple doors. And to trace each arm down to its hand where they were carved as gripping the earth. The temple ended at the base of the torso. The original design was for it to have legs and feet too but there simply had not been room on the piazza.

A curious quirk of the design was that there were few windows in Shorth. The grand doors let in light which was reflected about the walls by mirrors and white walls, but otherwise the builders had stayed as true to an elven body as they could. And so apart from a few light wells letting down onto contemplation chambers, the only windows were those adorning the fingernails at the ends of the hands, and of course the eyes.

Auum turned to look down onto the lawns and away into the city. The fight was almost done but magic had been cast. Auum frowned and felt a shiver through him.

'They are waiting for us to attack the doors,' said Marack.

Auum knelt and put his face and hands to the glass of the left eye. Warriors were scattered through the vast hall of the body of Shorth. He could see priests too. Moving about the business of the temple. An anomaly of normality. He wondered who they would help and who they would hinder given the opportunity.

'Ready?' asked Marack.

'It's a long way,' said Takaar.

'Like jumping from the centre rungs of the bore,' said Auum. 'But a blessed landing awaits.'

'Where's Katyett?' asked Takaar.

'Sweeping up. With us soon,' said Auum.

The Tai of Marack, Auum and Takaar, took a pace back, jumped and fell feet first through the eyes of Shorth.

Katyett saw them go and knew she was behind schedule. She raced around the last fire. A group of three mages stood there, defended by the same number of warriors. Merrat and Grafyrre came to her shoulder. From the left, Dravyn's Tai closed. From the right, Acclan's cell. Katyett threw a jaqrui. It bounced from an invisible shield in front of the warriors. She saw one of the mages wince at the impact.

The warriors had no idea which way to face. One of them turned round and shouted at the mages.

'Break!' shouted Katyett. 'Watch for the hands.'

The three cells scattered. Katyett ploughed straight on towards the swordsmen. She grabbed her second blade. In front of her, the warriors crouched. Behind them, a mage raised his head and laid out his hands, palms up.

'Clear!' yelled Katyett.

She veered right. The mage's casting howled across the piazza. A myriad flechettes of ice flayed into Dravyn's Tai. Shards needle-sharp and razor-edged slicing through clothing, ripping into skin and slitting face, eyes, neck and cheeks. Dravyn cried out, threw his arms about his face and stumbled on. The ice ripped the flesh from his hands, exposing bone faster than a shoal of piranhas. He pitched onto his face.

His cell brothers tumbled to the ground near his ruined body, blood draining from hundred upon hundred cuts. Flesh hung in strips. Gaping wounds opened where larger shards had carved through their meagre defences.

Acclan's revenge was swift. His cell stormed into the rear of the group. His swords came down left and right, taking the head from the casting mage. The decapitated body slumped forward. The cell took one mage each. In front, the warriors scrambled to their feet, shoving the body of the headless mage aside.

The first looked up. Katyett's boot smashed his nose across his face. She hinged it back and slapped it in again, time after time into his head and neck, driving him to the ground. She fell on him, her blades piercing throat and heart. Merrat dragged her off the body. Grafyrre and Acclan finished the other two.

'It's over,' said Merrat. 'It's done.'

Katyett ran to Dravyn, knelt beside him. He was still breathing.

'He needs help,' she called.

She turned him over and knew he was way beyond such need. Katyett's shoulders slumped. Dravyn was barely recognisable. Most of the skin was gone from his face. His eyes were bloody pools and his lips cut to ribbons. His throat pulsed blood and his cheekbones showed through the flesh torn away.

'Rest, my brother,' she said. 'Help is coming.'

'Liar,' managed Dravyn, mouth bubbling red. 'At least I am close for my soul to travel to Shorth.'

Katyett's tear fell on his cheekbone. She kissed his forehead, tasted his blood.

'Yes, you are. Sleep. Yniss protect you. He has tasks for you elsewhere.'

Dravyn smiled and his head fell to one side. Katyett rose. She stared at the bodies of men littering the lawns, defiling them with their blood. In the firelight the faces of her people were drawn at sight of Dravyn's fate. She wiped bloodied hands down her trousers and picked up her swords.

'Get human bodies to the edge of the piazza. Use them if we need to trigger wards to escape. Acclan. Your Tai to the roof. Look out and in. Keep us together. The rest of you. Form up. Out of sight. Not one of those abominations gets in here. Not one of them gets mercy. Send them all to the wrath of Shorth. He is watching. Merrat, Grafyrre. With me.'

Estok leapt onto the sailcloth-covered crates. He ran to the far end of the stack, turned a forward roll in the air and landed in front of his next victim. His blades sang, slitting leather armour at the chest and biting deep. He rocked back and cracked a foot into the soldier's knee, feeling it break. Estok stepped aside and let him fall.

He turned. The job was done. Diversion. Slaughter. Seventy of them idling on the dockside. Fifteen TaiGethen. Only ever one result. Estok called his cells to him. Two TaiGethen had been lost. He spoke prayers for the fallen and exulted at their victory.

He spun at the sound of running feet.

'Thrynn. Late for the fun. Shame for you.'

But Thrynn did not smile. 'They're coming. Hundreds of them. We have to leave. Now.'

'How did they . . .'

'They were ready, armed and drilled. Estok, please. We have to get back to the forest.'

Estok felt the joy drain from him. But he would not leave this way. Not run like some craven beast. Like Takaar.

'No. We can fight. We can win. Look at what we've done here.'

Thrynn shook his head. 'Do what Katyett asks. Your task is complete. Come on.'

Thrynn turned and with his Tai began to trot away back to the coastal trail towards the Kirith Marsh. Estok's cells looked to him. Some had already begun to follow Thrynn.

'We have to weaken them. Prove we can beat them,' he said.

Estok heard marching. No, a trot. Coming down the side of the ruined harbour master's warehouse. A TaiGethen ran to get a view. She backed away quickly. Estok stared. Thrynn had been right. A hundred and more. Swords and castings. Estok swore. They filled the dockside, heading straight for the TaiGethen.

'Estok?'

Estok stared away to where Thrynn was already gone. Cut off from them now.

'We cannot lead these to Katyett. Tais, we fight.'

The first castings exploded over their heads.

Auum's feet slapped onto the marble altar amidst a shower of glass. He crouched and rolled sideways to absorb the impact, coming to his haunches at the edge of the circle. Men were staring in disbelief. Takaar and Marack landed by him.

'Where?' asked Auum.

'Left arm first,' said Marack. 'Go.'

Ignoring the guards and priests in the grand hall, the three TaiGethen turned and ran towards the back of the temple. Shouts were raised behind them. A clamour for action and a call to arms sounded the same in any language. Takaar led, his speed taking him quickly ahead. He tore around the corner into the corridor of the left arm of Shorth and fetched up sharply, slithering to a stop and backing up, beckoning down the corridor with one hand and making a tiny circling gesture with the other.

Auum and Marack ran left, passing a priest cringing by a column. Takaar backed up further. Five men followed him, swords drawn. None of them was Garan.

'Shorth will remind you,' said Takaar, 'that a TaiGethen is never alone.'

Marack went low, Auum high. Takaar went right. Marack took the legs from the first soldier, bringing him down in a heap. Auum flew over his head as he fell, his feet striking the side of the second warrior's face and cannoning his head into that of the third.

Blood sluiced across the wall at the corner of arm and body. Takaar's blade swiped into the air, red slicking its surfaces, and plunged down again. Auum landed between the two men he had floored. The first was not moving. The second only groggily so. Auum grabbed him by the hair and slammed his face three times into the stone floor. A dark pool spread beneath his skull.

The three were up and running the moment the fight was done and before the guard from behind could catch them.

'Stairs up,' said Marack.

'Why?' asked Auum.

'Best living quarters up there.'

Stairways were located immediately right and at the end of the arm where the walls rose to meet the fingers. Marack took the first way, sprinting up them three at a time, turning and running up the second flight without pause. Auum was hard on her heels, Takaar behind them both.

Doors slammed down the length of the corridor, the last of them to the panorama room built inside the fingers, with windows out towards the rainforest and the Ultan.

'Easy place to become trapped,' said Takaar.

'We'll start far end. We know someone's in there and there's no way out but the windows,' said Marack. 'Silent running.'

Ears could have been pressed to every door and it would have made no difference. The TaiGethen whispered over the timber floor. Like in the forest tracking tapir or monkey, they couldn't afford to disturb anything.

Marack indicated Auum and Takaar stay left and right. Marack charged the last few paces, dropped to her backside and slid in hard, her feet slamming into the door at the first cross brace. The door thwacked back against its hinges. Arrows flew out over her head, skipping off the walls and bouncing uselessly onto the floor.

Auum and Takaar threw jaqruis through the doorway. Marack was on her feet directly after them. The jaqruis missed their targets but served their purpose. Archers ducked. Marack slashed her blades across in front of her, splintering bows in the hands of the two humans.

Both backed away, reaching for knives. Auum and Takaar moved up beside her. The men glanced at one another and put their hands above their heads in surrender. Auum shook his head. His blade licked out, taking the left hand man through the eye, Garonin style, and piercing his brain. Marack ran the other through.

Auum turned to assess the room. It was empty barring two *iads*. Ynissul. One of them was staring at Takaar and he met her gaze unwavering.

'*You*,' she said.

Chapter 39

Welcoming long lost friends is a risk until you know why they were lost so long.

'You have to admit he's clever.'

Garan edged his foot into one of the elven bodies and turned it over. The camouflage paint remained where the burns had not consumed it. Otherwise, the face was melted. The heat under the multiple orbs and the blistering drops of fired rain must have been devastating in the moments before death. The deluge had been spectacular. And the mages accurate enough to save most of the empty crates masquerading as supplies too.

Garan nodded. 'I never doubted his cleverness, Keller, only his planning and execution of military operations. It seems he's been learning. But I still don't agree with the sacrifice of so many of my men for so relatively few of theirs.'

'It's just mathematics, Garan. Simple equations and acceptable loss.'

'I'll be sure and include that in my letters to the bereaved.'

'He's bringing this fight to a quick conclusion. I for one am happy about that because it means I get to go home.'

'Don't pack your bags just yet,' said Garan. 'They aren't finished and there'll be more of them here somewhere.'

Keller rocked on his heels and his eyes unfocused. His mouth moved but no sound came. Garan waited. It was the only choice when Communion was underway. Keller was frowning and his fists clenched and unclenched. The contact was short, and when it was done, Keller was nervous.

'Perhaps he's not so clever after all. There are TaiGethen in the temple.'

*

'Yes,' said Marack. 'Him.'

Marack put the point of her sword under Llyron's chin. Llyron lifted her head but didn't take her eyes from Takaar.

'And he's unbalanced,' said Marack. 'Prone to sudden changes of mood and unpredictable actions. So, *cascarg*, you had better speak.'

'Speak?' Llyron dragged her eyes away from Takaar. 'You aren't here to kill me?'

'You flatter yourself. We're here for the man in charge, not the *iad* who betrayed us. Not yet. Consider this a stay of execution.'

'The people of Ysundeneth need their priest of Shorth,' said Takaar.

'Like they need their champion of the harmony?' said Llyron.

Takaar frowned. 'She isn't right. But I am not here to lead. Only to help. Never to lead. Only a pair of hands. It is not convenient in any way. Wrong again. But I can strike like a taipan, kill like a panther. Useful. Yes.'

Auum watched Llyron lean back gradually from both Marack's blade and Takaar's muttering. Marack cocked her head.

'Kill like a panther,' she repeated. 'Ready to speak?'

Auum focused on the other *iad* in the room. Silent for now and staring at the unfolding scene with open mouth and blank eyes. Sildaan looked beaten down. Gone was the cocksure expression and the arrogance of growing power. Replaced by a dull morbidity. Not triggered by the arrival of the TaiGethen either.

'Where's Garan?' demanded Auum.

Sildaan looked up at him. She wasn't about to say anything. Next to her, Llyron managed a dry laugh.

'Garan? He's down at the barracks. That's where the soldiers live. Why on earth would you care?'

'Like I said, we're here for the man in charge?'

Llyron laughed again and Marack pushed her blade a little closer. 'And you're looking for Garan? He's not in charge. You poor fools, why did you come here? You really have no idea of the power that has arrived on our shores, do you? It's over for the elves of Ysundeneth and so it will be for those of Tolt Anoor and Deneth Barine.

'All you can do now is run to the rainforest. Hide in the darkest parts of the canopy and wait for the inevitable end. Men are here. Magic is here. And you can do nothing to stop it.'

Auum saw Marack hesitate. Now he understood Sildaan's desolation. And his hatred of her deepened.

'So who is the man in charge?' he asked. 'We don't care who he is. We want him. No human is fast enough to beat a TaiGethen.'

Sildaan caught his gaze, and Yniss preserve him if there wasn't pity in her eyes.

'O Auum. So right about so much but so wrong about this. Please run while you still have time.'

Something in her chilled Auum to the core. 'What have you done? What have you allowed into our lands?'

'We are all of us only alive until our usefulness runs its course,' said Sildaan.

'Sildaan!' snapped Llyron. 'Enough.'

'Why?' asked Auum. 'What aren't you telling us?'

Sildaan didn't get the chance to respond. Takaar groaned. He stumbled back clutching at his head, doubled over and fell to the ground on his side, vomiting bile onto the timber floor and convulsing.

Both Llyron and Sildaan leapt up and backed away from him as he writhed and tried to cry out through jaws locked in pain.

'What's happening?'

'Magic,' said Auum. 'That's what. Lots of it. Either here or down at the dockside.'

Outside the windows, echoes of light could be seen flashing across the sky. Marack ran to the door and pulled it open. Auum, crouched by Takaar, could see down the corridor. It was empty but there were the sounds of fighting echoing up from the hall below. Katyett was inside the temple.

A door opened halfway down the corridor and an *ula* stumbled out, crashing into the wall opposite before turning his back to lean against it and jab a finger back towards the chamber.

'I will never bow to this. This is not what we planned. How can you countenance this genocide?'

The *ula* ducked. An arrow bit into the wall where his head had been. He looked left and right, saw Marack at the door and began running towards them. Auum growled and stood.

Hithuur.

The traitor priest dived headlong into the room.

'Close it. Bar it. Please.'

Other figures were emerging from the room. Marack slammed the door, ran to a heavy chair and dragged it across. Auum pounced on Hithuur.

'*Cascarg*. You killed my Jarinn. You murdered our high priest. Welcome to your execution.'

'No. What are you talking about? It was men. Men and magic. I loved Jarinn.'

Hithuur tried to scrabble away but Auum was too strong. He clamped a hand on Hithuur's throat and squeezed.

'Liar. Olmaat saw. And Olmaat lives.'

Hithuur's eyes widened. He gurgled, trying to force words out. Auum tightened his grip a little more. Marack pulled another chair in front of the door. Behind him, Takaar was moaning but his body was back under his control.

'Please,' croaked Hithuur. 'Or many thousands more will die.'

'And if I am one of them it will be worth it to see your soul to the wrath of Shorth,' said Auum.

'I. Deserve. It. Please. You can help them.'

There was an impact on the door. Marack braced herself against it and yelled for Sildaan to help. Sildaan did not move.

'Say nothing, Hithuur. Nothing,' said Llyron.

Auum heard her, spared her a glance and relaxed his grip.

'Speak. Speak now. Llyron cannot hurt you. I can.'

'Hithuur,' warned Llyron.

'Shut up. Shut up. Trying to save your own skin. Too late for that.'

Llyron rose to her feet but Takaar was in front of her and shoved her back down. There was another impact on the door. Heavier this time. The chairs moved. Marack pushed them back hard.

'There is a very powerful man in charge. A mage lord. He's sectioning the city. Dividing the threads.'

'Huh,' said Auum. 'You should be delighted. That's just what you wanted, wasn't it? The old order restored.'

'Ystormun, the mage lord, he isn't sectioning the city to bring back the old order. He's doing it because he's going to exterminate the threads he feels can't benefit him.'

Auum swayed back from Hithuur and looked at Marack to be sure he'd heard right. Hithuur had made flesh a fear that burned in every elf. To lose a thread is to lose a god.

'Apposans and Orrans he assumes will be useful. Ixii, Gyalans, Ynissul. Not so. And not just here,' said Hithuur. 'Across Calaius.

Every city, every settlement. We . . . we saved the archives. He has everything he needs.'

Door, chairs and Marack were flung aside as if tossed by the hand of Yniss himself. Marack fetched up against the wall under the windows. The chairs broke against stone and beam. Auum was on his feet, his swords out. Hithuur lay where he was and let out a feeble whine. His crotch grew dark.

A man strode into the room. It could only be Ystormun. Tall. Gaunt like a corpse on whom the flesh has weathered like leather. His head was shaved. Eyes sunken into dark-rimmed sockets. They were a stunning emerald green and brim-full of malevolence. He wore plain clothes. Grey and cream shirt and trousers. On his feet were light-brown boots. Beside him was a human with a bow. And just behind him was Helias. The final traitor.

Ystormun surveyed them all briefly. He reached out a hand. Black lines, like lightning, sprang from it and speared into Hithuur's body. The priest jerked and his tongue jutted from jaws that clamped down on it. Blood poured from his mouth. His clothing began to smoulder and his eyes flashed flame briefly before a shriek was dragged from his mouth and he lay still.

Ystormun moved further into the room, sniffing the air. He spared Sildaan and Llyron the briefest acknowledgement before focusing on Takaar, who had gripped the sides of his head and sunk to his knees when Hithuur had suffered his fate. Auum looked at Marack. She was moving but still down. Helias had positioned himself behind the archer, whose bow was trained on Auum.

'In my city, we call this an awakening. Painful is it not?' Ystormun's voice was barely more than a whisper yet it contained such force that Takaar raised his head to see. 'Often fatal if mishandled. Curious that one of you should be so blessed.'

Ystormun reached out a hand and placed it on Takaar's brow. Takaar's face relaxed, his pain faded on the instant. He breathed deeply. Ystormun withdrew his hand and wiped it on his trousers. His gaze moved and came to rest on Auum.

'TaiGethen,' he said. 'Impressive. Worthy of study. Perhaps one day I will create a force to rival you.'

The sheer strength of Ystormun's gaze forced Auum back a pace but he steadied and refused to blink.

'We will never serve you.'

'That will not be necessary,' said Ystormun. Auum tensed to strike but the mage lord merely laughed. 'Save it. If the archer does not hit you, I cannot fail. Savour what is left of your life. Put up your blades.'

Auum did so, though he didn't know why.

In the moments before the chaos unfolded, Helias sensed something. He had to have done because he was already moving when the archer's arrow thudded into the ceiling and his body hit the floor. Ystormun was turning and moving towards Katyett and her cell. Marack had scrabbled to her feet. Takaar was shouting. Auum could see it and couldn't stop it.

'No, Katyett, no,' shrieked Takaar.

Katyett did not or would not hear him. She slid hard and fast across the polished timbers, her feet striking Ystormun's ankles and upending him in a heap on the floor. Merrat and Grafyrre turned to defend the doorway from approaching soldiers. Katyett leapt on Ystormun, wrapping him in a crushing bear hug.

'Got him,' she said. 'Got him.'

'Kill him!' cried Takaar, dragging a sword from his scabbard and running forward.

'No. They told me downstairs. He's the one we want. We need him alive. Help me.'

Ystormun didn't struggle. He merely reached a hand up to Katyett's face and unleashed his black lightning. Katyett screamed as her face charred and split. Takaar howled and fell back, his hands about his head once more. Auum ran towards Katyett where she thrashed, her hold broken and her body smoking. Her hair caught fire.

Marack threw her arms about Auum and bore him back.

'No. You can't help her. You can't.'

Merrat and Grafyrre had spun from the enemy at the door. They surged towards Ystormun but his free hand spat lightning at them, drawing dark tears in their faces and hands.

'Get away!' screamed Marack. 'Get away!'

Katyett was dead. Her body ruined and smouldering. Ystormun stood, his fingertips connecting his hands and the black light spitting and hissing within the cradle. Merrat and Grafyrre made to move in again.

'Too late,' said Ystormun. 'Much too late.'

Blackened hands reached out on the end of arms from which flesh had been melted back to the bone. They grasped at Ystormun's ankles.

Pulled. Tripped him. Ystormun fell, the lightning in his hands vanishing and a scream more bestial than human escaping his lips. Hithuur turned an eyeless face full of the desire for death on Auum.

'Run,' he croaked. 'Run.'

Ystormun was already climbing back to his feet. Already muttering under his breath. Auum saw Hithuur shake his head as the Tai thought to attack the mage lord. Something in the gesture chilled him so deeply he shuddered. Marack was shouting for them to run. Grafyrre and Merrat were staring at Ystormun. Takaar moved.

He slid across the floor and scooped up Katyett's body. He was up in the same movement and heading for the door. The corridor ahead was crowded with men. Takaar stopped and turned. Ystormun was smiling. Sildaan and Llyron were mute, cowering behind chairs. Grafyrre and Merrat were moving to guard Takaar. But there was nowhere to go.

'Nails!' screamed Marack. 'Now!'

There was the merest hesitation. Ystormun opened his hands. The doorway filled with swordsmen. Auum ran. He barrelled into Takaar as he stood, screaming Katyett's name, and bore them both straight through the window, Marack and Katyett's Tai right behind him.

Takaar came back to himself as the window shattered across his back and he pushed away from Auum. He saw black lightning lick out of the shattered window and chase down the walls, cracking paintwork and splintering wood. He was spinning in the air. His next view was of the ground, rushing up fast. No time to get his feet under him.

Takaar struck the ground on the tumble. He let go Katyett's body. His shoulder took the first impact and he tucked his head in, rolling around his upper back. His momentum took him on. He came briefly to his feet, twisted, and on the next fall got his arms out over his head, turned a forward roll and came to a stop on his haunches.

He stared back at Shorth. Katyett's misguided actions had saved him. Saved all five of them. Pain rocked him. It surged through his body and in his heart. Ystormun's words had confirmed what he had already begun to suspect. Faces appeared at the windows. Auum pulled him to his feet.

Light filled the piazza and there was the sound of multiple detonations. Castings were striking the lawns and temples. Takaar moved to Katyett's body and scooped it up again. He stared down at her face. It was burned, barely recognisable. He moved away a strand of hair. It powdered in his hand. He began to weep.

'Takaar.'

'Leave me.'

There was nowhere else to go. Here was why he had returned. Here in his arms and stolen from him the moment he had found her again. Love for Katyett stormed his body. He would do anything for her. He would die for her.

I'm sorry, what did you just say?

'No.' Auum's grip on Takaar was strong and pulled him towards the piazza. 'We need you. We're attacked. What was it you said? Grieve now or make sure the deaths of those you have lost have worth?'

Takaar stared at Auum. From the nails of Shorth, arrows flicked down.

'I will not leave her to them. She deserves better than that.'

'Then bring her but come on. We have to get out of here.'

Arms were supporting him. Takaar looked. Merrat and Grafyrre. Marack was by Auum. The five of them, bruised from their landings, ran back into the piazza, keeping the windowless face of Shorth at their backs. Marack ran between Merrat and Grafyrre, whispering words to them, containing her own grief for their sake.

Orbs of brown and green flame were soaring through the air. The lawns of the piazza were ablaze with magical fire. If bodies lay there, they were less than ashes. They kept to the edge of the lawns, in the partial shelter of the temples that ringed them. Every ward at the end of every passage between the temples had been triggered. Flames soared into the sky, trapping them inside and the men without.

Takaar searched for the TaiGethen. They were there. Tucked into the awnings of Tual and Cefu and Appos. Some glancing down the approaches to the Path of Yniss. Forty yards away, the street was packed with men. Takaar's heart fell. Ahead of the main force of soldiers, mages stood, preparing casting after casting. The noise in the piazza was deafening. Down the street, men clashed weapons, issuing a challenge.

Marack ran to the nearest cell leader.

'Why didn't you go, Kerryn?'

'Why would we do that? You were not ready,' she replied.

Kerryn looked at Takaar. Saw the body in his arms. She let out a sigh, part disbelief part pure grief.

'The Arch of the TaiGethen has fallen!' shouted Grafyrre. 'Let your anger flow. Take revenge. There are men to be killed. Men are to blame.'

'No,' called Takaar, and he didn't know why he had done so. They could hear him above the tumult of the spells and the fire, he knew they could. 'We can't waste our lives. To do so wastes Katyett's too.'

'But we have nothing!' Merrat was screaming right into his face. 'We have no hostage. We have no leader and we have no escape. All we have is vengeance.'

Oh, how you must be enjoying this. You couldn't have planned it better if you'd tried.

Takaar stared briefly at the enemy forces not thirty yards distant and preparing to attack. Mages were falling back behind the lines of warriors. Someone had to speak to the TaiGethen, who were already praying for a glorious death.

Yes. Speak to them. Give them the big speech and then fail them.

Takaar's heart was rippling, or so it felt. The sweat was on his brow and back and the tremors had reached his arms. His vision tunnelled. They were close. So very, very close. Soon they would roll over these pitiful few and the TaiGethen would be finished for ever.

A quick elf, a lone elf, might get away. Unseen over the domes just beyond Tual. Too many would be seen and hunted down. Alone, you can make it. But only if you go now. Abandon that corpse in your arms. Do it. You must live. Someone must live to tell the tale of what happened here. You, Takaar. It has to be you.

Tantalising. The climb wouldn't even be hard. None would live to gainsay his version of events.

Think of the tale of glory you could weave. An ula *of your intelligence.*

Takaar walked forward beyond the first line of defenders already preparing for battle. Eyes followed him. Mistrustful eyes. Betrayed eyes. The TaiGethen possessed long memories and little room for forgiveness. Behind them, the temple doors had opened. Soldiers crowded the steps. Ystormun would be close.

Takaar looked at his escape route. He looked up to the heavens. Gyal's shroud was forging across the heavens. Shielding the eyes of the gods from the slaughter to come. Making the sky dark. It would rain hard enough to conceal an elf trying to escape his fate.

Takaar looked at the spires and slender towers of the temple of

Tual. The places for birds and monkeys to rest. Where lizards and insects could find shelter and safety within the city.

No. Don't even think about it.

'I told you I got to choose,' muttered Takaar. 'Well I've chosen.'

He lifted Katyett's body above his head.

'Will you let your Arch, your hero, go to Shorth with her death a waste? Tens of thousands of your people lie in their beds not even knowing that they are living their last. Aye, it is so. Extermination follows from the hands of men. We cannot let that happen. We cannot bargain so we must fight. We must free our people, any that we can. Even one life saved is a blessing on the elven race and a wound in the body of men. Because we must fear magic we must nullify it. You all know what we must do.

'We are TaiGethen. Born to serve Yniss and our people. We do not serve him by laying down our lives to send a few worthless souls to Shorth. I'll do it on my own if I must. But I will not leave our people to die. Not this time.'

Takaar embraced Katyett to him, feeling her dead weight and the slackness in her limbs like a sword dragged slowly through his soul. He laid her inside the porch of Cefu, where the rain would not hurt her face.

'I will not fail you again, my love. I will not.'

I cannot believe what I am hearing.

'Then go and listen to someone else.'

Takaar ran at the human army of thousands. Thirty-seven Tai-Gethen came in his wake.

Chapter 40

A superiority in numbers is one thing, the element of surprise is quite another.

Ystormun turned from the shattered windows. Hithuur was still breathing. Ystormun's hand flicked out casually and a stalk of lightning buried itself in his forehead, cooking his brain. He looked over at movement to his right.

'I see you managed to save your own skin, Helias. Good for you.'

Helias bobbed his head looking like nothing more than a child's toy, he was so pathetically grateful. Llyron and Sildaan were unscathed too. Remarkable. Ystormun moved swiftly to Llyron and grabbed her collars with one hand, pulling her upright and off the ground in a single powerful movement. She began to choke a little.

'What will they try to do?' he demanded.

'I have no idea,' said Llyron.

Ystormun felt a thrill of anger energise his tired body. 'High Priest of Shorth, I have been knocked down twice. It will not happen a third time. You know them. Tell me where they will try to go even though my army is pressing every corner of this ridiculous gathering of temples.'

'You killed their Arch,' said Sildaan, emerging from her hiding place. 'And they will kill you for that. But not tonight. Tonight they will seek to free those Hithuur told them were about to die.'

'They have no chance. They are pitiful in number.'

'You do not know them. You do not know their belief and their desire. And you do not know their speed and their skill. They will not try to beat you. Not tonight. But they will hurt you. That I promise.'

Ystormun let Llyron go and the high priest collapsed to the floor, gasping in grateful breaths. He loomed over Sildaan, whom he could see still retained a little of her courage. Plenty of time to extinguish that.

'You are free with your promises, Sildaan. How good of you to pledge so much to me. I will demonstrate my gratitude thus.' Ystormun snapped his fingers and his aide, a mage of some small talent, came to his side. 'Are we set?'

The mage consulted a parchment he had been clutching in his hands.

'Yes, my lord. The Ixii, the Gyalans, the Orrans, the Cefans and the identified militant Tuali are held and secure. The chosen places are the museum, two of the larger grain stores, a market square to the north of the city centre and the walled courtyard in front of Llyron's mansion. None of the identified elves has a way out. We await only your word.'

'Then the word is given,' said Ystormun. He swung back to Sildaan. 'There. See how easy it is?'

'How easy what is?'

Ystormun sighed. 'And I thought you were supposed to be among the smarter of your race. Garan told me so, but perhaps respecting his judgement was my mistake. I do not have the manpower to enslave your entire race. Indeed to harvest the resources we want I frankly don't need your entire race. Neither do I have the manpower, or the desire, to keep them imprisoned. Such a cost. Cruel too, to keep creatures that desire freedom under lock and key, don't you think?'

'I don't understand,' said Sildaan.

'What I don't want, I discard. That is the way to maximum efficiency, maximum profit and minimal chance of dissension.' Ystormun watched Sildaan's face crumple. He smiled. Power was such a wonderful thing to wield. 'Ah, now you're getting it. And since I do not want to risk any of my swordsmen getting injured during the process, I have asked my extremely talented and imaginative mages to carry out the procedure cleanly and quickly. This they can do at a distance. It'll be painless too, which is a mercy I am happy to bestow.'

Sildaan's face was as pale as a sharp-ears face could get. Tears were spilling down her cheeks and she could only gasp out her words. Near her, Llyron was too stunned even to speak.

'Please, my lord. You have imprisoned thirty thousand – *iad*, *ula* and child. Innocents.'

'No elf is innocent,' said Ystormun. He turned to his mage. 'Is it really as many as thirty thousand?'

'That's a good estimate, my lord.'

Ystormun raised his eyebrows. 'Really? Well, Sildaan, it's fortunate that you have such a large forest in which to bury them all.'

The TaiGethen spread across the Path of Yniss, running hard at the human army. Grafyrre and Merrat were centre. Calling orders. Their grief and their passion ringing in every word. And the TaiGethen responded, chanting a mourning dirge as they came, the words echoing against the blank wall of nervous human soldiers.

Takaar ran on their left, Auum and Marack flanking him. He could feel every one who ran as if they were touching him. Their energy, their faith and their belief. Their desire for purification and vengeance. Ahead, the human army was halted. Their line was forty abreast with room to wield their longswords, broadswords and shields.

Behind the front ranks of swordsmen, mages cast. Brown and green orbs arced into the night sky, heading for the piazza. The mages raised their heads to see their handiwork only to be confronted by the onrushing TaiGethen. Orders were barked. Mage heads dropped in concentration again.

Twenty yards to impact.

'Jaqrui!' called Grafyrre. Hands grabbed out crescent blades. 'Away!'

Takaar watched the deadly metal flash across the diminishing space. Shields were held out. Blades raised. Fear ran through the enemy. Takaar's jaqrui slashed into the cheek of his target as he ducked and turned his head. Other crescents thudded into shields or careered from sword blades, shattering on walls or slicing into those behind. Most found flesh or leather armour.

'Jaqrui!' called Grafyrre again. 'Away!'

An order rang out across the human lines. Swordsmen dropped to their knees. Many threw themselves flat, knowing what was coming in front and behind. Mages raised their heads, ready. Jaqruis whispered into their lines. Blades chopped into hands, heads and chests. Mages screamed. Castings bloomed dark as mages lost control at the critical moment. Ice and fire fell on the human lines.

Ten yards and closing. Other mages, calmer mages, steadied and cast.

'Evade and strike!'

Clouds of ice washed out towards the TaiGethen on a dread frozen wind. Tongues of flame leapt from the hands of mages even as jaqruis struck them down. Takaar saw the castings rush towards them and felt a moment's peace mingle with his nausea, lessened since the touch of Ystormun's hands. The din subsided and the energies about him caressed rather than sickened him. He recognised the state. Last time he had felt it was in combat with the Garonin. He breathed it in.

Takaar could see the individual shards of ice in the mass that came towards him. He saw the twinkling yellow reflection of torchlight. Saw them turning end over end or spinning around their horizontal axis. Beautiful. Beguiling. Takaar leapt, pushing off with his left foot and arrowing into the air, his arms straight in front of him. He angled his body horizontal and pushed his arms to the sides.

The ice gouged beneath him. He felt flechettes snip at his jacket and the toes of his boots. The cold air behind the ice shocked his lungs. He was past the cloud in a heartbeat. The enemy were below him. None had even registered what was coming at them. Bloodied bodies, jaqrui victims, writhed on the ground amidst those caught in the hell of their own castings.

Takaar brought his legs under him. He came down in a crouch, straddling a moving body. He jabbed out his hand, straight-fingered, crushing the man's windpipe. Takaar straightened. Enemies were everywhere. TaiGethen who'd rolled under the castings came to their feet. Others who had chosen to leap landed all around him.

'Strike forward, guard your backs!' called Merrat. 'Tais, we strike.'

The mage in front of Takaar raised his head. Takaar saw him mouth what was most probably a curse. Takaar swept a blade from his back and chopped it hard down the mage's face. The man fell silently. The TaiGethen surged forward, still singing the mourning dirge.

Keller wasn't lead mage for nothing. He'd seen what was going to happen and cast wings on his back rather than ice for his fingers. He shot straight up into the air past the diving and rolling forms of the TaiGethen and breathed a huge sigh of relief that he was not on the ground.

Garan had ordered seventeen hundred men up the Path of Yniss from the barracks and staging areas the moment the confirmation of the attack on the temple had been confirmed. Everything had been foreseen by Ystormun, but he had not understood the tenacity of the TaiGethen. Maybe he had assumed the temple would be reached but this, he could not have foreseen this.

A few TaiGethen had been trapped in the piazza. They could not get out to the sides or the rear. Sitting targets for spells and then blades to mop up the survivors. That they would *attack* was against all reason. But up here, where it was safe and the screams of the dying filtered up through the din of barked orders, the low elven chanting and the steady disintegration of order, Keller could see something more.

They weren't just attacking. They were trying to break through. Unbelievable. Keller flew back towards Garan. He could see the big general amidst his men, too far back to see what was happening further forward.

'Garan!' Garan looked up. 'You have to break your force. They're in amongst you. No room to fight.'

'We'll take them as we are.'

'You don't understand. They aren't fighting head on. They're trying to get through us. Order daggers drawn at least. Be ready.'

Garan glared at him. 'That is not the way to face this enemy. They're too quick. We need heavy defence.'

'Clear a break. Make room for spells, then.'

'Now that I might do.'

Keller nodded and rose again. 'Sooner rather than later.'

He flew back towards the fighting. In the gloom, he could barely follow it. More so because the elves were so damned *fast*. Three leapt above the men they were approaching, rolled in the air and came down striking out. Three men died. Mages behind them made to cast. Woefully slow. Blades licked out. Mages fell.

In the centre of the street a knot of soldiers had formed, facing in all directions and bristling with weapons. The elves ran at them, leapt over them, continued on down the street while the men scattered. Elves came from nowhere. Hands and feet struck out. Men were spun on their heels. Heads snapped back. Blades caught the torchlight. Blood misted into the night sky.

'Dear gods around us,' whispered Keller. 'It's a massacre.'

In the centre of their force, the humans were packed too tight to fight. They couldn't free their swords. They pushed for space. Angry shouts rattled across their lines. Panic was beginning to grow. Men were dying. Elves were not. Mages dare not cast in the confined space. More and more took the route of the coward and flew straight up, abandoning their comrades to the cold, disciplined fury of the TaiGethen.

'Forward!' called Grafyrre. 'Keep moving forward.'

Blood slicked the cobbles. Bodies of men choked the gutters and the central drains. Auum spun and kicked high, his foot smacking into the side of an enemy's head. The man fell sideways. Auum moved into the space. A sword came at him, hurried through waist high. Auum ducked it. The soldier couldn't control the sweep. The blade sank into the gut of one of his own.

Takaar ensured the man went down hard. He moved up. Marack blocked aside a downward cut. Takaar slid a blade through the man's ribs. Space. Auum moved up. Takaar paced forward and leapt. He twisted in the air, landed and hacked down. Blood surged from his target's shoulder.

Auum dropped, slid the feet from a mage. Marack hacked into his chest and moved into the space. The press was getting thicker. The pressure increasing from behind too. Auum felt his movements hampered for the first time. Ahead, men were slowly getting themselves together, holding their swords straight out and using them for stabbing. Overhead, mages were flying down the Path of Yniss. Not in confusion, with purpose. Auum saw them and knew in his heart that time was short for the doomed threads.

'Follow me!' yelled Takaar.

'Where?'

Auum diverted a blade coming for his gut and thumped the heel of his palm into his enemy's chest. The man fell back against the rank behind. Takaar pointed to the sky.

'Up.'

Auum smiled. 'Graf! Heads up and run.'

Grafyrre relayed the idea as an order and the TaiGethen reacted as one. The man Auum had just knocked down had been caught by those behind. Auum ran up the front of his body and launched himself from the man's face. He jumped high above the human army. He cycled his arms and legs, reaching out as far as he could, searching for the ideal landing point. He saw it catch the light of torches from either side of the Path of Yniss.

A helmet.

Auum glanced left and right. His clear view across the street afforded him the sight of TaiGethen elves soaring above their enemies. Faces were turning up, but those who had seen them were already too late to stop them, much less follow them. Marack was turning a somersault next to him, Takaar another of his horizontal flights, fierce and graceful. Grafyrre and Merrat were hand in hand, coming down on their left feet and pushing off in perfect balance.

Auum landed. The helmet's occupant grunted and ducked at the brief weight on the top of his head but Auum was already gone. Like running the sucking mud of the Mouth of Orra at the outflow of the River Ix, or the quicksands out at Palynt Reach. Quick steps, minimum weight down and the whole body canted forward at a steep angle. Always pushing away, never levering forward. Olmaat used to describe it as nothing more than a controlled fall.

A wave of incredulous fury followed in their wake. By the time soldier or mage had reacted, the elves were past him. Swords waved ineffectually and belatedly overhead. Fists punched empty space. Fingers grabbed at nothing.

Auum bounced left and right as he ran. His eyes searched four moves ahead, his mind trusting his feet to land without error. The TaiGethen passed across the heads of their enemies like the last mist blown from the surface of the ocean. Felt and gone.

'Cover on landing. Left turn. Orsan's Yard for muster,' said Grafyrre, his voice carrying across the soaring line of elven warriors.

Auum saw the back of the human lines. It was loose there and they could see what was coming at them. Auum growled a warning, his panther voice focusing the eye of every TaiGethen. He selected his landing point, straightened his body and slammed down hard with both feet on the head of his last mark.

The mage collapsed beneath him. Auum dropped, rolled and rose in one movement. The TaiGethen moved forward, a single unit. Auum drew his second blade. He jammed his left into the gut of a hapless soldier and spun past his falling body. He whipped his right blade into the neck of the man next to him, dragged his left clear and buried it to the hilt in the chest of the man behind. Takaar hurdled a body, Marack in his heel prints, and took the next man two-footed on the point of the jaw. Marack ran past him and tore the throat from a fifth with the ends of her fingers. Auum came to her left, blocked a wild slash and chopped into the hamstrings of a sixth.

Clear space but the mages would be turning and clear of the bulk of the army.

'Go, go,' said Auum, pressing a hand into Takaar's back.

They headed for the left turn to take them into Keeper's Row. Grafyrre and Merrat were ahead of them, the bulk of the TaiGethen around them. Ten yards to the turn, the first way off the Path of Yniss from the mouth of the temple piazza.

'Casters ready!' called a voice. 'Move!'

Takaar pulled Auum and Marack along, practically threw them around the corner. A freezing wind howled past the opening. Auum felt his hair crisp with frost. His blade gleamed with ice. The TaiGethen were already pounding away to the south, heading into the warren of the Grans.

Auum and Marack followed in Takaar's wake just in front of the rear cells. Abruptly, Takaar stumbled. He reached out a hand, which Auum was able to grasp.

'Takaar?' he asked.

Takaar carried on running but he'd slowed dramatically.

'Something's growing,' said Takaar. 'Something ugly and evil. Like Gyal building to a storm of wrath but beneath my feet. In the energy lines. In the magic. I don't think we have much time.'

'What are you talking about?'

'If Ystormun really wants to commit genocide on the lesser threads of elves he isn't going to do it with the sword,' said Takaar.

Auum remembered the mages flying fast overhead. He shuddered.

They ran into Orsan's Yard and faced fifty and more blades and axes. The two groups faced each other for a moment before Merrat broke and ran forward, dragging Pelyn into a fierce embrace.

'Yniss bless you and the axes of the Apposans. We need you now.'

'Couldn't quite bring myself to follow Katyett's last order,' said Pelyn. She frowned. 'Where is she?'

No one needed to speak the words. The first line of a lament to the fallen was whispered by every TaiGethen. Pelyn closed her eyes and tears escaped down her cheeks. Takaar, the nausea rising within him as the magic built in intensity, walked forward still using Auum for support.

'There will be time for grief, Pelyn,' he said. 'Tell me what you had planned to do here. Quickly. Time is short.'

Pelyn's stare was quick and angry but she could see there was no arrogance in his face. Only the pain of what was growing underfoot.

'There are more Apposans here. Others that will want to get out. We came to help them.'

Takaar nodded and there was smiling among the TaiGethen.

'You have chosen a path more vital than you know. And your Apposan axes will be the difference between life and death for hundreds, maybe thousands.' Takaar paused and breathed deeply. 'There will be fire and there will be panic. I will explain, but we must use these to our advantage. Grafyrre, we need to split to reach all the most vulnerable threads at once.'

Grafyrre's nod was curt and his eyes held the passion of the wronged. He turned to the elves and began to talk.

Garan knelt beside the body of the elf and turned her burned, wrecked face to the rain. He rubbed at his stubble and sucked in his bottom lip.

'We got one then,' said Keller, landing behind him and dismissing the spell at his back.

'No,' said Garan. 'We barely even nicked one of them. This one they brought with them. It's got Ystormun's sick signature all over it. She must have been important.'

Garan stood and turned back. Soldiers were filling the space around him.

'No one touches this elf,' he said. 'No one moves her; no one pisses on her body; no one takes anything from her. Do I make myself clear? Good. Pass the word. I will be checking back.'

'What's that all about?' asked Keller.

'Just a hunch,' said Garan. 'Tell you later.'

Keller shrugged. 'Whatever you say. Do you think they can do it? What Ystormun says they want to do?'

'I think that if the TaiGethen really put their minds to it, they could do pretty much anything they want. Their problem is there aren't enough of them.'

Garan turned to head to Shorth. The blackened walls and the smoking ruins of temples surrounding them saddened him. The elves had destroyed enough of it themselves. They hardly needed the help of men.

'Where are you going?' asked Keller. 'Action's this way.'

Garan didn't bother turning to look at Keller. 'I don't think so. I'm a soldier. I'm not a murderer of unarmed civilians. I will have no part in the massacre. Why would I want to watch the helpless be slaughtered?'

'It didn't seem to worry you in the Park of Tual.'

'They were agitators, problems to be dealt with. What we have left now are those desiring only peace. Why would I want them dead?'

'Because they're only elves and this is the moment when we assure victory and compliance.'

Now Garan turned and he was surprised at the contempt that he felt for Keller. Mixed with pity that his sight was so short.

'I thought more of you. But you're just a lackey to the mage lords. You know what should be worrying you is where this power of his comes from and why it's so different from yours. One day you'll need to be sure you're standing on the right side of the conflict.'

'What conflict?'

Garan chuckled. 'Don't take the piss. You're not that naive. You know the tension in Triverne. You know there's a struggle coming. The six are on one side. Every other mage in the circle is on the other. Has it really never occurred to you why Ystormun wants control here so quickly? Look at the resources. Look at the power they represent. One day, and it may not be for a hundred years, Balaian will fight Balaian for this place.'

'And what will you do in the meantime?' Keller's face dripped his scepticism. 'Keep your head down or resign your commission?'

'I doubt Ystormun accepts resignations with any grace, do you? No, Keller, I expect when I detail my men to shovel the ashes of the innocents away from the carcasses of their homes, I'll be thinking of heading into the forest and taking my chances with the TaiGethen. What about you?'

The earth rumbled underfoot. Flames spat hundreds of feet into the sky. There was a concerted groan and a thundering crash of timbers. Detonations echoed away into the clearing sky.

'It begins,' said Keller.

'It certainly does.'

Chapter 41

The TaiGethen need no shield behind which to cower, only the blessing of Yniss.

The TaiGethen ran. Apposans were with each of the three groups Grafyrre had detailed to seek and release, if they could, Gyalan, Ixii and Cefan prisoners. They did not know how they could achieve what Takaar desired but they did know they had to try. It was what the TaiGethen existed to do.

Auum ran with the cells closing on the museum. Pelyn had made a promise to Methian that she would try and help the Gyalans. And that was despite what had happened to a young Al-Arynaar at their hands just a few days before. This was not the time, Grafyrre had said, to be bothered by thread animosity. Elf could kill elf later, that was their right. It was not the right of humans.

They headed for the lights that bordered the quarter of the city where the Gyalans had made their homes for centuries. They were weavers, potters, artisans of all types. Famed for the verve of their creations and the flair of their construction. And now within moments of being dealt a potentially fatal blow. They were not an overtly fertile thread. They could not afford to lose such numbers from their stock.

Auum and Marack flanked a pale and shaking Takaar. Every pace brought a grunt of exertion. Every breath was pained and deliberate. He was not going to be of great use in a fight. Through the dark streets of Old Millers they came. Pelyn ran with them. Grafyrre and Merrat too. Thrynn and Corsaar guarded the Apposans. Ulysan brought up the rear. They were forty-five in all. Auum expected them all to die.

'Remember it'll be chaos,' managed Takaar. 'Use it. These soldiers need order. Take it from them.'

The museum of Hausolis itself was the centrepiece of the quarter.

Houses bordered it on all sides of a square that saw celebrations every year on the anniversary of the closing of the gateway. Other days, markets and itinerant performers used the space as their own. Other streets ran away to Old Millers, down to Mural and Glade and towards the spice market.

They rounded a corner into a street lined with torches. Swordsmen were patrolling and there were mages in groups along its length. The street let out into the museum square at the other end. Here it was houses and shops on both sides. A place where normal people lived. Every house was barred shut. Every shutter was closed and secured from the outside.

Grafyrre made a hand signal. Cells of TaiGethen climbed walls either side of the street. He and Merrat ran on. Auum and Marack moved ahead of Takaar. Belatedly, the guards saw them, pointed and shouted for help while backing away towards their comrades.

Mages turned. Heads were bowed.

'Apposans to every house!' called Merrat. 'Get them away towards Olbeck. Shove them, push them. Anything.'

Auum ran to the rhythmic sound of doors being smashed by axes. To the sound of screams and urgent shouts. To anger and fear.

'Target the mages,' ordered Grafyrre.

Two mages lifted their heads and spread their hands.

'Doorways.'

Merrat's shout triggered the street to clear. TaiGethen and Apposan sheltered in doorways, crashed through timbers into houses and dived into shutters, shattering wood. Countless thousands of shards of ice flew along the street. A fine mesh to flay flesh from bones, to strip away life in an instant.

Apposans pushed fleeing Gyalan civilians to the ground. Sacrificed their own bodies to save those they had released. The hail of ice came on a howling wind that cracked timber and widened the cracks in stone and tile. Auum heard the whisper of feet above him.

Abruptly, the castings were exhausted. TaiGethen ran back out on to the streets, leaving terrified Gyalans behind them – clutching each other, waiting for the Apposans to see them to safety. Auum checked Takaar and glanced outside. TaiGethen dropped from the rooftops. Mages died.

Auum sprinted down the centre of the street. Marack was at his shoulder, Takaar a little way behind. Merrat and Grafyrre moved past them. Soldiers squared up. Above and left, Thrynn chased along their flank. More mages were preparing to cast.

Auum thrashed into the shaky human barrier moments after Grafyrre sank his blade into the midriff of a scared soldier. Auum's fist cracked into his target's nose. He kicked down at the enemy's knee, taking him off balance, and rammed his blade into the man's side, butchering vital organs. Blood sluiced onto the ground.

Takaar barrelled into another, wrapping his arms around the man's trunk and bearing him down. The two of them rolled. Takaar came up looking a little dazed. The man had dropped his weapon. He opted to punch. Takaar caught his fist in one hand and straight-fingered into the man's throat with his other.

Auum ran on. Thrynn and his cell pounded to the edge of their rooftop and dived off. Below them, mages readied to cast. TaiGethen engulfed them.

'Straight to the museum,' said Takaar. 'They'll want to take it—'

Takaar stumbled and fell, clutching his head and screaming. Auum slithered to a stop, Marack by him. The TaiGethen faltered.

'No,' said Takaar, grinding the words from locked jaws. 'Go. It's coming. Help them.'

Auum pushed back to his feet.

'The museum. Now. Get it open.'

TaiGethen and Apposan ran. They burst out of the street and onto the museum square. Pelyn was there by Auum, her feet slapping on the cobbles. There was a ring of soldiers around the grand building, and the lines of the Tul-Kenerit which it mimicked brought unwanted memories to Auum's mind. Beyond the museum, the Path of Yniss danced with light. The human army was coming.

Torchlight washed the square. There were mages overhead, shouting orders. Soldiers were turning, moving away from their mages, forming a defensive line. From the north, a massive explosion rumbled through the ground and flames lit up the ocean sky. Auum swore. Even he could feel that in the pit of his stomach. He prayed as he ran that his brothers had been fast enough to beat it.

This time, the mages didn't turn. They were focused on the museum. Auum could see arms stretched out in effort. Limbs shook with exertion. Bodies trembled. A soft green light began to grow in the sky above. It coalesced, brightening quickly.

'Forget the warriors,' shouted Grafyrre. 'Two cells up and over. Apposans to ready. Pelyn, stand and face.'

Auum picked up his pace. He flashed across the square, feeling an increasing weight on his chest as the light grew and deepened. The casting was pulsating. Flashes of brown light could be seen within it. It was like one of the orbs only so much bigger. It would be seen right across the city.

Auum threw a jaqrui at the nearest soldier. He threw it high. The soldier ducked. Auum planted his right foot and sprang up. He tucked in his body, rolled in the air and came down on his left foot, already moving towards the first mage.

Auum took his sword in both hands and smashed it into the mage's lower back. The man pitched forward, dead before he hit the ground. Auum turned left, jabbed the blade into another's throat. Blood spurted out. The mage collapsed to his knees. Auum turned right. Marack beheaded one mage, spun and kicked out at the head of another, catching him in the temple and sending him sprawling. Merrat finished him, Above them, the casting guttered and blinked out.

Auum twisted and faced the soldiers. Pelyn and the Apposans were already on them with the balance of the TaiGethen. Above, the casting had begun to grow again. Grafyrre called for more to attack the casters.

'Right!' cried Thrynn. 'Force moving in on our right.'

Hundreds of men, backed by mages in the air and on the ground, poured into the square from the Path of Yniss. Auum cursed.

'To the doors. Apposans to the doors!' Pelyn shouted her order and led them across the open space to the rear doors of the museum.

They were barred and chained. Apposans fell on them with their axes, hacking and slashing at timber and steel. Sparks flew. Timbers began to shatter and crack.

'TaiGethen, defend the door.'

So like before. So like ten years ago. TaiGethen made a thin barrier in front of the Apposans. Pelyn came back to stand with Auum. Soldiers were filling the square, cutting off their way back towards Old Millers and relative safety. Back there in the street, Takaar still lay helpless.

Above their heads, the green globe grew and grew. It rotated. Lightning spat within it. Mages they would never reach controlled it. Brought their casting closer and closer to fruition. Behind, Apposan axes hammered at the doors. TaiGethen took down more mages.

Auum could hear the screaming of the Gyalans within and the shouts of their rescuers for calm. They would get none.

Ahead of Auum the soldiers had stopped moving in and were even backing up. Every eye was on the casting. None on the elves in front of them.

'Get that door down,' urged Grafyrre.

He stood to Auum's left, his eyes burning, his face ashen with the grief he fought to contain. The door went down. Gyalans, urged by Apposans, poured out behind the TaiGethen. The sky went silent. The pressure on Auum's ears built to a painful crescendo. Something was wrong. Auum glanced back and up. The globe was wobbling. Fire lashed from its sides. Lightning speared down. Auum followed its trail to where it buried itself in the heart of a casting mage. He heard shouting. Humans. Desperate and afraid.

'Run!' yelled Auum. 'Run!'

The TaiGethen broke their line and ran, forming a cordon around their Gyalan charges. The globe plunged down onto the museum. Men began running, scattering. Green light flooded the museum square. There was a sucking at the air. Wind pushed into Auum's face. He heard the shattering of a thousand tiles and then a dull bass thump.

'Down!'

Auum threw himself forward, hit the ground and rolled onto his back. He had to watch. Had to see.

Gyalans were still pouring out of the doors. Apposans literally throwing them into the square. Around him, most had taken his lead and fallen prone. Green light grew behind the open doors, deep within the museum. There was a crackle as of lightning buried in clouds. Next heartbeat, the museum exploded.

The walls either side of the doors bulged and disintegrated, hurling stone and timber hundreds of yards across the square. Flame blew through the open doors. Gyalan, Apposan, TaiGethen – anyone standing in its arc was gone in a blink. Bodies turned to ashes. Elf and man still standing were picked up and cast aside on the wind of the detonation. Bodies twisted and flipped as they bounced. Limbs out of control. Blood smeared the square.

Above, the roof of the museum was spat into the night sky. Lumps of masonry and wood, fragments of exhibits and what might have been bodies were thrown high and clear. The echoes of the explosion slammed around Auum's head. He stared up. Spiralling high, shapes tumbled end over end. Some small, some big, the size of oxen and carts.

They began to fall.

'Up!' Auum's shout was taken up by every TaiGethen at once. 'Up and run. Now.'

Auum pushed himself to his feet. A timber thumped to the ground where he had been lying. It splintered. He felt shards rip into his trousers and lodge in his legs. He stumbled and steadied. Auum ran from *iad* to *ula*. Dragging them up, pushing them towards the north. Towards Takaar.

Quickly, the movement gained a momentum of its own. Auum turned. Pelyn was racing past him. He followed her direction. Men were forming up again. Running back into the square. Just a thin line.

'TaiGethen.' The blessed sound of Grafyrre's voice. 'Make a path. Apposans to the rear. Tais, we move.'

Yniss's elite came together. Fewer now. Of Thrynn there was no sign. Nor Corsaar. But Merrat ran with Grafyrre. Marack, blood pouring from a wound in her forehead, fell in beside Auum and Pelyn. They simply ran at the growing line of men and took their revenge for the death of their Arch, their friend. Their sister.

Men were calling orders. Archers were running in from the right. Mages, those that could, were moving up behind the swordsmen. Auum feinted to swing at the man in front of him. The soldier flinched. Auum dropped and rolled between him and another. The man caught Marack's blade in the side of his head.

Auum stood and thrashed his blade through the guard of the next in line. The enemy's sword broke, the tip flying to lodge in his skull. He cried out and put his hands up to his head. Auum dug his sword in under the hapless human's ribs. Behind Auum, the Tai-Gethen washed over the front line of men. The whole moved back a pace under the pressure of the attack, giving Auum brief room.

A flight of arrows came in from behind, landing amongst the fleeing Gyalans. There was a roar from that direction too. More men spilling into the square. Auum straight-punched the man in front of him, knocking him cold.

TaiGethen flew over his head, dropping into the midst of the growing press of men. They were still four deep ahead. Auum and Marack moved side by side. Four blades blocking and chopping. Merrat and Grafyrre were by them. Pelyn was to Auum's left.

Another surge came from behind. Apposans. Less pretty, just as effective. Axes rose and fell. Blood sprayed into the sky. Auum took heart. He swayed inside a stab to the head and cracked the pommel of his blade into his attacker's face. Auum followed up with a straight kick to the groin. The man gasped. Auum stepped up and butted the bridge of his nose, splitting it open. The man fell. Auum stamped down on his throat and moved past him.

Marack jumped, spun and kicked out. Her foot caught the head of her target. He flew back. The man behind tried to fend him off but succeeded only in stabbing him low in the back. Marack chopped in, left and right. Both men died. More arrows at their back. Auum could hear them skipping off the cobbles.

Auum ducked a wild swing, hearing the blade clash against Pelyn's. He straightened fast. The soldier, surprised, swayed back. Auum stabbed into his exposed throat. Down he went. The soldier behind him was staring at Auum but wasn't about to strike. Blood was sluicing down his face. When he fell forward, Kerryn stood behind him.

'Clear!' shouted Auum. 'Push left and right. Graf. Get some through to the mages.'

The line of men broke. TaiGethen and Apposan chased them away. The square was still in uproar. What was left of the museum was collapsing in on itself. Fire scratched at the sky. Clouds were coming in again.

'Run! Run!'

The Apposans chanted in unison. They rounded up Gyalans and pushed them towards the street and the way out towards the Grans. Terrified *ula* and *iad* came past Auum. He fell in beside them. Behind them, more and more men poured into the square to give chase. Ahead, mages stood waiting. No longer were their comrades in line before them. They had clear targets.

'Graf! Mages!' shouted Auum, but Grafyrre couldn't hear him.

Auum could see him and Merrat over to the right. They took apart three men standing in a tight knot before turning to usher Gyalan and Apposan past them and away. Hundreds, thousands had been saved. The devastation at the museum had brought more onto the street, beating open their own doors and windows to join in the exodus. There was no need for questions now. No need for any elf to wonder if they should join the crowd. One look at the faces of men was all they needed. Any who stayed behind were as good as dead.

Auum powered towards the mages. They were together, seven of them. The sea of elves was about to engulf them but they stayed still, preparing. Auum broke through the line of running Gyalans and Apposans and closed on the enemy. But he would not make it in time.

As one, the mages opened their eyes and focused on their enemy.

They could not see what was behind them. A figure in the air, twisting as he came down right in their midst. Takaar. His swords blurred. Mages were hacked aside. A hand dropped to the ground, still opening and closing. A shoulder was chopped through. They tried to turn and defend but his hands were too quick and his feet too sure.

The last of them grappled with him, wrapping his arms around him and pushing him back. Takaar dropped both blades and stared at the mage. Auum slowed too, letting the rescued and rescuers flow past him. Takaar cocked his head. The mage did not know what to do next. He let go with one arm and felt for a knife, sensing a chance.

Takaar put a hand on the mage's chest and shoved him back just one pace. The other hand he placed on his face. Fire engulfed the man's head. It was a juddering mix of brown and green shot through with grey. His screams were agonised and brief.

Takaar took his hand away and stared at it, his mouth open and moving. Auum glanced behind. Gyalans still poured past him. Men were closing. Not as fast as even the slowest elf but even they would overhaul a TaiGethen who stood and waited for them.

'Takaar. Come on,' he said, though the words he wanted to speak were utterly different.

Takaar looked at him as he approached. Takaar swallowed and stepped back as if trying to retreat from his own hand.

'I felt it in me,' he said. 'And in him. Look at what I did. What did I do?'

An arrow bit into the cobbles right at Auum's feet. Another struck the smouldering dead mage. Auum grabbed Takaar's arm and felt a jolt through it like an impact. He wanted to let go but instead tightened his grip and pulled.

'Come on. Later, all right? Live now.'

Auum began to run. The last of the Gyalans were coming past him. Pelyn was with them. She was cut and bloodied but in her eyes there was victory.

'We did it,' she said, coming to Takaar's other side. 'We did it.'

Takaar looked at her once and shook his head.

'We did nothing. Saved a handful and let so many others die. We have lost Katyett and we have lost our city. Calaius belongs to the humans.'

Chapter 42

While a TaiGethen still has the forest, there is still hope.

For two days survivors trickled out of the city and into the canopy, where the TaiGethen found them and led them to safety. On the third day the humans were done with their slaughter and the city was sealed so tight that no *iad* or *ula* would find a way out.

They were not pursued into the forest. That was left, presumably, to another day. Victory, Pelyn had said, but Takaar had been right. They had lost. The elves had been expelled from their own city. It belonged to man now and they would soon be reaching into the forest to take the rest of what they desired.

So much death. Llyron would be busy for years, sending the souls to Shorth. Assuming Ystormun had kept her alive. And Auum thought that he had. He was clever. Brutal, evil. Clever. Auum sat with Serrin of the Silent on the cliffs above the Ultan. Heavily strapped and limping but very much alive, Serrin's sudden appearance had left Auum's feelings mixed. Serrin did not want to be here but had felt compelled to come. Auum waited to find out why that was while his discomfort grew.

They could sit here safely, looking into the city and seeing the devastation and the work of men. They could see their people too. Slaves now, he supposed. The thrill of the run to the museum was already a tainted memory. The attempts to free thread elves elsewhere in the city had been much less successful.

'Ridiculous, isn't it?' said Auum. 'The Ynissul are now the most numerous thread among the rescued of Ysundeneth.'

Serrin looked at him and shrugged. 'More will come.'

'Not from there,' said Auum. 'Not now.'

A few in excess of two thousand Gyalans had joined close to two and a half thousand Ynissul, half that number of Cefans and a mere few hundred Ixii. The fate of the rest within the city was wholly unknown. Handfuls from other threads had escaped that night, joining the exodus when they saw the chance.

But the truth was that those they had rescued made up a truly pitiful number. Pelyn estimated that more than twenty thousand had in all probability perished in Ysundeneth alone. TaiGethen and Al-Arynaar were already on their way to find out if Tolt Anoor and Deneth Barine had suffered the same fate.

TaiGethen. Almost all gone now. They could barely make up ten cells. Most of them had survived the attack on the museum. Others had perished going back into the city to find more Ixii, the thread that had been targeted most cruelly by the humans. Auum wondered why that had been. Takaar in a brief moment of lucidity had simply nodded knowingly and stared once more at his hand.

'We failed,' said Auum, feeling a desolation sweep through him that he hadn't felt ten years ago when the price in lives had been even higher. 'I'm not sure we can survive this.'

Serrin cleared his throat. 'I will speak freely, Auum, and it will be for the last time.'

Auum felt his heart lurch. 'I wondered why you chose to come back here. After what you said in the forest, I thought I had seen the last of you.'

'Things are changing,' said Serrin. 'Not just for the Silent. The balance of power has shifted away from the priesthood for ever. What Sildaan and Llyron and Hithuur started means priests will never rule the elves again, though in time they might be revered and trusted as keepers of their own faiths. Nothing more.'

Auum opened his mouth but Serrin shook his head.

'Hear me, Auum of the TaiGethen. You see numbers of warriors and you see defeat and extinction. But the coming of man to these shores to use their magic has awoken something within the elves that has lain dormant for thousands of years. Takaar exhibits it most clearly. So do I. So does at least one other Ynissul *iad* that Sikaant found in the forest.

'Did it never occur to you why so many failed to become Silent Priests or failed to become Al-Arynaar or TaiGethen? What man has awakened he will rightly fear. It exists in the subconscious of those of us who serve Yniss with the blade. It underpins your skill, your speed and your awareness.'

'You're saying there will be more of us now?' asked Auum. It sounded so far-fetched, yet coming from the mouth of Serrin it had the weight of inevitability about it.

'Many more,' said Serrin.

'I hope you're right.'

'But you will have to look for them. Sweep the forest clean. Katyett knew what she wanted to do. Build a new fastness at Katura Falls. Every free elf must be brought there. The Silent will keep watch over the temples. We will see that no stranger defiles any of them until the TaiGethen are numerous enough to guard them once more. The TaiGethen and Al-Arynaar must train and build their strengths. Add new talents to their ranks.'

Auum shook his head. It all sounded so perfect. So simple. Too perfect. Too simple.

'But we can never hope to take back our cities. Man is here to stay.'

'You're so sure? You think too much in the short term. Remember that without the rainforest to harvest, the cities are worthless. Empty vessels. Everything we have comes from within the canopy. Make them fear the canopy. Make them regret they ever set foot here so that when you do emerge once again, you are already halfway to pushing them back across the Sea of Gyaam.

'We have lost so much but we have gained much too, though it is hard to see it now, of course. The wounds and the grief are still too fresh.'

'Such as?' Auum knew he sounded petulant but he couldn't find the wit to care.

'You have Takaar.'

'Not necessarily. No one has seen him in two days. Whatever happened to him in Ysundeneth, it's sent him down again. Most likely he's run back to his hovel. Perhaps he'll let the taipan bite him this time or rub a yellow back on his tongue.'

Serrin chuckled. 'Oh dear. I see we have our work cut out to make you see beauty and harmony again.'

'Sorry.'

'No need. But don't worry about Takaar. He'll reappear. If there's one thing we know about him it is that he is a survivor, yes?'

Auum had to smile at that.

'Good,' said Serrin, getting up and brushing himself down. 'At last some humour. I have to go. You'll see me, my friend. The Silent will never desert the forest. And remember, there are two things that we have that the humans do not and can never have.'

'Yes?'

Serrin began to walk away. The sun cast him in silhouette. It was a memory Auum would retain all of his life.

'We have the rainforest and know it is untameable. Humans will never understand that and it is one reason they will fail.'

'Granted,' said Auum and he felt some crumb of comfort. 'And what else do we have that they cannot ever have?'

'Time.' Serrin moved away. 'Lots and lots of time.'

Garan was rewarded on his third night of vigil. He hadn't begun to doubt but he'd already heard the mutterings of his men. No matter. He sat quite still as the lone elf descended the wall of the temple of Cefu. It was quiet now. Night was full and the city was silent but for the cries of the grieving and desperate. And there were few who would raise their voices now.

The elf knelt by the body of his fallen. He whispered words Garan could not catch and lifted her stiff form into his arms. He eyed his climb. Garan didn't envy him it. He walked into the shadows of the porch.

'I can see you safely across the Ultan bridge,' he said.

The elf turned. His face was wet with his tears and his eyes held a wildness at odds with the control of many of the warrior class Garan had seen.

'I can kill you before you know I've moved,' said the elf.

Garan nodded. 'Probably. But then you'd still have to escape the city with your beloved in your arms. Difficult. Even for a TaiGethen.'

'Why would you help me?'

'Because the death of those we love is not constrained by race or victory or defeat.'

'You knew I would come?'

'I knew she had been laid there for a reason. The cloak is mine.'

The elf nodded thanks.

'She was Arch of the TaiGethen. I loved her,' he said.

'Then come with me. Let me help you respect her in death as I did her skill in life.'

The elf stared at him for a time, weighing him up. He muttered to himself, said some sharp words and walked forward.

'I am Garan.'

'We came to kidnap you,' said the elf.

'And ran into Ystormun instead. I'm almost sorry you didn't find me first.'

Takaar didn't reply. Garan walked with him into the Path of Yniss and away towards the Ultan bridge. Patrolling soldiers stared at them but he simply waved them away. Ordered them to continue their routes. Assured them he was safe.

At the far end of the bridge, beyond the last guard post, they stopped. The elf was staring out at the ground.

'You can see them, can you?'

The elf nodded. 'There is space to walk between them.'

He turned to face Garan, and if the man expected thanks he was disappointed.

'Tell your masters we are not done. Tell them we will return. Tell Ystormun that he should fear my name.'

Garan saw the strength in him and could not help but shudder. He forced a chuckle. 'You know I might just do that. What is your name?'

The elf lifted his head and his face bore a faded glory.

'I am Takaar.'

Acknowledgements:

Thank you to my wife, Clare, for putting up with sudden grumpiness when things weren't going right. To Simon Spanton who provided inspiration and strength. To Lizzy Hill who provided such insightful comment and criticism. And to Richard Griffiths for his unflinching support.